THE FARAWAY INN

Cozy Fantasies by Sarah Beth Durst

The Spellshop

The Enchanted Greenhouse

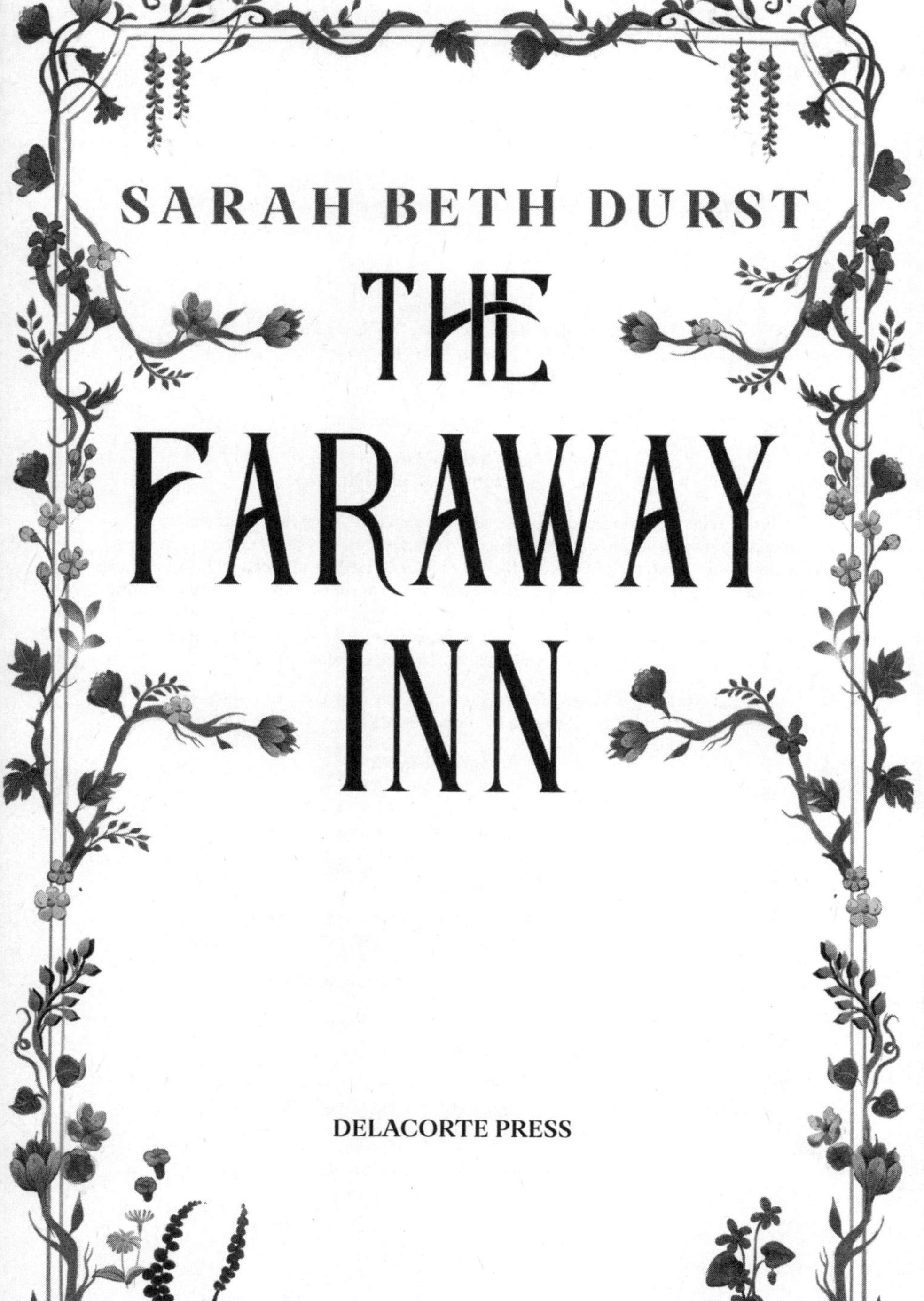

SARAH BETH DURST

THE FARAWAY INN

DELACORTE PRESS

Delacorte Press
An imprint of Random House Children's Books
A division of Penguin Random House LLC
1745 Broadway, New York, NY 10019
penguinrandomhouse.com
GetUnderlined.com

Editor: Lydia Gregovic
Cover Designer: Angela Carlino
Interior Designer: Cathy Bobak
Production Editor: Colleen Fellingham
Managing Editor: Tamar Schwartz
Production Manager: Shameiza Ally

Library of Congress Cataloging-in-Publication Data is available upon request.
ISBN 979-8-217-02430-8 (trade pbk.) — ISBN 979-8-217-02431-5 (ebook)

The text of this book is set in 11.2-point Warnock Pro.

Printed in the United States of America
4th Printing

The authorized representative in the EU for product safety and compliance is Penguin Random House Ireland, Morrison Chambers, 32 Nassau Street, Dublin D02 YH68, Ireland, https://eu-contact.penguin.ie.

For everyone
who needs an escape,
a refuge,
a moment to breathe

CHAPTER ONE

There were a lot of trees.

Calisa stood by the mailbox with her backpack and her suitcase and told herself very firmly that this was exactly what she needed.

Ahead of her was a forest, hemming in a one-lane road. Pine trees clustered together, the expanse of evergreens only broken by the occasional white-barked tree that stood out like a candle against the dark green. Overhead, the sky was a matte white, clouds blotting out the sun, which matched Calisa's mood—cloudy with a chance of rain.

"This is going to be an amazing summer," she said, as if saying the words out loud would act as some kind of spell to make them come true.

She just hadn't pictured what it would feel like to actually be here, by herself, in the middle of a truly excessive number of trees, away from everyone she knew and everything familiar. She'd been too focused on not being *there.*

A few weeks ago, she'd never have considered coming to Vermont by herself for two entire months, but after her world fell apart, she'd pounced on the invitation. She'd wanted to spend her summer anywhere but Brooklyn—anywhere but where Ethan, the boy who'd yanked her heart out of her chest and then stomped on it with the enthusiasm of a four-year-old in tap shoes, was going to be. It was essential self-care.

In retrospect, Calisa supposed she should have had the Uber driver take her all the way to her great-aunt's doorstep instead of just the mailbox, but after the hours on the train and then in the car, she'd wanted to walk.

Also, the driver wouldn't stop talking about fly-fishing. So, here she was.

It will be fine. She could tell from the clouds it wasn't going to rain until later. And if it did, she'd packed an umbrella, though she wasn't sure exactly where.

Everything is going to be fine.

Shouldering her backpack, Calisa hauled her suitcase down the road. On either side, the trees loomed over her. It smelled like pine and wet earth and not at all like the mix of hot gyro meat, bus fumes, coffee, and overripe trash that she associated with the street outside her family's apartment in Park Slope. Above, birds cawed to one another with sharp, biting cries that made her feel like an intruder. Listening, she thought she heard one softer trill, a cascading chirp that was more friendly. Squirrels leaped from branch to branch, causing the forest to rustle. She wondered if Vermont had wolves. Or bears. Probably not. Or maybe yes? This wasn't the city or even suburbia.

Bears weren't impossible. On the plus side, being attacked by a bear would make a unique party story. Or an excellent college application essay. She hadn't started writing hers yet. On the minus side, it would not be great to be mauled.

Close beside her, the trees rustled again, and Calisa jumped. She spotted a squirrel racing up the trunk of a pine tree. *Just a squirrel. Not a bear. Only my overactive imagination.*

In Google Maps, it hadn't looked that far from the main road to the bed-and-breakfast. She pulled out her phone. No signal. She shoved it back into her pocket and kept walking. Ahead, the sky was darkening as gray clouds seeped into the white.

The road twisted, and in front of her, on the left side, was a wooden sign, half devoured by ivy, with letters gouged into it that read:

THE FARAWAY INN

She exhaled and smiled.

"See," she said to the trees. "Almost there." She'd thought it was a melodramatic name—Vermont wasn't *that* far from Brooklyn—but now that she was here in a random, possibly bear-infested forest, she decided it fit. She felt extremely far away from everything, which was exactly what she wanted.

Cheered, Calisa walked faster—and it began to rain.

At first it was just a few drops, one on her cheek, one on her head, and a few spattering on the road around her, and then it increased to a drizzle. She shivered as she walked, wishing she had worn something warmer than her favorite Brooklyn Beans T-shirt (teal with a picture of a coffee cup and the words "Brew can do it!") and a pair of jean shorts. Mom-Kate had insisted she pack a jacket, even though it was summer, but it was shoved deep somewhere, probably with the umbrella. She didn't want to stop to dig either of them out and risk drenching everything else in her suitcase in the process. Better to just keep walking.

A few minutes and many raindrops later, the road rose up a hill and then, as it crested, widened to reveal a hollow between slopes thick with pine trees. Behind it was a panorama of the mountains, crowned in gray clouds.

And in the center of the hollow was her great-aunt's inn.

"Huh," she said out loud.

Calisa hadn't been here in years, not since she was five or six, and it did *not* match her memory. She thought she'd remembered a storybook inn, framed in roses and lilacs, with a burbling brook next to or behind it. Had she imagined all of that? She'd been young enough that it was one of those fuzzy kinds of memories that felt jumbled. But she'd still been expecting cute.

This . . .

It was not cute.

Well, she supposed it could have been charming once, but if so, that had been many, many years ago. Blinking through the droplets on her eyelashes, Calisa looked at the run-down inn and wondered what had happened. Auntie Zee's B&B was gray, drab, and . . . the kindest description she could think of was "vintage distressed." It reminded her of a squashed wedding cake. Three stories tall, it had faded and peeling paint that could have been white with ivory trim at one time but was now gray with dirtier gray. The roof was tilted, lopsided, and the shutters hung crooked on either side of the windows. One window on the second floor was boarded up with plywood. And the wraparound porch was so overrun with vines that half of it was buried beneath greenery.

It was all tremendously overgrown. The flower gardens, which Mom-Kate and Mom-Elise had gushed about while Calisa was packing—"Daffodils and lilacs and roses and lilies everywhere!" they'd said—were a mess. Okay, that was putting it mildly. Brambles and ivy from the forest sprawled across the flower beds as if trying to devour them. She couldn't even see the supposed burbling brook, if there still was one.

It looked as if the forest was on the verge of swallowing the inn whole.

To be fair, her moms had said Auntie Zee was having trouble keeping up the place. It was, in fact, the reason that Mom-Kate had the idea to send Calisa here. She could help Auntie Zee and recover from her heartbreak at the same time. "Two birds with one stone," Mom-Kate had chirped cheerfully. But Calisa didn't think her mother had any idea how run-down it really was. If it wasn't for a few lights inside, she'd have thought it was abandoned.

Calisa stood, staring into the hollow at the shabby bed-and-breakfast while rain slithered down her shirt and seeped into her sneakers. Her socks were already soaked, and her hair dripped on her shoulders. It wasn't the arrival moment she'd pictured.

At least Auntie Zee will be happy I'm here. There was clearly a lot of work to do. Calisa wasn't afraid of hard work. Just afraid of being pathetic. Far better to be the unpaid, overworked help than the heartbroken girl everyone felt sorry for. She'd cheerfully be Cinderella so long as it meant she didn't have to dance with any kind of prince.

Her original plan for the summer hadn't involved any of this. Before Ethan upended everything, she'd had it all nicely mapped out: she'd secured a job at a vintage boutique called Buttons and Bell-Bottoms, which would have been fantastic. She'd work there for a few hours every afternoon, primarily playing on her phone and trying on the most random outfits she could assemble. After work, she'd meet up with her friends. She, Maddy, and Crystal had set themselves a challenge to visit every single coffee shop in Brooklyn before the end of August. Every evening, she was going to meet Ethan at the bodega where he'd be working, downstairs from her apartment. They'd have dinner (sometimes with his family, sometimes with hers, sometimes just the two of them), watch movies, and cuddle, or go out and drop in on one of Ethan's friends' parties. It would have been a very, very different summer than this.

Now . . . even if she spent the entire summer on nonstop yardwork and housework and whatever else until she had blisters and calluses on both hands, it was still a better option than having to see Ethan every day when she walked past the bodega and feeling as if she were being ripped to shreds from the inside out all over again.

At least here, her heart would be okay.

If a bit damp.

She'd be able to start her life anew in the fall, with her head held high for senior year.

Calisa took a deep breath and continued down the hill toward the Faraway Inn. She hurried along the path, ignoring the way her socks squished inside her shoes. Her suitcase bounced over the uneven walkway as she pulled it behind her.

A gray stone statue of a woman with hands clasped in front of her watched Calisa pass. Rain dripped down her stone face and pooled in her blank eyes.

Hauling her suitcase up the steps, Calisa climbed onto the porch. She exhaled and resisted the urge to shake like a wet dog. Instead she just dripped. But it was an improvement: she was under a roof, though the porch roof clearly had multiple holes in it—rain collected in puddles every few feet.

She studied the front door, unsure if she was supposed to knock or just walk in. She was expected, and this was an inn, not a house. You didn't knock at a Marriott. But it had a knocker, made of brass and shaped like an owl. . . . Calisa told herself to quit delaying. She had nothing to be nervous about. She'd made the leap: backed out of her summer job, said goodbye to her friends and parents, and come here. The hard part was done. *Knock, then enter,* she decided.

She took a step forward—

And the wood planks beneath her snapped. She plunged through the porch, and her breath whooshed out of her. Her backpack caught on the unbroken boards, hiking up above her shoulders. Her suitcase sat innocently beside the hole.

"Gah!" The sound came out of her like a chicken squawk.

She wasn't hurt, was she? She took stock—knees, ankles, elbows. All fine.

She'd fallen up to her chest, and the hole was about as wide as she was, plus a portion of her backpack. Placing her hands up on the unbroken boards in front of her, Calisa tried to hoist herself out.

It didn't work.

At all.

Maybe if she hadn't been wearing her pack when she fell—but she had been, and now her backpack was wedged behind her. With it, she was a cork in a bottle.

Calisa tried again, jumping up while pushing with her arms and, after she was a few inches off the ground, bicycling with her feet. After huffing and puffing for a solid minute, she sank down again into the hole.

Okay, this is not good.

She was not going to panic, she told herself. It wasn't as if she'd fallen into a hole in the middle of the Vermont woods with bears and wolves and strange men with axes. She was on (or, more accurately, *in*) the front porch of a respectable bed-and-breakfast. If she yelled for help, someone would hear her and come to her rescue. Except this was *not* how she wanted to start her summer job. How did she say to her aunt, whom she hadn't seen in years, "Hey, Auntie Zee, I'm here to help, so I broke your porch"?

No, she'd figure out a way to get out of this herself.

If she squirmed out of the backpack first and then—

"Hello?" a voice said. Male. Youngish. "Are you hurt?"

Calisa felt herself blush, torn between relief that someone was here to help and embarrassment to be stuck in a hole in the first place. "I'm fine."

She twisted as much of her upper body as she could to see the owner of the voice. Standing on the porch above her, he looked to be her age (as far as she could tell) and handsome (*that* she could definitely tell), with tousled wet-from-the-rain hair. In addition to looking absurdly fresh-off-a-movie-set pretty, he was strong, which was obvious not just from the bulk of his arm muscles but also because he was carrying a large stone gargoyle on one of his shoulders like it was a sack of potatoes.

"I'm Jack. Groundskeeper," he said. "Or, technically, groundskeeper's son, but I help out." He was frowning at her as if she didn't belong here, which she thought was a fair assessment. She did *not* belong mid-porch.

"Uh, hi, I'm Calisa, Auntie Zee's niece. Grandniece." It wasn't the most poetic of introductions, but at least she hadn't stumbled over her name, which she had done the very first time she had set eyes on Ethan. He'd told her it was charming. But she had *not* come here with the intention of having another awkward meet-cute like that. In fact, she hadn't even considered the fact that she might have to interact with anyone her age at all. She'd thought the summer would be just her and Auntie Zee, with a few aloof adult guests who came and went. She did not want or need any complications. Like falling through a porch.

He pointed to the gargoyle with his free hand. "This here is

Zef. He's supposed to be in room eight. I'm just bringing him out of the rain before I get the cheese."

None of that made sense. "Cheese? For . . . Zef?"

Jack laughed, a nice, warm laugh that made her feel like she'd just successfully told a joke, even though she'd merely been confused. "The guest in room twelve likes cheese. And vegetables. But mostly cheese."

"I like cheese." She winced at herself. *Why am I incapable of holding a normal conversation with a good-looking guy? Is it maybe because I'm trying to be friendly while stuck in a hole?* "All except blue cheese."

"Never understood blue cheese," Jack agreed.

"The blue spots are supposed to be edible, but I can't get past the fact that they're mold." Why was she talking about mold? She did not want to be talking about mold. She wanted to be out of this hole. "I like cheddar. And goat cheese, the soft kind that you can spread. It's really good with fig jam."

"I especially like cheesecake."

"Everyone likes cheesecake."

"Except the lactose intolerant," Jack said.

"Mm-hmm, it's probably a cruel joke to them," Calisa said. "Cake but not."

Jack frowned. "You're right. In that case, we shouldn't serve it."

"Unless you use cream cheese with lactase."

"You can do that?"

She knew it existed, but she'd never baked with it before. "I made a regular cheesecake last year. Trick is you have to cool it gradually, or it cracks. Probably same process." Oh God, why was she still having this conversation? *If the universe expects me to swoon into his arms after he rescues me as some kind of cosmic apology for last month . . . Nope, not going to happen.* She did *not* want to have to be grateful to him.

"I had a slice of white chocolate raspberry cheesecake once," he said dreamily. "Fresh raspberries are the best."

"Blueberries are better," Calisa said.

"You clearly have never eaten a raspberry straight off the bush."

She hadn't, but that wasn't exactly her greatest concern right now. Calisa squirmed, trying to angle her arms better to lever herself out of the hole. "I'm sure it's delicious." She failed again and heaved a sigh.

With the careful tone of someone who isn't sure whether he's being rude or not, Jack asked, "Are you an invited guest? I mean, you said you're Auntie Zee's grandniece, but . . . she didn't mention you. Are you supposed to be here? Did she know you were coming?"

"She should," Calisa said. "My moms talked to her."

"Ah . . ." He looked relieved. Tentatively, he asked, "Are you okay?"

No. "Yes. But I think I'm stuck." Wait, did he think she was dangling halfway through the porch on purpose? Did he not see she very obviously needed help?

"Hmm," he said, examining the break in the porch as if it were a feature of the architecture, not an unintentional disaster. "Let me just return Zef to room eight, and I'll be back to rescue you. And then you should talk to Auntie Zee. She's the boss of everything that happens here."

Before she could ask for help *now,* not after he finished

his chores, Jack—the polite and handsome but ultimately unhelpful groundskeeper's son—had already disappeared inside. Calisa muttered to herself, "Okay, so definitely *not* a meet-cute." That was just awkward. What was with the are-you-supposed-to-be-here questions? It was an inn. Even if she wasn't invited, shouldn't they get people popping up unexpectedly all the time?

"Whatever." She had zero desire to be rescued anyway.

And even less desire to wait around to be rescued.

Climbing out wasn't going to work, though. She looked across the porch and out at the yard, but all she saw was the statue of the lady, with one hand outstretched, in between the weeds. "Thanks, but I don't think you can help," Calisa said.

She tried one more time to propel herself out. It failed again.

What about if she went down instead of up? Could she crawl out from beneath the porch? That wasn't a bad idea. Calisa ducked down easily, her backpack coming with her a second later and then thumping onto her back. It was dark beneath the porch, as well as damp, but she could see light to her left. Squatting, she waddled toward it.

Up ahead, she heard murmuring.

Shivers danced up her spine, and she stopped. "Hello?"

The murmuring ceased.

Could it be the voices of guests within the inn? Peering into the shadows beneath the porch, she didn't see any movement. She continued on with her awkward waddle, not wanting to crawl on the muddy ground.

Another cascade of whispers, this time behind her.

She turned fast. Again, no one was there. Her heart beat faster. It had to be the acoustics under the porch warping the sound from inside somehow, but there was an edge to the whispers that made every inch of her skin prickle.

Moving more quickly, Calisa hurried toward the light and emerged from beneath the porch. She stood up straight, facing the overgrown gardens and the mountains in the distance. The rain had lessened, and she could see streaks of blue breaking through the clouds by the peaks. The whispers were silent.

Returning to the front of the inn, she skirted the hole and approached the door carefully. She opened it without incident and stepped inside, bringing her suitcase and backpack with her.

She exhaled, feeling as if she'd achieved a minor miracle by simply entering the B&B.

Inside, the lobby was shadowed. Light filtered through the dusty windows to bathe the foyer in a soft haze. She waited for her eyes to adjust. On either side of her were open doorways, all hooded and silent. The lobby's peeling wallpaper was streaked with water stains. A mirror hung on one wall. It was so grimy that it looked as if it were reflecting smoke. Instead of her face, all she saw was a wispy smudge as she passed by. In front of her, between a set of stairs (which she assumed led to the second-floor guest rooms) and a hallway (which led who knew where), was the reception desk, with old-fashioned skeleton keys hanging from hooks on a board behind it. Only a handful of keys were absent from their hooks. She wondered if that meant the B&B was mostly empty.

There was a silver bell on the desk, and she wondered if she should ring it. Again, she wasn't a guest, and she wasn't sure what she was supposed to do. Her parents' instructions hadn't gone beyond which subway to take to Penn Station, which train to take to Burlington (as a parting blow, the train line was named the Ethan Allen—how far did she have to go to escape reminders of Ethan?), and what address to give the Uber driver. Plus she had clear instructions to text as soon as she arrived (or call if there was no Wi-Fi, though how could you have an inn without Wi-Fi?) so they'd know she was safe and sound and hadn't gotten lost in the mountains and been forced to eat squirrels and berries to survive. . . . Her moms were worriers, especially Mom-Elise, who raised parental fussing to an art form.

Calisa peeked through the first doorway on her left into what looked like a sitting room. It was gray with dust, matching the shade of the outside of the bed-and-breakfast. Formerly white but now dingy sheets covered half the furniture, as if the room had been partially put into storage. A tea set of tarnished silver sat in one corner on top of a tea tray with wheels. A cobweb stretched from the handle of the teapot to the edge of the tea tray. No one was in the sitting room, except for an elderly white cat who lay on a faded red velvet chair. The cat opened one eye to look at Calisa and then closed it again—a very clear don't-bother-me look. Respecting that, Calisa retreated.

Opposite the sitting room, on the other side of the lobby, was a library. It too was empty of guests or Auntie Zee but had clearly once been nice. The shelves were dusty, and she spotted a few cobwebs on the top shelf, but it had a perfect window seat tucked in between bookshelves and beneath an arched window. The shelves themselves covered every wall, filled floor to ceiling with books, and a ladder on wheels leaned against it so guests could reach any book they wanted—or just glide along the perimeter of the room. Calisa resisted the urge to try it out.

First find Auntie Zee, then play with the library ladder.

And pet the cat, if it lets me.

She peeked into the next open doorway, into the dining room, which looked as if it hadn't been used in years. A vase of dead flowers sat in the center of the table, and a chair with only three legs leaned against a wall. Beyond the dining room, tucked behind the stairwell, was another short hallway that looked as if it led to a handful of guest rooms.

On the other side of the reception desk, down the hallway she'd noticed before with peeling wallpaper, Calisa found the kitchen. It was old-fashioned, with a brick oven on one wall, rafters that had dried herbs hanging in batches, and a large butcher block island with a few rickety stools around it. Unlike the other rooms, it had been cleaned recently, but it still looked unused and unloved. Pots and pans were stacked on the stove, piled high as if the burners were never turned on, and the measuring spoons that hung on the wall looked more like permanent decorations than cooking tools. Overhead the dried herbs were desiccated nearly to the point of crumbling.

She crossed to the sink to look out the window at the backyard. Outside was an old and sprawling apple tree, with curved branches and a riot of leaves. She spotted a few unripe apples, small and green, between the leaves. Beyond the tree were the mountains. Sheathed in misty clouds, they looked ethereal, as if they might dissolve if she stared for too long.

Where is everyone?

If it weren't raining, she'd have suspected that some guests were out strolling through the forest or hiking up a nearby mountain. Just because she had zero interest in hiking didn't mean that the guests did. Or maybe they were out in whatever town was nearest, going antiquing or doing some other Vermont-ish activity? Or they were in their rooms, tucked away from the world, enjoying their escape from whatever disappointment or stress or heartbreak had sent them fleeing into the wilds of New England. . . . But where was Auntie Zee? She should at least—

"Little Cali," she heard behind her.

And Calisa turned to face the innkeeper, her great-aunt, Auntie Zee.

Auntie Zee was half a head shorter than Calisa and had startlingly white hair, skin so wrinkled that she very closely resembled a walnut, and sunken eyes with pupils rimmed with milky blue. She looked, Calisa thought, far older than her eighty-two years. "Hi, Auntie Zee," Calisa began. "It's great to—"

"You can stay the night," Auntie Zee cut her off. "But then you have to leave."

Calisa felt her mouth drop open.

"I neither need nor want you here."

CHAPTER TWO

"I can fix it," Calisa said immediately, thinking of the porch.

"Unlikely." Auntie Zee let out a mirthless laugh. "You're your mother's daughter."

Ouch. She meant Mom-Kate, who was Auntie Zee's biological niece and Calisa's bio mom and was not what one might call handy. She'd once infamously confused a wrench for a screwdriver. But Calisa thought she could figure it out, if she had an afternoon and access to a few YouTube videos. Also wood, a hammer, and nails. Plus a saw? "I can try."

"She couldn't help me, and she tried for years when she was your age. No, I have enough on my plate as it is. It's better if you leave now before you muck up anything for my guests."

She isn't talking about the porch, Calisa realized. This was broader than that. It was possible that Auntie Zee didn't even know about the hole. With a sinking feeling in the pit of her stomach, she said, "I thought my moms talked to you."

Auntie Zee grunted. "They talked."

So why didn't she—

"They didn't listen."

"But . . . I need to stay!" It was supposed to be her summer to recover and heal—to do self-reflection and find inner strength and practice self-care and all of her best friend Crystal's favorite phrases—before she had to face senior year, college applications, and the utter lack of regret in her ex-boyfriend's beautiful eyes. She needed this! And she'd come all this way. She couldn't slink back to Brooklyn jobless after one day and say her aunt didn't want her.

Auntie Zee shuffled to the kitchen window and made shooing motions, as if scattering a flock of pigeons. She then humphed and turned back to Calisa. "So melodramatic. You don't *need* to stay. You *want* to stay."

Glancing out the window, Calisa didn't see what Auntie Zee had shooed away. It looked the same as before: an apple tree in an untamed yard, the forest and mountains beyond, the darkening sky. "Please, Auntie Zee, I know I can be helpful. I like to cook. Or at least bake. Pretty good at it, I think. Or I could clean. Dust. Vacuum. Whatever."

Auntie Zee was shaking her head.

"How about dishes? I can do dishes! We don't have a dishwasher in our apartment, so I'm expert-level at dish washing, even vases that have had flowers in them so long that leaves and petals are practically glued to the inner glass—"

"I don't need your help."

Calisa gestured at the stack of unused pots, the desiccated

herbs, and the horrifically overgrown garden out the window. "You clearly need someone's help."

"Says a girl who knows nothing about running a bed-and-breakfast."

"Says a girl who has eyes and can see—" She cut herself off. She wasn't going to convince her great-aunt by insulting the state of her inn, even though it was blatantly obvious that the place was one strong sneeze away from collapsing into a pile of dust. Auntie Zee was looking at her like she was a clump of muck on her shoe. Calisa added in a smaller voice, "I *want* to help."

Studying her for a moment more, Auntie Zee snorted. "Why?"

"Because . . ." What reason would the old innkeeper like to hear? Should she say she thought it was important to help family (except she hadn't seen Auntie Zee in years)? Or that she thought it would add a necessary line of work experience to her college applications (except she'd barely begun to think about them)? Or that she had no other way to spend her summer that wouldn't involve her feeling as if she had been shoved through a vegetable slicer every time she saw Ethan with another one of his apparently multiple girlfriends that everyone had known about except her?

"The truth," Auntie Zee demanded.

"Because I walked in on my boyfriend with his hand up the shirt of Jocelyn Pullman," she burst out, "and I need to be as far from anything that makes me think about him as possible."

Auntie Zee stared at her again, and then she laughed.

Calisa felt herself blush. She wished she'd chosen a different answer, ideally one that sounded less pathetic. She glanced up at the rafters, down at the scuffed wood floor, then over at the cabinets with their faded paint. You could just barely make out the remnants of delicately painted roses and ivy that decorated the wood. She focused on the little roses while her eyes grew hot.

The laughter stopped. "I appreciate your honesty. A far better answer than claiming you want to help out a grouchy old lady who never even sent you birthday presents."

She looked back at her great-aunt, wondering if she had, against all odds, said the right thing. *I can't just turn around and go home.* What would she tell her moms? Mom-Elise would tell her she needed to learn to stand up for herself and understand her own value, while Mom-Kate would want to march up to Vermont to yell at Auntie Zee. Neither reaction would help with the core problem of what Calisa was going to do to make it through July and August without turning into a blithering mess of self-pity.

"My B&B has always been a place for people who needed to escape."

Yes. Escape. That was exactly what she wanted. She needed trees and mountains and so much work to do that she wasn't able to think. Hope rose into her throat. "So you'll let me stay for the summer?"

"Absolutely not."

The hope dissolved.

"No, that's a terrible idea. But . . . a few days, I think. You can stay three days, finish whatever moping you need to do to make yourself feel better, and then you go home." And with that, Auntie Zee waddled out of the kitchen.

Whatever moping she needed to do . . .

The entire point was *not* to "mope"!

Shaking it off, Calisa followed after her great-aunt.

Auntie Zee shuffled down the hallway into the lobby. She waved at the smoky mirror. "Ignore the mirror. It's a pessimist." And then she sidled behind the reception desk.

Calisa studied the mirror. That was a strange way to say a mirror was unflattering, especially when what it really needed was a wipe with Windex, which just seemed to be more evidence that she *did* know more about running a bed-and-breakfast than Auntie Zee thought she did. Not that she was going to say that out loud.

Thump.

She turned around to see that Auntie Zee had plopped a leather-bound book on the reception desk. Scowling, she flipped open the pages. Calisa drifted closer to see—

"Gah. Private." Auntie Zee shooed her backward.

Calisa took a step away but still tried to peer at the book. It was full of handwritten notes neatly spaced in columns, like a guest register. Or was it more than that? On one side of the page, she spotted a list of expenses, as well as supplies. It looked like Auntie Zee kept all the inn's records in this book, instead of, like, a spreadsheet. Given the state of the inn, Calisa supposed it wasn't a surprise to see that Auntie Zee hadn't upgraded to computers.

At least she'd progressed from ink and quills.

"Guests at the Faraway Inn are all afforded privacy," Auntie Zee said. "You will respect that for the three days you are here."

At least three days was better than "leave in the morning," which was where the conversation had started. She thought of the line from her moms' favorite movie: *Good night, Westley. Good work. Sleep well. I'll most likely kill you in the morning.*

Maybe after three days she'd be able to convince Auntie Zee to let her stay another three, and after that another three, until all of a sudden, boom, it was September and Calisa was fully healed from her heartbreak, emotionally stable, and ready to return.

"That's important: you must respect the guests' privacy. Do you understand?"

"Of course." She'd follow whatever rules Auntie Zee wanted, so long as she was allowed to stay. Clasping her hands behind her back, Calisa hoped she looked responsible and respectful. She wasn't certain that was possible after just pathetically pleading for mercy, but her goal now was to convince Auntie Zee that she'd be an excellent addition to the summer staff.

Auntie Zee added a notation to the guest book. "You can stay in room two."

"Great!" Before she could ask a follow-up question—such as "Where's room two?" or "Can I have the key?"—she saw a flash of movement out of the corner of her eye. She turned her head, but all she saw was the blurry streak of her reflection in the grimy mirror—hair matted from rain, shirt still damp, face a hazy smudge. *I look like a half-drowned mouse.* Pessimistic mirror indeed.

Calisa turned back toward the reception desk. The logbook was gone, squirreled away wherever Auntie Zee kept it, and, more significantly, so was Auntie Zee.

How had the old innkeeper scooted out of the room so fast? She hadn't seemed that speedy. Also . . . well, it was kind of rude. Calisa had just arrived. Granted, Auntie Zee didn't want her here, so she could hardly expect a tour or any kind of grand welcome, but still . . .

None of this is what I expected.

She stood for a moment, unsure what to do. Fix the hole she'd made? Change out of her soggy socks? Chase after Auntie Zee? Call home and tell her parents . . . what? She'd tell them she was fine, of course. She'd made it here safely. *I'll be fine.* Probably. Maybe.

Coming down the stairs, Jack said, "Ah, you're not in a hole!"

She glanced up at his cheerful face as he took the steps two at a time. "And you're not inexplicably carrying a gargoyle. How things change."

"He doesn't like rain."

She was ninety-nine percent sure he was joking. Eighty-five percent? It was hard to tell, given his excessively earnest face. As he reached the bottom step, she said, "Auntie Zee told me room two. Do I just take the key?" Calisa waved her hand at the wall of hooks with skeleton keys behind the reception desk. "Also, do you have a hammer, nails, saw, wood, and knowledge of how to fix a broken porch?"

"You talked to her! Great!" He looked enormously relieved, also surprised. More surprised than she thought he should be.

Then again, he probably knows how unfriendly his boss is. He added, "I was planning to fix the hole after it stops raining."

"I think it stopped." Crossing the lobby, she opened the front door and peered outside. "Sort of?" The rain pattered down in sparse drops, as if the sky were a dishcloth that was nearly wrung out. Out in the yard, the statue was sleek with water. Drops dripped from her outstretched hands.

He joined her in the doorframe. "Close enough."

There was still an hour or two of daylight left. Calisa had taken the earliest train she could so that she'd arrive with time to settle in. Plus the sun set late this time of year. She should have time to do a little carpentry before it was fully dark out. How long could it take to patch a few broken boards?

"And yes," Jack said, "if Auntie Zee said room two, then you should take the key for room two. But, um, don't go into any of the other guest rooms, okay? Even if the keys are there. Not sure if she said so, but Auntie Zee is very particular about that. She assigns the room, no changes allowed."

"Sure, no problem." Calisa had no intention of wandering into random rooms. "Let me just change my shirt and socks and then I'll be back to fix the porch."

"Um, sorry about doubting you before, whether you're supposed to be here. I just . . . I didn't know she'd invited you. She's been pretty adamant about not hiring anyone new. Dad's asked lots of times. Usually she just grunts, but sometimes she launches into this impressive monologue about the importance of self-sufficiency. She's run this B&B for decades. She doesn't want to let a stranger muck it up. Not that you're a stranger.

You're family. Guess that makes it different." He smiled at her, and it was like the sun coming out after the rain.

Wow, that was quite the smile. She wondered if she should tell him it was just a three-day probation. On one hand, it was embarrassing that her own great-aunt didn't want her to stay, but on the other hand, it was possible Jack could help convince her. "She didn't toss me out immediately, but she also didn't agree to the full summer. Yet."

The smile wavered. "So you know about the inn, right?"

"To be honest, no, I don't know anything about working at a bed-and-breakfast." She dropped her voice lower as she said that, in case Auntie Zee was listening. If Ethan were here, he would have told her to project confidence. He was a huge believer in blustering his way through any situation—it was one of the things she'd admired about him when they first met . . . and despised about him at the end, when she was the one he was lying to. But there was something about the way Jack was looking at her that made her not want to pretend to be more than she was. "I was thinking if I can fix the porch, it would help with Auntie Zee, except I've never actually fixed a porch before." Or anything, really. There wasn't much cause for carpentry in an apartment in Brooklyn.

Jack looked dubious, and she wished she could bring back that smile.

"I'm willing to try, though," Calisa added. That had to count for something, didn't it?

The pause went on longer than she liked. A lot longer. At last, he said, "Well, I can teach you how to fix a porch, if you're really up for helping me. It'll be easier with two people anyway. You hold the wood, and I'll saw?"

"Deal."

He still looked uneasy, and she was suddenly aware that they were standing side by side in the doorframe, inches from touching. If she shifted her hand a little bit, would he smile? Or would he flinch? "I'll just . . . um . . . put my stuff in my room, change, and then . . . um . . . meet you outside?" Calisa said, hating that she stumbled over half the words. *No,* she told herself. *Absolutely not. No rebound boys. He's a coworker. Just a coworker.* Who happened to have a nice smile, when he decided to use it and wasn't busy looking dismayed that she was here. That was all. Last thing she needed was to invite more heartache.

"I'll get the wood and tools." Skirting the hole, he hopped down the steps.

She watched him for a moment as he headed around the side of the inn. She felt prickles on the back of her neck as if someone nearby was watching her. There was no one there, though. Only the statue. Raising her eyebrows at it, Calisa said, "Don't judge me."

The statue stood silent as rain pooled in her stone eyes and cupped hands.

CHAPTER THREE

Calisa plucked the room key from the board and then dragged her suitcase down the hall behind the stairs. The hallway featured a faded blue carpet, a broken sconce, and a bathroom at the end. She could see the corner of a sink through the partly open door. It all smelled faintly of lavender. And dust.

Only two guest rooms budded off the first-floor hallway. She halted in front of the second door. Above the number two was an X painted in red.

She wondered what that meant. In need of cleaning? Not suitable for guests? Condemned for health reasons? Scene of a crime?

She unlocked the door and peeked inside warily.

It was adorable.

Or it had once been adorable, which was close enough.

She smiled as she walked in and dropped her luggage.

Looking around, she saw a queen bed with a canopy, a window seat with a view of the mountains, and a fireplace with a stone mantel. Yes, the quilt on the bed was frayed, the paint on the window seat was peeling, and the hearth of the fireplace was stained with years of soot, but it was all quaint as hell. The wood floor was covered by a faded rug with pictures of flowers, and the curtains were slightly tattered lace. A few leather-bound books were lined up on top of the dresser in between bookends shaped like cats. Everything was a little bit old, a little worn, but it was cleaner than the common rooms, and it smelled like the sprigs of lavender that were in little vases in various places around the room: on the bedside table, on the mantel, on top of the dresser.

I can live here, she thought. *If I'm allowed to.*

She liked that it was nothing at all like her room at home, where the walls were covered in photos of Ethan and her friends, the bed was rumpled and half buried in not-yet-put-away laundry, and her desk was stacked with stuff from school that she planned to ignore until September. And it was nothing like *his* room either.

This would be a fine place to spend the summer, with mountain views and lots of tasks to keep her busy and distracted. Now, if she could only find a way to convince Auntie Zee to let her stay for longer than three days . . . *I can start by fixing the porch.* At least Jack was going to let her help with that, even if he did seem less than thrilled she was here.

He'd been perfectly friendly while they were talking about cheese. It was only when he'd realized she wasn't one hundred percent invited that he'd gotten skittish. She supposed it made sense—he wouldn't want to piss off his boss by being overly welcoming to someone who wasn't actually welcome.

Calisa lifted her suitcase onto the window seat and changed out of her damp T-shirt and soggy socks. After she'd draped them over the back of a chair by the fireplace to dry, she checked her phone. No signal. And no Wi-Fi to log in to.

She'd said she wanted distance from Brooklyn, with zero updates from anyone about Ethan, so this wasn't tragic. She knew her friends would forgive her for a few weeks of silence. Before she'd left, her best friend Crystal had tried to convince her to drop off the grid entirely for the summer, and now it looked like she'd be doing that. Of course, she still had to call home, but luckily there was an old-fashioned phone by the bedside table, complete with a curly cord.

She reported in, reassuring Mom-Elise that the train was fine, the Uber was fine, and everything was fine and telling Mom-Kate that she'd met Auntie Zee, her room was very nice, and she'd packed dental floss, even though she had no intention of using it until, like, the day before her next appointment—who did?

She did *not* mention that the B&B was a wreck, or that Auntie Zee had said she could stay for only three days. Why worry them? "Gotta start work," she told them.

They dumped bits of advice on her (don't work too hard, don't *not* work hard, remember to eat a vegetable or two, call often, make friends, listen to Auntie Zee, don't leave wet towels in a heap on the floor) and smothered her with love ("I love you to the moon, I love you to Neptune, I love you to Pluto, which is still a planet in our hearts . . .") until she laughed and said goodbye.

After hanging up, Calisa hurried outside. Oddly, that call had felt more like a goodbye than getting on the subway this morning had. She was acutely aware of how far from home she was and how different this was from the summer she'd planned. Stepping out the front door, she took a deep breath. The air after the rain smelled so—

"Petrichor," Jack said.

She exhaled. "Sorry?"

"It's the name for the smell after rain. Petrichor. It's caused by . . . eh, I don't remember. A chemical in the soil that releases when it rains, but I always thought it was cool that it has a name." He was carrying planks of wood on his shoulder and had a tool belt strapped around his waist. Safety goggles dangled around his neck.

She helped him set the wood down on the unbroken section of the porch. He then contemplated the hole, first from one angle and then from another. There were two planks that she'd busted through. Broken bits of wood had fallen into the hole, and the bits that remained attached to the porch looked jagged and splintery.

"What do we do first?" she asked.

"Ever used a crowbar?"

"No, but if you say I get to use a sledgehammer, I'll love you forever."

He grinned, which went a long way to making her feel better about the fact that those words had just come out of her mouth in that order. It was the kind of thing she said to her friends, and it had spilled out without her thinking about the fact that she was talking to a near stranger, especially one that her mind had already labeled as very, very pretty. "No sledgehammer," he said. "But we do have to take the old boards out. Crowbar will be fastest."

"Sledgehammer will be faster."

"But it might break parts of the porch that we don't want to break, like the supports."

He put on his safety goggles and handed her a pair too. She put them on, aware they made her look a bit like a frog, but since Jack was looking froggy too, it was fine. They could be froglike in solidarity.

He then showed her how to use the crowbar, which was straightforward: slide it under the wood she wanted to remove and pry the wood out. While she worked to extract the broken pieces, he measured the width of the porch. It was simpler, he explained, to replace the two broken boards than to patch the hole. It would look nicer too, because the wood would weather at the same rate. She liked the way he explained things—he did it all with zero condescension. It was more like a kid showing off his toy dinosaur collection. He seemed happy to teach her, even if he wasn't sold on her being here.

"How did you learn to do this?" Calisa asked.

"My dad taught me."

"You said your dad's the groundskeeper?"

"And the carpenter, plumber, electrician, whatever else needs to get done," Jack said, pride in his voice. "He can do just about anything. If he were here, he'd already have the porch fixed and be on the roof, fixing those holes." He measured the width a second time and then marked the board.

"He's not here?"

"He's off on a trip," Jack said. "Picking up supplies for the inn for the summer season. He's supposed to be back soon, but not, you know, soon enough. Can you hold the other end of the wood? That'll keep it from breaking before I've cut all the way through."

Leaving the crowbar, she joined him and held the wood. He was going to cut it over the steps up to the porch, to avoid the risk of sawing through anything that wasn't supposed to be sawed through. "So, it's just you, while your dad's away? Anyone else work here? Who cooks? Who cleans? It can't all be just you." She hadn't seen any other staff. Surely Auntie Zee had other employees, didn't she?

"Just me. Until Dad gets back, I'm in charge of cleaning the guest rooms, washing the towels and sheets and everyone's laundry, preparing the breakfast trays, helping the guests with whatever they need, and fixing everything that breaks. Also supposed to take care of the grounds, but aside from the vegetable garden, I kind of . . . haven't. At all. It's been busy."

That . . . was a lot. How much work had she gotten herself into? Why was there no other staff? There must have been at some point. She was certain she remembered a few from when she'd been here as a kid. Had Auntie Zee fired them all? Or had they quit? Exactly how grouchy was she?

Positioning the blade over a mark he'd made on the wood, Jack began to saw. She held one end steady; he held the other with one hand and one knee as he sheared through the board.

"What's Auntie Zee like?" Calisa asked.

He paused and glanced at her in wary surprise. "She's your aunt."

"Great-aunt. And I haven't been here since I was a kid. Besides, the last time, I was entirely too distracted by the fact that there was a tower of chocolate-covered strawberries to think about what she'd be like to work for."

His expression warred with itself for a minute, as if he wanted to stay disapproving but couldn't help grinning again. He resumed sawing. "A tower of chocolate-covered strawberries?"

"I'm not going to tell you how many I ate."

"I hope it was a lot," he said. Even though she was holding it, the end of the board still thumped down on the steps when he sawed through the last bit. "Can't waste an opportunity like that."

"It was absolutely a lot."

Jack nodded approvingly. "Excellent."

He measured the second board, then began sawing it. Returning to the key question, she asked, "Auntie Zee? What's she like?" She also wanted to ask: Did he like working here? How long had he worked at the B&B, and when had it begun to fall apart? Did he know? Was he here full-time? Did he live at the B&B? Did he have a girlfriend? Did he like girls? Did he like her? *Whoa, Calisa, no,* she told herself. *That's absolutely not why you're here.*

"She's . . . Well, I've known her since I was a kid."

"You grew up here?"

"Yeah. Used to live just a few miles away. You're from New York City?"

"Brooklyn. You said 'used to.' Do you live at the inn now?"

"Yep, room six," he said. "We—that is, Dad and I . . . My mom died when I was born. Dad and I used to have our own place, not much, but home. Anyway, Auntie Zee needs us here now, so we're here. Hired us both, package deal." He shrugged as if that were a complete explanation of his life.

Together they began nailing in the new boards. She had at least used a hammer before, to help Mom-Kate put pictures up on the wall, but those had been gentle taps. It was a lot more satisfying to drive a nail into a thick board. She only missed a few times, denting the wood on either side of the nail.

"Why won't Auntie Zee hire more people?" Calisa asked. "I mean, I get the wonders of self-sufficiency and independence and all that, but it's an inn. It's supposed to have staff. Cooks and cleaners and maintenance people."

He didn't answer, and she thought he was focusing on the task at hand, but when she looked up, he was staring out at the garden as if she'd asked a complex question.

Finally, he said, "She doesn't want to."

"Uh, okay."

Jack returned to hammering the nails with greater concentration.

"She can't afford it?" Calisa guessed. She'd noticed how few of the room keys were in use, compared to the total number of rooms. It would most likely cost a lot to refurbish a three-story building and even more to hire additional full-time help. But if Auntie Zee couldn't keep the inn clean and not falling apart, then fewer and fewer guests would return. . . . She wondered how close the bed-and-breakfast was to failing entirely. *Maybe this is why she's so unfriendly.* "If she needs the help, though, why send me away? I'm a relative. Free labor."

He shrugged.

It could be pride. Auntie Zee didn't want to admit she needed help. Calisa could understand that. Her great-aunt had founded this inn, built her business on her own, and now she was supposed to be okay with accepting help? Especially from relatives she hadn't seen in years?

"I'll start cleaning tomorrow," Calisa said. "I think that's top priority." And also it was within her skill set. She'd dust everything first, then figure out where Auntie Zee stored the vacuum. She had to have one.

"Usually top priority is whatever just broke," Jack said. "Or whatever a guest needs, which is why the routine stuff doesn't get done."

"Do the guests usually need a lot?" she asked.

Hammering in the last nail, he didn't answer at first. He hit it one more time then rocked back on his heels. "Depends on the guest."

That was vaguely ominous. "Oh?"

"We once had a guest who loved bacon. Only bacon. Breakfast, lunch, dinner, tea. The whole inn smelled of bacon. He even got himself a hot plate and cooked up his own as a midnight snack."

"I mean, kind of excessive, but bacon is excellent."

"Yeah, but . . . Anyway, it was bearable until we got a guest who had a pet potbellied pig."

Calisa winced. "Oh no. He didn't."

"He didn't, but only because Auntie Zee had a talk with him. Otherwise, definitely would have been Bacon Fest. Wish I could've heard what she said." He sounded both wistful and admiring. "But, um, don't repeat any of that, okay?"

She opened her mouth to say of course, but he didn't give her a chance.

Jack stood up abruptly, as if he regretted how chatty he'd been. "I'll put the tools away," he said. "Can you get a broom so we can sweep up the sawdust?" He gathered the extra nails, safety goggles, saw, crowbar, and hammer as he spoke.

"Sure."

He darted away before she could ask where to find a broom.

He ran so hot and cold—it was as if the instant he noticed he was relaxing around her, he pulled back. How was she supposed to win him over if he so clearly didn't want to be won? Not that she needed to, but it would be nice. And he could help with Auntie Zee.

She guessed she'd need to find a broom closet to find a broom, but where exactly? Going into the B&B, she searched. Upstairs was unlikely—those were probably all guest rooms. Through the kitchen, she discovered a narrow hallway with multiple closet-like doors. She tried them, one after another:

Coat closet.

Pantry.

Towels.

Birdseed, potting soil, and . . . "Alligator feed?" she read the label out loud. *Ask later.* She closed the closet door. She hadn't imagined the inn would have so many supply closets. "Where are you, broom?"

She approached the next closet, a narrow and tall one, and opened the door. Inside, it was as black as a moonless night. Wind slammed into her face, and she heard a howling scream.

Calisa clapped her hands over her ears.

A wrinkled hand slammed the closet door shut in front of her, and she staggered back to see Auntie Zee glaring at her.

"Broom?" Calisa squeaked.

"I'm far too old for this," Auntie Zee grumbled.

A second later, Auntie Zee opened the same closet door to reveal a perfectly ordinary broom closet with a variety of brooms, mops, and sponges. Calisa realized she'd hung back, in case it was the howling darkness again. "Before—when I opened it . . ."

"You're tired. You had a long journey."

"Yes, but—"

"It's a broom closet."

Of course it was, but—

"First rule of the Faraway Inn: don't open doors without permission," Auntie Zee said. "Ever." Muttering to herself, she selected a broom and shoved it at Calisa before she began waddling away toward the kitchen.

Calisa grabbed it before it fell. "What are the other rules?"

From the kitchen doorway, Auntie Zee looked back at her. "Other rules?"

"You said that was the first rule. What are the others?"

Auntie Zee snorted. "Only one other rule."

"What's that?" Calisa asked. It would be better to know right from the beginning, so she didn't make any more mistakes. She only had three days to do everything right, make herself useful, and convince Auntie Zee to let her stay, as well as possibly figure out what on earth she'd just seen (and heard) inside that closet, which she didn't *think* had been caused by her overtired mind or her overactive imagination . . . except it must have been, because the closet clearly held cleaning supplies. The broom in her hand, solid and ordinary, was proof of that. "Auntie Zee, what's the one other rule?"

"Don't ask questions."

CHAPTER FOUR

Calisa walked outside with the broom in her hand and stood on the porch. She stared out at the jumble of weeds and brambles, the pine tree forest, and the winding road that led away from the bed-and-breakfast. The sun had set at some point while they were repairing the porch, and now dusk lay like a gray cloth over everything, muting the colors and deepening the shadows.

What had just happened?

I imagined it.

Or there was a malfunctioning light bulb that had flickered at just the wrong moment while the wind howled outside. Yes, that was much more plausible than her brain suddenly deciding to present her with a gaping void where a broom closet was supposed to be.

"Calisa?"

Except Auntie Zee's reaction had been so over-the-top that

it made Calisa feel like she must have experienced some kind of unusual—

"Hey? Calisa?" A hand landed on her shoulder, and Calisa yelped and spun, brandishing the broom like a sword. Jack jumped backward. He held his hands up in surrender. "You, um, want me to sweep the sawdust?"

Calisa felt herself blush. "Oh! Sorry! No, I can do it." She began to sweep, smacking the new boards with the bristles with more enthusiasm than was strictly necessary. Sawdust billowed into a cloud around her ankles. She was aware that he was watching her, and she wondered if she looked as unsettled as she felt. "The closet in the hallway . . ." She trailed off, not knowing how to complete that sentence in any way that made sense.

"Ah, you opened a door."

Calisa halted mid-sweep. "Yes. What did—"

"This place has old wiring. Sometimes if you open a closet too quickly, you hear creaks. Groans. Weird light stuff. Old houses get quirky over time, my dad says." He shrugged, as if that was an explanation, and maybe it was. It had only been a fraction of a second before Auntie Zee had slammed the door shut.

"But why would Auntie Zee react so—" A lace curtain flicked in the sitting room, and Calisa cut herself off. Was that Auntie Zee, eavesdropping? It could be. "Never mind. It's fine."

So her great-aunt owned an old, creaky inn and was very, very touchy about it. So what? This was still a far better place to be for the summer than Brooklyn. *I can make this work.*

She'd expected a little quirkiness as a side dish to the Vermont bed-and-breakfast charm. "I've never stayed at a bed-and-breakfast," Calisa said, trying to sound light and cheerful as she not very subtly changed the subject. "Except for visits when I was little, which I already told you I barely remember. What's it like living in one?"

"It's great!" Jack said. "Lots of, you know . . . breakfast. And beds." He winced, as if aware he was being less than profound. "Anyway, if you're hungry, there's food in the kitchen. You can just help yourself to whatever you want. We, uh, don't have a cook. But there's soup. And . . . cheese. Bread."

"I'm fine, but thanks." She'd bought a panini in Penn Station and eaten on the train. She might not be a natural with carpentry stuff—and Jack seemed to have that covered anyway—but cooking . . . *I could help with that.* Every Mother's Day, birthday, special occasion, and the occasional random Sunday, she'd make pancakes for Mom-Kate and Mom-Elise. The first time, when she was about six years old, they'd turned out so lumpy that it was like eating gummy pebbles, but she'd improved, thankfully, and she liked to think she now made excellently fluffy pancakes. If she made breakfast for everyone in the inn, would that impress Auntie Zee? "Do the guests like pancakes? I could cook pancakes tomorrow morning, if that would be helpful."

He perked up like a puppy who'd seen a squirrel. "You know how to make pancakes? My dad makes the best pancakes. When he's here. When there's time. It's his special-occasion breakfast."

If it was his dad's specialty . . . "I don't want to step on any toes. . . ."

Jack shook his head vigorously. "Pancakes would be awesome. We have the ingredients. Come on, I'll show you." He headed inside, and she followed with the broom. He strode through the lobby. "You're going to love our maple syrup. We buy it locally, and it's seriously ambrosia. Got a bunch of specialty flavors too. One guest said he was coming back every year just for the maple syrup, and he did until he got himself eaten. Auntie Zee sent him a care package with syrup, but he still hasn't made another reservation."

As she passed the mirror on the wall of the lobby, she saw a flicker out of the corner of her eye, like a wisp of smoke crossing the surface of the glass. She glanced at the mirror, and it was cloudy, as if it were reflecting only the shadows of what it saw. Had it gotten more dirty since she'd last looked at it? "Wait, did you say 'eaten'?"

"Ha! No. I meant he had an accident."

"An accident that involved being eaten?"

"Nope. A ladder."

Ah, that made more sense. Jack must have had breakfast on the brain. "You have to watch out for those man-eating ladders," Calisa said solemnly.

Jack laughed, though she thought his laugh sounded a little strained. Granted, it hadn't been a particularly good joke. It was nice he was being polite.

Reaching the kitchen, he dragged her from cabinet to fridge to cabinet, showing her where all the ingredients were: flour, sugar, eggs, whatever she needed. Oddly, in the wake of her joke, he had switched from friendly to hurried.

He plucked the broom out of her hands. "I'll put that back," he offered.

"That's okay. I can . . ."

He scooted down the hall, and she listened for a howl or for the old inn to creak and groan. All she heard was a door open and shut, and he was back a second later, beaming at her. "All right, then! Pancakes tomorrow, with the world's best maple syrup! Can't wait! You cook, and I'll clean." With a jaunty wave, Jack headed for the stairs. "Good night!"

"Good night?" That was it? It wasn't late—not even nine o'clock—and Calisa had about a thousand more questions to ask about the inn and her aunt and the guests and Jack himself. He was so different from any of the guys she knew—a mix of competent and innocent, kind and also kind of clueless, equal parts friendly and skittish. She wanted to know more about what his life here was like, what he was like, why the inn was such a disaster if he and his dad were both groundskeepers. But he was already out of sight. *Did I say something wrong? What just happened?*

She heard him thump up the stairs. A door opened, then shut.

And then the inn was quiet.

Alone in her guest room, Calisa changed into her nightshirt and flannel shorts. It felt strange not to say good night to her moms, not to text Ethan (*Don't think about him*), and not to talk with Crystal and Maddy until she fell asleep. She hadn't even seen Auntie Zee again or met any of the guests, even though she'd dithered in the kitchen until the quiet drove her into her room. Now it was just her, alone in guest room number two.

And it was, if possible, even more quiet.

She slid under the quilt and then switched off the lamp next to the bed. Shadows layered the room. She stared up at the lace canopy, which looked like a lattice of cracks in the faded-denim darkness, and she tried to figure out why it all felt so strange.

It's the moon, Calisa decided. She was used to shadows in her bedroom, either sharp from the streetlights outside or undulating like waves from the cars on the street below, but those shadows were always in motion. Here, though, they were soft and still, tinged with blue. She wondered if Ethan was—

No.

She switched to thinking about the broom closet.

She should absolutely *not* double-check it, especially since Auntie Zee had explicitly told her not to open doors without permission or ask questions. Clearly, Auntie Zee was a woman who valued her privacy, an odd stance for a person who made a living by routinely inviting strangers to visit.

Closing her eyes, Calisa tried to will herself to sleep. She'd woken early to catch the train from the city, had had a long journey, and needed to wake up in time to make the promised pancakes that Jack was so adorably excited about. *Go to sleep.*

She lay still for several minutes.

Gah, it was way too quiet.

Except for the crickets outside. *Those* were loud. She opened her eyes and stared up at the pale blue shadows of the lace canopy. She wished there was better cell coverage. It had been a long, slightly strange day, exactly the kind of day that required texts. She wanted to tell Crystal about the sad state of the B&B. She wanted to hear what Maddy would say about Jack. She'd probably say, *No rebound guy. Look after yourself.* And she'd point out that Jack didn't seem to like her very much—or didn't seem to want to like her, which was almost the same thing. She didn't need another guy she had to convince to value her. Calisa imagined telling Ethan about the broom closet, and she knew what *he'd* say. He'd claim it was all in her head. She thought of how he'd immediately tried to tell her she hadn't seen what she'd seen before he even had his hand fully out from under Jocelyn Pullman's shirt. "I can explain" were the first words out of his mouth, before he unleashed a string of lies that she'd wanted to believe so badly but couldn't when the truth was so obvious.

I saw what I saw.

Hadn't she?

She heard a clatter outside her room and a soft "Oof."

Calisa pushed the covers off and clicked on the light. It sounded like Jack hadn't actually gone to sleep, which was excellent since there was no way she was falling asleep anytime soon, not with the way her thoughts kept bouncing around in her skull, and if she lay here in the dark and the silence too long, she'd begin to brood. Or worse, mope. She had zero intention of moping while she was here, whether it was for three days or the entire summer.

She paused at the door, glancing down at her nightshirt and flannel shorts. The shirt was emblazoned with the silhouette of a superhero and a robot beneath the words "Fight Evil, Read Books." No holes. No stains. *Eh, it's fine.* She didn't want to delay to change into clothes and risk Jack heading back upstairs before she had the chance to talk with him again.

Taking her key, Calisa slipped into the hallway. The carpet felt like moss under her bare feet. It silenced her footsteps, making her feel like she was tiptoeing, even though she wasn't. She passed by the stairs, through the lobby, and into the kitchen.

Standing at the counter amid the stacks of pots and bowls was a fifty-to-sixty-year-old man, as thin as a skeleton, with wild white hair that poked out at all angles and skin so pale he looked nearly translucent. He was wearing all black—a black turtleneck, black slacks, and a single black gem earring—and humming "Ain't No Sunshine" as he poured milk into a bowl.

He had to be one of the guests.

"Hi," Calisa said.

"Gah!" His hand shook as he jumped, and milk splashed onto the counter. "Oh dear."

"Sorry!" Calisa rushed forward and grabbed a towel from next to the sink. "I didn't mean to scare you." She mopped up the spilled milk while he fluttered near her, flapping his arms like a bird.

"What a mess, what a shame," he said.

"It's fine. No worries."

"Oh no, dear girl, you shouldn't have to clean my disaster," he said. But she'd already finished. It hadn't been more than a spatter—the towel was barely damp. "Very kind of you. Yes, indeed. I am grateful."

"I'm the one who startled you," Calisa said. "Not your fault, and not a disaster at all."

"Of course, yes, of course." He beamed at her.

She smiled back, feeling awkward. What was a brand-new B&B employee supposed to say to a guest? Should she offer to help? Give him privacy? Ask if he was having a pleasant stay? She hoped he didn't report back to Auntie Zee that she'd startled him.

"What drew you out here, in the still of the night?" he asked. "Did I disturb your slumber?" He dropped his voice at the word *slumber,* as if he feared she was still asleep.

"It's like nine-thirty. You didn't disturb me. No worries." What was it with early bedtimes? Was this a Vermont thing, or just this bed-and-breakfast? He didn't sound like he was concerned about her bothering him; more like vice versa. She relaxed a little. Surely, Auntie Zee wouldn't kick her out just for interacting with a guest.

He sighed dramatically. "I'm relieved to hear it. I was assured it wouldn't be a bother if I used the kitchen facilities after-hours. I know we all come to the Faraway Inn for a sliver of peace to touch our souls, and I wouldn't dream of disturbing the repose of the other guests."

Calisa pressed her lips together so she wouldn't laugh. He reminded her of a man she'd seen at the renaissance fair that Crystal had dragged her and Maddy to last summer—a willowy man in a black cloak who'd spouted poetry while hawking corsets. Like that man, this guest enunciated every sentence as if it were a sonnet. "No repose disturbed," she told him. "And

I'm not one of the guests. I'm Calisa, Auntie Zee's niece. I'm working here for the summer." *Hopefully.*

He laid his hand over his heart, and she thought for an instant that he was going to bow. "Ah, a blood relation of our illustrious hostess! I'm honored to meet you. My name is Mulligan, and I am a regular visitor to this bucolic haven."

"Nice to meet you," Calisa said. "I just arrived today, so I don't know anything yet, but is there something I can help you with? What are you making?"

"Ah! This"—he gestured at the bowl with a flourish—"is a potion for the wounded heart. A salve for a shattered soul. A concoction to comfort those caught in the crushing misery of an unkind fate." He struck an actor-overplaying-Hamlet pose, arm raised, head back, silhouetted against the darkness of the kitchen window.

She wondered if Mulligan had ever done theater. "Sounds great."

He dropped his hand. "It is more colloquially known as 'hot chocolate.'"

Calisa grinned. "Definitely great."

"I make it from scratch with only the finest ingredients: whole milk, unsweetened cocoa powder, sugar, chopped chocolate, and the secret ingredient . . . vanilla extract from the highest-quality bean in all the known realms." He lifted a bottle of vanilla, displaying it as if it were a rare wine bottle. "Would you care to join me?"

She opened her mouth to say no, she was fine.

"It eases heartache."

"Sure, yes, that would be nice," she said. "Thank you."

Mulligan smiled so widely that the skin of his cheeks stretched thin. “Delightful indeed to have company in this time of sorrow, to share the pain of existence with a fellow traveler of the deepest part of the night.” He bustled over to the stove and placed a copper pot on it, and then he poured the mixture he'd been stirring in the bowl into the pot. “Low heat, and when it's ready, we shall add the chocolate. Would you be a dear, my dear, and chop-chop-chop?” He flapped his hand toward the counter.

She located the bag of chocolate, tied with a pink ribbon. As she opened it, the scent of chocolate rolled out, and she breathed it in, rich and luxurious. “Smells wonderful.”

“The most wonderful!” Mulligan agreed. “It is made from the rarest of cocoa beans, cultivated by the reclusive denizens of the forest of everlasting day and obtained from the Night Market.”

She wondered where that was. He *did* have a bit of an accent. Maybe British? Maybe Indian? She couldn't tell. “Sounds amazing. How much should I chop?”

“A generous amount, my sweet fellow seeker of solace.” He stirred the milk and cocoa while she spilled a handful of chocolate chunks onto a cutting board and located a knife. “Tell me, what has drawn you out of slumber and into the cold unflinching night?”

Again, it was only nine-thirty, but she wasn't going to point that out.

“You don't need to share if you don't wish to,” Mulligan continued. “I don't intend to pry. If you wish to hold your pain close—”

“Heartbreak,” Calisa said. “Really ordinary, embarrassing,

he-cheated-on-me-then-tried-to-lie-about-it heartbreak. It's not a very interesting story, and I'm hoping that this place will help me forget it." She said it as lightly as she could. *Not going to mope.* It wouldn't bring back the imagined dream of a future with Ethan, the summer she was supposed to have, the next school year, whatever followed. . . . She'd spent time worrying about how they'd fare with a long-distance relationship after graduation, if she went off to one college and he went to another. She'd nearly decided to pick the same city as him, when it came time. But they hadn't made it to senior year. Or even July.

"Ah, yes, the pain of life's inexorable cruelty. I know it well. I too am nursing a heartache, though of a different sort." He sighed even more dramatically than before. "Mine is the pain of regret, of failure, for I continue to fail the one I love the most." He gazed out the window for a moment at the darkened gardens and then said, "But I think you are perhaps not as cavalier about your wound as you pretend? It is new, yes?"

She felt a lump in her throat. It wasn't all that new—it had been a few weeks, and she had plenty of proof that she was better off without him. Other stories about other girls . . . He wasn't who she'd thought he was.

It still hurt, though. Like someone had reached into her heart and clawed out a chunk.

"Chop as fine as you wish," Mulligan advised. "It will only melt faster. Like joyful memories as time dissolves them in the never-ending night of loss."

"It's more that I miss who he should have been," Calisa said.

"What I thought I had. What I *did* have—I have all these joyful memories, yes, but I also had all these hopes and dreams." She sliced the chocolate into slivers.

"You mourn the loss of someone who never was," Mulligan said. "A future that never will be. That is as much a death as a true one."

"Except he's walking around, smiling and laughing." She chopped faster.

"He is not. That is a simulacrum. You carry the true him in your heart, or the him as he could have been, and there is no shame in that. Allow yourself to feel what your heart wishes to feel. Do not deny your pain."

That was . . . actually nice to hear. So many friends told her to forget him, that he wasn't worth a single tear, that he didn't deserve her pain, but that didn't make it hurt any less. "I'm not denying it," Calisa said. "I'm just hoping that being here and far away from his smiling and laughing simulacrum will, you know, make it better." She wasn't sure if it would work. She wasn't doing a good job distracting herself from thoughts of him so far. "Did you . . . Is that why you're here? Do you want to talk about your heartache?"

He smiled, stretching his skeletal face. "Not at present, but I thank you for your kindness in asking, and for your assistance with tonight's concoction."

She showed him the slivers on the cutting board. "Is this the right amount?"

He clapped his hands together. "Perfection! Now, bring them here."

She carried the cutting board over to the stove, and he swept the slivers into the milky chocolate. They fell like dark snow, and she inhaled the already-rich chocolaty scent. "It smells amazing," she reported as she washed the empty cutting board and knife in the sink.

"Its taste will transport you. Metaphorically, of course, not literally—though it is said that taste can directly link to memories. Ah, to remember happier times."

Out of the corner of her eye, Calisa saw a shadow shift and looked out the window over the sink. The sky was a sweep of dark blue and the mountains were silhouettes. The apple tree shivered in the night breeze. Beneath it was the statue of the lady.

Leaning forward, Calisa peered out at the statue. She wondered why someone had moved it from the front lawn to the back. And how. It had to weigh a ton. She thought of Jack carrying the stone gargoyle up to one of the guest rooms. She supposed he might just like to rearrange sculptures? Or maybe this was a different statue from the one in the front. That seemed more likely. She just hadn't noticed it in the daylight, when she'd been awed by the view of the forest and the mountains.

Mulligan claimed two mugs from one of the cabinets. Both looked handmade, slightly lopsided but glazed with colors like a sunset. He poured the hot chocolate into each, then took a sip. Closing his eyes, he swallowed. She waited a moment, expecting him to sigh dramatically, and he didn't disappoint. He sighed like the wind over the sea.

Calisa lifted the mug to her lips. The chocolaty steam rose

deliciously into the air until she felt as if she'd tasted it already. She took a sip, and . . . *Wow.* She'd had lots of hot chocolate before, some from really nice bakeries in Manhattan and one from a gourmet chocolate shop in Park Slope, but this . . . It tasted like the warmth of a hug from a friend who just wanted you to feel better. Closing her eyes, she took a second sip, larger than the first. She felt it warm her throat as it slid into her rib cage, and she imagined the chocolate spreading into her heart, enveloping it with rich sweetness.

"It's the vanilla," Mulligan explained.

"It's magnificent," Calisa said. She drank again, and this time it tasted like a toasty fire in a hearth while snow fell outside—not that she'd sat by many fireplaces; they didn't have one in their apartment, but it tasted the way she imagined a nice, cozy fire would feel.

Silence fell across the kitchen as they drank their hot chocolate, but this time it was a gentle quiet, and she didn't mind it. Outside the crickets chirped, a tuneless melody, and she thought she heard an owl, low and soft. The moon was three-quarters full, and its light fell across the counter, mixing blue with the amber of the kitchen lights.

"I hope your stay in this sanctuary soothes your heart wounds," Mulligan said.

Calisa lifted her mug in a salute. "The hot chocolate does help."

"I am glad to hear it."

"I hope it helps you too."

"We shall see." Setting aside his mug, Mulligan pulled a vial out of his shirt pocket. "I do continue to try. My hope is unflagging, and my heart forever true."

She blinked at the vial, wondering what he planned to use that for. It was made of murky glass and looked more like an antique than part of a chem lab experiment. The stopper was made of tarnished silver. He removed it and laid it on the counter.

He carefully poured hot chocolate into it while she watched. A few drops spilled onto the counter. He put the stopper back on and then cleaned the spatter. Finishing, he smiled at her with a mouth full of narrow bright white teeth as he tucked the vial back into his pocket. He patted it, as if to confirm it was safe.

Okay, that was odd. "Um, there might be a better way to transport the leftovers? Maybe a travel cup?" She crossed to the cabinets. "Or a jar with a lid?"

"This will suit my purposes," Mulligan said.

Maybe he just wanted a tiny sip of hot chocolate for later tonight? She wasn't sure how to ask without it sounding rude, and it really wasn't her business anyway. She thought of Auntie Zee's rule of no questions.

Humming to himself, a dirgelike melody in a minor key, he began putting away the vanilla, milk, and other ingredients. Calisa washed the pot and bowl, and he wiped down the counter and stovetop.

As they finished, he executed a slight bow. "I thank you again for your kindness, as well as your company." He then shuffled out of the kitchen, bringing only the odd little vial with him. She listened to his footsteps soft on the stairs.

Calisa took another sip of her still-warm hot chocolate.

She looked out the window at the garden at night. Stars were strewn across the sky, and a cloud drifted across the moon. She *did* feel better.

Everything is going to be okay. I'm *going to be okay.*

There was just one more thing she had to do, and then she thought she'd be able to fall asleep. Carrying her mug with her, she went to the end of the hallway of supply closets. She stopped in front of the broom closet.

Calisa took a fortifying sip as she contemplated the door, feeling a little silly for still thinking she saw and heard more than old hinges and a shadowy closet, and then she opened it. The door didn't shriek, groan, or howl. Inside, the closet held only brooms and mops.

She closed the door and went to bed.

CHAPTER FIVE

Outside the window, birds chirped like it was some kind of Disney movie.

Calisa yanked the pillow out from under her and squeezed it over her face and ears. It made the room somewhat darker, but the birds were still shrieking, *"Tweelee, tweelee!"* and *"See see see!"* and— "Gah!" she said.

Sitting up, she looked at her phone. Five-thirty-five? In the morning?

The songbird on her windowsill took off at her sudden movement. She heaved herself out of bed, intending to pull the curtains shut. She hadn't realized her room faced east, though even if she had, she wouldn't have guessed that was a problem. It wasn't an issue at home. Usually, the streetlights, the headlights from the cars, and the change of the nearest traffic light invaded her sleep. Morning came darkly, with a steady increase of noise, not with all this chirpy fanfare. Reaching the window, she looked out.

Mist curled over the forest, and lemon light stained the tops of the mountains. It felt as if she were looking at a painting. She stared out at it, her hand on the curtain, unwilling to close it. As the sun spread over the pine trees, Calisa decided she didn't hate the birds if they came with a view like this. She left the curtain alone.

Awake now, she trooped down the hall to the shared bathroom, showered, and dressed. It too was quaint, with a claw-foot bathtub as well as an archaic-looking shower, but the plumbing worked fine at least, once she figured out which knob did what.

As Calisa brushed her wet hair, she heard a low murmuring whisper outside the door. She stopped and tried to hear whose voice it was. "Hello? I'm in here."

Another whisper joined the first—or was that a third?—but now they sounded distant. She thought of the odd whispers she'd heard underneath the porch. These sounded like that, garbled and far away.

Finishing her hair, she cracked open the door and peeked out into the hall. "Hello?"

It was empty.

She listened, but the voices had vanished. If the inn had TVs, she would have said one had been switched off. Or maybe it was a guest on the phone? Anyway, it hadn't been anyone talking to her. Dismissing it, Calisa headed down the hall. She was humming to herself by the time she reached the kitchen.

Looking as if he'd been awake for hours, Jack was assembling multiple bottles of maple syrup on the counter. He brightened when she came into the room. "Have you ever tried blueberry maple syrup?" he asked. "Or salted-caramel maple syrup?"

"Never."

He picked up a bottle shaped like a leaf. "How about elderberry?"

"I don't even know what an elderberry is."

"It's a berry from an elderberry bush, which I realize as I say it is not so much of a definition, but it's good. Especially on pancakes . . . which you said you'd make?" Jack looked at her hopefully. He was one hundred percent a morning person, far too chipper for barely after dawn, but somehow he managed to be more adorable than annoying.

She laughed, despite how early it was. "Yes, I'll make them right now."

Calisa pulled out the ingredients, as well as the bowl that Mulligan had used to make his hot chocolate. She wondered how much batter to make. Should she double the recipe? Triple it? She usually made one and a half batches for her and her parents. "How many guests are in the Faraway Inn right now?"

"Four," Jack said, then paused. "Three."

"You're not sure, or you lost one?"

"I didn't . . ." He trailed off, composed himself, and answered, "Three who will eat pancakes. Actually, two, but the third is supposed to arrive soon, so I'd count her. Plus me, you, and Auntie Zee."

Two-soon-to-be-three was not a healthy number of guests. Still, she'd better make triple what she usually made for her and her moms. Better too much than too little, if she wanted to impress her great-aunt. She recited the adjusted recipe in her head as she cooked:

One and a half sticks of butter.

She unwrapped two sticks, chopped one in half, and set the butter to melt in a little pot on the stove. The inn lacked a microwave, which she hadn't noticed before, but a pot would work fine. "Is there a griddle? Or any kind of flat pan?"

He handed her a circular griddle, and she laid it on the stove and switched on the burners to preheat, before turning back to the ingredients:

Four and a half cups of flour.

Six tablespoons of sugar.

She added a half tablespoon extra. She always did. Learned that from Mom-Elise. You always need a little extra sugar, she'd say. Life lesson.

Seven and a half teaspoons of baking powder.

Three-quarters teaspoon salt.

"So, I was wondering . . ." He was looking at the stove, not at her, which she thought was a sign that he was about to ask something she didn't want to answer.

Six eggs.

She cracked each one and tossed the shells in the garbage. The yolks reminded her of the sunrise, plump on the mountain.

"Yes?" she said when he didn't continue.

"Why are you here? Not here in the kitchen, but here at the Faraway Inn this summer?"

Yep, she was right. She didn't want to explain again. It was bad enough that she'd told Auntie Zee and Mulligan. She didn't need her coworker with the very gorgeous eyes and floppy hair looking at her with pity. "I told you: to help Auntie Zee."

One and three-quarters teaspoons vanilla.

She thought of Mulligan as she added the vanilla and wondered what he'd think of her pancakes and if he'd drunk his vial of hot chocolate yet. It wasn't a big deal, but it was just so quirky that she couldn't stop wondering about it. Why save just a teaspoon of hot chocolate? She stirred, breaking the egg yolks with the spoon. The eggy flour clumped on its neck.

Three cups of milk. She poured the cups in, plus a splash extra.

"I mean, why now instead of other summers?" he said. "You came here as a kid, you said, with the chocolate-covered strawberries, but then not again. Why didn't you come back here before? Even to visit?"

A much better question. Also one that she wasn't sure she wanted to answer. *Or one I even can answer.* She wondered why Auntie Zee's no-questions rule didn't apply to Jack. Maybe it was more a loose guideline than a rule.

As she thought about how to answer, Calisa checked on the butter—nicely melted. She poured it in. "I think there was an argument? Between one of my moms and Auntie Zee. I was young, and no one ever told me what it was about. They made up, I'm pretty sure. At least they talk on holidays, and she agreed to let me come here this summer. . . ." Hadn't she? Auntie Zee hadn't acted happy to see her. Based on what she'd said, it was seeming more likely now that Mom-Kate had just plowed ahead with what she thought was best.

Stirring the batter, Calisa chased the lumps of flour around the bowl.

She should have had a longer conversation with Mom-Kate before she'd come here about what exactly the status of their relationship was. Or maybe it didn't matter, and it was in the past. Really, all she had to do now was convince Auntie Zee to let her stay longer than three days, which she'd have a better chance of doing if she made herself useful—by making everyone excellently fluffy pancakes. She didn't need to fix old family problems that weren't her business. Just like she didn't need to know why Mulligan wanted a single vial of hot chocolate.

She ladled batter onto the griddle. It spread into a circle. She added three more circles of batter to the griddle. "Spatula?" she asked Jack.

He produced a spatula, and she thanked him.

When the pancakes began to bubble, she flipped them. After waiting a minute, she turned to ask Jack for a plate—and saw that he'd laid out trays, each with a plate, a rolled-up linen napkin, a glass of milk, and multiple tiny bowls with various syrups. He was putting blossoms into tiny vases in the corner of each tray.

"How did you do that so quickly?" Calisa asked.

He shrugged. "Practice. Can't make pancakes but can set up a room service tray."

"The guests don't eat breakfast downstairs?" She shouldn't be surprised, given how dusty and unwelcoming the common rooms were, but still . . . shouldn't they?

"Guests always used to," Jack said, "but lately, they've

preferred to eat in their rooms. I guess because it's nicer—you've seen the dining room—or maybe they just like the privacy." As he finished with adding flowers to the trays, she transferred the golden and pillowy pancakes to plates and started the next batch.

He picked up two of the trays and carried them out of the kitchen. She heard his footsteps on the stairs. By the time he returned, she had pancakes on the last tray. He took that one to the third floor as she scraped out the rest of the batter, then piled the remaining pancakes onto a single plate.

Sitting on a stool at the counter, Jack helped himself to three of the stacked pancakes and then poured raspberry maple syrup on top of them, so much that it dripped down the sides of the pancakes and pooled on the plate.

She sat on a stool next to him. "Do the guests stay in their rooms all the time?"

He handed her the maple syrup. "Room eight usually only comes out at night, but once room three arrives, you'll see her and room twelve pretty frequently."

Only comes out at night . . . "Is room eight Mulligan?"

He glanced at her with surprise. "You've met Mulligan?"

Calisa waved her fork at the stove, then swallowed her bite of pancake. Oh wow, raspberry maple syrup! Jack was right—it tasted like pure summer, with a twist of maple. Belatedly, she answered, "He was making hot chocolate."

"Hot chocolate this time? Huh. He's tried stranger things."

She wasn't sure what he meant. Did Mulligan usually go

for other kinds of drinks during his nighttime appearances? She hadn't noticed any alcohol in the kitchen. "It was good hot chocolate."

"I'm sure it was," Jack said. "Mulligan uses the best ingredients." He looked as if he wanted to say more, but instead he shoved a forkful of pancake into his mouth. She wondered if she'd said something that alienated him again—they'd been doing so well for a few minutes there.

"Has he been a guest here long?" The way he talked about Mulligan made him sound like a permanent resident. She wondered if the current guests were long-term visitors. If so, how long did they usually stay? She'd assumed people came to a bed-and-breakfast for a weekend getaway. She didn't know what one did in the middle of nowhere for longer than that. It was miles and miles to the nearest town, and what was there to do in town, anyway? A few restaurants at best. An antiques shop or maple syrup store or something equally Vermont-y? Did the guests like to hike? There were certainly enough mountains to hike in. She tried to picture Mulligan in his all-black outfit, hiking up a mountain. It didn't seem like his style. What drew guests here, especially long-term ones?

"These are awesome pancakes," Jack said. A spot of syrup was on his cheek. She resisted the urge to wipe it away as he shoveled more pancake into his mouth. Even with his cheeks bulging like a chipmunk's, he was still cute.

Don't notice that, she told herself firmly.

"Thanks." Eating another bite, she made herself look out the window at the apple tree instead of at Jack. Hadn't there been a statue beneath the tree last night? She was certain there had been. She must have been looking out from a different angle before. It was most likely just out of sight. "So, is this the inn's offseason? Are there more guests in winter?"

He shifted uncomfortably on his stool, as if she'd asked a touchy question. "Well, it used to be our busiest season. We're just going through a slow patch. . . . Not all the usual summer season guests have returned, but they might still book. It's just the start of the summer."

That didn't sound great.

Only three rooms filled? And this was supposed to be the busy season?

Exactly how much trouble was Auntie Zee's B&B in?

She and Jack cleaned up from breakfast after they finished. He wrapped the leftover pancakes lovingly in plastic wrap and displayed the syrups on one whole shelf in the refrigerator. She spotted at least a dozen flavors, from vanilla to peach caramel. "I'll be on the roof if you need me," he said. "Gotta fix the leaks before it rains again."

"Do you need help?" she offered.

"Wow, no one ever asks that." Jack smiled sunnily at her. "But it's kind of a one-person thing. Not sure the porch roof can support two people on it."

Fair enough. "Got it. Don't want to repair another Calisa-size hole."

His eyes widened. "It's absolutely not personal!"

Calisa wasn't offended. She *had* crashed through the porch, and she had zero interest in repeating that performance on a roof. "It's fine. I'll find something else useful to do." It would have been nice to keep talking to him. She hadn't asked him anything about himself, about his life here, about why he thought the inn was so vacant, about whether he'd ever had his heart broken, about whether he thought hot chocolate and pancakes would be enough to heal that. *Stay focused.* The last thing she needed was to attach herself to another boy. *I'll admire from a distance. And not on a roof.* "How do you know what Auntie Zee wants you to do next?"

"I just try to spot what needs doing and do it."

"But how do you know if she really wants you to do that?" If this were an ordinary job, she'd be given assignments. She wasn't convinced there was anything ordinary about this place.

Jack shrugged. "Guess I don't? But when I fix stuff, she seems happy. Or at least she grunts in a kind of friendly way?"

Okay, at least she knew her goal: make Auntie Zee grunt happily.

As Jack headed outside, Calisa surveyed the kitchen. She'd made pancakes, but she had no clue whether Auntie Zee or any of the guests had liked them.

If she wanted to impress her great-aunt, she had to do more. A lot more.

She'd already boasted to Auntie Zee that she knew how to clean, and she did. Her moms believed in cleanliness, as well as the importance of chores. She'd been cleaning stuff since she was five or six. Granted, that was a tiny apartment, not an inn, but other than scale, it should be the same.

Plus she could pretend she was scrubbing Ethan out of her brain.

That sounded like an excellent plan.

Calisa located cleaning spray and dustrags in a closet next to the refrigerator. She hesitated when she realized she'd opened a door without permission and then shook her head at herself. Surely, Auntie Zee hadn't meant closets . . . except the door from the other night had been a broom closet.

She closed and reopened the closet. Just Lysol, sponges, and soap.

"Stop being ridiculous," Calisa told herself out loud. She'd start with the worst room, she decided, to make the greatest impact: the sitting room, where the majority of the furniture was hidden beneath sheets as if this were an abandoned Victorian house populated by ghosts and overdramatic widows.

The elderly white cat was curled on the red velvet chair again. As Calisa entered, the cat opened an eye to look disapprovingly at her.

"I promise I won't disturb you," Calisa told the cat. "I'm just going to clean."

Yawning to show all its teeth, the cat stretched and then lowered itself from the chair. It sauntered past Calisa, its tail flicking her ankles, and out of the room.

"I don't know whether that's permission or disapproval," she said to the retreating cat. She made a mental note to ask Jack its name and if it ever allowed anyone to pet it. It did not seem approachable.

Calisa turned back to the sitting room.

"I can do this," she said to the dust and the covered furniture.

She dove in, dusting and spraying and scrubbing every surface she could reach, from the floorboards to the doorframe to the windowsill.

She thought of Ethan and the promises he'd made her.

Forever, he'd said. *We're soulmates.*

Liar, she thought.

Playing music on her phone, not so loud that it bothered the guests but loud enough that it chased away the silence of the mountains outside, she danced as she cleaned. With each bit of the room she attacked, she imagined herself scouring away another memory. Another lie.

I'd never lie to you, he'd said. *You are my one and only.*

Traitor, she thought. *Cheater.*

She yanked the sheets off the furniture, sending up plumes of dust. The motes caught sunlight and created a hazy glitter in the air.

I only have eyes for you, he'd said.

Gaslighter, she thought. *Asshole.*

Underneath the sheets were couches and chairs and tables, but not just ordinary couches and chairs and tables—they looked like works of art. One couch was carved to look like a shell, with wood shaped like the spiral of a conch. Its cushions were blue-green, and the soft knit blanket on top reminded her of sea-foam. Another chair was shaped like the stump of a tree and carved with flowers and acorns. A thick moss-green cushion was sunk into the center of it. The top of a coffee table was a mosaic of pebbles, polished as if by a stream.

She wondered if he'd ever loved her. Had it always been lies?

As she made her way around the edges of the room, dusting

sconces and shelves and the mantel over the fireplace, she pictured his face and sprayed it with Lysol, then imagined she was wiping him away, word by lying word.

We're meant to be, he'd said. *It's destiny.*

He'd actually said those words with a straight face.

Worse, she'd believed him.

Working steadily clockwise, she reached the tea set in the corner that she'd spotted when she'd first arrived. Unlike the majority of the furniture, it hadn't been hidden beneath a sheet and was coated in a thick layer of dust, with cobwebs draped between the teapot handle and the stack of cups and saucers.

She was erasing their forever destiny with each cobweb she cleared. He was the past. She was leaving him behind and rediscovering her future, whatever it was. He had no place in it anymore. His promises were lies. His kisses were lies. His lips, liars. His eyes, liars.

Past. Over. Done.

She wiped down the tray table, kneeling to clean around the wheels, and then stood and began wiping the grime off the teacups. She wondered what her moms would say if they knew she was cleaning without being asked. *They'd be proud,* she thought. *And a little snarky.* If only her room weren't so messy.

When she finished with the tea set, Calisa scooped up all the sheets that had been covering the furniture. She had spotted a laundry machine at the end of the hallway of closets, beyond the kitchen. As she carried the sheets through the foyer toward the kitchen, she heard Auntie Zee say, "Welcome back, Kendra. Your room is ready for you."

She poked her head into the kitchen to see the new guest.

And then she blinked.

Auntie Zee was closing the closet door next to the refrigerator, and if Calisa didn't know better, she would have said it looked as if the guest had just stepped out of the cleaning supplies. Aside from the logistical implausibility of this, the new guest, Kendra, did *not* look like the kind of woman who ever touched a dustrag, much less emerged from a closet full of them. She was intimidatingly elegant, with white hair, dark skin, and fierce angular features. Zero wrinkles despite the white hair. She wore a tailored suit with a snow-white turtleneck under it. This must be the third guest, the one that Jack had said was due to arrive soon.

How, though, had she arrived without Calisa noticing? She hadn't heard a car. Or a plane or a helicopter or whatever this elegant, terrifying woman arrived in. *I was listening to music. And my own thoughts.*

"I trust the amenities will live up to my standards," Kendra said.

"Probably not," Auntie Zee said. "But the view is still the same."

"It'll do." She then fixed her eyes on Calisa, and Calisa froze as if she'd been caught mid-crime. Kendra's eyes narrowed. "I detest being watched."

As Auntie Zee turned, Calisa unfroze and bolted out of the kitchen.

She told herself there was absolutely no rational reason for her heart to be pounding. Of course the new guest hadn't appeared out of thin air, and Calisa shouldn't have fled when the guest looked at her. Sure, the woman looked intimidating, but New York City was full of intimidating women and she'd never fled from them. *I don't know why I panicked.* Running from guests was not going to impress Auntie Zee.

Obviously, I'm stressed and not thinking clearly.

She took a deep breath and inhaled the smell of tea. In the corner, the teapot rattled. Calisa turned and stared at it. Steam curled from its spout.

She'd just finished cleaning it. How was it suddenly full of hot tea?

In the fireplace, a nice warm fire crackled. She stared at that too. She'd just left this room less than a minute ago. Who had come in, lit a fire, and made tea?

Jack, she thought. Of course, it had to be. But . . . why?

Either he was trying to be nice, or it was the coziest prank she'd ever heard of.

CHAPTER SIX

Still carrying an armload of sheets, Calisa hurried outside and called, "Jack?"

She heard hammering from above her.

Stepping off the porch onto the weed-choked walkway, she looked up at the roof. Jack was straddling a hole in the shingles, a hammer in one hand and a chunk of wood in the other. In the morning light, his hair was a halo, and he looked like an angel perched on top of a shabby cathedral. A nicely muscular angel. She swallowed and dragged her mind back to the question of the sudden appearance of hot tea, a crackling fire, and the inn's newest guest. "Hello, Jack?"

The hammering stopped.

A second later, Jack peered down at her over the edge of the shingles. "Everything all right?"

"Sure, fine, but I need to ask—"

Squinting at her, he asked, "Are you looking for the laundry? It's at the end of the hallway off the kitchen."

"I know." It occurred to her that she probably looked ridiculous carting around an armload of random sheets. "But did you—"

"The detergent is on the shelf above it," Jack said.

"Thanks, but—"

"It's an old machine. Just use, like, a couple of teaspoons of detergent." He looked concerned, as if he thought she might break it. "If you need—"

"There's tea," Calisa said quickly, before he could tell her about fabric softener, stain remover, or whatever.

"Can't right now," he said, "but thanks for the offer."

Not what she was trying to say. *He might be angelically gorgeous, but gah!* It almost felt like he was being deliberately dense. Shifting the sheets to one arm, she pointed at the window. "I left the room for less than a minute, and when I came back, the teapot was full of hot tea. Was that you?"

He frowned, and then his expression lightened like he'd had a profound epiphany. "Ah, you must have accidentally hit the *on* switch."

The *on* switch? She hadn't seen any switch . . . or had she just missed it? She'd been more focused on removing the grime and cobwebs—and on scrubbing Ethan from her mind—than anything else. "You mean it's an electric teapot? But I didn't see a plug."

"Battery-operated," Jack said. "Honestly surprised the battery hasn't worn down. Guess sitting dormant didn't hurt it."

Oh. Right. A battery-operated electric teapot. She supposed that made a lot more sense than the idea that Jack had shimmied down from the roof, made a pot of tea, put it on the tea tray, and then scooted back in less than a minute, in order to surprise her.

"Sorry it surprised you," Jack said.

"How about the fire in the fireplace? Did you light that?"

"That must have been Auntie Zee," Jack said. "She likes a nice fire, even in summer. Says it's welcoming. Also, good for her joints or something?"

Calisa shook her head. "Auntie Zee was in the kitchen greeting the new guest." Thinking of the guest, she scanned the driveway and the road as far as she could see before the forest swallowed it. Since coming outside, she hadn't seen even a hint of a car. No taxi. No Uber. No limo. Not even a motorcycle. "Did you see her arrive? The new guest, I mean. Auntie Zee called her Kendra."

He smiled sunnily. "Oh, she came! Great! I was worried we'd have another cancellation."

So he *hadn't* seen her arrive?

Before she could ask, he said, "Always kind of a jumpscare when she comes. She likes to arrive on foot."

"On foot?"

"Kendra's a hiker," Jack explained. "Loves the mountains. Probably came in off a trail behind the inn. Yep, she loves to hike."

That seemed odd, given how impeccably she'd been dressed. On the other hand, Calisa had walked the last stretch to the inn herself. Maybe Kendra had also had an Uber driver who wouldn't stop talking about fly-fishing. But wouldn't she have luggage? Calisa tried to think whether she'd noticed any suitcases. She hadn't been paying attention to that.

"You should offer her tea," Jack said. "Or I can do it when I'm done with the roof, if you're busy with the laundry. We can all have tea when we're both done. If you want."

That sounded like an excellent idea. "All right, it's a date," she said, and instantly hated that she'd said those words. She felt her cheeks blush. "Not literally. Just an expression."

He didn't seem to notice that she was blushing. He was gazing off into the distance, toward the sky above the pine trees. "My dad told me that the inn used to have tea every day, with little sandwiches and cakes. All I remember are the cakes. I don't think I liked tea as a kid."

"Do you like it now?" The question felt ridiculous as she asked it, but she found herself wanting to know the answer.

"Sure. I mean, I don't know. The teapot has been broken for years, or I thought it was."

She stared at him for a moment. He did know there were other ways to make tea than a battery-powered teapot, didn't he? He could have just boiled some water on the stove or stuck a mug in the microwave. "We should restart afternoon tea, once I've got the front room clean."

He brightened. "Do you know how to bake a cake?"

"Not without a recipe," Calisa said, "but with one, yes. I didn't pack a cookbook." She'd made a birthday cake for Crystal just last month, and it had turned out pretty good. Lopsided but delicious. Chocolate with raspberry jam. She'd even made her own buttercream icing. "Does Auntie Zee like cake?"

"*I* like cake."

"How come you've never tried to bake your own?"

Now it was his turn to blush. His ears pinkened. "Um, well . . . Truth? Auntie Zee doesn't let me cook. One of her rules."

"Why not?" Because he was a guy? She knew Auntie Zee was grumpy, but she hadn't thought that meant she was sexist. Scowling, Calisa wondered if she shouldn't have volunteered to cook and clean. She hadn't meant to relegate herself to a traditional gender role. It was just that the inn needed to be cleaned and the guests needed breakfast, and she knew how to do both, thanks to her moms' love of assigning chores. It had been her choice, not a default assumption. In fact, Auntie Zee had given her no guidance whatsoever.

Jack ducked back so she couldn't see his full face over the lip of the roof. "I kind of almost burned the inn down about a year ago when I was trying to scramble eggs."

She bit back a laugh. He didn't deserve to be laughed at. It wasn't funny. "How . . . ?" Okay, no, it was legitimately funny. "Scrambling eggs? That's not even . . . What did you do?"

"Well, there was a bee inside the kitchen, and I kind of, well, overreacted. I was trying to get it out, and I was using a towel to, you know, scare it away—and I smacked the stove and knocked the skillet with the eggs onto the floor."

She still didn't see how that could almost cause a fire.

"I cleaned up, but I forgot to turn off the stove."

"You're blaming a bee because you forgot to turn off the stove?" Calisa said. That really didn't sound like it was the fault of the bee.

"It would have been fine, except I'd also opened the window.

You know, so the bee would fly out? And then, well, leaves blew in. It was fall. Really windy. Really dry leaves. Like, kindling-dry. Anyway, the leaves landed on the stove, a few caught fire, and they blew around the kitchen. . . . So, long story short, Auntie Zee won't let me cook anymore."

Calisa burst out laughing. She tried to stop—it wasn't nice of her—but the image of Jack fluttering around the kitchen with the bee and the fiery leaves . . . She hiccuped as she swallowed her laugh. As soon as she could breathe again, she said in a voice that only quivered a little, "So, is that why you don't make pancakes either? Or tea on the stove?"

"Yep. I was kind of hoping to avoid telling you that story, so you don't think I'm an idiot." His voice drifted down.

"I don't think you're an idiot," Calisa said. A little ridiculous. Adorable, even. But not an idiot. And she was relieved the cause of his ban wasn't rampant sexism. That made her feel better about her own choice of tasks at the inn. "It could happen to anyone."

"Yes! That's what I told Auntie Zee."

She imagined that Auntie Zee had scowled hard enough to curdle milk. There had probably been yelling, or at least a very disapproving grunt. "I do, though, think it's not entirely the bee's fault."

"I'll apologize the next time I see one," he said solemnly. He leaned forward again, far enough that she could see his face. His cheeks and neck were still pinkish from blushing so hard.

"Good. When I get a chance, I'll look for a cookbook that has a cake recipe." She wished she had internet access here, but whatever. Worst case she could call her moms and have them look it up. Mom-Kate liked store-bought cheesecake, and Mom-Elise always picked chocolate cake from the Little Cupcake Bake Shop on Vanderbilt for her birthday, but they could google a few recipes for her.

Calisa headed back inside. Auntie Zee and the new guest were nowhere to be seen, though she thought she heard voices drifting down the stairs. She dumped the sheets into the laundry machine and found the detergent where Jack had said it would be.

By the time she returned to the sitting room, Kendra was standing by the tea tray with a fresh cup of tea in her hands. "Oh! Hi!" Calisa said.

"If you had any training in innkeeping whatsoever, you would have offered me tea the instant I arrived." Her voice was low and soft, as melodic as a wave, if that wave were irritated and vaguely British. "But I'm told you're new and allowances must be made."

Jack had said to offer her tea, but Calisa hadn't had a chance.

"At least you've brewed a respectable beverage," Kendra said. "You people and your coffee. Sewage swill. *I* won't stomach it." She picked up the sugar, inspected it, then set it down.

"I only like coffee if it's mostly milk and sugar," Calisa ventured. "Really, just milk and sugar with a slight flavor of coffee. Better if it's got vanilla or hazelnut."

"Swill." Her eyes swept up and down Calisa, as if cataloging every detail for a scathing critique. "So . . . you're the niece." Turning her attention back to the tea tray, she picked up a saltshaker.

Calisa opened her mouth to tell her that was salt, but she

was too late—Kendra poured a healthy amount of salt into her tea. "Um, yes, I'm Auntie Zee's grandniece, Calisa."

Carrying her teacup and saucer, Kendra swept across the room and seated herself in the conch-shaped chair. "Since you're new, I will be clear: you will not disturb me while I'm at my repose." She stirred her salted tea elegantly. Calisa had the sense that Kendra did everything elegantly. "I come here for refuge, not to be gawked at, though I appreciate your admiration. I believe it's essential to have a place where one can rest and recover, do you not agree?"

"Absolutely," Calisa agreed fervently. That was why she was here, after all. She liked that framing a lot better than how Ethan had reacted—he'd told her she was running away and that if they wanted to fix the problems in their relationship, she had to stay and work through them. She'd told him the "problems" were his lies, manipulation, and rampant assholery, and so no, staying was not going to fix anything, unless he wanted to take himself to the local veterinarian to "fix" himself so he wasn't tempted to cheat anymore.

That conversation hadn't gone well.

Kendra sipped her tea. "Ahh, exactly as I remember."

With salt? Odd, but whatever. "What kind of cake did Auntie Zee used to serve with afternoon tea?" Calisa asked. She was liking the idea of restarting a daily tea. Already one guest was clearly pleased to have the front room available again and tea served.

"Rest and recover," Kendra repeated. "In peace."

"Sorry."

Sinking farther into the chair, Kendra closed her eyes as

she swallowed. Calisa wondered if she should keep cleaning or leave the room. This guest was almost as unfriendly as the inn's cat.

"Victoria sponge cake," Kendra said into the silence.

Hmm, that sounded potentially complicated to bake.

"Soft, tender, fluffy." Kendra licked her lips, as if imagining it. "Cream and raspberry jam sandwiched between the layers of cake. I'd never tasted anything like it back home."

"Where's home?" Calisa asked politely.

Kendra's eyes opened. "One does not ask that question here. Didn't Auntie Zee tell you that?"

Calisa flinched. Auntie Zee *had* said not to ask questions, but she'd thought the standard where-are-you-from fell in the realm of acceptable small talk. *Guess it's not just a loose guideline.* "Sorry." She wished she hadn't asked. It *should* have been okay to ask where Kendra was from, but maybe the stately woman was here to escape where she came from and who she was there. *Maybe she's someone famous.* A movie star. She did have a dramatic flair to her, a confidence in the way she flowed through the room. Probably Mom-Elise would have recognized her—she loved old movies. "Since we don't have cake right now, is there something else I can get you?" She had no idea what was in the kitchen, but there must be something to offer guests.

"Just the tea is sufficient." Kendra rose from her seat. "I will finish it in my room. In peace and solitude." She swept out of the room, her shoes soundless on the rug, her silent exit pointed.

Calisa winced. *That could have gone better.* At least she'd seemed to like the tea, despite—or because of?—the salt. And at least the room was clean. Scanning it for any remaining cobwebs or spots of dust, Calisa noticed the fire had gone out in the fireplace, leaving an unburnt log.

Over on the tea tray, the teapot continued to rattle and brew merrily.

CHAPTER SEVEN

Calisa was considering which room to tackle next when Auntie Zee appeared in the doorway to the sitting room. Scowling, the innkeeper waved at the sheet-free furniture and cobweb-free mantel. "Who told you that you could do this?"

So much for a friendly, approving grunt. "I thought . . ."

Auntie Zee snorted. "You didn't think."

"I didn't need to think hard," Calisa said. "It was drowning in dust and cobwebs."

This time her great-aunt's snort sounded a little more amused.

Encouraged, Calisa added, "The guests like it." Or one guest, at least. She didn't need to know that the guest had retreated to her room out of irritation. "I hoped you'd like it too." It was, after all, a highly visible part of the Faraway Inn and had been decorated with care, once upon a time.

Crossing her arms, Auntie Zee surveyed the sitting room. For a long moment, she didn't say a word. She simply scowled at the room as if she could swallow it in her wrinkles. "I can't maintain this. That's why I mothballed it in the first place—it's too much."

"That's why I'm here," Calisa said. "I can help maintain it. If you let me stay."

Auntie Zee glared at the tea tray as if it had wronged her, then shifted her glare back to Calisa. "I told you already. You can't stay."

She didn't know why those words hit her as hard as they did, but they felt like a fist to her stomach. She'd been working as hard as she could, trying to please Auntie Zee, who clearly didn't want to be pleased. "Why not?" *Why don't you like me?*

"You just aren't the right fit," Auntie Zee said.

Ouch.

Hadn't she been demonstrating that she wasn't useless? Jack liked her pancakes, she'd helped fix the porch, and she was cleaning nonstop, voluntarily, without any instruction or help or encouragement.

Auntie Zee added, "And I told you: don't ask questions, especially of guests." She then stalked out of the room, leaving Calisa to feel like she'd been dunked in cold water.

Now what?

It was clear that Auntie Zee didn't want her here.

It was clear that Calisa had to change her mind.

She wasn't going to just leave, not so soon after she got here, not when she didn't have a backup plan, and not when she hadn't yet tried everything she could to make this work. Like she'd tried with Ethan, until he'd revealed his true colors and made it impossible. Crossing her arms, Calisa stared into the cold fireplace, thinking, until a minute later she came to a decision:

I'm going to clean the bathrooms.

It wasn't glamorous, but it was a chore that always impressed her moms. She was certain even Auntie Zee wouldn't be able to resist the allure of a sparkling toilet. And she could drown her thoughts of Ethan in the toilet, flush them away where they belonged. It would be cathartic.

Visiting the kitchen, Calisa scooped up the cleaning supplies and headed upstairs with renewed determination.

The guest bathroom on the second floor was at the end of the hall, a white door with a rose painted on it. She knocked first, then opened the door.

It was, as bathrooms went, adorable: an old-fashioned claw-foot bathtub, a linen shower curtain embroidered with leaves and vines, and a sink with a faucet shaped like a flower. On the windowsill was a row of vases with sprigs of dried lavender in them. It had been cleaned much more recently than the common rooms, thankfully, but if you looked, there were still streaks on the mirror over the sink, hair around the shower drain, and grime behind the toilet that said it wasn't done daily or thoroughly, or had been done by someone with less exacting standards than Mom-Elise. Setting her cleaning supplies down, she opened the linen closet to check if—

Thump.

Calisa shrieked as a large, lizard-like reptile tumbled out of the linen closet and landed in front of her, its clawed feet splayed out. She jumped backward.

What the hell—

Lifting its bulbous head, it looked at her with marble-size amber eyes.

She shrieked again.

It's alive. And huge!

Like, Australia-wildlife huge. It was at least a foot long, not counting its whiplike tail, with a narrow body and four beefy legs. It looked like a . . . She didn't know what it was. Iguana? Alligator? Not an alligator—that was absurd. She thought of the alligator feed in the supply closet. *No. Not an alligator.* It was the wrong shape for an alligator anyway—they had elongated snouts and, like, alligator jaws.

She stood rooted in the doorway and stared at it. It stared back.

Its head was the size of her fist and covered in knuckle-like ridges. Its skin was gray-green and rough, like leather that had been clawed and shredded. Loose purplish-brown flaps of what looked like shed skin covered its back.

It's molting, she thought.

And then: *I don't care if it's molting. It's in the bathroom.*

Why was it in the bathroom? Specifically, why was it in the closet in the bathroom? How did it get there? And what was she supposed to do about it? She very badly wanted to scream again. Her heart was thudding hard in her chest.

Behind her, she heard Mulligan, concerned. "Miss Calisa, are you well?"

Calisa jumped again and bit off a third screech. She spun around to face Mulligan and pulled the door shut behind her. She leaned against it. Her heart was racing from two jumpscares when she'd expected zero. Bathroom jumpscares were the worst. "Fine. Sorry. Just . . . this bathroom is out of commission right now. Would you mind using one on the first or third floor?" She smiled a fake smile at Mulligan.

He was dressed in just as much black as the other night, except this time he wore a thick quilted bathrobe. He held a towel over his arm. "Of course, but you have not injured yourself?"

"Nope. All good here." Except for the presence of the lizard. She didn't think any guests needed to know about loose reptiles in the towel closet. Unless it belonged to one of them? "You didn't happen to, um, lose a pet, did you?"

"I have lost my light, my joy, and my happiness, but no, not a pet."

"Cool. Um, if you see Jack, like on the roof of the porch, would you mind sending him my way? I have a maintenance question for him. Just a routine bed-and-breakfast thing. Absolutely nothing to worry about." She tried not to wince at how very suspicious that sounded. She was a terrible liar.

"Of course. I would be delighted to assist in any way I can."

She watched him retreat down the hall before she reopened the door and looked down at the unexpected addition to her chosen chore, which hadn't budged from where it'd plopped. "You shouldn't be here."

The lizard shifted its weight to face the bathtub. It looked as if it were contemplating a nice soak, preferably with bubbles.

She could pick it up with a towel and transport it to . . . where? If it was the pet of one of the guests, it should be returned, but she didn't want to knock on each door and ask if they owned a stray lizard she'd found in the bathroom. She imagined the kind of reviews guests would leave after an episode like *that.*

Calisa heard someone jogging up the stairs, then down the hall, and she peeked out. Jack! She felt relief flood through her veins. He'd know what to do without alerting Auntie Zee. He must have encountered this kind of situation before.

"Are you okay?" he asked. "Mulligan said there was an emergency."

"I didn't say *emergency*—"

"He said you required assistance and waxed on about one's duty to those in distress."

She was *not* a damsel in distress, though she conceded there could be a lizard in distress. "I just have a question," Calisa said. *So many questions.*

He reached her, and she widened the bathroom door so he could peer inside at the lizard, which still hadn't moved from where it had plopped on the tile floor.

Jack's eyes were nearly as wide as the lizard's. "Um, that's . . . not supposed to be here."

Okay, so maybe he wasn't an expert in all aspects of innkeeping. "Does it belong to anyone? If it's a pet, I'll return it to its owner. If not . . ." She wasn't sure what to do if not. Call animal control? That seemed extreme. It hadn't done anything alarming. It was just sitting there.

"As far as I know, it's no one's pet," Jack said, still staring at it as if he wished he were anywhere but here. "It must have gotten in from the garden."

"And let itself inside the closet?" Calisa asked.

"Guess so?" He was backing away, looking as if he wanted to bolt. His eyes darted right and left, as if he was deciding the fastest exit.

"What are we supposed to do about it?"

If there were a window nearby, Jack would have climbed out of it. *He's not good in a crisis,* she thought. *Or maybe just not good with wild animals?*

He swallowed hard and said, "We should, um, probably remove it?"

"Fine, but you really think it's from the garden?" Calisa asked. "What if it's an invasive species? We can't just release it into the wild if it's not supposed to be there."

"It's not supposed to be *here*." He had retreated a quarter of the way down the hallway, which would have been funny except she still had the problem of the unwelcome lizard and no clue how to handle it. "Sorry," he said. "Just not a fan of lizards. Or snakes. Or turtles."

"What's wrong with turtles?"

"I don't know. They're just . . . squishy inside their shells."

"People are squishy inside too."

"I didn't say it was rational," Jack said. "Just that I don't like to be near them. Tortoises are fine, maybe because they're drier? Turtles seem moist."

The lizard wasn't moist. Its skin looked rough and dry, even flaky. She didn't think pointing that out was likely to make Jack feel better.

He offered, "I can ask Auntie Zee . . ."

"Or we can find a solution on our own." Calisa didn't want Auntie Zee thinking she was helpless or useless. She put her hands on her hips and looked down at the reptile. "All right. This isn't a disaster. It's just a little hiccup."

"What do you think we should do?"

It was nice that he was asking her. She appreciated the vote of confidence. Also, he hadn't actually fled yet, which was another point in his favor. He was, though, less useful than she'd hoped. Like when she'd been stuck in the hole in the porch.

I got myself out of that. I can get myself out of this.

She returned to contemplating the lizard. It shuffled sideways to face the window. She wondered if it could jump and how fast it could move. Should she worry about it escaping the bathroom? She really didn't want to get caught up in some cartoon chase all around the bed-and-breakfast. "We need a safe place to keep it until we can figure out where it came from. Ideally, not the guest bathroom. Someplace outside, like a garage or a shed or—"

"How about the greenhouse? It's kind of a mess, but . . ."

A greenhouse! Perfect! "It has to be better than a linen closet." Stepping into the bathroom, Calisa picked up a towel. The lizard regarded her quizzically.

"What are you going to do?" Jack asked.

"Catch it." That seemed the obvious next step.

"Be careful," he said. "It could bite."

"It won't bite." She had no idea whether lizards bit or not. She supposed anything would bite if it felt cornered. *I would.* She eyed the lizard, silently ordering it not to bite.

"You don't know that. Plenty of lizards bite. Like Gila monsters. You don't want to be bitten by a Gila monster. Their venom is a nerve poison. Also, Komodo dragons—their bite is fatal."

"Is it a Gila monster?"

"Um, well, no."

"Or a Komodo dragon?"

"No."

"Are you sure?"

"Gila monsters are black with pink splotches. And Komodo dragons have thick necks. Also, they live in Indonesia, not Vermont."

"Are there any venomous lizards in Vermont?" Calisa asked.

"We have newts."

She kept her eyes on the lizard. "Venomous newts?"

"Just newts."

"Is this a newt?"

"No."

Calisa wanted to glare at Jack. He was *not* helping.

"We also have salamanders. Not venomous either. Anyway, it's not a salamander. It's a reptile, not an amphibian. It's got dry skin. Plus scales. Amphibians don't have scales."

She *did* glare at him this time. Just a quick glare, and then she returned to watching the impassive lizard. It clearly had dry skin with scales. Jack knew an awful lot for someone who didn't like lizards. If he hadn't seemed so genuinely freaked out, she would have accused him of planting it here. "You seem to know a lot about lizards for someone who doesn't like them. Do you know what it is?"

"Um, no."

Calisa stared at the ceiling and counted to ten. "Can you tell me if I'll die if it bites me?"

He peered over her shoulder at the lizard. "I don't think so? But maybe don't let it bite you just to be on the safe side?"

"Cool, cool, cool." *Do not strangle the gorgeous, helpless, hopeless boy.*

Jack retreated again back into the hall. "This is where I should be manly and offer to catch it for you, because I'm a fearless, outdoorsy type of guy who has no problem with spiders or bats or skunks."

"I feel like you're not going to offer."

"It's not a spider, bat, or skunk."

"Close the door," she told Jack. He darted forward to obey, shutting the door.

Now it was just her and the large reptile that wasn't a Gila monster or a Komodo dragon.

She squatted beside it. "Okay, I'm going to pick you up now. I won't hurt you. I promise. I just want to take you somewhere you won't alarm anyone." She knew the lizard wouldn't understand her, but hopefully if she kept her tone soothing and moved slowly . . .

It didn't move.

Stepping behind the lizard, she wrapped the towel around its body and lifted it. It didn't try to squirm. It merely twisted its neck to look at her with mild interest. She kept a firm grip so that it couldn't twist enough to reach her with its mouth. "Okay, got it!" she called to Jack.

He opened the door, and his lips quirked.

"What?" she asked.

"It's just . . . When you arrived, with your suitcase and your hair all wet from the rain and you got yourself stuck in the porch, I thought you were too much of a city girl to stay here even if Auntie Zee did hire you. But here you are, completely comfortable picking up a random unidentified lizard that may or may not be venomous."

"Just because I'm a city girl doesn't mean I've never encountered an animal. I'll have you know that, where I'm from, there are rats large enough to eat this lizard for a snack." Not precisely true. She'd only seen ordinary-size rats, and they were mainly in the subway, not ever in her bathroom, but he didn't need to know that. "This is fine."

"Just saying, I'm impressed."

"So happy to hear it." Could she say she was not impressed with him? No, that would be rude. He had other good qualities besides lizard wrangler. *He's a good listener,* she reminded herself. *And he has a nice smile.* Right now, that was the sum total of his positive traits that she could think of. "Can you show me where the greenhouse is? Really don't want to be holding this guy all day. I did *not* have this on my bingo card for fun summer activities."

Keeping his distance from her and the unidentified lizard, Jack led the way out of the inn, through the kitchen door into the backyard. Outside it was still damp from the rain or the dew or whatever, but the sky was robin's-egg blue, streaked with thin white clouds. The grass in the yard was knee-high, and flowers bloomed within it, daisies and lilies and roses crowded in by weeds. Jack waded through the grass, past the apple tree, and toward a structure she hadn't seen from the kitchen window. It was octagonal and all glass, with a small cupola on top, decorated with a weather vane that looked like a bird. As they drew closer, she saw that a few of the panes of glass were riddled with cracks, mostly near the roof.

Jack opened the door—he had to yank it before it budged. The hinges had rusted, and the weeds in front of the door had grown thick, but it opened with enough force. Carrying the lizard wrapped in the bath towel, Calisa followed him inside.

It wasn't very big, and it had clearly been abandoned, which wasn't a surprise given the state of the rest of the inn. Several pots with dead plants were on shelves, and the garden equipment—trowels and clippers and gloves—was covered in clumped dirt, dust, and cobwebs. But the place was large enough and sturdy enough for a single reptile, even of this one's ample size.

"It'll need water," Calisa said. "And food—I guess?" She wasn't sure what it ate. Insects? She pictured herself chasing flies and grasshoppers around the yard. How about the alligator feed from the supply closet?

This was not what I expected to be doing this summer at all.

But she was doing it. She set the lizard down beside one of the empty flowerpots. It didn't try to run anywhere, just surveyed its new surroundings. She couldn't tell if it was happy, upset, afraid, chill, or gassy. It was just . . . a lizard.

Extracting a bucket from the heap of supplies and shaking off the cobwebs, she handed it to Jack. "Can you bring some water? He could be thirsty."

Several of the pots were seated in shallow trays that didn't have drainage holes the way the pots did. If she could fill them with water, her new acquaintance would have plenty to drink or soak in or whatever lizards did. When Jack didn't move, she said, "It's a bed-and-breakfast, isn't it? We want our guests to be comfortable. And not, you know, die."

He broke into a grin, and then he darted out the door. She closed it behind him so the lizard wouldn't get any ideas about exploring the garden, at least before they were sure it should be allowed to explore the garden. It had to be someone's pet, didn't it? How else could it have gotten inside, much less into the bathroom closet?

While Jack fetched the water, Calisa rearranged the greenhouse. She neatened the tools, stacked the pots, and removed the dead plants, piling them in a heap. By the time Jack returned, she had it looking less abandoned and more as if it were patiently awaiting a gardener.

She laid out a tray in front of the shelves, and Jack poured in the water. Interested, the lizard waddled closer to it. "I think that'll work," Calisa said. "Do you think there's anything we can give it to eat?"

"Um, pancakes?"

She glared at him again.

"Or there are worms in the garden," Jack said. "A lizard this size . . . probably eats insects and worms, as well as mice and . . . I don't know. Whatever it finds?"

She picked up two of the trowels and handed him one. "Let's find a few worms." At least it was more likely that the lizard would eat worms than pancakes.

Jack was looking at her with an expression that she didn't recognize, and she wondered if he thought it was odd that she was asking him to dig up worms with her. *It's definitely odd,* she agreed. "He's been in a closet," Calisa said. "He's probably hungry."

She shooed him out the door before her. She still had to finish cleaning the second-floor bathroom, and who knew what she'd find on the first and third floors? Also, she wanted to figure out a recipe for cake.

Outside the greenhouse, Jack was still staring at her.

"What?" Calisa said.

"Just . . . what I said before . . . it's true," Jack said. "You really aren't anything like what I thought you would be."

She hoped that was a compliment.

CHAPTER EIGHT

By afternoon, Calisa had finished cleaning the bathrooms, and Jack had finished patching the porch roof. "It'll hold until it rains," he said confidently as he joined her in the kitchen, where she was putting away the latest batch of cleaning supplies.

"Just until it rains? Isn't its entire purpose to block the rain?"

"Sure, but I don't want to overpromise." Jack pulled a glass jar out of the refrigerator and held it out to Calisa. "Soup for lunch? Could you . . . you know, the stove? If you don't mind . . . Absolutely don't want to take advantage, but you haven't been banned from cooking yet."

She took the jar. "What did you do before I showed up? Just eat cold soup?"

"No?" he said, as if it were a question.

Calisa located a pot and dumped the soup into it. It looked like a chicken soup with carrots, celery, and pasta. She turned the stove on. "No?"

"Yes."

She raised her eyebrows at him.

"I also eat a lot of sandwiches."

He sounded so pathetic that Calisa couldn't help but laugh. "Do you think she'll ever lift the ban on you cooking?" At some point, Auntie Zee had to admit he'd learned his lesson and forgive him, didn't she? She doubted he'd make the same mistake again. "How long can she hold this against you?"

Jack shrugged. "How many years did you say it's been since your family visited?"

Fair point. Auntie Zee had proved she could hold a grudge an impressively long amount of time. He was probably doomed. "I hope you like sandwiches."

"Goat cheese and fig spread, you said? I'm going to try that sometime." He pulled two bowls out of the cabinet. "As soon as I find a goat."

"I'm going to assume you're joking, and you know they sell goat cheese in the grocery store," Calisa said as she stirred the soup. She liked that he'd been listening to whatever cheese-related nonsense she'd spouted while she was stuck in the hole in the porch, even if he hadn't helped her climb out of it. "Do you think the guests want any soup? Or Auntie Zee?" She realized she hadn't seen Auntie Zee in a few hours. She wondered what the innkeeper was busy doing. Had she noticed the clean bathrooms yet? Would she care?

"I don't make it to the grocery store often," Jack said, hovering over her shoulder to watch the soup heat. "Auntie Zee gets most of the supplies for the inn herself."

As soon as the soup was warm enough, she ladled it into

the bowls while Jack set out spoons, napkins, and glasses of water. She sat on a stool next to him. "Who made the soup, if there isn't a cook? Auntie Zee?" It didn't look store-bought.

"You ask a lot of questions," Jack observed.

"I know I'm not supposed to."

"It's kind of the Faraway Inn policy," Jack said. "Guests are supposed to come here to escape whatever they left behind. So that means we don't remind them of where they came from or who they are."

Calisa wondered if he'd overheard her with Kendra and winced. "So, we aren't supposed to talk to them?" she asked. She ate a spoonful of soup. Herbs exploded on her tongue, and the warmth slid down her throat. "Wow, seriously, who made this?"

"You can talk to the guests," Jack said. "Just don't ask them questions about themselves. If they choose to share with you, fine, and if you want to share with them, also fine. But Auntie Zee really believes in respecting everyone's privacy."

"Including yours?"

He shrugged, which wasn't a no.

"Come on, I want to know your story." She poked his shoulder lightly. "What do you like to do? When you're not fixing things around the inn . . . do you have hobbies? Obsessions? Shows you watch? Wait, is there no TV in this inn?" She hadn't seen one, and she already knew there was zero cell phone coverage, which with no Wi-Fi meant no streaming anything. Ugh, no wonder there were vacancies.

Jack laughed. "I don't know why you'd want to know about me. I'm boring."

"Where do you go to school?" she asked.

"Homeschooled," he said. "Just got my GED."

"Are you planning to go to college?" Her moms had been talking about college for the entire past year. If she hadn't come to Vermont, she was certain she'd have been brought on a dozen college tours. As it was, she didn't know what she wanted to do or where she wanted to go. She figured she'd just apply to as many places as she could manage and then work it out after that, depending on who said yes.

It was better than getting her heart set on a college that was only going to say no. She'd made that kind of mistake already, with Ethan. *Don't wish for what you can't have.* Besides, it was a Future Calisa problem anyway.

"Been thinking of applying to the University of Vermont."

"And?"

"And?" he repeated.

"You can't just apply to one," Calisa said. She thought of her guidance counselor, a woman with perfect makeup, straight-as-hay hair, and a flower brooch on every blazer. She'd have had fits at the idea of any senior applying to only one school. She had very strong opinions about applications and a track record of being nearly always right. "What if you don't get in?"

He shrugged. "Then I won't go."

"Huh." She tried not to sound like she was judging him, but she was totally judging him. Who applied to only one college and just trusted fate? Your future was a very large thing to leave to chance. And shouldn't he have already applied, if he had his GED? Unless he was taking a gap year? "What does your dad think you should do?"

Jack looked down at his soup. "We haven't talked about it much. He knows I don't want to leave the inn—not when it needs me—and he's fine if I delay college. What I want . . ." He took a deep breath. "What I want is to convince Auntie Zee to hire me full-time as a permanent employee. She hasn't committed to that yet, even though . . . Well, what about your moms?"

He said moms, plural. He *had* been listening when she'd talked about them. *He listens. Not just about goat cheese.* It was a very nice trait. She couldn't help but like him a bit more. Just as a friend.

"They *say* they just want me to be happy," Calisa said, "but Mom-Kate has made a spreadsheet of all potential colleges within driving distance of Brooklyn, and Mom-Elise just keeps buying books about how to decide what to do with your life and leaves them around, as if she's being subtle. . . . And I don't know what I want to do with my life. Crystal—she's one of my friends back in Brooklyn—gives annoyingly good advice: she says I need to know *who* I am before I can know *what* I want." She stirred the soup and spoke directly to the noodles. "That was one of the reasons that I liked being with Ethan so much. When I was with him, I thought I knew who I was. I was who he saw me as. Someone he wanted to spend time with. Except apparently that wasn't enough. *I* wasn't enough." She didn't know why all these words were spilling out of her or why he would care, except that she knew he'd listen. She stopped talking, looked up from the soup to his face, and waited for him to reply with some kind of platitude or make an excuse to leave.

But he didn't.

He swallowed a spoonful of soup and then asked, "Who do you want to be?"

"Really, really good question."

"Yeah. I know. Please don't ask *me* to answer it," Jack said. "It just seemed like the right question to ask . . . I mean, since it's your choice. Not your moms'. Not that guy's, Ethan, who I'm going to assume is your ex?"

"Cheating ex, yes." She lifted another spoonful of soup, then lowered it. It was supremely delicious soup, but thinking about how it all ended with Ethan made her not want to eat any of it. She wondered how she was supposed to stop thinking about him. Cleaning had helped distract her, but it hadn't excised him completely—he was still creeping into her thoughts all the time. *Time, yes. I need time.* Time away from him, from them, from everyone who knew who she was and had opinions on who she was supposed to be. She needed to take a power washer to the whole inn and blast Ethan out of her heart. "I need to stay longer than three days."

"If you'd like, I could vouch for you."

"You'd do that?" She met his eyes. *He has really nice eyes.* Open and honest. The kind of eyes that made you feel like you were seeing straight into his soul. She was absolutely *not* looking for a rebound guy, but she liked thinking she could make a friend.

"You can make pancakes and heat up soup," he said, scooping more soup as if in proof. "Also, how you handled that lizard shows you can deal with the unexpected, which is, like, half of the work here. But I have to warn you: Auntie Zee never listens to anyone. Least of all me. You'd have better luck asking the cat."

"Does the cat have a name?" She'd been meaning to ask.

"Portia. But don't actually ask her. That was a joke. Also, don't try to pet her. You'll lose your hand. Or at least bleed copious amounts, and it's hard to get bloodstains out of stuff."

He worries a lot. She resolved not to become one of the things he worried about. She'd find her own way to convince Auntie Zee to let her stay. Still . . . his view of her had clearly changed, which was nice. She'd have to remember to thank the lizard.

The next day, Calisa started on the dining room. She was fairly certain there was a table underneath the layer of dust, and it was absurd that no one had thrown out the very dead flowers in the vase. As she was tossing the brittle blooms into the kitchen trash and filling the vase with hot sudsy water to soap, Auntie Zee entered. "You're still here? I said three days."

"It's day two," Calisa said.

"You arrived day one, yesterday was day two, and today is day three," Auntie Zee said.

She heard footsteps thump down the stairs, and then Jack jogged into the kitchen. "Calisa, I found a cookbook!" He waved a tattered book with a gingham cover in the air and then froze. "Oh hi, Auntie Zee." He looked as if he wanted to pivot and bolt.

"Jackson Thomas Jones." Auntie Zee bit off each of his names.

He held the cookbook slightly behind him, as hidden as he could manage while trying to make it look casual. "I'm, uh, planning to fix the electrical outlet on the third floor today. Going to try to unstick the window in room eight after."

"I told you, you're not allowed near the stove or the oven." Her voice was a thunderstorm, containing the threat of floods and fire within the rumble of her syllables.

He hadn't done anything to deserve either drowning or electrocution by words. Calisa jumped in to defend him. "He hasn't touched them. Not once since I got here."

Snorting, Auntie Zee didn't glance at her. Her eyes were fixed on Jack.

"I'm the one who cooked the pancakes and said I'd bake a cake," Calisa said stoutly. She didn't know why Auntie Zee was being so hostile to Jack. Near as she could tell, Jack was the only one who'd been helping with the bed-and-breakfast, especially with his father out of town. She wondered if this was what had happened with the rest of the staff: Auntie Zee had chased them all off.

Except Jack has nowhere else to go. This is his home.

That makes it so much worse.

"Ah, I see," Auntie Zee said, still glaring at Jack. "You found a loophole."

"Um . . ."

"He wouldn't need a loophole," Calisa said, "if you'd just let him cook. He'll be careful. He's learned his lesson." It was absurd that the punishment had continued for more than a week, much less however many months it had been.

"He nearly burned down the whole inn," Auntie Zee said. "That boy can't be trusted."

He studied his shoes.

Calisa felt a curl of anger. "People make mistakes. You don't punish them forever. He knows he messed up, and he has no intention of doing it again. You could try forgiving him."

Auntie Zee scoffed. "You know nothing about it."

"I know he lives here, which makes him practically your family," Calisa said. The unfairness of it—of everything Auntie Zee said and did—crept up into her throat, the curl of anger uncoiling into a flame. It was fine if her great-aunt was in a perpetual bad mood; it wasn't fair that she weaponized her grumpiness against people who cared about her, or who wanted to care about her. Like Jack. Like her moms. *Like me.* "Is this how you treat family? Not forgiving them for mistakes? Is this why we haven't been back since I was five? Did my mom—"

Scowling harder, Auntie Zee cut her off. "You know nothing about any of that."

"What did Mom-Kate do that was so terrible?" Calisa pressed on, undeterred. "No, never mind. I don't care. Whatever it was, was it really worth losing her over it? Pushing her away? Pushing *me* away?" She wondered if any of this was about her at all. It could all be about whatever happened between Auntie Zee and Mom-Kate. *I'm just collateral damage.* "Because it's not logical to send me away. You clearly need help, and I'm here, willing and able—"

"Enough!" Auntie Zee snapped. "I told you when you arrived: you aren't wanted here." In a softer voice that seemed more tired than kind, she added, "It is nothing personal."

Calisa snorted. "You said I'm not the right fit. How is that not personal?"

"Girl, you don't understand—" Her storm-cloud eyes were focused on Calisa now, but Calisa wasn't intimidated. She'd weathered Jocelyn Pullman's smirk, Ethan's fury that she wouldn't give him another chance, and the pity of everyone who already knew he was a lying cheater.

She cut her great-aunt off. "I definitely don't understand." She waved at the window with the view of the mountains and toward the foyer. "Look at this place! It could be amazing, but you've let it fall into ruin, and now you won't let anyone help you save it—"

"Why do you care about saving it?" Auntie Zee said. "You've been here two days!"

"Ha! I told you it was just two days. I have one more day to prove—"

"This is *my* bed-and-breakfast, *my* home, and I can withdraw my hospitality—" Auntie Zee cut herself off this time. Her wrinkles smoothed into a smile as Kendra glided into the kitchen and halted by the butcher block island. "Ah, Kendra. We disturbed you. I'm very sorry. We were just clearing up a little internal matter."

Kendra simply looked at Auntie Zee, her eyes full of disdain.

The moment stretched.

Calisa heard the sound of dripping water and realized it

was from Kendra's bathrobe. She must have just emerged from the shower. Briefly, Calisa contemplated ducking into the hallway of supply closets to retrieve a towel but decided this wasn't the moment to move.

At last, Kendra turned to Calisa. "Is there tea?"

"Ahh . . ." She hadn't touched the teapot to turn it on yet.

A look crossed Auntie Zee's face that Calisa couldn't interpret. Resignation maybe? "Come, it's in the front room."

Kendra pivoted and strode to the front room.

Calisa and Jack exchanged looks and then followed a second later. The teapot was already steaming, and Kendra had a cup in her hand.

"Earl Grey," she said with a sniff. "Acceptable."

How had it brewed that fast? It must have already been heating up. Perhaps Auntie Zee knew her guest would want tea and flipped the on switch earlier?

"Kendra . . ." Auntie Zee began.

"I heard mention of cake? Will that be offered with tea?" She addressed Calisa without even glancing at Auntie Zee. "I am tired of being disappointed."

"That's up to Auntie Zee," Calisa said pointedly.

Kendra raised a sculpted eyebrow at the innkeeper.

Auntie Zee sighed heavily. "Calisa will be baking a cake with tea tomorrow. I'll take care of obtaining the ingredients later today."

Don't cheer. Play it cool. Calisa glanced at Jack. He cheered silently and then stopped when Auntie Zee glared at him. Heroically, she kept herself from smiling. It was only one more day that she'd won, but it still felt like a victory worthy of an Olympic athlete.

With a nod, Kendra swept out of the sitting room. In the foyer, by the stairs, she looked back, every inch regal, despite the dripping bathrobe. "Also, I wish to thank you for your re-housing my unwanted companion. It was never my intention to attach him to me."

Calisa stared at her, unsure what she was talking about but not wanting to admit that in front of Auntie Zee. "Um, you're welcome?"

"He has not yet come into his fire, but he will serve you well when he does," Kendra said. "I hope you will enjoy his companionship in the meantime." She then proceeded up-stairs, leaving a trail of droplets behind her.

There was silence for a moment.

"Calisa," Auntie Zee said behind her, much closer than be-fore, "what did you do?"

She turned to see that Auntie Zee had crossed the room and was standing only inches away. "I'm not entirely sure," Calisa said. *Unwanted companion?* She didn't know what Ken-dra was talking about, unless she meant—

Jack let out a nervous false laugh. "Just a little hiccup. We took care of it."

Lower, softer, Auntie Zee repeated, *"What did you do?"*

Together the three of them trooped out to the greenhouse, with Jack in the lead and Calisa just behind him. Auntie Zee followed, and Calisa tried not to feel the weight of her stare boring in between her shoulder blades. She'd already explained how she hadn't wanted to simply release the unidentified reptile into the wild, since she didn't know whether it was either an invasive species or not suited to the environment.

Auntie Zee merely huffed as she strode through the grass, which could have been either from exertion or disapproval, Calisa couldn't tell.

"So, Kendra arrived with a pet and then decided she didn't want it?" Calisa asked Jack in a low voice. What kind of person did that? Not a nice one. Or maybe there was another explanation? "What did she mean about 'come into his fire'?"

"Ahh . . ." Jack said.

Behind her, Auntie Zee said crisply, "We don't ask questions of guests."

She wasn't asking the guest; she was asking Jack. But Calisa pressed her lips together and decided it didn't matter if Kendra was being cryptic deliberately or accidentally. All that mattered was whether Auntie Zee was going to be pissed at her when she saw the relocated lizard. Jack opened the greenhouse door, and Auntie Zee waddled past Calisa to enter first. Calisa followed.

It was crowded inside with the three of them.

Four, if you counted the uninvited lizard.

The lizard was lounging next to the tray of water. His loose leathery skin hung from his back—he still hadn't finished his molt yet, if that was what the excess skin was. Calisa wasn't certain now that she saw him again. The flaps seemed firmly attached, and she thought she saw a hint of a bone running along the edge of the leathery skin. He lifted his bulbous head as they entered but otherwise didn't stir.

Auntie Zee's hands were on her hips. She grunted.

A friendly grunt?

"You did well," Auntie Zee said. The words sounded as if they hurt her throat.

Calisa wasn't sure if she was talking to her, Jack, or the lizard. "I did?"

Auntie Zee studied the lizard for a minute more and then turned and marched out of the greenhouse. "Leave the door open so he can come and go. He won't hurt anything but the local rodent population, and that could do with a little diminishing. If he still seems hungry, he can eat the alligator feed in the closet—don't look alarmed. That's just the brand name; it's made neither from nor for alligators. Keep him out of the inn. He's exclusively an outside pet. I don't want to see his little footprints in your morning pancakes."

Following her out of the greenhouse, Calisa stopped and watched her great-aunt toddle back to the inn and then up the steps into the kitchen. She didn't look back. Jack stood next to Calisa. She'd gotten a friendly grunt for the lizard, as well as permission to bake a cake tomorrow *and* tacit approval of her pancakes—did that count as official permission to stay? "Do you think that means I can stay for the summer?" Calisa said to Jack.

With a shrug, he handed her the cookbook.

She looked down at it. Across the gingham cover was a

handwritten title: *Jones Family Recipes.* Jones . . . Where had she heard . . . "That's your last name. Is this a family recipe book?"

"My dad's. Found it in his room."

Jack should be the one allowed to make the recipes inside. "She shouldn't treat you that way," Calisa said. "You're doing everything around here."

"She used to be kinder. Happier."

"What happened?"

He shrugged again. "Time, I think. She's angry that she's older, that she can't do it all, that the bed-and-breakfast is not what it was, that she can't keep everything the same."

That was very understanding and empathetic of him, but it didn't excuse Auntie Zee acting that way toward someone who was obviously doing his best. Being mean to Jack was like kicking a puppy. He clearly threw his heart and soul into this place—for his home, for his job, for his father. She didn't know him well enough to be sure exactly why, but she *did* know he didn't deserve to be treated like he was some kind of screwup for one mistake. "Auntie Zee has issues," Calisa said as she cradled the cookbook. "I suppose Kendra does too." She nodded in the direction of the greenhouse.

"I think Kendra was trying to help, in her own way," Jack said. "She practically praised you in front of Auntie Zee."

"Why did she bother to bring a pet if she intended to abandon it?"

He shrugged. "She's quirky."

Or she was terrible, in addition to terrifying. *Poor lizard.*

"And I don't understand why no one has an explanation for why the lizard was in the bathroom closet."

Yet another shrug. "Maybe he just wanted to go home?"

Calisa raised both her eyebrows at him.

"Or maybe he's quirky too."

CHAPTER NINE

The birds woke her again the next morning, and Calisa found them marginally less annoying now that she knew to expect them. Opening the curtains, she looked outside. The morning sun bathed the forest and mountains with a golden glow as a misty haze rose off everything green. "Wow," she breathed, transfixed once again.

There was so much green.

Actually, too much green.

She instantly knew what she wanted to tackle today: a task that would solve all her great-aunt-not-liking-her problems and secure her position here . . . or at least make Auntie Zee give another friendly grunt . . . aka saving the gardens.

The only flaw was that she didn't know how.

After making pancakes for the guests and eating her share with Jack—this time she tried the blueberry maple syrup, which was just as delicious as the raspberry—she said, "What do you know about gardening?"

"Um, you know. Groundskeeper's son. What do you want to know?"

She dunked the last bite of pancake into a pool of blueberry syrup. "I live in an apartment. Our only plant is a spider plant that's basically indestructible. So assume I know nothing." While Jack turned toward the sink, his back toward her, she dipped her finger into the last of the syrup.

"Well, it's pretty much just common sense." As he talked and cleaned the pancake batter bowl, she eyed her plate and decided it would not be classy to lick it. "You just give the plants what they want—if they like sun, you plant them in the sun. If they need shade, you plant them in the shade. Give them room to grow. Clear out any weeds. Water them if they need it. Don't . . . I don't know . . . stomp on any plants? Why do you ask?"

Continuing to resist the urge to lick the rest of the maple syrup off her plate, she carried both plates to the sink, handing them to him. He dunked them into the soapy water. "I'm thinking that today we could try to make it look less like the plants are taking over and more like an actual garden," she said. "Unless you have other plans?"

Jack looked out the back window. She could see the doubt etched on his face, even in profile. *He's not going to agree,* she thought. "It's gotten kind of out of hand," he said. "I thought it could wait until my dad got back, but . . ."

Calisa glanced out the window at the rampant overgrowth. *Kind of out of hand?* It could hide an entire family of bears easily. "How long has your dad been gone? You didn't say." When

Jack said he'd gone for supplies, she'd assumed it was only a couple of days, but the yard couldn't have gotten *this* out of control that fast. It wasn't days of growth out there or even weeks. Could it be months?

He didn't answer.

"Jack? You okay?" Had his dad been gone for months?

He rinsed the plates, then put them on the drying rack, wiped his hands on the dish towel, and completely failed to answer her question.

She eyed him and decided not to push. He'd open up when he was ready. Or not. *It's not my business.* Especially if she didn't want to risk driving him away. "Where do you think we should start? Front of house? Near the porch? It's the first impression for any guests." She wouldn't be surprised if potential guests saw the botanical disaster before them and just turned right around and went to a different bed-and-breakfast. All the weeds and brambles made the inn look abandoned.

Jack's shoulders relaxed minutely. "Sure, front sounds good."

Auntie Zee hobbled into the kitchen. "Good for what?"

"We're going to weed by the front porch?" Calisa couldn't help it coming out like a question, and she immediately wished she'd sounded more forceful, like she knew what she was doing, even though everyone knew she didn't.

Calisa held her breath, expecting Auntie Zee to scowl, glower, or tell them not to. But instead, she said, "Gardening tools are in the greenhouse."

"Ah, okay, great." Wow, she had not expected Auntie Zee to

say something helpful. *Maybe she's coming around on us fixing the inn.* "Thanks."

"It's pointless, though," Auntie Zee said. "It'll just all grow back."

"Not immediately," Calisa protested.

"Years ago, there were beds of flowers around the inn. Daffodils and tulips in the spring, then the peonies and daisies. And the lilacs. You should have smelled the lilacs. I even had climbing roses on the porch." For an instant, Auntie Zee looked wistful, then she scowled again. "It was a lot of work."

"But worth it for the flowers, right?"

"Flowers die. Or they're eaten by deer and rabbits. And then the deer and the rabbits call all their friends and have a banquet, and you might as well not bother." She paused. "But you two do as you want."

Well, that was *almost* an endorsement.

Before Auntie Zee could change her mind and tell them not to, Calisa pulled Jack out through the kitchen door into the inn's backyard. It was a beautiful day. The summer morning sun was like a kiss, and she lifted her chin to feel it on her skin. The sky was cloudless and as blue as a kindergartner's drawing of a landscape. She waded through the grass past the apple tree toward the greenhouse.

The door was propped open, as they'd left it. Jack entered first and stopped. "Huh."

She peeked in behind him.

The lizard was lounging on the highest shelf. One of the leathery flaps on his back had unfolded, and it reminded Calisa of a bat wing. She guessed he wasn't molting after all—the leathery flaps were part of him. "Did he *fly* up there?"

"Lizards don't fly," Jack said.

He certainly looked like he could have.

"Well, except flying lizards," he amended. "But they live in Asia, and their 'wings' are more thin skin between their legs, kind of like flying squirrels."

If she had access to Google, she'd have looked it up, but as it was . . . "He has wings." Studying them, she could see the thin bones that stretched through the delicate skin. "They're like bat wings. Kind of pretty."

Jack handed her a pair of gardening gloves. "See if these fit."

She shook the dirt off them. They were stiff, but no holes. She tried them on, and they fit fine, loose around the fingers but workable. "I'm going to name him Draco. You know, because he looks like a mini dragon."

"That's a terrible name," Jack said loudly.

She shot him a look. That was a particularly vehement opinion from the usually laid-back Jack. So far, he hadn't been anything but sunny and occasionally anxious. She hadn't thought he was capable of arguing about anything.

Less vehemently, he said, "He, uh, doesn't look like a dragon at all."

"He's a lizard with wings," Calisa said. "He totally does."

"You're going to give him a complex, making him think he's something he's not."

"Or it'll give him ambition."

Jack handed her clippers. He took a pair of shears with

long handles and held them over his shoulder. "I just think he doesn't look like a Draco."

"What do you think he looks like?"

He thought for a moment. "He looks like a Steve."

She laughed. "Okay. Bye, Steve. Let us know if you need more worms."

With the gardening tools and gloves, Calisa headed out of the greenhouse and walked with Jack through the tall grasses and weeds around to the front of the bed-and-breakfast. The gravel driveway led out of the pine forest and curled up to the front door. It had once been lined with rosebushes and hydrangea bushes and probably countless flowers. Now it was all overrun with weeds. Vines crept over everything, especially the bushes in front of the porch. She could see why Jack had just given up on it. It was overwhelming, and this was just the front yard. Calisa tried to make out the intended shape of the yard, but it was all far too overrun.

"How do I tell what's weed and what isn't?" she asked.

Standing next to her, Jack was surveying the disaster too. "A weed is just any plant that's growing where you don't want it to grow."

Fair enough. She continued to contemplate the vast expanse of bushes, brambles, and vines. How on earth had it gotten this bad? What had Jack been doing with his time? And his dad? He was supposedly the groundskeeper. Why wasn't anyone keeping the grounds?

Nearby, the statue of the stone lady stood in between grapevine-covered rosebushes with her hands clasped in front of her. Calisa wondered if it had been moved again or if she was just misremembering. She opened her mouth to ask, but before she could, Steve the lizard waddled out of the grass and plopped himself at her feet as if the journey had been utterly exhausting and he resented every inch of it. "Oh. Hey, Steve. Are you going to help?"

Angling himself so his back faced the sun, he sprawled on one of the walkways, which couldn't have been a more clear *no* if he'd spoken.

"Guess we have an audience." Calisa turned back to the B&B and put her hands on her hips. "How about we start on the left side of the porch? And then we can work out from there?" That should make it feel like less of a Herculean task.

"Sure," Jack said.

Steve gave a contented snort and rolled onto his side.

Together they attacked the bushes. Calisa yanked vines away, while Jack clipped them free. She winced as branches scratched her arms and thought she should have worn long sleeves, but after a while she started to sweat and was glad for the short sleeves and shorts.

Leaves showered down on her as she tugged on a knot of vines, and she leaned backward for leverage. With snaps and pops and creaks and groans, vines separated from the porch in one massive kraken-like tumbleweed. She staggered backward, then caught her balance. Jack joined her, and together they dragged the debris to the edge of the forest and left it in a tangled pile.

They waded back through the weeds to the porch.

As they began to yank down the next wad of vines, which were wrapped around the sides of the porch and clumped on top of the shrubbery, the front door of the inn flew open, and a girl a few years older than Calisa, possibly early twenties, raced outside. Very pretty. Very angry. Her hair was dyed hues of brilliant green. Her face was furious. She wore a flowery dress that flowed behind her as she ran down the steps, across the gravel driveway, and into the midst of the bushes and brambles.

Halting, she shrieked at the yard, the sky, and the forest, *"Why do you scream?"*

Calisa glanced at Jack. She hadn't heard any—

The stranger spun in a circle. Her skirt flared around her, along with her bright green hair, and then she stopped and leveled a finger directly at Calisa. "You!"

"Me? Um, what? Hi. I wasn't . . ."

Head down bull-like, she charged across the lawn toward Calisa and Jack. The brambles bowed on either side of her as she marched through them. Out of the corner of her eye, Calisa noticed that the statue was reaching out a hand as if to slow the girl. She had just enough time to think, *Weren't her hands clasped?* before the green-haired girl, her fists clenched and her shoulders shaking, reached Calisa.

Dropping his clippers, Jack jumped in front of Calisa. In a pleasant the-customer-is-always-right voice, as if the strange girl weren't rushing toward them as if she wanted to tackle them, he said, "Melidor, can I help you with something?"

"Yes!" Melidor tried to dodge him to reach Calisa, but he moved with her.

Holding a bunch of just-pulled weeds in front of her like they were a shield, Calisa retreated toward the corner of the porch. "Hi. Hey, hi. What's wrong? Are you okay?"

"How can we help?" Jack asked.

Melidor spotted the clippers that Jack had dropped, and she let out another high-pitched shriek. Her cheeks flushed with an oddly greenish tinge. "You're hurting them!"

"Who? What?" he asked, his voice still soothing.

Melidor was trembling as she stared at Calisa's hands.

Calisa looked down at the mat of vines she was holding in front of her. She'd asked Jack if everyone at the inn was quirky, but this . . . "Are you talking about the plants?"

Jack jumped in quickly. "We're just doing some gardening. That's all." He looked as if he wanted to be anywhere but here. Still, he kept his position between Melidor and Calisa. Calisa stared at him, or, more accurately, at the back of his head. That was . . . sweet. Incredibly sweet. She wondered if he thought Melidor was dangerous, if he thought Calisa was helpless, or if he was just the kind of guy who automatically thought he had to be everyone's hero; then she wondered what Ethan would have done. *Probably try to charm his way out of it. Or turn it into one vast joke.*

Melidor wasn't joking. With a wail, she shook her head hard with her hands pressed against her green-tinged cheeks. "Cutting! Tearing! Ripping! Killing!"

She *was* talking about the plants.

Okay, this was . . . Whatever this was, Auntie Zee would *not* be happy one of her guests was upset. She wondered where Auntie Zee was. Watching from a window? Or off doing whatever innkeeper things she did when she wasn't busy disapproving of Calisa? "We're saving the bushes," Calisa said firmly. "The vines are choking them. Look at them—they can't get any sun under all the vines. They'll die if they aren't helped."

Jack nodded. "That's right."

"Look around, Melidor," Calisa urged. "You know this isn't what it's supposed to look like. The plants can't breathe. They're all growing on top of one another. We're *helping* them."

Slowly, Melidor lowered her hands. "Helping?"

"Yes, helping," Jack said.

"Oh." She blinked and then took a step backward.

Calisa didn't move, waiting to see what Melidor would do next.

Heaving himself upward, Steve the lizard waddled toward them, past Melidor and Jack, and then plopped himself at Calisa's feet. All of them stared at him for a second. He opened his mouth and hissed at Melidor.

And then he yawned.

"I'm so sorry," Melidor said to him. "I was asleep in my room, dreaming. . . . No, it was a nightmare, not a dream, and I thought—oh my, oh yes. Of course! The poor bushes!"

It was such an abrupt shift that Calisa didn't know what to do or say.

Melidor darted toward a bush that was smothered in vines. Muttering, she began unwinding the vines from its branches. "We have to help them!"

Calisa bit back a hundred questions about why, how, who,

what. She looked down at the winged lizard. Steve rolled onto his back, tucking his wings under him and exposing a pale white belly. She bent down and scratched his stomach. He purred like a pleased cat. "Thanks," she told him.

Shooting glances at Melidor, Calisa returned to (cautiously) clearing the vines from the porch. If she hadn't just seen her rampage across the yard, Calisa wouldn't have thought Melidor was the dangerous type. She looked sweet and innocent. Her cheeks were as plump as a toddler's, and her eyes were round and very, very green. Her hair was dyed multiple shades of green, emerald to lime, and her dress swirled around her, a flowy fabric stamped with images of flowers and leaves.

As if she felt Calisa staring, Melidor confided, "The dreams have been getting worse. I know they've been sending them to hurry me along."

"I'm sorry," Calisa said.

"I can't run forever. At some point I need to face my responsibilities."

Calisa wanted to ask who she was running from and why. Instead she said, "A stay at a bed-and-breakfast isn't forever. It doesn't mean you're running away permanently. I think it's okay to take a break and regroup, if you need to, before facing . . . whatever you need to face."

Pausing her work, Melidor stared at her thoughtfully. She had unnerving eyes, as wide as a Disney princess's, with bright green irises that seemed far too large, crowding out the whites. *Colored contact lenses?* Calisa wondered.

"Yes," Melidor said. Then she repeated: "Yes, yes, yes!"

Gripping one end of a vine, Melidor whooped, then pivoted and ran toward the forest. The vine trailed after her, unraveling from the bushes with improbable ease, like it was a thread pulled from a sweater. She didn't stop when she reached the pine trees. Cawing wildly, she plunged into the forest until she disappeared, the vine flying after her like a kite string.

Both Calisa and Jack stared after her.

Utterly uninterested, Steve flopped on top of Calisa's foot and began to snore.

"Ahh . . . should we . . . go after her?" Calisa asked. She didn't want to run blindly into the forest, but was Melidor okay? Did she need someone to chase after her? "You know, ask her what's going on?" She glanced at the house, wondering if Auntie Zee was by a window, watching all of this.

He sighed. "We don't ask questions, remember?"

"*Why* don't we ask questions?" Calisa gingerly nudged the heavy lizard off her squashed toes. If Auntie Zee was watching, wouldn't she be concerned? She cared about the guests' well-being, didn't she? "I feel like we *should* ask questions."

"And risk losing the few guests we have?" Gently, sympathetically, Jack said, "Look, if you aren't comfortable here, you don't have to stay. You can go home to Brooklyn and your moms and your friends and your life and not have to worry about weeds and dust and out-of-place lizards and a perpetually grumpy innkeeper and quirky guests. I'll understand. Everyone will. It's okay."

Calisa rocked backward. She felt as if the oxygen had been knocked out of her lungs. Jack wanted her to leave? *No, that's not what he'd said.* He'd said, nicely, that if she couldn't take the heat, she should get out of the kitchen. A sudden thought popped into her head:

He's scared.

Of what?

She took a breath.

She wasn't certain why she knew he was scared—it didn't make any sense; what did he have to be scared of?—but she was certain of it all the way to her bones.

Steve wrapped his tail around her ankle, and she bent down to pet his jowls.

Jack returned to clipping brambles. The clippers snapped shut like the jaws of an angry dog, over and over again. Still petting the winged lizard, Calisa faced the tangle of front yard, with the statue in the center and the pine forest behind it.

I could leave.

She stared at the statue. It was facing her, and its blank eyes seemed to be looking directly at her. *I can't leave. Not until I know what's going on here.*

CHAPTER TEN

After clearing the vines from the bushes in front of the porch, Calisa felt coated in dirt and sweat. Jack had located a wheelbarrow and was hauling the displaced plants to the edge of the forest. Melidor hadn't returned. And the statue was still staring at her.

I need to talk to Auntie Zee. The innkeeper was the one with all the answers. Not that she was likely to want to share them, but Calisa could try.

"I'm going to shower and then start baking a cake," Calisa said when Jack returned with the empty wheelbarrow. She directed her words to both him and Steve. She made herself sound casual, as if she didn't plan to corner Auntie Zee. Also, she did need a shower.

"Sure," Jack said, with zero of his earlier enthusiasm for cake. "Just going to do a little more out here."

He didn't glance at her again, and she wondered what she'd

see in his eyes if he did. Instead, he just piled another armful of greenery into the wheelbarrow. Still, she hesitated—did he really think she should go back to Brooklyn? Or was he afraid she would? Or afraid she wouldn't? She didn't ask any of that out loud, though. Instead, Calisa asked, "You think Melidor is okay?"

"She's in the woods," he said. "She'll be fine."

Calisa didn't think those two sentences really went together. "What if she gets lost? Or hurt?" She'd gone racing off in between the trees. She could have tripped on a root, fallen off a cliff, or been eaten by a bear. "Do you know if she at least has a phone with her?"

Jack pointed behind her. "She's fine. See?"

Turning, Calisa saw Melidor just at the edge of the forest, halfway up a pine tree. She was seated on a branch, which bowed beneath her, and her mouth was moving as if she was in the middle of a conversation. She was too far away for Calisa to hear what she was saying. Her green hair was caught in the pine needles, halolike.

Calisa wasn't certain she'd call that "fine." But she guessed so long as Melidor didn't fall . . . "All right, I'm going inside." *It's time for answers.*

After one final pat for Steve, she headed in.

As she passed through the lobby, she glanced into the sitting room. The sheets were still absent from the furniture, despite Auntie Zee's protests. The teapot sat quietly in the corner, as if waiting for its time to shine. The elderly white cat, Portia, was curled on the same faded red chair. As Calisa walked by the doorway, Portia hissed half-heartedly.

The guest bathroom on the first floor was thankfully empty of both guests and lizards. She showered, rinsing leaves and twigs out of her hair and scrubbing dirt off her palms. She dug her nails into the soap to try to clean them and then stared at the little crescent moons she'd left in the bar as all the questions that she wasn't supposed to ask tumbled through her head.

Wrapped in a towel, she retreated to her room to put fresh clothes over her fresh skin. Her wet hair smelled like lilac. She was surprised to see a fire had been lit in the fireplace. It was low, a few flames that danced over the logs.

Yet another question: Who had lit the fire (again)?

As she dressed, she stared absently at the flames and wondered if it was a peace offering from either Jack or Auntie Zee, wanting to make her feel more welcome. It did make the room feel cozy, though it seemed odd that anyone would light a fire in summer. *Maybe it's a Vermont thing.* Or maybe Auntie Zee could explain it all.

All the little mysteries kept piling up, and Jack's smile, as nice as it was, wasn't enough to keep her from noticing them. She understood she was new here, but that didn't mean she had to be completely clueless. Dressed, Calisa headed out, determined to find Auntie Zee. Despite her commitment to grumpiness, she had to tell Calisa *something,* didn't she, if directly asked?

Calisa checked downstairs first—the library, the sitting room, the dining room, the kitchen—and then she went upstairs to the guest floors. "Auntie Zee?" she called softly.

It was as quiet as snow on the first and second floors.

She reached the third floor . . . and she heard whispers.

Familiar whispers.

As before, when she'd been crawling under the porch, as well as yesterday morning when she'd heard voices outside the bathroom, she couldn't tell what the whisperers were saying—the syllables blurred together into a rising and falling hum.

Following the voices, she walked down the hallway and stopped in front of room twelve. The voices, still overlapping, were clearly coming from inside.

This had to be Melidor's room. Mulligan was eight, Kendra was three, and Jack had said his was six, which left twelve for Melidor. It couldn't be Auntie Zee's—Jack had said the guest in room twelve liked cheese. Pressing her ear against the door, Calisa heard the whispers louder, but they still weren't understandable. She wasn't sure she even recognized the language, if it was one.

So far as Calisa knew, there wasn't anyone staying with Melidor in her room. There were only three guests in the inn, Jack had said. Possibly four. No more than that. But she heard multiple voices from behind the door, in exactly the same cadence as before.

Who's in there?

She knew one way to find out.

Knocking, she raised her voice and said, "Room service."

No one answered.

The whispers continued.

Okay, so I need a second way to find out. Calisa knocked again, louder. She tried the knob, locked. "Hello? Who's in there? Auntie Zee?" It didn't sound at all like Auntie Zee. In fact, it didn't sound like anyone in the inn she'd heard.

She stepped back and stared at the door.

Really, it wasn't any of her business who was inside. If they wanted to ignore her knocks, they could. But the whispers didn't sound like a normal conversation. The voices slithered and wound around one another, overlapping like a song without a tune. She couldn't just pretend she didn't hear it. Could she? Should she?

Leave it alone, she told herself. She should just walk away, keep looking for Auntie Zee or try to talk to Melidor or Jack. Or she could forget the B&B's little mysteries and just bake the promised cake. She certainly shouldn't even be considering trying to get a peek inside.

Auntie Zee had only two rules: don't ask questions (which Calisa kept breaking right and left) and don't open doors (which she had not, so far, broken, unless you counted the bathroom linen closet door, which, now that she was thinking about it, almost certainly counted, given that opening it had resulted in Steve). Okay, she was failing this test hard.

Don't do it, Calisa. Find another way to get answers.

The whispers were enticingly soft. It felt like if she could just listen harder, she'd be able to understand everything she ever wanted to know. What if she didn't actually open the door but just cracked it a little bit? An inch. Or two. Just enough to hear what the whispers were saying, to identify how many were speaking, to see if they were guests or . . . What else could they be? Squatters? Hallucinations? She supposed she could be hearing things. That wouldn't be great. *I won't know until I look.* Staring at the door, straining to hear, she felt as if she had to know. Her frustration over all the unanswered (and unasked) questions churned in her stomach. Auntie Zee wasn't anywhere nearby. She'd never know if Calisa took one little peek. There was no harm. All she wanted was answers. Besides, if she was imagining voices, wouldn't it be better to know?

Obviously, she was going to talk herself into this, so she might as well just do it.

Tiptoeing downstairs, Calisa peeked into the sitting room. She didn't see Auntie Zee. Jack was still outside, presumably, with Melidor up in a tree. She guessed that Mulligan and Kendra were both in their rooms. In the lobby, she slipped behind the front desk.

There had to be extra keys to the guest rooms, in case of emergency. Or a master key that worked all the locks—Auntie Zee had to be able to get into all the rooms to clean and change the sheets and do the usual innkeeping stuff, and she'd need a special key for that.

It didn't take Calisa long to find what she was looking for: it was the only item in the top drawer, a skeleton key with a silver ribbon. *Clearly, Auntie Zee has never lived in Brooklyn.* You didn't just leave a key like this where anyone could find it. But she wasn't going to complain.

With the key in hand, she scampered back upstairs. Her heart was thumping harder than it had the time she and Ethan had sneaked onto the roof of their high school.

Outside of room twelve again, Calisa had second thoughts.

And then third thoughts. She was on her fifth but-what-if thought as she stuck the key into the lock and turned it.

The door creaked as she pushed it open. Just a sliver. Calisa listened as the whispers rolled over her like a wave, still indistinguishable. She couldn't even tell how many voices, except that it seemed like a crowd.

Another inch open. She pressed her face against the crack, trying to see as much of the room as she could. Green wallpaper, with images of vines. She saw the frame of either a painting or a mirror, ornate gold-painted wood, and the corner of a rug that had a floral pattern. She didn't see any movement, and the voices were louder but not clearer.

No one within seemed to have noticed the cracked-open door, and so Calisa opened it wider until she could see more of the room: all green. A carpet of plush green. A bed piled high with green pillows and floral blankets. She opened the door farther. A chair with green velvet upholstery. A footstool carved with the picture of a pine tree. A fireplace with a painting of a bouquet above the mantel. A dresser with a vase of daisies and roses.

It was an adorably floral and (most important) empty guest room, yet the whispers still rolled toward her. Calisa swung the door open wide and stepped inside.

Across the very ordinary, very green guest room was an open closet door.

And what was inside was *not* ordinary.

Instead of clothes on hangers or even a bare closet, she saw a swirl of colors, like a slick of oil in the sunlight—purple, yellow, and black spiraling within the closet. She thought of the broom closet from her first day here, except this time there was no howling. Only whispers.

What. Is. That?

It was an impossibility.

An inexplicable impossibility.

Tucking the key into her pocket, Calisa walked toward the closet. She stopped. Stared. But it didn't vanish.

It was undeniably real. And beautiful.

Closer, the whispers tumbled over her as if she'd stepped into a waterfall and they were crashing over her head and shoulders.

The sensible thing would have been to turn around, leave the guest room, and ask Jack about it. Or better still, Melidor. Or Auntie Zee herself. But then, of course, she'd have to admit that she'd let herself into the room without permission, in direct violation of both Auntie Zee's rule and forgivable behavior. Also, even if she was able to hide that she'd snuck into Melidor's room, would they even answer her if she asked, or would they freak out because she was asking questions about something she was definitely not supposed to know anything about?

Obviously I'm not going to be sensible.

Calisa plucked one of the daisies out of the vase on the dresser and held it by the stem. She pushed the petals toward the swirling closet opening. It slid into the dark rainbow without any resistance. She counted to five and then pulled it out again.

It looked fine. Still blooming. Gently, she touched one of

the petals, and it felt alive and perfect, as soft as a butterfly wing. She returned the flower to its vase, where it was indistinguishable from the others.

Reaching out, Calisa touched the swirling colors of the doorway with the tip of her finger. It felt like a kiss. Emboldened, she put her whole hand through the swirl and pulled it back. Completely normal. She turned her hand over and examined it, clenching and unclenching it. It both looked and felt fine. Whatever the swirl was, it didn't eat flesh, which was good to know.

Behind her, she heard footsteps on the stairs. She glanced back—she'd left the door to Melidor's room open. If anyone passed by, they'd see her here, inside a room that wasn't hers, uninvited and unwelcome.

There was only one choice. . . .

Actually, there were plenty of choices, but only one that she liked. She didn't think too hard about whether she was using the footsteps as an excuse.

Calisa plunged through the iridescent swirl.

For an instant, she felt as if she were within a kaleidoscope: colors spun around her, streaked in velvety black. Her skin was swaddled in a warm breath, and then it was over and she was blinking into the sunshine.

Except the sun wasn't right.

A field of flowers unfurled at her feet, and the purple-tinted sun bathed it all, casting deep-purple shadows that felt more like midnight than day. It made the field look bruised.

Unearthly.

The wind felt sharp, as if it held microscopic shards of glass.

It bit at her skin. She rubbed her hands over her bare arms, but she didn't feel any cuts. *I shouldn't be here.* She had the overwhelming sense that she didn't belong.

All around, the whispering rose and fell, and she realized it was coming from the flowers themselves, calling to one another as the breeze blew through their leaves.

She heard a high-pitched sound, half like a giggle and half like a scream. Prickles chased over Calisa's skin, and a roselike flower ran past her. Its roots were like feet, its leaves pumped like arms, and its petals were flattened back as it darted by. It was the thing making the horrible giggle-like sound. Calisa felt her jaw drop.

A woman with green skin, green hair, and a silvery dress chased after the flower.

She slowed when she saw Calisa.

Calisa froze. She was only a few steps from the closet. She could flee—

"You." Her voice sounded like a wind chime, bell-like and scattered, but discordant. It hurt Calisa's ears, and she nearly clapped her hands over them.

"Me?" Calisa squeaked.

"You are from Auntie Zee," the green woman said. "You look like her."

Calisa wondered which piece of her looked like her great-aunt. Also, why was this woman chasing a flower? Also, why was a flower running? Also, why was she green and the sun purple and why did it all hurt? *Where am I?* "I, um . . . yes? You know Auntie Zee?"

Faster than her eye could follow, the green-skinned woman

darted close to Calisa, uncomfortably close. Her breath filled Calisa's face, and she smelled of soil and cut grass. She cocked her head. "You tell that daughter of mine that the time for indulging herself is over. She needs to plant her seedlings."

"Daughter?" Calisa echoed. *Seedlings?*

"Melidor!" The woman's voice ricocheted inside her head, sharp as a shriek. "I know she's checked herself in as a guest. 'To prepare,' she said. But she has not returned, and she is not heeding any of our songs, though we have sent them wide to infiltrate both her waking hours and her dreams." She gestured behind Calisa, and Calisa turned to see the swirling, door-shaped rectangle, the closet door, standing without any kind of support.

"I'll, um, tell her?" Her head began to pound.

"She cannot hide from her duties. The seasons turn, and she has responsibilities. Pretending they don't exist will not make them disappear. You tell her that, since she will not listen to us."

The breeze pricked her skin painfully. It was hard to think, with the whispering flowers and the biting breeze and the bruise-like shadows that looked not quite right and the pain from the throbbing in her head. Every cell in her body felt as if it were screaming that she didn't belong here.

The green woman, Melidor's mother, swiveled to face another plant that had uprooted itself and was now running away, giggling in a high-pitched voice. "Root yourself right now! This is not the time for such behavior!" She charged after the running plant, her silvery dress unfurling behind her.

Calisa stared and stared, as if her eyes could drink it all in.

She then stepped backward through the iridescent swirl into the charming but ordinary guest room, with its floral accents and forest vibe, and she breathed. Ordinary air. Ordinary light. She rubbed her arms, feeling the memory of the bite of the wind.

Where was I?

And: *Does every room have a closet like this?*

She had a theory. It was an absurd theory, but that didn't mean it wasn't true. Without letting herself think about what it meant or whether it was possible or even if she should, she spun around and crossed the room.

Sticking her head out of the door to the guest room, Calisa checked both directions—whoever she'd heard on the stairs seemed to have gone. She shut Melidor's door behind her and locked it.

After less than a second's hesitation, she used the master key to open the next guest room, number eleven, one she knew was unoccupied. She slipped inside. Instead of florals everywhere, this room was draped in silks that hung like buntings from the wooden rafters on the ceiling. The blankets and sheets on the bed were gold, and the headboard and posts of the canopy were painted gold as well. But her eyes went immediately to the closet door.

Crossing to it, she took a deep breath, then opened it—and she was greeted with another swirling portal. This time, it was black and gold, as if gold paint was being stirred into oil.

Giving herself zero time for freaking out, she stepped through.

It was dark. No, there was light: stars. So many stars! And a moon hung heavy and full, low in the sky over the gray silhouette of distant stone spires.

How did it become night?

In front of her, down a grassy hill, were row after row of tents, lit by torches and lanterns. It looked to be some kind of nighttime farmers market, with vendors at each tent hawking fabrics and fruits. The air was full of smells that she didn't recognize: meats and spices, she guessed, but nothing she could name. On the hills around the market were dozens of other door-size rectangles of swirling colors.

Calisa stepped backward through her portal into the guest room and daylight and closed the door. Her closet had nothing like this. She thought of the red X painted on her guest room door and wondered if *this* was what it meant. X for no swirl. No . . . wherever that was.

Checking the hallway, Calisa emerged from the unoccupied guest room and shut the door behind her. She was shaking, and she felt as if her thoughts were swirling inside her, as mixed up as the colors in the portals—that's what they had to be, didn't they? Portals to . . . somewhere else?

Auntie Zee knows.

So does Jack.

As did every guest staying at the Faraway Inn. . . . She thought of Kendra apparently stepping out of a supply closet, and how there were never any cars outside.

Exactly how far away are Auntie Zee's guests from?

CHAPTER ELEVEN

The fireplace in her room was cold when Calisa returned, and she stared at it for a moment, then shook her head. She had much larger questions than an inconsistent fire. She felt as if the very foundation stones beneath her feet were crumbling. If what she saw was real . . . then everything about the world was different than she thought it was.

Calisa picked up the phone on the bedside table, and before she could talk herself out of it, she dialed her home number. It rang. And rang. And rang until voicemail picked up. She didn't leave a message. She tried Mom-Kate's cell phone. Voicemail too. She tried Mom-Elise.

After one ring, Mom-Elise answered, "Calisa!"

There was background noise: voices, music. Mom-Elise must be out somewhere. It was Tuesday—errand day. *I can't have this conversation while she's in public.* "Hey, just . . . calling to say hi," Calisa said.

"So good to hear your voice!" In the background, she heard a man asking Mom-Elise whether she wanted a quarter pound or a half. "Quarter of the cheddar. Half of the cranberry Wensleydale." To Calisa, she said, "Honey, I'm at Brew Cheese. Can I call you when I'm home? Is everything okay?"

"Everything's fine," Calisa said. She paced beside her bed, as far as she could before the phone cord went taut. "Just had a question. Actually more of a question for Mom-Kate."

"She's got work meetings all day, but I'll tell her. You can call back tonight, if you want? Are you sure everything's all right? Do you feel okay? Is Auntie Zee being nice to you? I know she can be . . . brusque, but she'll warm up to you, I'm certain of it."

"Listen—do you know if . . ." She had no idea how to ask the question, especially in any way that Mom-Elise could answer while she was out in public. Stretching the phone cord, she crossed to the window and looked out at the mountains blanketed in pine trees. "Is there something special about the inn that I should know about?"

"It is a special place, especially to Kate," Mom-Elise said. More carefully, she added, "I think she's hoping you'll discover all the things that made it special to her, when she was a kid."

That . . . was a kind of answer all on its own. Unless Calisa was reading into it what she wanted to hear? "I think I'm beginning to?" She didn't know how to put what she'd seen into words, or if she was ready to. If she said it, it would make it real, and she wasn't sure she was ready for it to be real. She wasn't even sure what *it* was.

"No, half pound of the Wensleydale." Then to Calisa

again: "Give the inn a chance. I know it's not what you were expecting—"

"Yeah, you could say that."

"—but it could be wonderful. And I think . . . Yes, half pound. I think you're exactly what that place needs. You'll give it a chance, won't you? Open a few doors, both metaphorically and literally?"

For an instant, Calisa couldn't breathe.

"Calisa?" Mom-Elise sounded worried.

She felt dizzy, and her knees wobbled like Jell-O. Leaning her head against the window, she looked down and saw Steve curled on top of the statue's head, beside the apple tree. "I'll give it a chance," she promised.

"That's my girl," Mom-Elise said. "Love you to the moon."

"Love you to the stars," Calisa said, staring down at the statue with Steve sunning his lizardy body. "And back."

The phone clicked, and she returned to the bedside table and placed it on the receiver. Staring at it, she reminded herself to inhale and exhale.

Across the room, the fire began to inexplicably blaze in the fireplace again, flames dancing over the logs. "No," she told it. "No. I have to think."

She grabbed Jack's father's cookbook and bolted out of the room, refusing to look back at the weirdly temperamental fire. She had too many questions. She felt as if they were all swirling inside her, threatening to rise up into her throat and choke her.

She'd bake the cake, and then . . . she had a *lot* of questions for Auntie Zee. Of course, she wasn't sure if she'd be allowed to ask any of them, and she had no idea where to begin.

First, make the cake. And breathe. She needed to remember to breathe.

In the kitchen, Calisa read the recipe twice, three times, before actually focusing on the words. *I'll need flour, sugar, eggs, butter, vanilla, salt, baking powder, vegetable oil, milk. . . .* A minute later, she had all the ingredients out of the cabinets and strewn across the counter. After a bit of searching, she found two cake pans. She'd make a two-layer cake and spread jam between the layers. She'd seen some raspberry jam in one of the cabinets. It was almost like a Victoria sponge cake, minus the cream.

No thinking. No questions.

Not yet.

As Calisa mixed the dry ingredients, she glanced out the back window and saw that the statue was no longer with the lizard beside the apple tree. Instead, it was on the path to the greenhouse. Its hands were clasped again, and it was in profile, as if looking out at the mountains. Calisa paused, gawked for a moment, and then turned back to stirring even more vigorously.

"It could be wonderful," Mom-Elise had said on the phone.

She knew, Calisa realized.

"Open a few doors, both metaphorically and literally?"

She absolutely knew.

Maybe both her moms had known all along, even back as far as the visit with the chocolate strawberries. *I can understand them not telling me then. But why not* before *I got on the train?* Even a hint. Or a warning. Would that have been so terrible? *Hey, just a heads-up, Calisa,* they could have said, *there's something about the inn we think you should know.*

Whisking the sugar with the milk and vanilla, Calisa tried not to feel lied to again. It hadn't been Mom-Elise's secret to spill. Or even Mom-Kate's. They must have felt they couldn't tell her. Maybe they'd expected Auntie Zee to fill her in.

Or maybe they thought I wouldn't believe it until I saw it.

She began to stir less vigorously.

That could be true. She would've thought they were joking. She might not have even come if she'd believed it was all some elaborate prank. The more she thought about it, the more Calisa thought that was likely it. Her moms had both encouraged her to go to Vermont, despite the fact that they'd hated sending her away to one measly two-week camp the summer after eighth grade—she'd also hated that camp, mainly because her roommate had been the world's most devoted pessimist, who talked exclusively about how much her boyfriend (also an eighth grader) had wronged her by not loving her nearly as much as his Nintendo Switch. But she'd so obviously needed a distraction from mourning what she'd lost with Ethan. . . .

Behind her she heard footsteps. She didn't turn.

"Are you making a cake?" Jack asked, eager.

She looked out again at the statue. It was in the same position, at least for now. *Jack has answers,* she thought. But would he tell her the truth if she asked? She wanted to think yes—she liked him—but she couldn't be certain. Besides, how did she phrase the question she really wanted to ask? Should she hint around it? Coax it out of him? Hope he volunteered it? *Eh, screw it.* She'd never been good at subtle.

"Yep, a cake," Calisa said. In a cheerful perky-casual voice, she asked, "So, are the guests from other worlds?"

He blinked. "What?"

"Just wondering."

"Ah," he said.

"Because there seem to be portals in the guest room closets."

He looked as if she'd dumped a bucket of ice water on his head. She considered that maybe just jumping into the question non sequitur–style had not been the best approach.

She stirred harder. *Come on. Tell me the truth. Please.*

"Uh, no. What? Portals? Closets? Haha . . ."

He was choosing to lie to her.

Like Ethan.

Ethan had lied to her again and again, and when finally caught, he'd tried to gaslight her into disbelieving the overwhelming evidence in front of her eyes.

It didn't feel good to have that happening again.

"Of course there aren't," Jack said. "You must have been dreaming. I have the strangest dreams sometimes—this one time, I dreamed I was a moose, and I had these really heavy antlers, which was funny because I don't actually have antlers—"

"You're lying to me," Calisa cut in. "You've been lying to me since the second I got here, and you're continuing to try to lie to me. Badly. Really, really badly."

He slumped. "I . . ."

"You have your reasons, I'm sure," she said flatly. She tried to match Auntie Zee's thundercloud glare, imagining that a lightning bolt would strike him if he lied again. "But whatever they are, you can stop now. I've seen the portals—are they portals?"

He glanced at the window as if he were longing to jump out of it and run off into the forest like Melidor, cawing wildly all the way.

"If you don't start talking," Calisa said, "I'm going to go to Auntie Zee and ask her every question I have."

His body jerked, and he paled. "She'll fire me. Instantly. I can't lose this job. You don't understand. It's more than a job; it's my home. It's my future."

Calisa continued to glare. She was *not* going to be distracted by how uncomfortable and unhappy he looked. She didn't care how puppylike he was. Or how angelically handsome. He'd lied to her with every word and every smile.

"I can't lose my place here," Jack pleaded. "You haven't been here long enough to know, but this inn . . . it's special. When I was a kid, it was full every single night, with a waiting list a mile long. Our guests were desperate to come. Even now, when it's falling apart and we can't even guarantee breakfast, much less tea, our regulars still come back. . . ." She could hear the worry in his voice, woven into each word. "It's still special."

He's scared, Calisa realized, and she felt some of her anger drain away. He wasn't the one who had really lied to her. That was Auntie Zee. And her moms, if they knew, which she thought they probably did.

Unable to keep looking at his wide, bright eyes, Calisa

poured the batter into the two cake pans. In a calmer voice, she said, "Look, Jack, I'm here, and I'm figuring things out. Slowly and clumsily, and it's way too late to stop now. If you'd rather that I didn't do something irreversibly embarrassing for the inn that will piss off Auntie Zee, it would be best to tell me what's really going on here. I'm not going to stop wondering, so don't you think it's safer for everyone if I'm not just bumbling around trying to find answers on my own?" She slid the cakes into the oven and then turned to face him.

He looked like a rabbit cornered by a wolf. She almost felt sorry for him.

"Jack? I'm right, aren't I? About the closet doors?" Calisa asked.

He shook his head. Squeezed his eyes shut. Opened them. And then he said, "It's any door. Sometimes. And sometimes not. I don't know exactly how it works, but certain doors open to certain places. Except when they don't."

And there it was.

Unless this was a joke.

It's not a joke. She'd seen it, walked through it, visited . . . "certain places." "Where do they go? How do they work?" *How is any of this possible?*

"Auntie Zee is the only one who can make the doors cooperate at all."

She thought of the first door she'd opened: the broom closet with the howling darkness. After Auntie Zee had slammed it shut, it was an ordinary broom closet. She should have guessed that Auntie Zee herself was a key element.

Jack continued, "Auntie Zee is, like, the caretaker of the

inn's doors. She's the one who says whether a door works as a portal or as, um, you know, a closet or bathroom or whatever." His eyes slid to the foyer, as if he were expecting Auntie Zee to charge into the kitchen and demand that they stop talking.

"What *do* you know?"

"The bed-and-breakfast is a nexus," Jack said. "A nexus of realms."

She absorbed that. "And what exactly does that mean?"

He shrugged. "Lots of doors to other worlds."

Again, for an instant, Calisa couldn't breathe. She'd been right—there really were other worlds through those doorways. *Actual other worlds. I've been to other worlds!* That was why the sun had felt and looked so strange and why the smells from the night market had been so unfamiliar. There wasn't anything like it on Earth, because she hadn't been on Earth. She'd known it, but she hadn't *known* it. *A nexus of realms.*

"It's rare, a place like this," Jack said. "That's why it's so special. It's a place where people can come to escape. A real getaway, for whoever needs it."

"So the guests . . . they're actually from other worlds? Realms, you said?"

"I think of them as 'realms' because, as my dad explained to me, they're not other planets. At least not other planets in our solar system. It's not like Kendra is from Venus, and Mulligan is from the moon or even Alpha Centauri. They're just from other places. Faraway places. Like pocket dimensions, if you want to sound all sci-fi about it, which you shouldn't because Auntie Zee hates that."

"Wow." She tried to wrap her mind around this. "How

many . . ." No, that wasn't what she wanted to ask next. "Are you from another realm?"

He shook his head. "Vermont born and bred. Like my dad."

"And Auntie Zee?" Calisa asked.

Jack looked surprised by the question. "I never asked."

From upstairs, Auntie Zee called, "Jack, third floor!"

Both of them froze. Had she somehow heard them talking? *She couldn't have.* Did she find out that Calisa had opened doors that she shouldn't have opened? *She could have.* What was Auntie Zee going to say? And what was she going to do?

I can't go home! Not now!

Auntie Zee called, "Bring the plunger!"

And both Calisa and Jack exhaled in unison.

CHAPTER TWELVE

While the cake cooled and Jack plunged the third-floor toilet, Calisa made the icing. She didn't need a recipe for this: it was just powdered sugar with milk, butter, and vanilla. She'd made it for the cupcakes she'd baked for Mom-Kate's birthday, the ones that had tasted like churros.

A flicker of orange caught the corner of her eye, and she glanced at the kitchen fireplace to see a flame dancing over the logs. *That's still weird.* What else was in the Faraway Inn that she'd failed to notice because it should be impossible? How about the teapot that heated instantly and didn't seem to have an on switch, despite Jack's claim that it was an electric kettle?

Checking on the cakes, she decided they were cool enough. She smeared raspberry jam on the first layer and then laid the next layer on top. Jam oozed out the sides and dripped onto the plate, bleeding into the white icing and causing it to smear pink. She should have waited until the cake layers cooled more, but it was late afternoon already. If she delayed any longer, it would slip from teatime to dinner, and she'd latched onto the idea of reinstating a real teatime with homemade cake and tea from a possibly enchanted teapot.

If she could keep Kendra happy, then Auntie Zee would let her stay longer. And the longer she stayed . . . *the more answers I can find.* Had Kendra come out of the cleaning-supply closet? What about Mulligan? Why had he filled a vial with hot chocolate? She needed to know more! And for that, she needed to finish this cake.

She wished her hands would quit shaking so hard.

Nexus of realms. The words ricocheted inside her head.

Calisa smoothed the icing around the sides. It wasn't bakery quality—the icing was uneven, and the cake itself leaned to one side. Jam clumped around the base, and she wished she knew how to make icing flowers to cover up the issues. It was, however, clearly a cake, which had been the goal. And as for her goal in coming here . . . well, an inn full of otherworldly guests was certainly a distraction from Ethan. She barked a laugh.

"It looks delicious," Jack said behind her, and she jumped.

"How long have you been there?" Had he heard her cackling to herself? Almost certainly. Had she talked out loud? She didn't think so.

"Not long." His eyes slid toward the door, and she glanced out the window to see the statue just outside, looking in with her stone-blank eyes.

A shiver danced down her spine. "New question: How long has *she* been there?"

"Longer," Jack admitted.

"Can she talk?" Calisa asked. To the statue, she asked, "Can you talk?"

The statue was silent and motionless.

Crossing to the window, Calisa stared at the statue. Her eyes were smooth gray. No pupils. No irises. She had a crease where eyelids would be, but no lashes. Her lips were closed. "Is she like the Weeping Angels? Only moves when I'm not looking?"

"What are Weeping Angels?" Jack asked.

"From *Doctor Who*. Never mind. Is she friendly?"

"She's stone," Jack said.

"That's not a helpful answer."

"It wasn't a reasonable question."

She thought it was very reasonable. There was, really, a ludicrous amount Calisa didn't know about all of this, but it would be helpful to know if the shudder she felt was warranted. She skipped to the most important question: "Is she going to murder me?"

Jack rocked backward. "Of course not!"

"How do you know, if she can't talk?" The statue still hadn't moved, not even to flinch at the suggestion that she was murderous.

"She wouldn't," Jack said stoutly.

A point in the statue's favor: Jack hadn't been murdered yet. "I guess statistically I'm more likely to be murdered by a random human than a statue."

"Can we stop talking about murder and talk about cake instead?"

Calisa grinned. That had sounded so adorably pathetic, like

he'd been craving cake for his entire life and would perish without a bite of it in the next ten minutes. It was impossible to stay mad at him. It was like trying to stay mad at a puppy dog, especially one with nice eyes, nice hair, and incredible muscles, who actually listened to what she said and cared what she felt and had stepped in front of her when an irate guest had charged toward her—*Focus, Calisa,* she told herself. "I have more questions."

He sighed. "Of course you do. Can you just . . . not ask Auntie Zee? I'll answer whatever I can. Just please don't let her know you know."

"But I *do* know, and she can explain all of it."

"Yeah, but she'll ask *how* you know, and she'll never believe I didn't tell you. I'll be fired, and you'll be sent home."

Calisa opened her mouth to say she'd defend him—but how would she explain how she'd figured it out? She'd broken one of Auntie Zee's only rules, rather flagrantly. She'd absolutely be sent home if she admitted that. "You'll tell me what I want to know? No more lying?"

"I'll do my best."

She could live with that.

"Okay, so how does it work? The portals, I mean. How do the doors become portals? How do they connect to other realms?" Was it a wormhole? A magic spell? Were they special doors, or had something special been done to them? Did each door connect to a specific realm, or could they open to different ones? Could Auntie Zee control which realm she reached? How did she "take care" of the doors? What did that mean? Did she control them somehow? Program them? "How does Auntie Zee do it?"

Coming into the kitchen, Auntie Zee asked, "How does Auntie Zee do what?"

Calisa saw panic cross Jack's face. He stopped breathing, and his entire body went rigid. "Ahh . . ." She tried to think fast. "How does Auntie Zee find so many flavors of maple syrup?"

Auntie Zee narrowed her eyes.

"I've only had plain pancake syrup before," Calisa said.

With a disdainful sniff, Auntie Zee said, "Corn syrup."

"Yeah, um," Jack said. "I was about to tell Calisa that there's a local maple syrup farm that specializes in different flavors." To Calisa, he said, "You need to try gingerbread maple syrup. Apple-cinnamon maple syrup. Rhubarb-flavored, which is a lot better than it sounds."

"Wow," Calisa said. Inwardly, she winced at herself. *Wow?*

But Auntie Zee didn't question it. Instead she turned to Jack. "There's a light on the second floor that's flickering, and it's not the bulb. I need you to look at the wiring."

"Sure, yeah, right away."

"I'll show you." After a glare at Calisa, as if to blame her for the faulty lighting, Auntie Zee led the way out of the kitchen.

Following, Jack mouthed at Calisa, *"Thank you."*

She shrugged as if to say it was fine, even though it was absolutely not fine. All the questions were burning inside her. And if she couldn't ask Auntie Zee . . . *Maybe there's someone else I could ask instead.*

Leaving the nearly finished cake, she marched outside through the kitchen door.

And she took a deep breath.

The backyard of the inn overlooked the mountains, and the sun bathed them in amber. She tilted her head to feel the ordinary sunlight on her cheeks. An ordinary breeze wrapped around her. It smelled of flowers, but familiar flowers. By the greenhouse she spotted the statue.

She crossed to it, to her.

The statue was facing the mountains. She looked as if she'd just emerged from the greenhouse. She was frozen mid-stride, one hand still on the door handle.

"Hi," Calisa said. "I'm Calisa, Auntie Zee's grandniece, and I know you aren't going to move or talk to me while I'm looking at you, so I'm thinking that I'll ask you a question and then turn my back and then you can move or whatever, if you want to answer me, okay?" The words spilled out of her—she could hear her own nervousness threaded through her voice, but she couldn't help it. She still knew so very little about what was going on and whether any of it was safe, or whether it would have been smarter to run screaming back to Brooklyn. She tried to pick a yes-or-no question, ideally the most important one, but which was the most important one? What did she really want to know?

Everything. I want to know everything.

She ran through a list of questions in her head and then settled on one: "Do you need help?"

Calisa turned her back to the statue and looked at the inn.

Prickles crept up her spine as she wondered what the statue was doing, if she really moved when no one was watching, what she wanted, why she was here, and whether she was dangerous. A few seconds later, she turned around.

The statue had moved her head to the left, gazing at the forest.

"No? Okay, good." The statue didn't need help, which was excellent news, since Calisa didn't know what she'd have done if the statue had said yes. Had she been born a statue? That was probably too personal a question to ask, and it wasn't really at the heart of what Calisa wanted to know. "Are you from here? From Vermont? From this world?" She turned her back and counted to five.

When she spun around again, the statue was looking in the opposite direction.

Another no.

Not from this world.

Calisa swallowed hard. She was actually communicating with a statue. "Do you want to be here? Are you here willingly?" Again, Calisa turned away and waited a few seconds.

This time, the statue's head was lowered, her chin near her neck—a frozen nod.

That was good to know. She wasn't from here, but she wanted to be here. Calisa considered what to ask next. It had to be yes or no.

From across the garden, she heard Jack call, "Calisa?"

To the statue, she said, "Thank you. You've been really helpful. If you need anything . . ." She wasn't certain how to complete that sentence. "Well, I'll, um, come talk with you again, if you don't mind."

Calisa trotted across the unmowed lawn toward Jack, who was frowning at her. "I should have said this before," Jack said, "but really important: you shouldn't go through any of the portals. If you're tempted."

She thought of the two worlds she'd already stepped foot in. She'd barely seen either of them. She wanted to explore, to see what else was out there. What other realms were hidden within guest rooms? Or through broom closets? She thought of the linen closet in the bathroom where she'd found Steve—could the lizard have come through a portal? He wasn't like any ordinary Vermont lizard. He could have come from . . . elsewhere. "Why not?"

"You go through a portal without Auntie Zee's okay, she'll fire you. She'll fire me."

"But why?"

"She thinks . . . it's not safe. My dad . . ." Jack paused, swallowed. "He went through one to look for a way to help the inn. He . . . hasn't come back."

"You said . . ."

"I said he went for supplies for the inn," Jack said. "That wasn't a lie, or not entirely a lie. I simply didn't say *where* he went. I don't even know where he went. He didn't tell me. Just that he was going through a door, and he'd be back soon."

She had the sudden urge to wrap her arms around him. He looked as if he were about to crumble. "What about Auntie Zee? Can't she tell you where he is? Can't she go get him?"

Maybe she couldn't ask Auntie Zee questions, but Jack had known her aunt for years, possibly his whole life.

"She says . . . some of the doors don't work anymore. She can't open them again."

Gazing at the three-story inn with myriad guest rooms and bathrooms and clothes closets and supply closets and linen closets, she wondered how many portals were inside it—and how many had failed. Calisa thought of her guest room with the red X—a room with a broken door? Was that what the X meant?

He continued. "That's what Dad was trying to fix. He was looking for something that would fix the problem with the broken portals. After he went through . . . that door quit working too. It won't reopen, at least not as a portal."

"But . . ." What was he saying? Was his dad *gone*? Permanently?

Could that have happened to me?

"Isn't Auntie Zee doing anything to try to get him back?" Calisa asked.

"She's tried," Jack said. "She's still trying."

Calisa looked at the inn again, at the weeds and brambles that surrounded it, at the broken shingles and occasional boarded-up window. The condition of the bed-and-breakfast . . . It was too dilapidated for it to have been a few weeks, as he'd originally implied. There was too much neglect here.

Softly, she asked, "How long has your father been gone?"

"Three years," Jack said.

CHAPTER THIRTEEN

Calisa wanted to reach out and hug him. The way he said "three years"—she could hear every morning and every night of a boy waiting for his sole parent to come home, every question that went unanswered, every explanation that wasn't enough. "I'm sorry."

He shrugged.

It was the kind of shrug when you don't trust yourself to speak. She wished there were more she could say or do. "How can I help?" she asked.

"You can't," he said. "Not unless you can fix whatever's wrong with the inn. And you didn't even know there was anything special about this place until, like, ten minutes ago."

Ouch, but true. "But what *is* wrong with it?"

He shrugged again, and this time it was the kind of shrug that said you were so frustrated that if you didn't shrug, you'd explode. "It's falling apart. You can see that for yourself. Every bit of it. And that includes the portals. It used to be that the inn was full of guests all the time, every room booked. You never knew who or what you'd meet. Once there was a man with a three-headed dog—I played fetch with that dog for hours. Another summer, we had a woman who floated six inches above the ground."

She wished she could have seen that. "They don't come anymore?"

He shook his head. "It's not just the portals shutting down, though that's the worst and largest problem. It's the place itself. No one wants to come to an inn with a leaky roof and temperamental plumbing and hit-or-miss breakfasts. Dad says that this place used to be fit for royalty. And now look at it."

Looking at the inn, Calisa tried to imagine it: if the brambles were cleared, if the outside were painted, if the broken windows were fixed, if it didn't look as if it had been abandoned a decade ago and was now home to a family of feral raccoons, could it be fit for royalty again?

"There used to be a gardener and a cook and a housekeeper, an actual staff," Jack said. "But then it became this downward spiral: guests don't come, which means we can't afford staff, which means guests don't come, which means . . . You get it. I think I was ten when the cook left, and she was the last to go."

Calisa didn't know what to ask that wouldn't make it worse. His father had been gone for three years? "Your dad . . . Is there any . . ." She wished she hadn't started that sentence; she didn't want to ask whether there was hope if there was none.

"He'll find his way back," Jack said, not looking at her. Turning his back to the inn, he fixed his gaze on the pine trees in the distance. Calisa shifted to look with him. The wind whistled through the tops of the trees, swaying them. It made it look as if the mountains were breathing. Above, the sky was streaked with clouds. If she moved her hand just a few inches, she'd be touching his. She didn't move. She waited for him to speak again. At last, he continued. "He can't get here directly anymore, and we can't reach him. So he has to find another nexus and then world-hop until he can find a different door that connects. But the Faraway Inn needs to stay in business so he has a place to return to."

Three years! There had to be a way to help him find his way home faster. She thought of all the other portals she'd seen on the hills around the market. "Do you know where the portal led? If we went through a different one—"

"No," Jack said.

She flinched. "I'm sorry." The last thing she wanted to do was make things worse for him. It had to hurt to have to explain any of this to a near stranger. She stood silently for a moment, wondering if she should take his hand, watching the pine trees become still, then sway again. A hawk circled high above. Just because she had questions didn't mean he had to answer them. *This isn't about me anymore.* "We can talk about something else, if you want. How about cake? What's your favorite kind? Chocolate? Carrot? Angel food?"

Jack didn't even seem to hear her. "I tried to find him. For months. I stopped doing anything around the inn, and I searched. Went through every portal I could find. Eventually, Auntie Zee noticed. And that's when she told me that the portal he'd used had closed and wouldn't reopen—I can't find him, no matter how many portals I go through, no matter how hard I look; he has to find me. After that, I couldn't bring myself to do anything for a while. A long while."

Calisa laid her hand on his arm lightly, ready to remove it if he didn't want to be touched. "You aren't doing it alone anymore. I'm here to help, however I can." She'd already restored the sitting room and reestablished afternoon tea. If they could finish fixing up the gardens . . . paint the inn . . . would that be enough to help keep the B&B in business? At least long enough for Jack's father to come back? "After tea and cake, we'll continue restoring the gardens. Make them look idyllic. The porch already looks better without the brambles." She strode toward the kitchen and was halfway there before she realized that Jack wasn't following her. She halted.

He was crouched on the ground, his face in his hands. The statue was beside him with one of her hands near his back, an inch above him, as if she wanted to comfort him but couldn't quite touch him.

"Jack? Are you okay?"

He took a breath and his shoulders shuddered. He then stood up—the statue remained bent behind him, motionless, comforting the empty air. "Yes. Sorry. It's just . . . Sorry." He trotted toward her, and she saw his eyes were overbright, like he'd just cried. "It's been just me for a long time."

Calisa felt a knot of anger curl in her stomach. *Someone*

should have helped him before now. He shouldn't have had to shoulder all of this alone. He was only a year older than she was, if that. He should be having fun with his friends, applying to college, beginning his future. She wondered if he had any friends, if he had time for anyone. She doubted it. He probably hadn't let anyone see how bad things had gotten for him. "Hey, it's okay. We'll fix everything. We'll make this place fit for royalty again. Guests will flock back."

She held out her hand, and he took it.

"Your dad will have a place to come home to," Calisa promised.

As she finished up the icing on the only slightly lopsided and accidentally pink cake, Calisa ordered Jack, "Get plates, forks, and napkins, and meet me in the sitting room."

He jumped into action while she carried the cake out of the kitchen.

Over her shoulder, she called, "Also, a cake knife."

In the sitting room, Calisa set the cake on the table with the mosaic of pebbles. Her concoction looked lumpy and amateurish on the elegant table, but it was incontrovertibly cake. She supposed if that was all you could say about it, that was fine. She'd do better on her second attempt. *If I get to make a second attempt.*

"Want to do the honors?" she asked Jack, offering him the knife handle.

"First slice is yours. You made it."

She shook her head. "If it's terrible, I don't want to be the one to eat it first."

He grinned. "So I'm your poison tester?"

"Yep. I *think* I used sugar instead of salt." When his smile wavered, she added, "I'm kidding. Probably." God, he was adorable, and it said a lot about *how* adorable he was that she was still noticing that on the day she'd discovered that the inn was a magical nexus.

He cut through the cake and angled the knife for a wide slice. "We once had a guest who would only eat sugar. Like—literally. She'd pour sugar in water, on top of toast, over her burgers and fries—" He cut himself off. "Kendra! Um, cake?"

"I do hope that I am not spoken of when I'm not in residence," Kendra said crisply. "There is an expectation of privacy that I value in this establishment."

Jack looked adorably panicked again. He wore that expression often. "Nope. Did I say guest? I meant a friend from school."

He had absolutely said "guest," plus Calisa knew he'd been homeschooled, but their elegant guest let that pass. "You have baked a cake," Kendra observed.

"It's vanilla with raspberry jam filling," Calisa offered. "Not quite Victoria sponge, but close—it's my first attempt."

Jack hurriedly cut a slice for her.

"Never apologize for trying," Kendra said. She accepted the slice while Jack dove into his own portion, shoving enormous bites into his mouth. Kendra took a more reasonable bite. "Acceptable," she determined. "You will do better next time."

"Thanks?" At least Calisa hadn't driven her out of the room yet. That was an improvement. And she knew she could do a better job with baking a cake when she wasn't distracted by monumental discoveries about the nature of the universe.

Crossing to the teapot, Kendra declared, "I would like some tea."

Obligingly, the teapot rattled, and steam curled from its spout. And then it rose into the air, tipped forward, and poured fresh tea into a cup.

"Delightful," Kendra said.

Calisa felt her jaw drop.

Kendra didn't seem remotely surprised. She merely added salt to her cup and sipped neatly before carrying her tea and slice of cake to her preferred seat, the one with the sea-foam blanket.

Swallowing hard, Calisa watched the teapot float back down onto the tea tray. She was one hundred percent certain she hadn't imagined it and equally certain that Auntie Zee wouldn't appreciate it if she freaked out about it in front of a guest. Instead, she looked at Jack and raised both eyebrows.

"The teapot was a gift from a guest," Jack said, as if that explained it.

She wondered what excuse he'd have tried to make if she'd seen it float before she'd discovered the portals. "Must use impressive batteries."

"Uh, yeah."

Out of the corner of her eye, Calisa saw movement out the window. She turned quickly, hoping to catch the statue in motion, but instead she saw Melidor, scurrying in between the rosebushes. In her wake, flowers bloomed. "Jack, could you cut me another slice of cake, please? I want to offer it to Melidor."

After Jack cut another slice, Calisa carried it outside, cradled in a napkin. She smiled, trying to look as friendly as possible, then worried she was smiling too hard and toned it down. By the time she was off the porch, she was certain she looked like a doll with a painted grimace. But she kept walking forward and holding out the cake. "Melidor?"

Melidor jumped up from between a patch of irises and a clump of out-of-control grass. "Fire? Where?"

Calisa halted. "No fire. Just cake."

Sighing, Melidor squatted back down between the irises until only the top of her very green hair was visible. She murmured wordlessly in a singsong voice.

"I brought you a slice of cake, if you'd like it," Calisa said, crossing to her, cake outstretched. "It doesn't look gorgeous, but it tastes good. Vanilla and raspberry."

"I like raspberry." Melidor snatched the plate and fork out of Calisa's hands.

Calisa considered how to tell her that she'd broken into her room without permission, crossed through the portal, and talked with her mother. . . . *Yeah, that's not going to go over well.* Maybe she could ease into it. "I wanted to apologize for . . . before. You know, hurting the plants." She was fairly certain that Melidor had forgiven her already, but it never hurt to apologize extra. It might work as a good conversation opener. Establish trust and all that.

Melidor waved the fork. "You had to hurt in order to save. It's like that sometimes."

"What's like that sometimes?"

"Life."

"Ah, yes. I guess it is." *How can I tell her?* If she did, chances were good that Melidor would complain to Auntie Zee, and if the innkeeper found out that Calisa had opened those doors and, worse, gone through one . . . *I can't risk it. Not yet. Not until I understand more of what's going on.*

Melidor crumbled bits of the cake and dropped them onto the dirt between the plants.

"Do you not like it?" Calisa asked. "I can make a different flavor next time." Assuming Auntie Zee let her stay to make another one.

"I'm sharing."

"With the plants?"

"With the worms," Melidor said. She knelt and pressed her cheek against the soil. When she lifted her head, she had dirt clinging to her cheek and dusting her eyelashes. "They're grateful."

Normally, Calisa would have walked away slowly after that kind of display, but now she wondered if Melidor actually could talk to worms. "I've never talked to a worm. Do they have a lot to say?" She hoped she sounded sincere. It *was* true; it was just that the words felt ridiculous on her lips.

Melidor looked at her as if she were the absurd one. "They're worms."

Fair enough.

Regardless, it wasn't really what Calisa wanted to know. What she wanted to know was . . . *Everything. I want to know everything: what she is, why she's here, why she hears plants scream and how she talks to worms and where she went and what she did when she ran into the woods.* She had no idea how to begin to ask any of that. "Can you talk to everything?"

"Sure," Melidor said. "Trick is: Does it talk back?"

"Well, um, does it?"

She shrugged. "If it has something to say."

Crouching down, Melidor pressed her cheek to the dirt. She hummed to herself and closed her eyes. Calisa waited to see if she said anything else, but she seemed done. *Don't push,* she told herself. She'd delivered her peace offering; it was time to back away. Later, she could ask more questions and figure out how to deliver her mother's message. "There's fresh tea inside, if you'd like."

Melidor stayed on the ground, her lips moving silently. She'd gotten icing all over her fingers and smeared on one cheek, mixing with the dirt.

Calisa retreated to the inn.

Inside, Jack was on his second slice, and Kendra was still sipping her tea. She had a pile of pink icing on her plate. "Melidor is feeding the cake to the worms," Calisa reported. "Can she actually talk to them?"

Jack mumbled around the cake.

"Manners!" Kendra snapped.

"Sorry," Calisa said. "I'll, um, take a piece up to Mulligan."

Shoveling another bite into his mouth, Jack put down his plate and cut a slice for Mulligan. It flopped over onto the plate. She noticed that he had a dot of icing on his cheek, just where a dimple would be, and suddenly wished she could make him smile. But nothing witty popped into her head. He handed her the plate, and she just said, "Thanks."

Climbing the stairs, Calisa puzzled over how she could learn more. Even outside of Auntie Zee's rules, it wasn't socially acceptable to just walk up to someone and ask their life story, but she wanted to know everything about everyone here.

Especially Auntie Zee.

And Jack.

And why Mom-Elise thought it would be good for Calisa to be here, aside from the fact that hello, nexus of realms, very cool. Or was that precisely the key fact?

She knocked on Mulligan's door. She didn't hear any movement. Pressing her ear against the door, Calisa listened. She knocked again. "Mulligan?"

He didn't answer.

She wasn't certain he was in there, though she hadn't seen him in any of the common rooms or heard him on the stairs.

"There's cake, if you'd like some," Calisa called through the door. "I'm going to leave the piece here. Try not to step on it, okay?" She set the plate down beside his door and turned toward the stairs.

Opening the door, Mulligan stuck his head out. He smiled broadly when he saw her. "Did I hear you mention cake?" His eyes lit up as he spotted it, and he bent to pick it up. "Delectable! Sugar is a balm for the wounded soul."

Calisa smiled and tried to figure out a polite way to ask if he had a magical portal in his closet. "It's vanilla cake with raspberry jam filling."

He put a hand to his heart. "You are an angel sent from above."

She wanted to reply, *And where are you from?* But that kind of made it sound like she thought he was from hell, which would be rude. "Thanks. Um, did you enjoy your vial of hot chocolate?"

His smile drooped and his shoulders sagged within his black robes. "Alas, it was not enough to entice him to wake."

Never mind the portal; she couldn't leave a statement like that just hanging out there. "Entice who to what?" She wondered if Mulligan was going to slam the door shut in her face or snap at her like Kendra for asking. If he did, she wouldn't blame him—well, she'd blame him a little because it wasn't an unreasonable question.

He hesitated.

"It was great hot chocolate. Even *magical*." Calisa added as much emphasis to the word as she could, stopping short of either wiggling her eyebrows or winking.

"Ah!" His smile broadened so wide that the skin of his cheeks was stretched taut over his bones. "You know! Excellent. I had thought, given your ancestry, that you must, but you gave no indication of it the other night, and I did not wish to presume."

"A lot has changed."

"Sadly, no change for me." Mulligan opened his door wider so she could see inside.

His room was painted black, with a plush black rug on the floor, black blankets and pillows on the bed, and all shades drawn closed—the only light was from lit candles on the mantel and bedside table, as well as the glow of a fire in the fireplace. In front of the fireplace was the gargoyle that Calisa had seen Jack lug into the house when she'd first arrived.

Mulligan heaved a mighty sigh. "It was an accident."

She raised both her eyebrows.

"In my hubris, I attempted a feat beyond my skill. My beloved Zef paid the price."

"You, um, turned him into stone?" she ventured. She knew she should be horrified, but wow. This revelation chased all other questions out of her head, at least temporarily. "And you came here to . . ." She trailed off, hoping he'd fill in the blank. She'd secretly half decided he was a vampire, based on his pale skin and only coming out at night, but now? Could still be a vampire. Could be an evil wizard. Could be an incompetent wizard. Or a chocolate-fueled incompetent evil vampire wizard . . .

She wished she knew more about magic, beyond: *Surprise! It exists!* A nice YouTube video titled "Everything You Knew About the World Was a Lie But It Will Be Okay" would have been very helpful. Bonus points if it had animation.

"I required peace and quiet for my studies," Mulligan explained. "I have been devoting myself to seeking a remedy. To my despair, all attempts have failed."

"Your attempts included hot chocolate?"

"My theory is emotion will break the spell. If Zef can understand and accept that I never meant to harm him, that I love him more than words, then he should be able to free himself. And so, I have been striving to create a potion that will convey that. Hot chocolate, I hoped, was the perfect solution—it's rich and decadent, yet with a taste of sweet innocence—but to my overwhelming sadness, it had no effect." Another mighty sigh.

"Is there anything I can do to help?"

"Doubtful, but it's kind of you to offer. Perhaps Zef and I are doomed to be the subject of ballads, to live on immortal in the tales of those who sing of sorrow and loss." He sank into the velvet chair beside the fireplace and laid one pale hand on Zef's stone wings. The other held the slice of cake, the fork neatly between his long fingers. "You are welcome to keep me company, if you wish, while I ease my sorrow with this confection."

Calisa pulled the desk chair closer to the fireplace and sat. She stared at Zef, wondering if he was aware he was stone, if he could hear or see. She hoped not. She hoped it was like being asleep and that someday he'd wake.

Mulligan tasted the cake and sighed happily. "Delightful."

"Thank you. I . . ." She trailed off. In the fireplace, the flames danced across the logs. Out of the corner of her eye, it looked like a bird—flames for feathers, darker flames for legs, a wisp of a beak . . .

Frowning, she gazed directly at the fire, and all she saw was a chaotic mix of flames, splitting and joining and twisting and blazing. Calisa looked at Zef again, and again out of the corner of her eye, the firebird danced from log to log, its wings wide.

"So," Calisa said, "there's a bird in the fire, isn't there."

"Yes, they like to visit."

She thought of the times she'd seen a random fire in one of the inn's fireplaces. She hadn't noticed it looking like a bird before, but then again, she hadn't been expecting impossibilities everywhere she looked before.

"I am told that the firebird is a permanent resident," Mulligan said, after swallowing another bite. "They were seeking a new home, after the loss of theirs, and Auntie Zee offered the inn, in exchange for helping to heat the rooms in winter. An equitable exchange."

"Firebird? You mean a phoenix?" Mentally, she patted herself on the back for keeping her voice so level and quiet. She thought she was doing a really good job of staying calm in the face of all of this: conversations with worms, floating teapots, and living fires.

"Not precisely, as I understand it," Mulligan said. "A phoenix is a bird that regenerates after spontaneously igniting and turning to ash. Our friend here is a bird made of fire."

"Ahh." That answer implied that phoenixes also existed, which was awesome. She wondered what else existed and what else she'd discover, if she were allowed to stay. And if the inn were able to stay open.

Mulligan, the sugar-loving possible vampire wizard, savored another bite of cake. "Spectacularly delicious, my dear. You have a gift. I wonder . . . have you mastered other kinds of cakes? Chocolate, perhaps?"

Calisa grinned. “I can look for a recipe.” She added hopefully, “If it’s not too much to ask . . . since you like the cake . . . could you maybe put in a good word for me with Auntie Zee?”

“I’d be delighted.”

The firebird danced on the logs, as if in agreement.

CHAPTER FOURTEEN

Maybe Mulligan *did* put in a good word for her, or maybe it was a combination of the lizard and the cake, because that evening, Auntie Zee didn't send her home. She didn't even mention the possibility. But she didn't say anything about the inn's magic either.

Determined to earn her trust, Calisa spent the next several days dusting, scrubbing, and mopping. Auntie Zee was frequently nearby, puttering in the kitchen or sitting in the now-cobweb-free front room or just following Calisa around to check on her progress.

She got a friendly grunt for the dining room. Plus an almost smile for the laundry.

"Your last cake was dry," Auntie Zee said as Calisa wiped the grime from the corners of the stove. Her great-aunt was perched on the stool. Steve the lizard was outside on the windowsill, gazing mournfully into the kitchen, his wings drooping as he watched her with his marble-like eyes.

"I overbaked it."

"You should try it again for tea tomorrow."

Casually, Calisa said, "You know, if we're able to draw in more guests, I could make a whole bunch of cakes and we could offer different flavors."

Auntie Zee glared at her. "We don't have more guests."

"Or we could expand the menu and offer little sandwiches. Like in England. Cucumber sandwiches, though I feel like cucumber isn't enough to really make it an actual sandwich. Jam sandwiches? You've a huge collection of jam in the kitchen, in addition to the maple syrup. Or I could learn to make pastries. How about croissants? Everyone likes croissants. I know you have to layer in the butter and fold it a billion times. Complex, but I could try. What did your guests used to like? Did they have favorites from wherever they're from?" *Tell me about the portals.* If Auntie Zee would just open up to her, Calisa could ask about the inn and the guests and how it all worked and maybe be able to help more with keeping the inn in business.

"Don't get grand ideas. You'll only be disappointed."

Calisa stared at her. "Wow. What terrible life advice." And it said so much about Auntie Zee and her worldview. Had she always been this pessimistic?

Auntie Zee scowled back. "You have an attitude. Did your moms ever tell you that?"

"Where do you think I learned it?" Calisa said.

Her lips quirked, and Calisa wondered if that was almost a smile or just an involuntary twitch. "You don't understand the difficulties of running an inn."

"Then teach me."

For an instant, an expression crossed Auntie Zee's face that Calisa couldn't place, then it vanished, and she shook her head. "That would be pointless. You'll be gone at the end of the summer and not look back. Just like your mother."

Ah, was that the source of their issues? She pounced on that little bit of insight. If she could fix whatever was broken between Mom-Kate and her great-aunt . . . fix the inn, fix her family, fix herself . . . that was a worthy goal for the summer. . . . Wait, did Auntie Zee just say "end of the summer"? Did that mean she had approval to stay for the entire summer? *Unlikely,* Calisa thought. "Did you want Mom-Kate to stay?"

"Your mother wasn't suited for this place," Auntie Zee said, as if it didn't matter to her one way or another, but Calisa knew she was onto something. Perhaps the inn had been handed down generation to generation, and Mom-Kate didn't want it? Or Auntie Zee thought she couldn't handle it?

"Did she want—"

Auntie Zee interrupted. "You should continue with the gardens. Tell Jack not to overprune the roses." She waddled out of the kitchen without another word.

Calisa followed Auntie Zee into the lobby, intending to continue the conversation, but Auntie Zee was nowhere in sight. There was only the cat, Portia, in the sitting room, and the firebird burning softly in the library fireplace.

Following Auntie Zee's directive, Calisa resumed gardening with Jack. After two days of weeding, she had blisters on her hands from the clippers, she ached in muscles that she didn't know she had (who knew forearms could ache? biceps, yes, but forearms?), and she'd been scratched so much that her skin was speckled with red dashes. But the front yard had been stripped of brambles and weeds. There were patches of bald soil from where the weeds had driven out the flowers, but elsewhere it looked as if the bushes and plants could finally breathe.

She hadn't seen Auntie Zee except briefly when she'd served leftover cake for tea, and then her great-aunt hadn't done more than grunt at her. But Kendra continued to enjoy the cake, and even Mulligan had appeared briefly (in daylight, which doomed her vampire theories—she was still sticking with chocolate wizard) to claim a slice, even though it wasn't chocolate. She hadn't attempted chocolate yet. The recipe in Jack's dad's cookbook had looked tricky.

After finishing weeding around another rosebush, Calisa walked between the plants in the front yard and frowned at the bald patches. Beside her, Steve waddled at a sedate pace. Occasionally, he paused to contemplate the soil. "You're right. It needs something," Calisa said. She asked Jack, "What's that bark-like stuff called that people put around plants and shrubs to make the gardens look neater? Especially people in the suburbs?"

"Mulch?" Jack said.

"Yes, mulch. We need mulch."

"Can't afford it," Jack said.

That was a shame. It would have made the flower beds look intentional instead of haphazard and kept the weeds from immediately growing back. She crossed her arms and studied the yard. At her feet, Steve nudged her toe and then rolled over onto his back. She reached down and scratched his belly the way he liked as she considered the issue of mulch. Mulch was definitely the kind of thing that a well-manicured yard at a well-maintained inn would have. "Can we make our own? It's just wood chips, right?"

"A lot of wood chips."

She had no idea how to make wood chips, but there was plenty of wood—a whole forest's worth of it. Seemed like they had the raw ingredients.

From behind a rosebush, Melidor popped up. "I can do it."

Calisa jumped.

Flopping over, Steve hissed and spread his wings.

She'd had no idea Melidor was there. Granted, Melidor was rarely inside—possibly avoiding the voices of her relatives from her closet—but Calisa still hadn't expected a jumpscare. She thought of the green woman's message, the one she hadn't passed along yet. She still hadn't figured out a way to phrase it that didn't make it obvious she'd been in Melidor's room uninvited. "It's okay," Calisa soothed Steve. "It's just Melidor."

The lizard folded his wings again.

"What do you mean you can do it?" Jack asked Melidor. "You'd have to cut wood. With an axe. We can't ask that of you."

"It's just wood chips, right? I'll ask a couple of beavers to gnaw a bunch of logs." She used her fingers to mime teeth chomping. "Gnash-gnash-gnash."

Calisa stared at her. "You'll . . . really?"

"They like me," Melidor said.

What are you? Calisa wanted to ask. But there was no way that question would go over well, either with Melidor or Auntie Zee, if she happened to hear it. "Great. Go for it."

Whistling, Melidor skipped toward the woods.

"Do you think she can actually talk to beavers?" Calisa asked Jack.

"Honestly? No idea."

They both waited for a few minutes, but Melidor didn't emerge from the woods. Calisa went back to weeding. Now that they'd cleared the largest tangle of weeds, there were an endless number of smaller weeds that filled the flower beds. Calisa was becoming adept at recognizing them. She piled them in a heap on the flagstones that led to the front of the porch. Steve nibbled at them as if they were a salad buffet.

"Have you thought about trying a chocolate cake?" Jack asked.

"You're making specific requests now?" Calisa asked. "I didn't know our relationship had progressed to that."

"If you don't want to . . . I mean, you don't have to. I just . . ."

She resisted the urge to smile. "I'm going to try one soon," Calisa told him. "Mulligan loves chocolate too. He's already asked. It's just the recipe is tricky. It calls for ganache and a mirror glaze, and I've never made that before."

As they continued to weed, they chatted about the best chocolate cakes they'd ever eaten. Calisa told him about her sixth birthday, when her moms had splurged on a special lunch at the American Girl doll café in Manhattan, where you sat your doll in its own seat at the table. She didn't have a doll like that, but she'd brought her teddy bear in a doll's dress. Jack told her about a chocolate cake a guest brought that, when you cut it, shot miniature fireworks into the air a foot above the cake.

After about a half hour, Melidor trotted out of the forest.

Behind her trailed six beavers.

Alarmed, Steve flapped his wings and flew to the roof of the porch.

It occurred to Calisa that she'd never seen a beaver in person. Surprisingly enormous, each was the size of an overfed corgi. They waddled in unison, dragging their wide leathery tails behind them. Their fur was wet and slicked back, and she wondered if they'd fluff up when they were dry. Their whiskers vibrated as they sniffed the air, wrinkling their noses. One of them was making a soft huffing noise.

Calisa and Jack (and Steve) stared as Melidor directed the beavers to fan out at the edge of the forest. The oversize rodents swarmed over fallen branches and logs, and soon the air was filled with the sound of a half-dozen beavers gnawing their way through deadfall.

Melidor hurried up to them with a huge smile on her face. "They'll make the mulch."

"That's amazing," Jack said. "Thank you!"

"How—" Calisa began.

Jack shot her a look.

"Thank you," Calisa said instead. "Is there anything we can help you with in return, while the beavers are, um, mulching?"

Jack was nodding as if he approved of the question. It was

an offer to help, not prying into her personal life, though Calisa was secretly hoping that Melidor would open up about why she was here and why her mother was so concerned.

"I'm good!" Melidor trilled.

"Are you sure? The other day, while I was passing by your room"—Calisa was *not* going to say she'd broken in; so far, Auntie Zee had not noticed that anyone had touched her master key—"I heard someone mention seedlings? Absolutely not trying to interfere, but if there's any way we can help, then I—"

Melidor shrieked, high-pitched, then cascading down into a hum, then silence.

All the beavers stopped munching and stared at her. She waved at them, and they resumed. Perched on the porch roof, Steve reared onto his hind legs and flapped his wings before settling back down again. Calisa and Jack clapped their hands over their ears.

"I can't," Melidor said matter-of-factly, as if she hadn't just screamed like an ambulance siren. "I'm supposed to, but I can't."

"Ah," Calisa said, lowering her hands. *Please say more.*

Melidor did not disappoint.

"It's something that every dryad has to do for herself," Melidor said. "It's how we enter adulthood. We coax seedlings to plant, and when they blossom, your family hosts a festival. It's elaborate and awful, and everyone will be looking at me." She put her hands over her face. "I'm not ready for it, that's all."

Dryad.

She's a dryad.

All right, then.

It occurred to Calisa that she'd had more unusual conversations in the past week than she'd had in, well, ever. Since she'd come here, she'd been continually surprised in both tiny and worldview-changing ways. She wondered if Jack still felt that surprise. *He couldn't have expected mulch-making beavers.* Still . . . dryad or not, Calisa recognized someone being pushed too far too fast. "If you aren't ready, then take the time you need. Listen to yourself."

"I've already delayed six months! Coming here . . . this was my final idea for putting it off. I thought if I could disappear, they'd lose interest. . . ."

"Is there a deadline?" Calisa asked. "Will anything bad happen if you wait?"

She lowered her hands from her face. "Well, no. Not exactly. It's only that everyone expects me to have already planted by now. It's traditional."

"What's the worst case if you wait until you feel ready?"

"My family would fuss."

"And if you ignore their fussing and don't listen?"

Melidor considered this. Her eyes flicked from flower to flower, as if drawing strength from them. In the background, the beavers nibbled and gnawed, a steady chomping hum.

"Is there anything that says the tradition can't wait?" Calisa asked. "Any end time by which it has to be completed or you miss out?"

"No . . ."

"So it's just the pressure from what others want?"

"Yes."

"Then stay here, talk to the beavers, run through the forest, and don't listen to the fussing. Close your closet door until you're ready to hear them again. And listen to when *you* feel ready. You're allowed to grow up at your own pace."

Jack nodded enthusiastically.

Melidor's eyes were wide, and Calisa noticed that the flecks of green looked like leaves winding on a vine around her pupils. "You truly think I can do that?"

Calisa backtracked. "I don't know your family or your traditions or your . . . realm." She stumbled over the last word. "Only you know that. But you can't force emotions. If you don't feel ready, I think it's okay to take a step back if you need to."

Melidor nodded. "That's why I came here in the first place. I just needed to think. To breathe. I felt like I couldn't breathe at home, with everyone telling me how excited I was supposed to feel."

"There's no shame in needing time and space," Calisa said firmly. "That's why I came here too. I had some stuff to process, and I thought distance would help."

"Is it helping?" Melidor asked.

Given that she hadn't so much as thought the name Ethan in days . . . He didn't fit into a place with portals and cake and magic and a friendly winged lizard and an infuriatingly hot groundskeeper who may or may not have the answer to every question she wanted to ask. "Definitely yes."

Melidor launched herself at Calisa and hugged her so tightly that it felt like being wrapped in vines. She then released her and scampered to the edge of the woods, where she began chewing on one of the downed logs, alongside a beaver.

"You're good at this," Jack said to Calisa.

She glanced at him, and he was smiling at her, his warm brown eyes like a mug of hot chocolate. She felt like she'd picked the right words, but it was tricky to give advice when you knew little about the person, their background, or their world. "I hope I said the right thing and didn't get her in trouble with her family. Any idea what she meant by planting seedlings? Do you think they're magic seedlings?"

"Highly likely."

"Cool."

Both of them watched Melidor chowing down on a log.

Waving at her, Calisa said, "It's not just me who thinks that's odd, right?"

"Not just you."

"Mmm . . ." She watched Melidor spit out chunks of wood. There was a growing pile of wood chips beside each of the beavers. "Honestly, it's making me hungry."

"Chocolate cake?" Jack said hopefully.

Calisa headed for the inn. "Lunch."

Above, the lizard launched himself off the porch roof, circled once, and then landed neatly on Calisa's shoulder. She carried him inside, while Jack trotted after her. Behind them, Melidor and the beavers continued to gnaw and chomp.

CHAPTER FIFTEEN

Sitting on a stool in the kitchen, Calisa flipped through the cake recipes in the cookbook while Jack pulled out a loaf of bread, two jars of peanut butter, and several jars of jam. On the wall, the clock with the carved birds watched them.

"Crunchy or creamy?" he asked.

"Creamy. Crunchy is just incomplete peanut butter. Like someone forgot halfway through that they were supposed to be mashing it." She studied the ingredients in a lemon drizzle cake and wondered if there was any cake that a beaver would like.

I said the right thing to Melidor, she reassured herself. She was mostly certain about that. The inn was a refuge for the dryad, just like it was for Calisa. Everyone needed an escape, and this place . . . *It fills a need. An important need.*

The more she thought about it, the more she was convinced

there was no reason for the inn to only have a handful of guests. Human, dryad, whatever—the need for an occasional escape was universal.

"Raspberry, strawberry, rhubarb-strawberry, or orange," Jack offered. "Orange-lime? That does not sound like it would go well with peanut butter, but whatever you want, I'll make."

On the kitchen counter, Steve stretched, then settled his wings. "Raspberry would be great," Calisa said. "Maybe Steve wants some?"

Calisa returned to the cookbook while Jack offered the lizard a variety of treats: a bit of bread, a spoonful of orange-lime jam, a grape. He accepted the grape and swallowed it whole, before hopping back outside to lie in the sun on the window ledge.

"Once we're finished fixing up the inn, we should have a grand reopening," Calisa said. "Invite back all the prior guests." There was absolutely no reason that the bed-and-breakfast couldn't be full for the rest of the season.

As soon as she said it out loud, she felt excitement bubble inside like just-opened soda. She'd already transformed the sitting room, and she was confident that with a couple more weeks of work, they could have the grounds looking less like an exploded salad and more like someone cared. Maybe it wouldn't be fit for royalty, but it could be ready for an influx of guests.

"Do you think we could do it?" Jack asked.

Sure, yes, absolutely. Probably. It just needed—

Entering the kitchen behind her, Auntie Zee said, "Foolishness." She crossed to the stove and turned on the kettle, which seemed a redundant thing to do with an enchanted teapot in the other room, but Calisa was too distracted by her abrupt dismissal to comment on it. After a quick glance to make sure Calisa wasn't watching (which Calisa saw and pretended she didn't), Auntie Zee grabbed a handful of breadcrumbs and dumped them on the clock. The carved birds began to peck the crumbs while the minute hand ticked enthusiastically forward.

"We've already made a lot of progress," Jack said stoutly, as if he hadn't just been questioning whether it was possible two seconds earlier.

"You know nothing about running a bed-and-breakfast," Auntie Zee said.

A lot of it seemed obvious: keep everything clean, make everyone comfortable, and offer breakfast. For the rest, she could ask Jack. He'd devoted his entire life to this place. Or . . . a novel thought . . . perhaps Auntie Zee herself could help. At least she could give them some direction. Advice. Instructions. She'd been running this place for years; she knew what had to be done. For example, she knew that the wooden birds on the clock ate bread. Calisa wouldn't have guessed that. "Don't you want this place to succeed?"

Auntie Zee leaned against the counter and gazed out the window, beyond the sunbathing Steve. Calisa didn't know if she was seeing the mountains or seeing memories. "This place used to be wonderful."

"It can be again," Calisa said.

"Its time has passed. You'll learn as you get older that

endings are inevitable. I have simply been slow to let go, which is my fault."

"You can't let go!" Jack yelped.

"If you let go," Calisa said, "what will happen to the B&B? To your guests?" She thought of Melidor outside, happy amid the forest and the flowers, safe from the pressures of her family. "To you? To Jack?" She thought but didn't say: *To Jack's father?*

Auntie Zee sighed. "The guests will return home, and the B&B will close." She shuffled to a cabinet and took out a mug that was painted with blackberry bushes.

"This *is* my home," Jack said.

"People need this place," Calisa insisted.

"They'll find another."

"There's no place like this," Jack said. "Not for me. And not for the guests either. It's special, and if you just let it close—"

"I don't *want* it to close," Auntie Zee snapped, "but I can't take care of it the way I used to." She lifted her hand and studied the wrinkles. She closed her fingers into a clawlike fist, and her knuckles looked like pearls through her thin skin. "I don't have the energy or the strength."

"That's why I'm here—" Calisa began.

"For a summer," she interrupted Calisa. And to Jack, "And you, for how much longer? You're going to move on, and that's as it should be. You've your own life to live, and you've been stuck here long enough, waiting on someone who can't return."

Jack looked as if he'd been punched in the gut.

How could she say that? Calisa imagined how she'd feel if

one of her moms had been gone without word, without hope, for three years. "Auntie Zee . . ."

"Don't get old, kids." She poured water into her mug and added a tea bag. "Alternative is worse, they say, but still." She shuffled toward the door to the garden. "I'll try to keep the inn open for the rest of the season, if I can, but don't get any grandiose ideas. Just keep these guests happy, and then it will end on a good note. That's all I want at this point. One good note."

Calisa tried again. "Auntie Zee, you can't—"

"I'll make another supply run this afternoon so you can keep baking your cakes," Auntie Zee said. "But don't think grander than cakes." After sipping her tea, she stepped outside. "I'll be back by dinnertime."

The door swung shut behind her.

Jack slumped against the counter. "She's given up. Dad . . ." His voice cracked, and he pressed his lips together hard.

Calisa didn't know what to say. He was right—it did sound like Auntie Zee had given up, both on his father and on the inn, despite all the progress they'd made in such a short time. She sagged onto a stool.

What's the point of fixing up the bed-and-breakfast if Auntie Zee has already decided to close it? No, she couldn't think like that. "She could be having an off day."

"She doesn't think he's coming back," Jack said. He had picked up a slice of bread and was squeezing it in his hands. "If she did, she'd never let this place close down. He— I don't . . ." His voice rose with each sentence.

Crossing to him, Calisa took the slice of bread out of his hands and then put her arms around him. She held him, not saying anything, trying to think of what to say that would help.

Jack breathed into her hair, a shuddering breath, and then she felt him begin to relax minutely. She felt the warmth of his chest pressed against her. Ethan would have never let her comfort him like this—he would've never let her see any kind of vulnerability—but Jack didn't hide how much he cared and how deeply he felt. She thought that made him a stronger person. She tried not to notice how nice he smelled, how solid and strong and gentle his arms were. "Just because she's giving up," Calisa said, "doesn't mean you need to. The inn isn't closed yet. The portals are still open. He could come home."

"It's been too long," Jack said. "If he was going to make it—"

She pulled back but didn't let go—just far enough so she could look into his eyes and so he could see hers. Their faces were only a few inches apart. His eyes were fixed on her. "You don't know that," Calisa said. She put as much conviction into her voice and eyes as she could. "He could walk into this inn tomorrow. You don't know."

He looked lost, and it made her want to hold him tighter. "Isn't that Auntie Zee's point? I don't know if he'll ever come back. What if I'm holding on too long?"

Maybe he was. Maybe his dad wasn't going to return. Maybe his dad *couldn't*. It could be that something terrible had happened to him, out there in another realm. Or there were no other open portals in whatever place he was. By now, his dad could have resigned himself to a new life, to never returning. Like Auntie Zee, he could have given up.

Or maybe he hadn't.

"Give it the summer," Calisa said. "We keep fixing this place up. Make it as nice as we can and see if we can make Auntie Zee change her mind."

He nodded. "Sorry for, um, kind of falling apart."

"Nothing to be sorry about. You're allowed." Their arms were still wrapped around one another, and Calisa didn't want to step away. Her eyes drifted to his lips. He had kissable lips. She made herself step back. *Not the time. He's in pain.* He needed a friend right now, not a complication or a distraction.

She felt cold without his arms around her. He glanced away, toward the window and the mountains, and she doubted he was thinking about her and her lips. He was most likely and understandably thinking about his father and the future.

"She'll change her mind about the inn," Calisa said as firmly as she could. "The same way she changed her mind about me." She crossed to the cookbook. "Now, I think I found a chocolate cake I want to make after lunch, without the mirror glaze. Come tell me what you think."

She was going to keep moving forward, even if Auntie Zee didn't want to.

The inn was saturated with the scent of chocolate.

Calisa breathed it in as she opened the oven. The cake had

risen, with a crack at the top that made it look like it was about to ooze molten chocolate. Wearing oven mitts, she pulled it out and tested it. Perfectly done.

As it cooled, she mixed the icing, dumping in enough cocoa to make it as rich as she liked. Since the raspberry jam had worked so nicely with the vanilla cake, she used the same jam again between the two layers, and then she spread the chocolate icing around the sides and smoothed it over the top. It came out far less lumpy than her first attempt. *I'm learning.* By the end of the summer, she'd be a master baker. Or at least reasonable.

But what would happen *after* the end of the summer?

Would enchanted tea with cake at the Faraway Inn continue, or would it all just stop—the inn shuttered, the garden left to be swallowed by the forest, and the portals permanently closed? What would happen to Jack? And to the guests like Melidor who needed a place to escape, away from all the expectations and stresses of life?

Auntie Zee seemed to think it was time.

What if I can't change her mind?

Or what if it really was time?

It couldn't be. When Auntie Zee got back from her supply run, Calisa would try to talk with her again. That wasn't the end of the conversation. A grand reopening could revitalize both the inn and Auntie Zee.

Calisa carried the cake into the sitting room. As if it had sensed her coming in, the teapot began to rattle and then steam. She glanced out the window to see Jack spreading

Melidor's mulch around the flower beds. She opened the window and called outside, "Cake's ready!"

He waved back. "Awesome! Be there soon!" He turned toward the forest. "Hey, Melidor, do your friends like chocolate?" *How does he do it?* she wondered. How did he keep going while carrying all that loss and fear? He let himself feel it—she'd witnessed that—but then he just . . . kept moving forward. Kept living fully. *That's strength.* Glancing toward Calisa, he smiled as bright as the sun. She felt her insides melt like icing on too-warm cake.

"Their favorite is aspen!" the dryad called. "Followed by birch, maple, and willow, though the large fellow over there is partial to oak."

"So, not chocolate?" Jack confirmed.

"Not chocolate!"

From the doorway, Mulligan said, "I am partial to chocolate, my dear." He came into the sitting room, keeping to the shadows as far away from the window as possible, and took a seat by the fireplace. "It was Zef's favorite."

He hasn't given up on Zef, Calisa thought. He wore his despair on his voluminous sleeves—today he wore a billowy silk shirt and black wide-legged pants—but he still tried to break the spell. How did he keep trying failure after failure? She wished there were a way to transfer some of Jack's and Mulligan's resilience to Auntie Zee.

Kendra joined them shortly after, and Calisa cut slices of the cake for both of them, as well as a thick slice for Jack, for whenever he was done outside. She placed his slice on an end table and tucked a napkin under the edge of the plate.

Carrying her slice to the conch chair, Kendra sat, her back straight and her skirt dripping quietly on the carpet. Mulligan chose a winged armchair by the fireplace.

"I was hoping I could ask your opinion on something, if you don't mind," Calisa said to the two of them. Her eyes flicked to the lobby, but she didn't see Auntie Zee, only the white cat strolling through toward the kitchen. "You've both been coming here for years. What did this place used to be like?"

Mulligan answered first. "Glorious, serene, vivacious. Ah, I do remember those days fondly. Every room full. Lively chatter over breakfast. Strolls through the garden and the surrounding hills. I have heard it claimed that the High King of the Goblins himself once chose to stay here in disguise, and that Auntie Zee simultaneously hosted the famed enchantress Isatre and her mortal enemy, the ruler of the Elind, without a single incident. They sipped juice at breakfast together and spoke of spring flowers, utterly unaware of who the other was."

"That was a long time ago," Kendra said, clipped.

"The glory days," Mulligan agreed.

Calisa asked the more important question: "What do you think it would take to bring the inn's old guests back?"

"Cake is a start," Kendra said, piercing another bite of the chocolate cake with raspberry jam. "But is this what Auntie Zee wishes? She has run this inn for many, many decades. She deserves her own rest."

Calisa hadn't considered that. It was possible that her great-aunt wanted to retire, sell the inn, and move to Florida, where she'd befriend a few alligators and flamingos or whatever retirees did in Florida. Maybe Calisa would have believed that if Auntie Zee had seemed happier about the idea. She hadn't, though. Surely she didn't want her inn to die with a whimper. Wouldn't it be better to leave it thriving? Sell it to another innkeeper, one who could keep the portals open. Not just let it wither away. This place was Auntie Zee's life's work.

Besides, there was also Jack and his father to think of.

And me. She'd just discovered this place and its magic and portals and firebird and adorable friendly flying lizard. To lose it all after only a summer . . . There was still so much she hadn't seen or learned. She still didn't know who or what the statue was. Mulligan hadn't restored Zef. Melidor hadn't planted her seedlings. As for Kendra . . . "Do *you* think it's time for Auntie Zee to close the inn?" Calisa asked her.

"Of course not. I value this place greatly. Every year it's been a restorative retreat. The one place I can go where no one makes any demands on me. I can simply *be*."

All right. That was at least a start. "Do you think Auntie Zee wants it to close?"

"I do not. But it is a heavy responsibility, and time and age come for us all. I understand the weight of it. Perhaps she cannot see a way to carry it any longer."

"If she could, though . . . what would you fix first?"

"The stream behind the inn," Kendra said without any hesitation. "It used to be a lovely spot to visit. Now the weeds have choked the walk."

"The library," Mulligan answered. "I used to spend hours

in that room. Frankly, I was disappointed to discover how unwelcoming it had become."

Kendra agreed.

They continued on, listing the flaws they'd noticed. Breakfast had been irregular until Calisa arrived. Tea, nonexistent. There were no planned picnics in the gardens by the burbling brook like there had been in past summers. Instead the gardens were mostly impassable, current progress aside, and the brook was buried beneath a thick mat of green. They missed sitting on the porch in the evenings with a view of the fireflies, a nice drink, and pleasant music. Auntie Zee used to plan excursions into town and provide disguises for those who needed them—that amenity was gone. Every Saturday, a traveling musician from a different realm used to come to entertain them in the library. Oh, and then there were the holiday feasts. . . .

Fetching a piece of paper and a pen from the lobby desk, Calisa made a list.

Some of it was beyond her. She wasn't a musician and didn't know any. She had no idea how to plan a trip into town—or even where town was or how to get there—beyond calling a too-expensive Uber. But she could do picnics in the garden. She and Jack could restore the stream and the porch. The library could be cleaned. Tea was already restored, but she could ensure it continued, perhaps with a variety of cakes.

Maybe if she did all the doable tasks, the guests would return, Auntie Zee would change her mind and see it wasn't time yet, and the inn would be saved. Jack's father would continue to have a home to return to. The guests would return. Kendra could keep her refuge, Mulligan could keep his retreat, and Melidor could continue to find peace.

Auntie Zee might be done trying, but I've barely begun.

And as soon as Auntie Zee got back, Calisa would make that crystal clear.

CHAPTER SIXTEEN

Auntie Zee wasn't back by dinnertime. And Calisa witnessed firsthand exactly how much her great-aunt did behind the scenes at the Faraway Inn.

It was Mulligan who came into the kitchen with a request first.

Calisa was perched on a stool, studying a new cake recipe in the cookbook and wondering what she could substitute for milk if Auntie Zee didn't get all the supplies, and Jack was scowling at the innards of a malfunctioning bathroom fan—he had the pieces splayed out on the butcher block island.

"I hate to intrude on your reverie," Mulligan said, "but is it known when Auntie Zee will return with my cocoa? There's a new variation I wish to try tonight, for Zef."

"She should be back soon," Jack said.

Calisa glanced at the clock. It was close to eight, and the wooden bird on the clockface was preening its wooden feathers.

They thumped together lightly, in rhythm with the minute hand. "We'll let you know as soon as she's back," she promised.

Mulligan executed a tight bow and retreated.

Quietly, Jack said, "She said she'd be back by now."

"Is that . . . Should we be worried?"

"Probably not. It's Auntie Zee." He looked worried.

She'd noticed that Jack had two standard expressions: deeply concerned and delighted at the world. She imagined that both were an outgrowth of living in a magical inn. Or maybe it was just Jack's personality. He cared a lot—about the inn, his dad, Auntie Zee, the guests—and he wasn't afraid to show it. Earnest, that's what he was. It was nice. But it did make clear when he actually was worried.

"I'm sure she's fine," Calisa said.

"It's not her I'm worried about," Jack said.

Next to complain was Kendra, who swept into the kitchen and regarded the parts of the bathroom fan as if they were filth covering the island. "I have not received my dinner."

"Auntie Zee will be back—" Jack began.

"I will have chicken potpie," Kendra declared, "as well as a glass of chardonnay. For dessert, I desire pudding. You will add a swirl of whipped cream on top."

Calisa and Jack glanced at each other.

Jack looked slightly panicked. "Um, I don't . . ."

"It is in my agreement with the Faraway Inn," Kendra said sharply. "I am guaranteed dinner. If Auntie Zee is not available to provide it, then it falls to you. I hope you will not disappoint me."

Calisa flipped through the cookbook, searching for a chicken potpie recipe. How hard could it be? It was just pie crust with vegetables and chicken inside. Cornstarch for thickening? "It has to bake for almost an hour. Would you rather—"

"I will wait," Kendra said, and spun to sweep out of the kitchen.

She swallowed. "I don't know yet if we have all the ingredients. . . ." Kendra was already gone. She wasn't the type to stick around to hear excuses, even valid ones.

Jack jumped off his stool. "You read. I'll check."

"Chicken and vegetables, first off," Calisa said. "Then: salt, pepper, celery seed, garlic powder, bullion, milk, egg . . . I know we're out of milk, but I can use cornstarch with water instead." They scrambled to assemble the ingredients, and Calisa began to mix the dough for the pastry crust.

Her fingers were deep in the butter and flour when Melidor raced into the kitchen. "Auntie Zee didn't replace my sheets, and mine are full of mulch."

"I'll check the laundry," Jack offered.

"Also, she promised me vegetable soup for dinner tonight."

Calisa had no idea that Auntie Zee provided dinner as well as breakfast at her B&B, though she supposed it made sense. None of the guests could easily trot into town for a meal, not without drawing attention to the inn. She supposed she could reheat soup, if there was any. After rinsing the pastry dough off her hands, she checked the fridge and spotted a jar of soup with carrots and string beans floating in broth. "I can heat up—"

But Melidor was already gone.

She started a pot of soup heating on the stove and then

finished up the dough, before starting on the chicken potpie innards. She was searching for a carrot peeler when Jack emerged from the hallway with an armload of towels. "I'll fix up her room," he offered.

"I'm taking care of the soup. Auntie Zee . . ."

"She'll be back," Jack said. "She's Auntie Zee."

Calisa was halfway through slicing the carrots when Mulligan appeared to ask for milk and strawberry syrup, for Zef, as well as a slice of leftover cake, for himself. Shortly after that, Kendra returned to demand her chardonnay. Jack sprinted up and down the stairs, carrying sheets and towels for all the guests to and from the linen closets, and then returned to the third floor with the toilet plunger.

By the time the chicken potpie was baked, the toilet fixed, the linens replaced, and everyone satisfied, it was late. The birds on the kitchen clock had closed their eyes, as if asleep. And Auntie Zee still wasn't home.

The next morning, it was raining so hard that the trees outside Calisa's window looked as if they were crying. Everything was coated in a silvery gray, and the clouds were so thick that she couldn't even tell where the sun was.

Worse, Auntie Zee still wasn't back.

Calisa made the usual pancake breakfast, thanks to Jack's early-morning run to the store for milk. Jack delivered the trays to the guests, but he barely ate more than a few bites of his pancakes, and he almost used honey instead of maple syrup.

"What do we do?" Calisa asked. She could call her moms, but it wasn't as if *that* much time had passed. And it wasn't as if they could do anything about it. *Except for tell me to come home.* No, she wasn't going to call her moms.

Jack frowned at the honey as if it had wronged him and then picked up one of the maple syrups, cardamom-flavored. "I don't know."

"Has this happened before?"

He was silent for a long moment. "Yes."

Calisa winced as she remembered his dad. He'd left for supplies and hadn't come back. Could Auntie Zee have been trapped behind a malfunctioning door? *She couldn't. Not possible.* "Auntie Zee controls the portals. You told me that yourself. She *can't* be trapped behind one. She's just been delayed." There were a zillion other explanations that were much more likely, such as she'd decided to spend the night visiting with magical beings.

He nodded, and she saw a shred of relief in his eyes. "You're right. I know you're right. It's not possible. She's not lost; she's just late. She's been late before. Every so often, she does this. Vanishes for a while."

"Why?" Calisa asked. "Does she say what she does or where she goes?"

"Auntie Zee isn't big on explaining," Jack said. "You may have noticed."

"Someone should tell her it's not okay."

"Yeah, that won't be me. Until then . . . we just do what we were going to do today, and try to keep everything running okay until she gets back." He added, "And we keep it from the guests."

She raised her eyebrows. "Lie to them?"

"If they know she isn't here and that we have no idea when she's coming back, they'll leave," Jack pointed out. "You saw how they were last night—they like things the way they like them. So, we have to pretend we know what we're doing, and that it's supposed to be this way."

"Fake it until we make it. A time-honored tradition for people who are completely in over their heads and know it." She and Jack had gotten through last night. Even the potpie hadn't turned out terrible. They could keep the inn running until Auntie Zee returned, couldn't they?

Jack nodded. "How about we tell them she had to go farther afield for supplies this time, and she'll be back in a day. Two days?"

"A week?" Calisa suggested. There was so much worry in his eyes that she added quickly, "She'll be back sooner than that. This is just what we tell the guests."

He looked relieved.

"Okay, I guess since we can't garden today, I'm going to clean the library?" There was no point in just waiting for Auntie Zee, and it was next on Calisa's list of rooms to improve.

Jack scraped his half-eaten pancake into the compost bin and washed his plate. "She'll be back soon." He sounded as if he was trying to convince both Calisa and himself.

She tried to think of what to say, but there wasn't anything to say that would make it better. *Someone really needs to tell Auntie Zee she can't just vanish.* She'd be happy to be the one to do it, if she had any idea where her great-aunt had gone. *If*

I could go bring her back right now, I would. But Calisa didn't know how or even where to begin. She did, however, know how to clean a bunch of bookshelves.

After the breakfast dishes were washed, Calisa claimed several dustrags, a broom and dustbin, and a cleaning spray that smelled like lavender. She carried them through the lobby to the library and deposited them on the window seat.

Out the window, on the porch, Steve was pressed against the glass. He looked in at her with wide, sad eyes. Apparently, he didn't like the rain.

"Don't drip on the books," she told him as she opened the window.

Steve waddled inside, hopped down to the window seat, and circled like a cat before settling on a pillow. He let out a happy chirp as he folded his wings on his back, wrapped his tail tight around his body, and closed his eyes. He was snoring in seconds. Leaving him on the pillow, Calisa began to clean the library around him.

As she worked, she chewed on a question: If Auntie Zee didn't return on her own soon . . . *could* they find her and insist she come home? Calisa had dismissed that as an impossibility, but what if it wasn't?

The most immediate roadblock to that was how to figure out where she'd gone. It was clear Jack didn't know, and she doubted any of the guests did either. As Jack had said, Auntie Zee wasn't big on sharing information.

Calisa stepped onto the bookcase ladder to dust the higher shelves, and the ladder zipped down the bookcase. She let out a yelp and hung on. It halted, and she caught her breath. *That was unexpect—*

It flew back to where she'd begun.

"Whoa! Slow down!"

Steve lifted his head and hissed.

"It's fine," Calisa told the lizard. "I was just surprised." A moving library ladder. She took a second to absorb this, then said, "Everything's fine."

The ladder wobbled as if apologizing, and then it hopped inch by inch to the left.

"You don't have to move," Calisa told it. "Just let me dust these shelves, okay?"

It halted.

Reaching, she dusted the top two shelves. "A little to the left?"

The ladder scooted a foot to the left.

"Perfect. Thank you."

She continued to dust the shelves, and Steve settled back down on his pillow. She felt a smile tugging at her lips. There was so much magic here, and the inn wasn't even at its peak. *What must it be like when it's full of otherworldly guests?* She wanted to see that.

But if Auntie Zee stayed away from the inn for too long . . . they'd lose what few guests they had. She wasn't as confident as she'd tried to sound to Jack that they could keep everything moving smoothly without Auntie Zee. She'd seen last night how demanding the guests were and how much the innkeeper did to cater to them.

Not to mention: What if Auntie Zee was in trouble? Hurt or

sick somewhere? Calisa didn't want to even think about that. It didn't seem plausible. Not Auntie Zee. She was too ornery for that. Regardless . . . *We can't wait for her to come back on her own.* If Auntie Zee did this regularly and if Jack had never said anything, she might not realize how many problems her absence could cause. She had to be told and brought back.

What they needed, she decided, was access to Auntie Zee's records. If they had that, they could figure out where she'd gone. Calisa had gotten a glimpse when she'd first arrived—a large leather-bound book with handwritten notes. It had looked to be where Auntie Zee kept all her info about the inn: guest registration, expenses, supply lists . . . Maybe there was a record of where those supplies came from? In fact, the more Calisa thought about it, the more likely she thought it was.

Unfortunately, Calisa hadn't seen the logbook since her first day. It clearly wasn't kept anywhere visible. "Do you know where Auntie Zee keeps the inn's logbook?" she asked the ladder.

It wobbled under her, as if she'd confused it.

"I doubt she keeps it in the library. You don't need to get upset." Climbing down from the ladder, Calisa patted the rungs. "You're doing a great job."

The ladder seemed to stand up straighter at that, and it occurred to Calisa that she had adjusted remarkably well to weird stuff happening, if she was complimenting a ladder without even pausing to think about it.

Her first guess was that it was in the lobby desk. If Auntie Zee were here, she was positive she wouldn't be permitted to touch it. She checked the kitchen, the sitting room, and the dining room to be sure no one was watching. All were empty. Jack was upstairs, cleaning the bathrooms. She could hear the faucets turning on and off. Outside Melidor was lying in a muddy puddle, talking with the shrubbery. The stone statue was closer to the inn, beneath the overhang of the porch roof, shielded from the worst of the rain. Drops rolled down one of her shoulders and along her arm.

Looking out at her, Calisa wondered if she should invite the statue inside. Had she ever been invited? Did she want to come in? *Could* she come in? Considering it, Calisa wondered how she'd manage the steps up to the front or back door.

Once Auntie Zee is home and everything is back to normal, I'll ask Jack if there's wood to make a ramp. There was nothing she could do about the second and third floors, but everything on the first floor should be made accessible, and not just for the statue. Other guests might have other needs . . . if they ever had other guests.

Certainly wasn't going to be an issue if they couldn't find Auntie Zee.

Filing the idea away for later, Calisa searched the desk, checking every drawer.

No logbook.

She *did* find a pine cone, a pair of scissors, and a yo-yo.

Calisa sank into the stool behind the desk. What if Auntie Zee had hidden it, to preserve the privacy of her guests, instead of merely putting it away? Given that the primary draw of her inn was discretion, that seemed likely.

"Where would she keep her book?" Calisa asked out loud.

What if it was in Auntie Zee's room?

If Auntie Zee didn't want Calisa to open doors, she was *not* going to like it if Calisa broke into her bedroom. Her great-aunt would likely send her back to Brooklyn instantly. . . . Of course, Auntie Zee would have to be *here* before she could do that.

Weighing the risks, Calisa absently watched the shadows in the mirror swirl.

If I wanted to hide something and I lived in an inn full of portals, why just hide it in my room? Auntie Zee could have hidden the book anywhere, in any realm.

"Any chance you're a magic mirror?" she asked the mirror.

The swirls seemed to deepen, and she glanced behind her to see if they reflected any movement. When she looked back, a single word was displayed on the mirror's surface in black newspaper font:

No.

"Seriously? That's not . . . Okay, yes, that's kind of hilarious." She crossed to the mirror and, hands on her hips, stared into it. "Magic mirror on the wall, do you know where Auntie Zee keeps her records book?"

The smoke swirled.

Yes.

"Where?"

More smoke.

Calisa waited, but it didn't resolve into any more words. "Can you only answer yes-or-no questions?"

No.

"Then will you please tell me where I can find the inn's logbook?"

No.

She blinked at the mirror. That was not what she was expecting. "Why not?"

I don't want to.

"Um, okay, is there anything I can do or say to get you to change your mind? Is there anything you want or need? Are you . . . trapped inside the mirror? Do you need help?"

I'm fine. Go away.

Despite herself, Calisa laughed. "That's a whole mood right there. Wow, this place." She turned away from the mirror to study the lobby. If the mirror, which was stuck to the wall, knew where the records book was, then it was likely someplace visible from the mirror's vantage point, which also made sense given how quickly Auntie Zee had accessed it when Calisa checked in.

She contemplated the desk and the wall of keys, which was clearly in the view of the mirror. And she noticed there was a hinge on one side of the board that held keys.

Like a door hinge.

Huh.

Striding toward it, Calisa pulled the board open and faced an iridescent purple swirl, about two feet by two feet. She shot a grin at the unfriendly shadow mirror and then reached into the portal.

She felt cold prick her skin, and she wondered if the air in other realms was ever toxic. Or radioactive. Or just generally unfriendly. She reminded herself that Auntie Zee had done this, and Calisa hadn't seen her wear gloves. Feeling around, her fingers brushed against what felt like hard leather. She put her hand down flat. A book?

She grabbed it and pulled.

The logbook fell out of the purple portal into her hands.

"Yes!" Calisa shouted, and then immediately regretted the shout.

Glancing around, she saw no one except for the mirror. It had returned to swirling smoke. She hoped it was ornery enough not to tell anyone what she'd done. She clutched the registrar to her chest and darted down the hall and into her guest room.

The firebird danced on the hearth as if it was happy to see her.

"Our little secret, okay?" she asked the firebird.

It flapped its wings over the logs, fanning the flames higher, and she wasn't sure if that was a yes or no or if it understood her at all. She waited a moment, but the bird didn't seem as if it planned to flee with the news that she'd absconded with Auntie Zee's hidden logbook. Perhaps it knew she'd stolen it in order to find the missing innkeeper? Perhaps it approved? *Or perhaps it's just a bird. Made of flame.*

Opening the cover, Calisa studied the pages.

It began with a date that was 150 years ago.

She'd had no idea the Faraway Inn was that old. She wondered who had owned it before Auntie Zee. A relative? Was this a family business, passed from one generation to the next? She wondered if Mom-Kate had ever thought about staying and running the inn. She tried to imagine what it would have been like to grow up here, to be surrounded by doorways to realms and guests from places she didn't know existed . . . to grow up alongside Jack. If her mom and great-aunt hadn't fought, she could have had that life. She could have always had magic from other realms.

Even more, if Mom-Kate had stayed, the inn wouldn't have fallen into disrepair.

But maybe Mom-Kate hadn't wanted that to be her life. Brooklyn was a long way from Vermont. She could have wanted a different adventure, with Mom-Elise.

Calisa couldn't imagine not wanting to be at the Faraway Inn if she'd had a choice. She wondered again what their fight had been about, why they hadn't returned for a visit in over a decade, why Auntie Zee was still so angry at Mom-Kate that she hadn't wanted Calisa to come and help when she clearly needed help.

Had they fought about the inn?

It was a leap to assume that. They could have fought about anything. But it was certainly possible. *Focus on this,* she told herself. What was past was past. She had to fix the future.

Calisa flipped pages, noting the records—name, date, and guest room. Sometimes there would be additional notes, such as *Allergic to beets.* Or *Likes mountain view.* Or *No apples.*

Most notes were cryptic, but once in a while, the innkeeper would stop the lists and instead write out more of a paragraph—a kind of journal entry.

Opened portal to the Night Market of Elyacor.

Good prices from Rin, third stall in the fifth row.

Ate a spiced meat pocket. Moon was gibbous.

It wasn't much of a diary, but in it were snippets of

adventures into other realms, mostly centered around either guest recruitment or shopping expeditions. This was where all the food and supplies for the inn came from, especially to please the varied palates of the guests.

Calisa heard a scratching at the door. She instantly tucked the logbook under the quilt before opening the door.

Steve waddled inside.

In the fireplace, the firebird flared brighter, and Steve chirped at the bird. He trotted across the room and lay down in front of the hearth. The firebird shifted its fire closer to the grate so it could warm the lizard.

Smiling at them both, Calisa retrieved the book and returned to her chair.

There were hundreds of entries for guests, each with dates scrawled next to them, as well as how much they paid—first in their original currency and then converted into dollars. A few paid with magical items. She found the entry for the enchanted teapot. It came from a realm called Versinar. Or was that the name of the guest? Every page sparked its own set of questions. New realms. New people. New creatures. She skipped ahead to near the end.

She wasn't certain what she was looking for.

Perhaps a nice, clear note detailing where Auntie Zee had gone last night and what to do if she didn't return as scheduled?

Or a record of where Jack's father went?

Or a clue as to when and why it all went wrong?

But there was nothing like that. Just a steady decline of guests. Maybe that's all it was: over time, Auntie Zee had slowed, and she'd lost the ability to care for the inn by herself. No grand event or traumatic moment. Just time, which Calisa supposed was traumatic enough.

"Why didn't she ask for help sooner?" she asked out loud.

In the fireplace, the bird halted its dance over the logs. It cocked its fiery head. Its eyes were embers sunken into the shifting flames.

"Do you know?" she asked it. "Why does she keep pushing people away?"

The firebird only stared at her.

"Steve, what do you think?" Calisa asked.

Steve let out a snort. He was asleep again.

She kept reading. In addition to every name of every guest and every realm they came from, there were records of where Auntie Zee purchased her supplies and how much she paid. Of all of them, one place kept cropping up more than any other:

The Night Market.

What's the Night Market?

And more important: *How do I get there?*

CHAPTER SEVENTEEN

Intent on finding Jack, Calisa hurried downstairs. She paused by the smoky mirror in the lobby. "Is that where she went? The Night Market? Do you know?"

Who?

"Auntie Zee."

New phone. Who dis?

"Ha. Very funny. How do you even know that? Never mind. Do you know if Auntie Zee went to the Night Market for supplies yesterday?"

Don't know. Don't care.

"You are determined to be unhelpful, aren't you."

Yes.

She glared at the mirror, and then she searched the inn for Jack. Calisa found him cleaning the bathroom on the third floor. Leaning against the doorframe, she asked as casually as she could, "Hey, want to go on an adventure?"

Jack did *not* want to go on an adventure, thank you very much.

She explained what she'd found and what she planned: a trip to the Night Market to see if they could locate Auntie Zee. And she explained her reasoning: the inn needed Auntie Zee, and just waiting passively for her to decide to return was a greater risk than going to find her.

"It's absolutely *not* a greater risk," Jack objected.

"We can't run the inn without Auntie Zee," she said. "I don't see there's much choice. She said she'd be back by dinnertime yesterday, and she's way overdue. We need to find her and tell her she can't do this. Not without telling us where she's going, when she'll be back, or what we're supposed to do while she's gone. She has responsibilities, whether she wants them or not."

He protested for about five minutes more, gesturing with the sponge that was still in his hand. He kept his voice low so the guests wouldn't hear. It was a terrible idea, he said. Much too dangerous. Auntie Zee wouldn't want Calisa to risk herself, her moms wouldn't want her to risk herself, Steve wouldn't want her to risk herself. . . . What she heard under it all was: *I don't want you to risk yourself.*

He didn't want her hurt. Or lost. Or to have anything bad happen to her. As the one with the most experience at the Faraway Inn, he considered it his responsibility to keep her safe.

The word *responsible* was made for people like Jack, Calisa decided.

Mom-Kate would have said, *He has integrity.*

It was rare.

And sweet.

He was absolutely not the kind of boy she was normally drawn to. She would have said she liked boys with a hint of danger—the kind with an attitude, as Auntie Zee would have said. But Jack wasn't like that.

So why did she even want him to come with her through the portal? She could do it by herself. And why didn't she get tired of spending time with him? He should have bored her. He was so *nice* and *good*. He shouldn't have been her type at all.

She let him spool out all his arguments until he ran out of words. She just looked at him, and he looked back at her. He sighed heavily. "You're still going anyway, aren't you."

"Yep."

And with that Calisa simply walked out of the bathroom. Leaving behind the cleaning supplies, he tagged along as she went downstairs to the second floor, to the guest room where she'd seen the nighttime farmers market. She thought it was a pretty safe bet that it was the Night Market that Auntie Zee had mentioned repeatedly in her logbook.

"Just once more, for the record, I think this is a mistake," Jack said. "My father was going for supplies when he went missing. Now Auntie Zee, same situation: going for supplies, and then missing."

"Not doing anything is a mistake," Calisa said. "Besides, you said she's disappeared before. It's not the same as your father."

"And if the door malfunctions and we're trapped on the other side?"

Then that was a Future Calisa problem. "It won't."

"You don't know that."

Yes, it was a risk, but she'd read every entry in the inn's record book, and the Night Market was the most common origin for guests, as well as the source for many of the supplies that Auntie Zee used to feed her guests. According to the notes, the Night Market was like the inn: a nexus, with customers and vendors from multiple realms, which meant the people there were accustomed to random, clueless visitors. Besides, she'd been there once already, even if she hadn't immediately realized it. The wind didn't hurt like it had in Melidor's world, and the whole place practically screamed to be explored.

She unlocked the guest room with the master key. "We can't run the inn without Auntie Zee." She didn't add: *And your father can't return without the inn.*

"I know that, but . . ."

She scooted inside, and he followed her, closing the door behind him. "This is a portal that's been stable for years—Auntie Zee went through hundreds of times. If there's any portal that's safe, it's this one, and if there's any place she's most likely to be, it's through here."

"Okay, but what if there's danger on the other side?" He didn't sound like he was going to say no. He was staring at the portal as if he wanted to walk through and just needed reassurance that it wasn't a terrible mistake.

She couldn't promise it wasn't, but she'd already stepped through this doorway once before and survived fine. "We'll stick together," Calisa said, "and if you feel uncomfortable or there's any sign of trouble—"

"We run? Like frightened rabbits."

"Like rabbits," she promised. Tentatively, she added, "Your father . . ."

"I know," Jack said. "We need to find Auntie Zee. For a whole lot of reasons." He hesitated one more minute, and then he took her hand.

She liked the way his hand felt in hers—it fit, warm and comforting. She could feel the calluses from all the work he did, and she wondered if he could feel her newer ones, or if he was paying nearly as much attention to the feel of her hand as she was to his.

Calisa opened the closet door, and the gold swirled through the black. "Brave heroes," she said, "venturing into the unknown, ready to flee."

"I've never wanted to be called brave."

"What would you rather be called?" Calisa said.

"I'd settle for not stupid," he said.

She wasn't sure if he was saying this idea was stupid or if he just meant in general, but either way she—

Before she could finish the thought, Jack stepped forward into the portal. It swallowed his body, and she followed quickly, still holding his hand. Coolness wrapped around her, and she couldn't feel anything but his fingers closed around hers.

A second later, they stepped out of the closet and into another world. Jack released his grip. She wanted to grab his hand back, but there was no rational reason.

It was night again. Or still? It was literally called the Night Market, according to Auntie Zee's notes. It could be perpetual night. She looked up. The moon was higher in the sky than before, blanching the blackness around it. The stars looked like jewels strewn across the sky, disappearing then reappearing as clouds shifted over them. Below, the Night Market was just as active and lively as before—rows of tents with customers strolling between them, alone and in groups.

This is another realm.

She let the words wash over her, and she felt her heart beat faster. A smile tugged at her lips, and she felt like laughing out loud.

"Any clue where we start?" Jack asked.

She'd memorized the relevant parts of Auntie Zee's logbook. "'Good prices from Rin, third stall in the fifth row,'" she recited. Good prices for what, she didn't know, but she hoped it meant this Rin person would be friendly. "He's mentioned often. I think we start with him, ask if he's seen her, and see what he says."

Together they walked down the slope to the Night Market. Voices welled up around them—shoppers and vendors—and music, unfamiliar music from instruments that Calisa didn't recognize, blended in a cacophony of sounds. The smells too rolled over them: spices and meats and fruits and breads, sweet and savory, so thick in the air that Calisa's mouth watered. They walked past a stall that sold stalks that looked like grasses, each a different shade of blue, with tufts of hay at the top. Another sold birds in cages—each bird was jewel-colored, with beaks that curled and feathers spread behind them with zigzags and swirls in patterns that Calisa had never seen on any bird she knew. A third was what she guessed was perfumes: tiny bottles that the customers sniffed. She caught a scent of the ocean, and then it was replaced by a heavy, fruit-like scent that she couldn't name.

She took Jack's hand again as the crowd pushed around them.

"If this is another realm, why are they all speaking English?" Calisa whispered to Jack.

"Portal magic," Jack whispered back. "It translates . . . well, it does this thing with our brains so it translates whatever we speak and hear."

"Convenient."

"Necessary." He paused. "Just don't, like, concentrate too hard on the syllables you're hearing. Let it wash over you."

She immediately started listening to the words around her, and they clashed as the syllables her ears heard overlapped with the words she understood. She winced and focused on the sound of the night breeze through the tents instead until the voices stopped warring inside her.

Despite the fact that most of the market's customers were dressed in draped fabrics while she and Jack were in shorts and T-shirts, no one stared at them. There was enough variation in the shoppers and the vendors that their differences were unremarkable: skin colors from blue to coal-black to pink to bronze to metallic silver. A few shoppers were covered in fur. One woman sported beige-colored wings. She had on a necklace of bird bones that fell down to her stomach. Another had talons instead of hands. He clicked them together in rhythm with his footsteps. Calisa could have wandered through the stalls forever, filling her eyes with all the impossible people and the beautiful oddities on display.

"This is the fifth row," Jack said. "Which stall did you say?"

"Third stall. Rin."

It didn't take them long to find the right one. If they hadn't seen it, they would have smelled it. It smelled like heaven—and looked it too.

Gorgeous, shiny, decadent baked goods filled the tables of Rin's stall. Honey-colored loaves were stacked in a pyramid. Rolls dotted with fruit filled a basket. Cookies and crackers were piled high. An elaborate wreath of bread laden with strawberries was the centerpiece, displayed on white linen. She inhaled the luscious fresh bread smell before noticing the seller behind the table. Once she spotted him, she couldn't stop gawking.

The baker, Rin, was a man from the waist up: silvery translucent shirt, blue-black hair, bushy beard, and a wide smile. From the waist down, he was a horse.

"You're a centaur," Calisa blurted out.

Jack elbowed her.

"Sorry." She winced at herself. "First time at the Night Market."

Rin's face lit up. "Ahh, then you must try the vella-berry bread. It is delectable and for the low, low price of only fifteen lercats."

"Actually, we aren't here to buy," Jack said.

"To sell, then?"

Calisa frowned at him. "And fifteen lercats is three times what Auntie Zee paid. She specifically said your prices were reasonable."

Now it was Rin who winced. "You're from Auntie Zee?"

"She's my great-aunt," Calisa said. "Literally. Not just

because everyone calls her Auntie. She's my mom's mom's sister. I'm helping out at the bed-and-breakfast this summer."

"Ah. You should have said that to begin with. My prices are always reasonable . . . for Auntie Zee." He spread his arms wide to encompass all the baked goods and pastries before him. His tail flicked away a fly.

Jack sounded outraged. "You were trying to cheat us before?"

"Not cheat," Rin protested. "Just offering an introductory price. But now that I know you're from Auntie Zee . . . Does she want her usual order, or something special?"

Jack glanced at Calisa—this was her idea, his look said, and he was letting her take the lead. She appreciated that. Ethan would have jumped in to run the conversation, but Jack didn't seem to need to feed his ego by speaking first and loudest. *He trusts me.* Even though he disagreed with her, even though he hadn't wanted to come and especially hadn't wanted her to come, he still trusted her.

"We were hoping that she'd placed an order herself," Calisa said. "Have you seen her recently? Like, yesterday?"

Rin shook his head, and his mane-like hair rippled. "She hasn't been to my stall in weeks." He looked from Calisa to Jack and back. "Why do you ask? Has something happened?"

"Probably not," Calisa said. "But she didn't come home when she said she would."

"We're concerned," Jack said. "She's older, and . . . we're just concerned. It's not like her to be late to return, and we want to make sure she's okay."

"Ah, merely late to return? You have nothing to worry

about," Rin said. "This is Auntie Zee! She'll be fine. You said she was supposed to return yesterday?"

Calisa nodded. "She was supposed to be back by dinnertime."

"Perhaps she had to wait for an order to be ready and elected to spend the night. Perhaps her hosts invited her to stay and dine with them, and it grew too late to return. Travel between realms can be somewhat unpredictable. She could have encountered any one of numerous delays."

It was possible she'd just lingered longer than she'd meant to. In fact, it was likely. But then someone needed to tell her to hurry back. Sure, Auntie Zee was tired, but the inn still needed her. "You're sure she didn't come here? Could she have gone to a different vendor?"

"If she didn't visit me, then she didn't come to the Night Market," Rin said with certainty. "But I'll ask around if anyone has seen her. We have many travelers from many realms who come through our stalls. Someone may have news. Come back in a few days if she doesn't return, and I'll share what I've heard."

That was at least something. "Thank you," Calisa said.

"We can discuss payment when you visit again," Rin said. "And if you find her in the meantime, no charge." He smiled broadly, and she noticed that his teeth were fat, wide, and even, like a horse's teeth. "Truly, I wouldn't worry. Auntie Zee is a force of nature. She'll show up when she's good and ready. There is nothing in the realms that she can't handle. But if you're impatient, you could check with her suppliers in other realms."

The logbook *did* list out other realms where Auntie Zee had purchased supplies. The Night Market was the most likely one, with Rin her most common supplier, but she could have gone to any one of a dozen of them. *We* could *check them all. . . .*

It would mean opening more doors.

A lot more doors.

Calisa wasn't going to admit it out loud to Jack, but she very much liked that idea.

CHAPTER EIGHTEEN

Throughout the following days, Calisa and Jack continued to slip through iridescent doors into other realms, using the records book as a guide for where to go and who to talk to. They tried to be careful: only choosing frequently used (and therefore hopefully stable) portals, keeping the visits short, and sticking together. Given that Auntie Zee had gone for supplies, it seemed very likely that one of her regular suppliers would have seen her, and it was just a matter of time before they found the right one. Calisa didn't think it was her fault that all those regular suppliers happened to live in wondrous new realms. It was just a wonderful bonus.

They visited a seaside village where mermaids flocked to the docks to deliver fish to local fishmongers, a labyrinth made of bones where the skeletal guard at the gate swore to pass the news to those within, a vast forest populated by creatures who resembled mushrooms and lived at the bottom of a tree that spiraled above them and blocked every hint of the sky. They spoke with a bone-like creature who covered its body in the pelt of a bear and to a family where the parents were made of bark and leaves and the children were twigs with wisps of grass for hair.

And in between their otherworldly visits, they kept fixing up the inn.

Despite worrying about why Auntie Zee hadn't come back yet and what was going to happen to Jack and the inn and her future and everything she knew she was supposed to be worried about . . . Calisa was the happiest she'd ever been.

Coming outside just after dawn, she could hear the stream burbling and bubbling, but she couldn't see it—it was beneath a shroud of brambles. Kendra had talked about picnics in the garden beside it. Even Calisa's moms had mentioned the charming brook that skipped over rocks and meandered between flowers. Today they were going to set the stream free.

Joining her, Jack handed her one of his shirts, a long-sleeve button-down. "To protect your arms from scratches," he said. "I'm seeing a lot of thorns."

It was sweeter and more thoughtful than being handed a bouquet of roses.

Calisa stared at him for a long second and wondered if she should kiss him. He'd taken this new loss—all the uncertainty about Auntie Zee and when she'd return, as well as all the muck it dredged up with his father's absence—and was still thinking of others, still being kind. It was extraordinary.

He only smiled at her, completely oblivious to that fact that she was wondering if he'd be a gentle kisser or one of those kissers who want to swallow you whole. She wondered which she wanted him to be.

"Thanks" was all she said out loud. She pulled on the shirt, and it smelled faintly of him—a little like pine needles, a little like maple syrup.

Jack handed her a pair of clippers and kept one for himself.

They didn't mention Auntie Zee. Or the future of the inn. Or their future. Side by side, they began clearing the brambles that blocked the streambed. They piled them in a heap beside the greenhouse. Later, they'd ask Melidor if she wanted her beaver friends to haul them off into the forest, for use in their dams or whatever beavers did. Calisa wasn't entirely clear on the lives of the local forest animals, and she didn't particularly care—all her focus was the brambles. She didn't want to think about anything else right now.

As the sun rose higher over the mountains, she began to sweat in the long-sleeved shirt, but she was still grateful for the sleeves. At least half the brambles had thorns that seemed to want to drink her blood.

"Hey, hold on one second," Jack said.

She quit clipping. Leaning over, he plucked a twig out of her hair. His face was inches from hers. *If I were braver, I'd kiss him.* Her eyes fixed on his lips. He tossed the twig onto the stack of plant debris.

"There used to be lilies that grew by the stream, until it got overrun," Jack said. "It was beautiful. I shouldn't have let it get so bad."

"You were trying to do everything by yourself," Calisa said. *Breathe*, she reminded herself. She shouldn't be thinking about kissing anyone while she was slicked with sweat. "You're lucky you didn't completely burn out. Didn't Auntie Zee see you had too much on your plate?" She winced inwardly—she hadn't meant to mention Auntie Zee.

Jack gave a shrug that could have had a million different meanings, none of which were connected to kissing her. "She told me not to do more than I could. But if I didn't, who would? She couldn't. Can't." He clipped the brambles as if it were their fault that he'd been forced to take on the burden of keeping the bed-and-breakfast running practically by himself—and now exclusively on their shoulders. She was acutely aware that she barely knew anything about running a bed-and-breakfast. Except how to bake a cake. And clean a room. And yank out weeds.

Wings wide, Steve glided over her head and then landed in the middle of the stream. With a sizzle-like sigh, he settled into the water. Burbling around him, it flowed over his belly and legs and tail. He folded his wings across his back and lowered his snout to take a drink, lapping the water like a cat. He let out a pleased chirp.

"One guest approves," Jack said, amused.

They continued to clear the weeds and brambles from around the stream until you could trace its entire path out of the forest, through the gardens, past the apple tree, and back into the forest. It wasn't exactly picnic-ready, but it was visible. A vast improvement. And enough for what she wanted: an idyllic view from the windows of the inn. The lizard seemed very appreciative of their work, basking in the water.

Together, Calisa and Jack hauled the debris to the edge of the forest for Melidor to distribute to whatever woodland creatures she chose. When they were finished, Jack put away the shears, clippers, and gloves, while Calisa went inside to shower. He must have done the same, because when they met up again in the kitchen, his hair was wet as well, with strands clinging to his neck. She caught herself staring at the bob of his throat before she dragged her eyes up to his face.

"Either we'll find her or she'll come back," Calisa said.

Jack nodded. "When I'm with you, I think I believe it."

After another visit—this time to a dark, fungal world where inhabitants lived in enormous mushrooms—Calisa returned with Jack to serve cake at teatime: a leftover carrot cake from the day before. Between all the search missions and gardening and innkeeping tasks, she hadn't had much time to devote to baking. She should have chopped the carrots finer, and she wished she knew how to make fancy icing designs to draw a rabbit on the top, but it had turned out reasonably well. She had settled on spreading the cream cheese icing as smoothly as she could, so it looked as professional as possible. If she were home and not jaunting off to other realms regularly, she would have watched a slew of how-to videos by now, but here she just had her instincts and Jack's father's cookbook.

Once tea was set up for the guests and after she'd offered

Portia a bit of tuna fish, which the cat had grudgingly accepted, Calisa went outside to invite Melidor in for a slice. The carrot cake had been her favorite, she'd said. It had both a cream cheese icing and a featured vegetable. She was partial to veggies and cheese.

Near the porch, Melidor was making snow angels in the mulch around the hydrangeas. She squinted at Calisa when she came into view. "Carrot cake?" she said hopefully.

"Yep. That's what I was coming to tell you." She was glad there were leftovers to offer the dryad.

"Yay!" She hopped to her feet, and little green sprouts tumbled out of her arms onto the ground. They bounced, and Melidor shrieked, then immediately cooed, "You're fine, you're fine, I'm fine, everything's fine."

"Are those—" Calisa began to ask.

"My seedlings." Melidor dropped to her knees and began to gather them all into various pockets in her skirt. "They need to be planted to grow, and I was thinking . . . that is, I was *hoping* . . ." In a rush, she said, "I want to plant them here. I know it's not my home, but I think it would be such a lovely birthplace for them, in the peace and quiet, without all the expectations and pressures. Can I plant them here?"

Calisa opened her mouth to say yes, of course, but she stopped herself. "Your seedlings? Wow. Um, will you be staying to take care of them? If not and you plant them here, who will take care of them? What do they need?"

"The sun, the rain, the soil." Melidor waved at all of it. "But don't worry. It only takes a few days before they're mobile, and then they'll follow me home."

"Mobile? Wait, I thought you said you were going to plant them. Like, roots in the ground. Stationary, planted plants."

Melidor laughed. "Oh no, they're not plants! They're babies."

Calisa gawked at her.

"Baby dryads. You have to plant them—that's how they're born, how I was born."

Understanding suddenly blossomed in her mind. "You came here to decide if you were ready to become a mom. And these will be your children." Wow, no wonder the dryad had needed time and space to decide. That was huge.

"Yes," Melidor said. Shyly, she added, "Would you like to help me plant them?"

Calisa felt her eyes widen even more. That wasn't a question she ever expected to be asked. She was flattered. Honored. Slightly unnerved. "Will that make me their parent too?"

Another laugh. Her laugh sounded like wind through pine trees. It crinkled as it whooshed. "Of course not. They came from *my* flowers, which makes me their only parent. You'd be more like an aunt."

I could be an aunt. "That doesn't come with any babysitting responsibilities, does it?"

"You may have to occasionally feed them carrot cake, whenever we come back to visit."

Calisa smiled. "I can do that."

"I think behind the inn, with a view of the mountains . . ." With Melidor carrying her sprouts in her pockets, they headed around the inn. Seeing the stream, Melidor squealed. "That would be the perfect place! Fetch a trowel, please."

Calisa found a trowel in the greenhouse and joined Melidor

by the side of the brook. Nearby, the lizard watched them lazily from a rock in the middle of the water. He'd spread his wings out wide and was drying them in the sun. He didn't flinch when the seedlings chirped at him.

"Dig where it's soft, beside that moss," Melidor instructed.

Calisa knelt on the moss and stabbed the dirt with the tip of the trowel. It slid in easily. "How deep and how many holes?"

"Three inches will do. Sixteen holes."

She paused. "You're going to have sixteen babies at once?"

"This season," Melidor clarified. "The first dryad spawning season is always only a few. Next year it will be twice as many."

I'll have to bake a lot of carrot cake. "There must be a lot of dryads."

"One per tree in my realm." Looking at the pine forest that spread over the mountains, she admitted, "It can be overwhelming, which is why I came here. I wanted space to think for myself, to decide if this is what I wanted, for me. There are no other dryads here. It's quiet."

Such a major life decision. How did she know what the right thing to do was? This would change the course of her life. "How did you decide?" Calisa asked as she dug.

"This morning, I woke up and felt the golden sun on my face, and I just knew that this was what I wanted to do next," Melidor said. "I think I needed the quiet to decide. Or maybe my heart always knew, and it was waiting for me to have enough peace and quiet to listen?"

"You don't have any doubts?"

She flapped her hands dismissively. "Of course I do, silly.

Doubts. Worries. Fears. But . . . I'm going to love these babies. I already do. So how can I say no to that?" Melidor smiled beatifically at her pockets.

She seemed so at peace with her decision, which was very different from the first time Calisa had met her when she'd raced off into the woods, cawing like a furious bird. *Being here helped her.* It gave her distance and time and quiet and carrot cake. *Auntie Zee* has *to come back. This inn has to stay open.*

As Calisa finished the first few holes, Melidor dropped the sprouts in. She cooed to them as she tucked the dirt loosely around them, allowing the green tip to poke through the soil. In a few minutes, they had all sixteen planted.

Wiping her hands on her shorts, Calisa stood up. "Okay, that's sixteen—"

Melidor popped up and threw her arms around Calisa. "Thank you!" She then sprang back and jumped into the stream, ankle-deep, singing as she skipped from stone to stone, kicking the water so it sprayed into the air.

Calisa glanced at Steve, who was still sunbathing on his rock. He flicked out his tongue, unperturbed. A lick of flame unfurled from the tip of his tongue and then fizzled in the air. He then looked at her expectantly.

She stared at him. "Um . . . congratulations?"

Pleased, he closed his eyes and began to snore.

Did her lizard really just breathe fire?

CHAPTER NINETEEN

"We can't keep doing this," Jack said. It was the next day, and they'd just returned from another visit—this one to a realm where the people were silent but their shadows spoke. "We've been lucky so far."

"Not lucky enough," Calisa said. "If we were actually lucky, we would have found her. Or at least found someone who'd seen her." She slumped into the window seat in the library.

The ladder wiggled hopefully.

"Sorry, I can't read now," Calisa told it. "Having a crisis."

"After my dad . . ." Jack's voice hitched. He stopped, swallowed, and continued. "After my dad went missing, I searched for him. Every door I could open, I went through. Calisa . . . I've done this before. It didn't help."

"If we don't look for her, who will?" Calisa asked. It wasn't the kind of thing you could go to the police for: *Hello, 911, my great-aunt is missing in another dimension.* Besides, she wasn't really missing. Just . . . they didn't know where she was.

Calisa kept expecting to find her visiting with friends or taking a mini-vacation, but they'd been to multiple realms now and no one had seen her. They were nearly out of places to look. They'd visited nearly every realm that had been mentioned as a source of supplies.

She saw movement out of the corner of her eye and glanced toward the lobby, but it was only the cat sauntering by. Calisa sighed heavily.

"Rin said she'll show up when she's ready to show up," Jack said, "but what if she doesn't want to be found? What if she didn't go for supplies at all, and that's why none of her usual suppliers have seen her?"

"What do you mean?" Calisa asked. *Why would she want that?*

He leaned against one of the bookshelves. Nearby, the firebird crackled, as low as embers. "What if she just . . . went away? You heard her before she left. She's tired. Maybe she needed a more permanent break."

That . . . was possible.

It could be that the reason no one had seen Auntie Zee was she didn't want to be found. This place, the Faraway Inn, was an escape for the guests—a break from their lives. Auntie Zee could have decided she needed an escape too, *from* the Faraway Inn. In that case, she could have chosen any portal to any realm. She could have even shut the door behind her.

Jack said hesitantly, "I think . . . we may have to wait for her to come back on her own. Unlike my dad, she can open the doors herself. She'll return when she's ready."

"I'm not giving up."

"I know. I don't . . ." He ran his fingers through his hair and sighed. "Maybe I just need some sleep."

Maybe they both did. Maybe one of them would come up with a new idea in the morning. Maybe there was a supplier they'd missed. Or maybe they should be looking at other locations, the less commonly visited realms, without obvious suppliers? They were still a few doors they hadn't tried. . . . *Or maybe we've pushed our luck far enough, and we should try being patient.* Auntie Zee had her own way of doing things, and she could have a perfectly good reason for her absence, which she'd explain as soon as she returned.

Or maybe something has happened to her and she can't *return?*

As always whenever that worry reared its head, Calisa shoved it back down. Nothing could have happened to Auntie Zee. She was the caretaker of the inn, the keeper of the doors, and she was fine. Just . . . absent.

Possibly intentionally absent.

The guests had started to notice. No one had said anything directly yet, but Mulligan had hinted at it a few times, and Kendra had made pointed comments about the decline in service. It was only a matter of time before one of them demanded to speak to Auntie Zee, and then what would they do? How long could they keep pretending she was on her way back or "Oh, so sorry, you just missed her"?

After saying good night to Jack, Calisa returned to her room and changed into her nightshirt and flannel shorts. Looking out the window, she saw the stream (finally free of the brambles), a shiny black ribbon in the light of the moon, winding out of the forest. Standing beside it, near where the seedlings were planted, was the statue. She looked as if she were guarding the baby dryads. Perhaps she was.

Beyond, the stars were sprinkled above the mountains. Calisa lifted up the window and leaned against the sill. Outside, crickets chirped. She heard the wind rustle the leaves in the trees. It smelled sweet, like earth and pine, and she didn't know how Mom-Kate had ever left this place. Brooklyn felt so far away, and she wasn't sure—

The phone on the bedside table rang, and Calisa jumped.

She'd forgotten there was a phone. Her moms. They'd been intent on giving her space, waiting until she reached out to them so that they wouldn't intrude on her time here. In fact, they'd showed impressive self-restraint. So why were they calling now? Did they know about Auntie Zee? They couldn't—there was no one here who'd think to tell them. Had something happened at home? Were they okay? Calisa hurried across the room.

She picked up the phone. "Hello? What's wrong?"

A familiar male voice said, "You aren't here. That's what's wrong."

Ethan.

She felt a lurch. Her knees bent, and suddenly she was sitting on the edge of the bed. She felt catapulted back into her old life more forcefully than walking through a portal. "Ethan."

"It's good to hear your voice, Cali." He was the only one who'd ever called her that.

"Why are you calling?" she asked. "How did you get this number?"

"Charm," he said. "Pleading. Patheticness. Please, Cali, just hear me out. It took me days to work up the courage to call and hours to figure out what I wanted to say."

Half of her wanted to hang up the phone. But her fingers curled around the receiver, and she couldn't seem to make herself move.

"I'm going to assume you're still there, because I haven't heard any kind of click. Okay, here goes: I am calling to say that I know I screwed up, I'm sorry, and I want you back. Whatever you need me to do, I'll do it. Grovel—I'll grovel like no one has ever groveled before. Public apology—I will buy a billboard if that's what it takes. I made a colossal mistake, and I am begging you to forgive me."

Well.

Wow.

This was it, the apology she'd so desperately wanted to hear but thought she never would. She never expected he'd so much as offer up a cavalier "my bad" much less a full-on monologue. "Did you write that out?"

There was a beat of silence. "Yes?"

"Did someone else write it for you?"

"I may have had some help. But it's my feelings, Cali love. All my heart."

She wasn't sure if that made it better or worse. He'd cared enough to enlist help—was that nice? "Who helped you?" It better not have been Jocelyn Pullman. . . .

"Crystal."

She sucked in air, feeling as if her heart stuttered. Crystal? Her best friend Crystal? She could guess now who had given him the phone number. She must have gotten it from Mom-Elise.

She thinks this is what I want.

It had been what she wanted. Before coming to Vermont, she'd had countless daydreams of Ethan begging her forgiveness, wanting her back—

"Why?" Calisa asked.

"Because you're the one for me," Ethan said. "I can see that now."

"You cheated on me, multiple times with multiple girls, according to, well, everyone. That was a choice—a choice you kept making over and over. It wasn't an accident or an out-of-control moment. It was a pattern of behavior, and you've now changed?"

"People change. Hey, you've probably gotten all crunchy granola up in Vermont. Made friends with bears and stuff. Are you dating a lumberjack? Is that why you're being so cold to me?"

Now she was going to hang up.

But his voice softened. "Cali, I screwed up. You didn't deserve it, and it was never about you. It was all me and my ego."

That was exactly what Crystal had said, when Calisa first went crying to her after catching Ethan and listening to his flimsy excuses. Clearly he wasn't lying about talking to Crystal, which was a surprise—first because he'd never liked Calisa's friends, and second because Crystal usually didn't put up with bullshit. But the greater surprise was that he'd actually listened to her. He sounded sincere. . . . Then again, this was also the boy who'd deceived her for months and she'd been blithely unaware, completely swallowing every one of his lies about where he'd been, whom he'd been with, and what he'd done. "How do you expect me to trust you?" she asked, gripping the phone so hard that her hand started to sweat.

"I'll make it up to you," Ethan promised. "Whatever you need me to do or say . . . If you want to check my texts . . . If you want to hire a random kid to spy on me . . . Whatever it takes."

Calisa laughed. She didn't mean to, but the image was hilarious—a fourth grader skulking after Ethan as he chatted up various girls who caught his eye. Ethan couldn't help being charming. That was one of the things that had drawn Calisa to him. He was at ease everywhere he went, with zero effort. Everything always came easily to him, to the point where he never had to work for anything or doubt that he'd get what he wanted. *It's his self-confidence. He knows what he wants, assumes he deserves it, and goes for it.*

This time, he wanted her back.

"Why?" Calisa asked again.

"What do you mean? Because I love you. And I realize I was an idiot not to treat you the way you deserve to be treated."

"Why do you love me?"

"Because . . . you make me feel like no one else. You *see* me."

She wondered if he saw her. She thought of how Jack listened to her, truly listened, both to her babble and her ideas. Had Ethan ever done that? She wondered if he knew what kind of cake she liked, what books she'd read, what her favorite season was.

He continued. "You complete me."

Calisa snorted. "You saw that in a movie." Or more accurately, Crystal had seen it. She'd been on a rom-com binge last winter, some good and some that had not aged well.

"That doesn't make it less true." He was dripping with sincerity, and she didn't trust a word of it.

"You're just a boy, standing in front of a girl, asking her to love him?" she quoted.

"Yes, exactly!"

"I've bewitched you, body and soul?"

"Um, what?" he said.

She guessed Crystal hadn't shared all her favorite lines with him. Just the ones spoken by a narcissist. "What is it that you love about me?" she pressed.

"I love that when you look at me—"

"That's still about you. What do you like about *me*? Is it my sense of humor? Is it my smile? Is it the way I think? Do you think I'm smart?"

"Of course! You're all those things. Smart, funny, beautiful."

She had wanted him to say these words, to admire her the way she'd admired him, but now that he was saying them, she felt . . . fine. She wasn't swooning or melting.

Maybe it's because I don't believe him.

A flicker caught the corner of her eye, and she glanced at the fireplace. The firebird danced over the logs, and suddenly the very last thing that Calisa wanted to be doing was debating the depth versus shallowness of Ethan's feelings. She just . . . didn't care anymore.

Huh. That's a surprise.

She thought of Melidor and how she'd suddenly known she was ready to plant her seedlings. Somehow, between weeding and scrubbing and worrying about Auntie Zee and venturing through portals into other realms, Calisa had moved on, and she knew it with as much certainty as the dryad.

"I have to go," she said, interrupting Ethan. "Sorry. Bye." She hung up and then stared at the phone for a few seconds.

It began to ring again.

She didn't answer.

"One more trip to the Night Market," Calisa said after pancakes. "It's possible that Rin will have news for us. He said he'd ask around. If he doesn't . . . I'll call my moms." They'd overreact definitely, and they'd insist that Calisa come home, but if Rin had no information, she didn't think she had much choice.

Jack nodded, but she got the feeling that he was just humoring her. He didn't believe Rin would have any news. "Let me just restock." He always brought a backpack full of snacks when they went on their otherworldly search missions—that was another thing she liked about him. Never undervalue a boy with snacks.

After he'd stuffed a few plastic containers into his pack, they headed up to the guest room that had the portal to the Night Market. Inside, the firebird was already waiting. It had raced ahead through the chimneys, and it crackled happily as it danced over the logs. She wondered briefly what it thought of what they were doing—it always watched their comings and goings, following them from room to room. She liked to think the firebird was rooting for them.

She opened the closet door onto the iridescent swirl. They walked through without hesitation, and she was instantly bathed in moonlight. She let her eyes adjust to the pale light while her ears adjusted to the cacophony of voices from the farmers market below.

"I brought payment for Rin," Jack said. Shucking off his backpack, he unzipped it and pulled out a plastic container. Inside was a slice of chocolate cake with raspberry jam, squished.

"He's a professional baker," Calisa said. "I'm not sure my attempt at a cake is going to count as payment." She'd learned through Auntie Zee's notes that the Night Market took payment in coins called lercats. Or the occasional cursed object.

"It's a *chocolate* cake." He grinned at her. "I asked Mulligan what counts as currency in the Night Market, besides lercats. Apparently chocolate is ludicrously expensive in Elyacor, due to the high demand—you don't want to know how much he paid for his hot chocolate ingredients. He advised that we bring a couple of slices, one for Rin and one to splurge on something to 'console our weary hearts.' This was after waxing poetically about chocolate, the market under the stars, and the ephemeral nature of life for about fifteen minutes."

"He's a bit dramatic," Calisa said.

Jack returned the slices to his backpack and zipped it shut.

"Auntie Zee once made the mistake of showing him some old vampire movies. He loved them."

"Wait. Are you telling me he's like that not because he comes from whatever world he comes from, but because he likes Dracula? Specifically, Bela Lugosi's Dracula?"

"Also, he reads a lot of Shakespeare." Swinging his pack over his shoulder, he grinned at her and headed down the slope toward the market. She hurried to catch up. Her feet skidded on the slick grass, and they ended up half sliding and half running until they reached the first tent. She stopped several feet before colliding into the canvas, and he grabbed her hand to stop his own forward momentum. He lost his balance, and they collapsed into a heap next to the tent.

Jack burst out laughing, and it was infectious. Soon, she was laughing too. She didn't know why she was laughing when Auntie Zee was still missing, but under the starry sky, with Jack, she couldn't help feeling like it was all going to be okay.

He got up and held out his hand. She took it and hopped to her feet.

It felt like the most natural thing in the world to slip her hand into his as they strolled. On either side, the vendors called to them, each claiming to have the most beautiful, the most unique, the most unusual wares. She knew they should head to Rin's stall, but once they did . . . If Rin had no news of Auntie Zee, she'd have no choice but to call her moms and admit that Auntie Zee had pulled a disappearing act, and then all this would end. No more trips through the portals. And if he *did* have news of Auntie Zee . . . well, then all this would end too. Auntie Zee would put a stop to their adventures. So,

Calisa wasn't eager to reach Rin. She wanted to enjoy their last stroll through the Night Market.

Jack didn't seem to be in a hurry either. *He thinks she doesn't want to be found.*

They lingered by a stall that sold scarves that shimmered like the sky—you could see sunset spread across the fabric, deepening from pale blue to rose and orange, then to deep blue scattered with stars. Jack wrapped one around Calisa's shoulders, and she held the fabric up to her eyes, watching it twinkle between her fingers.

"Beautiful," she said.

"Yes," he agreed.

He was looking at her, not the scarf.

Calisa felt herself blush as she unwound the scarf and placed it neatly back on the table. She headed for the next stall, which had a towering stack of hats. "Here, you try this on."

Picking up one, she dropped it onto his head, and his hair instantly lengthened and deepened to coal-black. When she lifted the hat, his hair retreated to its ordinary length.

"Handsome," she told him.

"Twelve lercats," the vendor interjected.

"Just browsing for now." Jack returned the hat and then patted his head as if to reassure himself his hair was still there.

They kept strolling toward Rin's stall, slowly. If it weren't for the ever-present worry about Auntie Zee, it would have felt like a date. She wondered if Jack felt it too. There was no not-awkward way to ask, but she kept sneaking glances at him as they browsed. What did he think of her?

Lingering by a glittering stall, they studied a spread of

jewels that crawled around the table before nesting into the settings of necklaces and bracelets.

"Jewelites," the vendor told them. "Rare crabs that live within caves. Once they find a setting they like, they'll reside within it for decades."

"They're alive?" Calisa leaned over to touch what looked like a bright green jewel. She would've thought it was an emerald, except it instantly skittered away.

"The jewel creates the jewelry," the vendor claimed grandiosely.

She wanted to ask why and how, but before the questions poured out of her mouth, she heard a sweet cascade of notes. It transfixed her. The notes seemed to dance in the air, drifting up toward the stars. "Do you hear that?" she asked Jack.

"Yeah." He twisted, trying to see its source.

Pulling Jack with her, Calisa followed the lure of the music. Two rows over, she found it: a harpist, playing at a stall that sold dozens of small, colorful bottles. The harp was more elaborate than any Calisa had ever seen. It had three tiers of golden and silver strings, and it towered over the seated musician. Eyes closed, the harpist ran her fingers over the strings so rapidly that the music cascaded like a waterfall.

"Come and view the rarest potions ever sold," the vendor called, his voice slipping between the notes as if it too were part of the music.

As the music enfolded her, Calisa drifted closer to the harpist. She didn't even notice her feet moving—the melody pulled her. Vaguely, she noticed others drawn closer too. Beside her, Jack was just as enraptured.

The harpist herself was as lovely as her melodies. In her hair, she wore braided flowers that bloomed from buds while she played a rising arpeggio and then closed their petals when the melody fell. Calisa noticed that her ears formed delicate points.

"We need to talk to Rin," Jack said to Calisa. But he didn't move.

"One minute." Shifting to view the potions as an excuse to keep listening, Calisa studied the colorful glass bottles. Each was tiny, holding no more than a few drops of whatever was inside. "What are these?" she asked the vendor, a man in all purple with a matching purple beard. His eyes, she noticed, were black. No white around an iris. Just all black.

He pointed to one bottle with a slender finger, his nail tipped with a diamond. "This one holds sadness." Another. "Joy." Another. "Regret." He picked up one and spun it so the colored glass sparkled as it caught the moonlight. "This is the distilled essence of the moment a mother sees her child for the very first time." He placed it down carefully and lifted another. "And this is the flush of first love."

"You're selling emotions?" Calisa asked. She wanted to ask how that was possible. Also, what were you supposed to do with it? She studied the bottle of first love. "Is this, like, a love potion? If you want someone to love you?"

He blanched. "Never!"

The harpist paused, her fingers raised over the strings, and the music instantly vanished, like a stolen breath. Calisa felt an ache, as if she'd misplaced something important.

Jack jumped in quickly. "We didn't mean any offense."

"Our potions would never control another," the vendor said indignantly. "No, these are for communication. They are for understanding. For empathy. Choose the one that matches your emotion, and when your loved one drinks it, they will know how you feel on a visceral level."

Wow, that was . . . She didn't know what that was.

She thought of Mulligan. It was his idea to bring two slices of chocolate cake. Could he add this potion to his hot chocolate? "How about one that captures how much you miss someone?"

"Ah, yes, a variation on regret with a strong dollop of hope and longing." His fingers danced above the bottles until he selected one in purple glass. "You'll want this one. Be warned: it's very strong and can momentarily overwhelm all else."

"It's perfect."

"For payment . . ." the vendor began.

Calisa turned to Jack. "You said we had a spare slice?"

Jack opened his backpack. "We offer this as payment," he said solemnly. With a flourish, he lifted the lid on the Tupperware, and the thick, sweet smell of chocolate wafted out.

Both the vendor and the musician ogled the cake. "Done," the vendor said swiftly. He smiled as he wrapped the vial in a bit of fabric and tied a ribbon around it.

Calisa pocketed the vial, while Jack handed over the slice of chocolate cake. The vendor breathed it in and sighed happily, and the harpist leaned over to ask for a taste.

Moving on, Calisa and Jack soon reached the fifth row.

As they approached the baker's stall, Rin called to them, "My friends from Auntie Zee! What a delight to see you, a timely delight!" Standing beside him were two women, both drenched in jewels. Calisa and Jack trotted over.

Calisa's first thought was: *They have news of Auntie Zee!*

Her second thought was: *They're not human.*

Smiling widely, Rin boomed, "Calisa, Jack, it's my honor to introduce you to the queens of Irisday. Your Majesties, these are the representatives of the charming bed-and-breakfast that I was telling you about."

Queens?

Calisa stared at them.

Both were thin and tall, but in a stretched way—their faces, their necks, their arms all looked too long, and their eyes were too wide and glowed a radioactive green. Their ears tapered into points, like the harpist's, but on them, it looked unnatural. Everything about them was unsettling, especially the way they were staring at Calisa and Jack.

"Fae," Jack breathed beside her. "Be careful."

Calisa wasn't sure if she was supposed to bow, curtsy, or shake hands. She settled for an awkward bow with a smile and hoped she hadn't offended the clearly not-human women. The portal magic ensured there wouldn't be a language problem, but it didn't translate customs. Or deliver warnings.

The two fae queens inclined their heads, which was a good sign. She hadn't offended them yet. Both were coated in makeup—the woman on the left had blue paint streaked on her cheeks with black kohl around her eyes, while the woman on the right was painted bronze. The blue queen wore silver roped necklaces with amber pendants around her neck and a crown of amber on her head that held a silk veil in place over her hair. The bronze queen was swathed in black from her neck to her ankles. Both were works of art.

"Tell us about your otherworld establishment," the bronze queen demanded.

Calisa's tongue felt thick, and she couldn't stop staring. She remembered Jack saying that the inn used to be fit for royalty. She wasn't sure it was anymore.

"Speak," the blue one said, her voice gentle, coaxing.

"It's peaceful, it's beautiful, and it's quiet," Calisa said, the words spilling out. "Except for the birds. They sing you awake every morning, and if you wake to their singing and go to the window, you can watch the sun rise over the mountains. It turns the sky lemon and pink before it brightens into a light blue. We serve breakfast every morning for our guests."

"Pancakes," Jack put in. "They're delicious."

"If you're looking for an adventure, you should find another vacation. The Faraway Inn is an escape," Calisa said. "It offers a few days to just breathe. To think, if you want, or not think. To be calm. To heal, if you need to. To have space and quiet."

"It's in a place called Vermont," Jack said. "There are mountains and trees. We have gardens with flowers and a stream that you can sit by. We serve tea every afternoon, and there's a library with shelves full of books. It's not fancy, but it's nice."

"It is," Calisa agreed.

The two queens exchanged looks.

The blue-painted queen smiled and said, "It sounds like precisely what we need."

"We'll tell the innkeeper, when she returns," Calisa said. There was no way they could host these two terrifying women without Auntie Zee, and she was certainly not going to invite anyone through the portal without the innkeeper's permission. "We can't . . ." The words died in her throat. Both fae queens were staring at her now, their expressions hard. She felt the urge to bolt and hide under something very large for a very long time.

Rin sighed heavily. "She still has not returned? This is hard news. I hoped she'd gone home of her own accord. Alas, I have heard nothing of her whereabouts."

Calisa felt her heart sink.

She hadn't realized how much she'd been hoping that Rin would have the answer—he could have talked with someone who'd seen Auntie Zee, he could have gotten word to her that they were searching for her and she needed to come home, or he could have found her and been here with her, ready to return.

Now what do we do?

CHAPTER TWENTY

Calisa heard Mulligan before she saw him: humming a dirge, mixing and stirring. Entering the kitchen, she found him at the butcher block island, creating a new concoction. She was fully aware she was dragging her feet on calling her moms—they were not going to be happy that Calisa didn't know where Auntie Zee was or that she'd kept it from them for so long—but despite all that, she smiled when she saw Mulligan. "Another attempt?"

"I had an idea! A new, brilliant, glorious idea that came as if on the wings of night, gliding softly over the mountains, to roost in my mind. If I can re-create the exact drink that Zef and I shared on the night we first met, he might wake."

"I think that's a beautiful idea." She waffled for a half second, wondering if she was overstepping, but then placed the bottle from the Night Market on the counter anyway. "I bought this for you. A new ingredient, possibly? I don't know if it'll work, and if you don't want to try it, I promise that's fine. I won't be offended or anything."

He lifted it up to the light and squinted at the liquid inside.

"The vendor who was selling it says it holds an emotion, specifically regret."

Mulligan lowered the bottle and stared at Calisa.

Calisa felt herself flushing. Weakly, she said, "I was thinking of you and how you said you just needed to make Zef understand it was a mistake, and I thought you could combine it with your hot chocolate or love drink or whatever?"

He swallowed, and she saw his Adam's apple bob in his thin throat.

"Or not." She shouldn't have bought the potion at all. This really, really wasn't her business. She'd way overstepped this time, and she knew it. It had been one thing to try to fix the inn when Auntie Zee thought it was pointless; it was another to meddle in a guest's personal life, especially when it involved magic. "It was just a thought. I don't know how magic works or, really, anything about anything."

Mulligan let out a little chirp-squawk noise, bustled around the counter, and enfolded Calisa in his robe-clad arms. She felt as if she were being hugged by a giant bat. His limbs were thin and bony, but the robe was voluminous. When he released her, tears were streaming down the hollows of his cheeks.

"This will work," he said. "I feel it."

She felt herself smile. His intensity was . . . intense. "How can I help?"

Following his instructions, Calisa hand-shredded fresh mint leaves. He scurried around the kitchen, singing tunelessly and happily, as he gathered more ingredients: strawberries, sugar, club soda . . . He puréed the strawberries, forcing them through a mesh strainer.

"Tell me about Zef," Calisa said as she inhaled the scent of mint and strawberry that filled the kitchen. "What do you like about him? I mean, when he's not a gargoyle."

Mulligan smiled, his eyes misty. "Zef, my Zef. He's kind and gentle. Once, a bat flew into our home, and he spent hours coaxing it down from the rafters with offers of fresh berries and aged cheese. That bat dined like royalty." He chuckled at the memory. "It was only later we learned that the bat *was* royalty, third in line to the throne of Umbre. The succession line in that realm is based on prophecies, which means their rulers are occasionally animals. They use regents for the actual ruling, of course, but the bat or wolverine or hawk or what have you is given a luxurious life."

"Huh." So many questions.

He topped off the drink and then carefully poured it into a test tube–size vial of club soda. "I believe it is nearly ready." Holding it steady, he added the few drops from the purple glass bottle. Only three drops. They swirled into the vial. "I shall save the rest for a second attempt, if necessary."

He then stared at the vial for a moment longer.

"Do you think it will work?" Calisa asked.

"If it does, I owe it all to you," Mulligan said with a smile. It was a sad kind of smile, and she realized that in his heart, despite the tears of joy, he didn't believe it would work. He'd tried so many times . . . but he kept trying, even with only the thinnest sliver of hope.

Softly, she asked, "How long has it been? Since Zef . . ." She trailed off, realizing she didn't know the word for what had happened to his partner.

"Eternity."

Oh.

He carried the vial out of the kitchen, and she, unsure if it was okay for her to follow, hesitated by the counter. From the lobby, he called, "If you would like to lend your support, I shall be glad of it."

She hurried after him, passing Portia, who was curled up on the registration desk. The cat opened one eye as Calisa trotted by, then closed it.

"I didn't know if you wanted privacy," Calisa said to Mulligan.

"I have had too much of privacy." He climbed the stairs. "It is companionship that I have missed. Zef and I . . . We used to be inseparable."

With a half bow, he opened the door to his guest room and welcomed Calisa inside.

Thick black shades were drawn over the window, which—combined with all the black on the walls and the bed—made the room feel like a cave. She wondered at the bat story and how Jack had said that Mulligan admired Dracula. It was all a bit on the nose. She thought about asking if he drank blood too but decided that would be rude, especially after she'd clearly seen him drink hot chocolate. Also, she'd seen him in the sitting room at teatime, which had made her previously dismiss the vampire theory, but had he ever been in direct sunlight?

Mulligan crossed immediately to the gargoyle, who was positioned beside the hearth on top of a golden pillow. "Zef, my love, it's time to try again. Wake for me, please, I implore you. This is not the life I wanted for either of us. This is not what's meant to be."

Calisa saw the firebird float down the chimney and lower itself onto the logs. It burned silently, watching. She wondered if it observed everything that happened in the inn—and why. It felt a bit like a wordless, fiery cheerleader, urging them on.

The firebird crackled encouragingly as Mulligan lifted the vial to Zef's fanged stony lips and poured. Calisa expected the liquid to drip down the gargoyle's stone face, but it pooled in the cracks between his teeth and then was absorbed.

As the stone drank, the firebird held still, its feathers draped over one of the bits of wood in the hearth as if clutching it in anticipation. How many times had Mulligan tried, and how many times had the firebird served as witness? *Please work,* she thought at Zef. *Wake up.*

Mulligan rocked back on his heels. His hands were clasped in front of him, so tightly that she could see his knuckles and the veins raised blue against his pale skin.

Calisa studied the statue. She'd expected him to transform, like the Beast into a prince, or the frog into a prince, or Pinocchio into a real boy.

He did not.

But he did *thaw.*

The gray of his stone softened, and the pebbly surface seemed to smooth until it more closely resembled flesh. The gargoyle's clothes brightened into scarlets and emeralds as they changed from stone to cloth. His face stayed gray and still looked caught between a monkey and a bat. But his eyes, which were once blank and gray, changed: a black iris and white around it. His eyes fixed on Mulligan's face.

Mulligan was sobbing silently. His shoulders shook. Tears streamed down his cheeks. "Zef," he croaked. "My Zef. I am so sorry. Please . . . I am so sorry. I have missed you so much, my friend, my love, my joy, my life."

"Well then," Zef said, his voice as gravelly as Calisa could have imagined, "you should have said so."

Mulligan threw himself forward, his arms and robe wrapping around Zef.

The firebird flew up the chimney, and Calisa backed out of the room with a smile on her face. She felt dampness on her cheeks and lifted her fingers to touch tears.

I need to tell Jack.

We have a new guest.

She wished Auntie Zee were here to see this.

Calisa found herself standing in front of Auntie Zee's door. She knew that the innkeeper wasn't inside, but she wanted to knock anyway. Her great-aunt had missed Melidor planting her seedlings and Mulligan's reunion with Zef. Who knew what she'd miss tomorrow? "Come back, please."

It was time to call her moms. Way past time. She'd delayed long enough. But it wasn't like there was anything they could do—their most likely response would be to make Calisa come home, which wouldn't help anything. Calling them felt like giving up on not just Auntie Zee but also Jack and the inn and all the guests and all the potential future guests who could someday need this place. She wished she could think of something else to try, some other way to reach Auntie Zee. . . .

"Ah, you've discovered the disaster too," a clipped voice said behind her.

Calisa turned and saw Kendra at the top of the stairs. Water was sloughing off her, pooling at her feet and then cascading down the staircase—far more water than if she'd come straight out of the shower. It seemed to be emanating from her, as if her pores were faucets. It welled up from her skin and flowed down her face, neck, and arms. It dripped off her fingers.

"I assumed it was merely my portal," Kendra said, as if she weren't a living fountain flooding the stairs. "But now that I see you here, in a near panic, I must surmise that mine is not the only portal that will not open."

"What?" Calisa said.

It was, she admitted, not her finest reaction—but considering a guest was literally gushing water from her skin, it was the only one she could summon.

Frowning, Kendra enunciated as if Calisa were incapable of understanding English: "My portal, which I need to pass through a minimum of once a week, as Auntie Zee well knows, is not functioning. It is an ordinary closet, no matter how many times I close and open the door, and this is simply unacceptable."

That . . . did sound unacceptable.

And like a potentially very bad problem.

Also, again, she was gushing water, which was definitely a very, very bad problem. She thought of Jack's father and how the door he'd passed through had never opened onto a realm again. What if the portal in room three was permanently closed? What if Kendra couldn't return to her home? "Show me?" Calisa asked.

Pivoting, Kendra strode down the stairs.

Calisa held on to the railing. The stairs were slick with seawater. She'd need to find towels and dry them before any guests hurt themselves by slipping and falling. But priorities. She and Jack *needed* Auntie Zee to return. This wasn't a good time for the portals to malfunction. "Has this happened before?"

"On occasion," Kendra said, "but never for more than a few moments. I am growing increasingly concerned. I am not some minor jellyfish. I am the sea witch for the Eastern Seaboard, and I *cannot* be absent for an extended length of time. Auntie Zee understands this. If I am unable to return within twenty-four hours, there will be havoc."

Reaching room number three, Kendra flung open the door. Calisa was struck by the stench of seaweed. Sea witch, did she say? What was a sea witch?

Eastern Seaboard?

As in the Atlantic Ocean?

Kendra strode across the room, and seawater sloshed around

her feet. *I'm going to need a* lot *of towels.* The sea witch reached the closet and opened the door with a flourish.

Inside was an empty closet. Just a few hangers, swinging from the wind that Kendra had generated when she opened the closet door so vigorously.

"Before, what did it—" Calisa began to ask.

"My ocean," Kendra said. "The lovely deep blue."

"How did that work? Did the portal keep the ocean inside, like a force field? Could you see fish?" She thought back to the piercing wind of Melidor's world—the portal must keep the realms separate while allowing travelers to pass through.

"The point is," Kendra said sharply, "my ocean is *gone*."

Calisa swallowed. Yes. Yes, that was a very good point. "I don't know how the portals work or why one would close."

"Then you will find out," Kendra commanded. "Locate Auntie Zee. Fix this. Immediately."

There was zero softness in her voice.

Calisa backed out to the hallway. Her socks were soaked, but she didn't even look down. She closed the door to Kendra's room and stared at it.

Half a minute later, she ran, jumping over puddles, to Jack's door.

She'd never gone to his room before, always meeting him in the kitchen or outside, but she didn't hesitate—she knocked loudly. He also had a red X on his door, matching hers. She wondered if Auntie Zee intentionally gave staff the rooms with broken portals. She filed that on her list of items that she'd probably never have a chance to ask. "Jack? It's Calisa."

She heard a thump, then heard Jack swear. He opened the door a second later, and she caught a glimpse of a chair that had been knocked over. "Are you all right?" he asked.

"Yes. No. Kendra's portal won't open."

She saw his face freeze, and she knew he was thinking of his father. She'd thought of that already. What if the doors all failed and none of the guests could return home? "Do you know if any of the others have had issues? Is it only Kendra's portal?"

Grimly, he said, "We should check. *Without* alarming the other guests."

Calisa nodded. Her heart was galloping. She hadn't really thought about what she'd do if something actually went wrong at the bed-and-breakfast. She always assumed that Auntie Zee would be back before anything serious happened. *I'm not supposed to be in charge.*

Panicking wouldn't help. Calisa took a deep breath. "Okay, let's check the doors we've used recently, and the ones the guests have. Get all the information we can on how widespread this is, *before* we panic." She grabbed his hand and pulled him downstairs to the lobby. She yanked the drawer of the desk open and scooped up the master key.

She marched first to the guest room with the Night Market . . . and the closet door opened to the familiar swirl. She heard Jack exhale beside her. "Check a few more?" he suggested.

Methodically, they checked room by room.

Miraculously, the other portals were intact.

"It's only Kendra's room," Jack said.

They returned downstairs to find the sea witch in the sitting room. She was pacing in front of the fireplace as she dripped seawater. Grabbing towels, Jack scurried behind her, sopping up water before it saturated the rugs. The white cat was on the windowsill, her fur fluffed and her body tense as she glared at the sea witch. Outside, the winged lizard was perched on the window ledge, looking concerned. Or hungry. She couldn't tell which.

"I don't think you understand the scope of this disaster," Kendra said without any preamble. She wrung her hands, and water splattered onto the walls, sliding down the wallpaper. "If I can't return, there will be no one to regulate the storms."

"We're going to find Auntie Zee," Calisa promised.

And then it hit her: If previously stable portals were malfunctioning, maybe Auntie Zee *had* been trapped behind a closed door? Maybe, for whatever reason, her magic wasn't allowing her to open it? Or she was sick and couldn't open it?

She hated that explanation.

But it did make sense.

All this time, she'd been assuming that Auntie Zee had chosen to stay away. But now . . . *What if I was wrong? What if she hasn't come back because she* can't?

Hoping the dismay she was feeling didn't show on her face, Calisa crossed the sitting room, her wet socks squishing, and held out her arms to the cat. "Portia? Will you let me carry you to a dry room?" The cat had never allowed Calisa to pet her, but this time she seemed to feel the situation was suitably dire. Portia allowed Calisa to carry her into the library, where Calisa deposited her on the window seat. "We'll fix this. I don't know how yet, but we'll think of something. Don't worry."

The cat hissed.

"It'll be okay," Calisa said, as much to herself as to Portia.

She hurried back to Jack. He looked near panic, his eyes wide as he mopped the puddles as quickly and thoroughly as he could—it was a losing battle, though, as the sea witch continued to ooze seawater.

"It's time to check Auntie Zee's room," Calisa said. "Maybe there's a clue there." Kendra's portal closing changed everything. Auntie Zee *couldn't* be staying away voluntarily, not if she knew this was what could happen in her absence. As grumpy as Auntie Zee was, she cared about the Faraway Inn too much to be that reckless with her legacy.

Calisa expected Jack to argue. But he didn't protest or even say a word. Just handed her the key. Maybe he knew it too. This was far more serious than Auntie Zee simply needing a break.

She charged up to the third floor, and then she stopped. They hadn't searched Auntie Zee's room because they'd assumed either they'd find her or she'd return on her own. Entering it now . . . that was tantamount to admitting that she couldn't come back.

Immediately, Calisa's brain helpfully supplied images of what could have happened to Auntie Zee to prevent her from reopening a malfunctioning portal, all the possibilities she hadn't let herself consider because this was *the* Auntie Zee. *What if she's hurt? What if she's sick? What if she's unconscious?*

What if she's— Not letting herself complete the thought, she stuck the key into the lock, twisted, and pushed the door open.

Auntie Zee's room was a wondrous kaleidoscope of color: scarfs and tapestries were draped over the walls, while mobiles made of prisms dangled from the ceiling. Gold, silver, and blue pillows were piled on the bed beneath a ruby-and-emerald-colored canopy. Multicolored rugs covered the honey-colored floor. Every surface was stacked with treasures: boxes carved from seashells; tiny sculptures of creatures that shouldn't exist, like dragons and centaurs; little paintings that hung on the wall depicting worlds with impossibly high waterfalls, many moons, and castles. Coming inside, Calisa saw one etching of the labyrinth with its bone guards.

These were souvenirs of her travels. Or perhaps gifts from visiting travelers. She'd made her room a shrine to all the wonders that the nexus could bring. *She loves this place.*

Looking around, Calisa was now completely and terribly certain: Auntie Zee wasn't staying away voluntarily. She had to be trapped . . . elsewhere. Far away.

She saw a warm glow from the fireplace. The firebird was here, watching her. It occurred to her that the firebird was always where she was, anticipating where she planned to go. She decided that was a good sign—she was supposed to be here, looking for her aunt.

Addressing it, Calisa asked, "Do you know where Auntie Zee is?"

The firebird flew up the chimney, and the room dipped into shadow.

She didn't know what kind of answer that was. Maybe none at all.

Calisa couldn't tell when her great-aunt had last been here. The sheets on the bed were rumpled, but when had they last been slept on? She studied it, as if the creases would hold the answer. Stray white hairs lay on the pillow, or perhaps tufts of fur . . . All that meant, though, was that Auntie Zee let the cat sleep with her. It didn't tell her anything useful either.

Calisa took a breath and then checked the one place she hadn't yet dared: the closet.

Girding herself, she opened the door.

Inside were only clothes on hangers and a pile of shoes at the bottom. She stared at the mess and wondered what it meant.

Had this once been a portal that closed? If so, how long ago had the portal failed? Years ago? If not, why no X on the exterior door? So, did that mean it failed recently? Was Auntie Zee, like Jack's father, stuck on the other side? Lost?

No, it couldn't have been recent. The closet wouldn't be filled with shoes if it were an active portal. All the other portal closets had been empty.

Except the broom closet, on the first day I was here.

Okay, never mind. She had no way of knowing if this was a recently failed portal or not. It was equally possible that it had never been a portal at all. Auntie Zee might not have wanted a portal in the same room where she slept.

Ugh, there's so much I don't know! It was infuriating. If Auntie Zee had just explained everything on day one, even a short this-is-how-the-magic-works primer, she wouldn't be feeling so helpless now.

Calisa took a deep breath.

Calm down. Think.

In her admittedly limited experience with the inn, in most cases, a door was either a portal or not a portal. Except for that first broom closet. After that day, the broom closet had behaved like an ordinary broom closet, filled with mops and dustbins and so forth. Calisa had used it often, but the very first time she encountered it . . . She tried to re-create the memory of that moment in her mind. Auntie Zee had shut the door on the howling void and then reopened it on brooms. How? Had she done anything special? Said anything? Cast a spell? Calisa was fairly certain the answer was no. All Auntie Zee had done was shut it and reopen it.

Calisa closed the closet door, waited three seconds, and then opened it.

Still shoes and clothes.

She chewed on her lower lip as she thought. Not panicked. Not yet. As far as she could tell, they now had two problems: Auntie Zee was missing, and the portals were malfunctioning.

The best option was to solve problem two and hope that fixed problem one.

How, though, did she fix a portal to another realm?

CHAPTER TWENTY-ONE

After knocking loudly to no answer, Calisa let herself into Kendra's guest room with the master skeleton key. She splashed through the film of water that had soaked the floor, and she opened the closet door. It was, as expected, empty. She stared at it, closed the door, and reopened it. Unlike Auntie Zee's closet, she knew this had been an active portal recently.

She closed and reopened it again.

On the fifth try, she heard a noise behind her and turned.

"Is it doing anything?" Jack asked plaintively.

"Where's Kendra?" Calisa asked. "Is she okay?"

"I convinced her to go outside," Jack said. "The salt water won't be good for the plants, but she agreed to pace on the gravel driveway. It can't hurt the rocks."

"Good idea. And no, it's still not working." Calisa crossed her arms. "Tell me everything you know about how the portals work."

"Well, um, they're magic."

Calisa glared at him.

"I don't know. They're just *there* sometimes. . . ."

"What do you mean *sometimes*? Be detailed." If she could identify a pattern . . .

He ran his hand through his hair. "Auntie Zee doesn't exactly welcome questions. You know that. Sometimes a closet door opens onto a portal, and sometimes it doesn't. Sometimes you just get shoes or brooms."

Okay, that wasn't helpful. Didn't he have any clue how it worked? He'd lived here for years. "Is there any kind of pattern to when a door opens to a realm and when it opens to just a closet? Any common factors?"

He considered it. "Well . . . Auntie Zee, of course. She's the only one who can change an ordinary closet into a portal, and vice versa."

"So we know it's not just the doors themselves." It wasn't new information. He'd told her that before, but it was a place to start. "That means it's not random, right? Auntie Zee must *do* something to them. Any guesses what? What does she do, in as much detail as you know, when she opens a portal that was previously an ordinary closet?"

"Um . . . I've never seen her do it."

Calisa had witnessed her converting a portal to an ordinary closet but not the reverse. She didn't think she'd seen Auntie Zee doing anything special, but then again, she'd been distracted by the howling darkness. "She never let you see, or you just didn't notice?"

"The first. It's not like I'm not curious. I've tried to watch. Lots of times. She shoos me away pretty much instantly. Last time, the statue ratted me out. She was standing outside the window, and Auntie Zee saw her pointing right where I was hiding."

Fine. So he never saw it happen.

Could someone else have seen?

How about the statue?

Calisa wasn't sure what the right yes-or-no questions would be to figure it out, but it was an option. There was, though, someone else a lot more talkative who could have seen. Someone who had lived here before Jack. "I need to call my mom."

There was a phone on the bedside table—thankfully only splashed, not soaked, in seawater. Before she could talk herself out of it, Calisa lifted the receiver and punched in the numbers to Mom-Kate's cell phone. She tried not to think about how awkward this phone call was going to be and instead focus on how to convince Mom-Kate to tell her exactly what she needed to know.

Mom-Kate answered immediately. "Hello, baby girl, how's fresh air and unblemished skies?" she said chirpily.

"Great. All good. I mean, well, actually . . . we're kind of having a bit of a problem here—I'm fine, totally healthy, nothing broken, and I didn't break anything."

"Okay. Good," Mom-Kate said, less chirpily. "But that intro makes me think you absolutely did break something."

"Not exactly, but yes, something is broken. Um, so . . ." What if Mom-Kate didn't know about the portals? What if she had no idea there was anything unusual at the Faraway Inn? What was she going to think if she didn't know and Calisa started talking about portals and realms and sea witches? "All right, please hear me out and don't judge me, and if you don't know what I'm talking about, pretend I saw it all in a TV show, and we'll just hang up and forget this conversation ever happened, okay, Mom-Kate?" She was clutching the phone so hard that her hand started to sweat.

"Cali, you're worrying me. You know you can tell me anything."

Calisa squeezed her eyes shut, as if that would make the words easier. "I need to know how to reopen a portal. To another realm."

There was silence on the phone.

"Mom-Kate?"

"Oh, sweetie. It's okay. It didn't work for me either, and I tried so hard. It's . . . it's an innate thing. Either you can do it or you can't. I'd hoped it might have just skipped a generation. . . ."

Her brain stuttered as it tried to catch up with what Mom-Kate was saying. "Wait. Are you saying . . . you know about the realms? You know what the B&B is? That it's a nexus?" After Mom-Elise's cryptic comment about opening doors, she'd guessed that her moms might know, but she hadn't been certain. Hearing Mom-Kate talk so matter-of-factly was a shock. *I should have called them sooner.*

"Of course." Her voice cracked as the phone connection wavered, then stabilized again. "I was supposed to take over for Auntie Zee eventually, but I lack the ability. It's inherent, you see. You have to be born with it." She sounded wistful.

Calisa glanced at Jack. "An inherent ability?" Did he know anything about that?

"Of course, it takes training and practice too," Mom-Kate said, "but that's useless without whatever gene I didn't get. I'm so sorry, Calisa. I hoped you might have inherited it. Given Auntie Zee's age and how much she wants the inn to continue, I thought it was worth sending you, in case she was willing to have you try. But if Auntie Zee has tried to teach you with no luck—"

"Auntie Zee hasn't tried to teach me anything," Calisa said. "She isn't here."

There was silence that made her wonder if the connection had failed before Mom-Kate said, "Sweetie?"

"She's missing," Calisa said. "And the portals . . . Some of them are closed that shouldn't be closed." Jack was standing beside her. She felt his hand on her shoulder, and she looked at him. "My mom says it's an innate ability, to open the portals. She didn't inherit it."

"Did you?" Jack asked.

"I don't know."

She returned to the phone. "Mom-Kate?"

But Mom-Kate was talking with Mom-Elise, explaining that Auntie Zee had abandoned Calisa and they needed to look up train times to Vermont right then.

Calisa raised her voice. "Mom-Kate!"

"Yes?"

"You coming here won't help," Calisa said. "Not if you can't open the portals. But what if *I* can open them? You said Auntie Zee tried to train you, right?"

"She tried. . . ."

"So train me."

Silence.

"Mom-Kate? I have to try."

"All right. But if this doesn't work, we're coming to Vermont."

"Fine," Calisa said. She faced the closet. "What do I do?"

"I love that you called me for help, Calisa," Mom-Kate said. "You know you'll always be my baby girl, and I will always be proud of you."

That was nice. Very nice. But not relevant. *"Mom-Kate."*

"Sorry. Okay. I'll be your Obi-Wan."

"Thanks." Calisa inhaled and then exhaled. She felt as if her heart were beating as fast as a hummingbird's wings.

"Wait," Mom-Kate said.

Her stomach clenched, and she froze.

Concern in her voice, Mom-Kate said, "Didn't Obi-Wan make Darth Vader? Because I don't want you turning evil."

Sighing hard, Calisa rolled her eyes. "Please don't try to make jokes. Everyone here is pretty keyed up. Especially the sea witch. She needs to get back to her tides or waves or storms or whatever. She has fish who need her."

Another breath of silence. "So you're having a good summer?"

"Mom-Kate!"

"Sorry. All right. It's just . . . been a while. I don't know what I've forgotten, so bear with me. . . . First, you need to quiet your mind and focus. Concentrate on your breath. It requires your touch and your breath and your mind. Use the word *open* like it's a mantra."

Steadying herself, Calisa focused on her breath. In. Out. In . . .

"Now, stand before the door," Mom-Kate said. "Run your fingers over the doorframe. You'll need both hands for this, so can you put me on speaker?"

Right. Both hands. She didn't think this old-timey phone had a speaker function. "I'm handing the phone to Jack. Tell him to tell me, and I'll do it." She handed him the receiver. "Jack, could you . . ."

Jack took the phone. "Hello, ma'am? Yes."

She couldn't hear what Mom-Kate said, but Jack blushed.

"Mom-Kate!" Calisa raised her voice.

Jack didn't repeat whatever had made him blush. Instead, he said, "She says you need to run your fingers over the whole doorframe. Don't miss an inch."

"I didn't see Auntie Zee do that."

A brief pause, and then Jack reported, "She was closing a portal that she'd opened herself; your mom says that's different. She also wants to know if you've been happy and if you're eating enough."

Calisa laughed, slightly hysterically. "Please tell her to remember what I said about an unhappy sea witch. I really don't want to be responsible for flooding the bed-and-breakfast."

He relayed that. "She says you want the door to know you, to recognize you. It would help if you whispered to it? Auntie Zee used to have her spend days in doorways, learning how it felt to be in a liminal space." Into the phone, he said, "I don't know that we have days."

Calisa hoped he didn't over-worry them. They were experts

at over-worrying. On the other hand, the situation was a bit on the dire side. Or at least the wet side.

"As you're touching the doorframe," Jack parroted, "focus on what it means to cross a threshold. To change. To transform. To grow."

That was . . . rather mushy. And vague.

"She says she never really understood it either. But Auntie Zee was insistent that portal openings were about being open to change, to new experiences, to new emotions."

"Well, I'm feeling brand-new anxiety and fear, does that count?"

Jack relayed that. "That's not precisely what she had in mind. I think it has to be a positive emotion?" He paused, listening, and then said, "She said that to unlock your potential, you have to experience a fundamental positive change while in the doorway. You need to experience an epiphany."

"Seriously? How am I supposed to do that?"

He asked the question and then reported, "She says she can't tell you. It's different for everyone, and it has to be true and honest. You need to unlock yourself before you can unlock a gateway to a realm. Especially the first time. You've got to free your power."

She glared at the phone, as if Mom-Kate could feel her glare across the miles. "Tell her that this is not at all like Luke Skywalker's training."

He relayed that. "She said it kind of is. 'You will find only what you bring in.'"

Calisa snorted. "Anything else?"

He asked and then shook his head. "She said that's the first step. You need to master this before you can proceed. Unlock yourself, and you'll unlock the magic within you. After that you'll be able to command the portal to open. Theoretically. She says she never got past the first step, she says she believes in you, and she's proud of you no matter what." He paused, listening. "Um, she says she loves you to Pluto and back?"

"Okay, tell her thank you and I love her and I'm going to try."

He repeated that, then said, "She said, 'Do or do not; there is no try.'" He hung up the phone and then came to stand by her.

Calisa took a deep breath and then another. It was possible she couldn't do what Auntie Zee could. Her mother couldn't. But she could try. "That's bullshit advice. There's always try."

"I think it's supposed to be motivational. Like, it means believe in yourself?"

I do believe. She'd seen incredible things from the moment she'd arrived. She'd walked into other realms! She'd talked with magical beings! She'd served them cake! It was entirely possible this would work. After all, she was descended from Auntie Zee, as she'd told Rin; she could have inherited the "ability."

Inch by inch, she ran her fingers along the doorframe. She concentrated, digging deep, looking for the kind of revelatory bolt of self-confidence that would let her do something magical, a positive epiphany—she needed to believe that she could do something unique, needed, and wonderful.

A voice whispered inside her, *What makes you special?*

I'm Auntie Zee's grandniece, she answered.

So? What makes you think that matters? Your mother

couldn't open portals, and she grew up here. Mom-Kate had seen magic throughout her childhood and still couldn't make it manifest in herself.

What kind of epiphany would unlock her power, if she had any?

Did she have to want it badly enough? Was that the key? *I do want it!* She wanted to help the bed-and-breakfast. She wanted it to succeed and last.

Why?

Why. That was an excellent question. She'd only known that magic existed for a few weeks. As for the guests, they weren't family or friends. Not yet. She liked them. She wanted Melidor to be able to raise her seedlings, knowing she could always return to visit. And Mulligan and Zef—she wanted them to be happy. She wanted Auntie Zee to come back.

She also wanted Jack to keep his home, to be able to continue to wait for his father to find his way home. She wanted to ease that stress and fear that she saw lurking behind Jack's smile. This was all he had. And she had the chance to save it for him.

Why did she care?

She barely knew him.

Except she *did* know him. She'd walked into other realms with him. He'd told her secrets that she knew he'd never shared with anyone—about the magic, his childhood, his father. He'd trusted her in a way that no one ever had before. He listened to her. He respected her.

Opening her eyes, Calisa turned to look at Jack.

He shifted, glancing behind him. "What?"

"Come here," she said.

He took a step toward her until he was nearly in the doorway to the closet as well. Inches from him, she knew what to do.

"Kiss me," Calisa said. She added, "Please?"

CHAPTER TWENTY-TWO

He could have made it awkward. He could have asked questions. He could have accused her of using him to find her "epiphany" or started an uncomfortable what-do-you-want-out-of-this-relationship conversation. He could have said no.

But he didn't.

Jack cupped her face in his hands and lightly brushed her lips with his.

He then drew back and looked into her eyes, and she felt something inside her melt, like chocolate in the oven. Calisa covered his hands with hers, and she leaned in to kiss him.

Kissing her back, he stepped forward until their bodies touched, and she felt the warmth of his skin through the fabric of their shirts. He wound his hands through her hair, and she wrapped hers around the back of his neck. His lips were soft. Her breath matched his breath, her heart thudded fast against his, and she felt aware of every inch of her skin, as if her entire body were vibrating.

The kiss deepened, and she pressed herself against him as he gathered her closer. She was within his arms, and that's all there was—the outside world may as well have ceased to exist. It felt as if everything had condensed to just this moment and just the space around their two bodies, so close that they were one breath, one heartbeat.

The kiss ended, and Jack looked at her as if he never wanted to stop looking at her. She reached up and tucked a strand of his hair behind his ear. She knew she was smiling goofily, but she couldn't seem to stop—and didn't want to.

"Hi," she said.

"Hi," he said back.

She wondered what she should say. There didn't seem to be words big enough to hold everything she was feeling. She felt as if she were floating.

"Do you want to try the door?" he asked.

Door?

Calisa stared at him blankly. *Oh, right, the portal!* She stepped out of the closet doorway, pulling him gently with her. She liked the way her hand fit in his, like it was meant to be there, puzzle pieces that clicked together.

She pulled the closet door shut.

"Open," she said to it softly.

And then she opened it—and the portal swirled blue, filling the doorframe.

Jack squeezed her hand. "You did it."

"Wow." Calisa gawked at the shades of blue that spun and danced in the watery portal. She reached out and touched it lightly with her fingers. She wasn't imagining it. *It worked!* A part of her was shocked, but another part simply felt content, as if of course it worked. "We need to tell Kendra."

"Right. Yes, we do." He didn't release her hand, and they headed together for the stairs. Her head was still spinning, and she felt as if she could float down the still-damp steps without needing to touch them. With her free hand, she held on to the handrail. Every step, she glanced at him.

I should say something. About the kiss. About him. About us.

She should tell him it wasn't about the portal, that it meant something to her—obviously it did or the portal wouldn't have opened. *An epiphany.* She'd felt a change within her, which wouldn't have happened if she hadn't fallen out of love with Ethan . . . and into love with Jack. And in love with this place. And its magic.

A very nice change.

She wondered if she'd scare him off if she used the word *love* this quickly. She wondered if he thought it was just about the portal. She wondered if it had been just about the inn for him, or if the kiss had felt as magical to him as it did to her.

Jack released her hand and sloshed into the sitting room. Puddles were everywhere, soaking the rugs and covering the floor in a watery sheen. All the towels he'd left were soggy lumps. "Kendra?"

She hadn't stayed outside, where she could drip harmlessly on gravel and grass. Instead, Kendra was curled, morose, in a chair. Her arms were wrapped around her knees, and seawater was sloughing off her.

Calisa wanted to say, *You can stop your temper tantrum now,* except that wasn't fair, since she had no way to know how seriously the sea witch needed to return home. She cut straight to the point: "Your portal is open."

Gasping, Kendra shot to her feet—seawater sprayed everywhere in a fine mist—and then she bolted toward the stairs, hitching her skirts up so she could run faster.

Calisa heard a cry of relief—and then silence.

Jack grinned, and then his smile faded as he surveyed the sitting room. "Guess I need to figure out how to get saltwater stains out of upholstery. Fresh water? Carpet soap? Probably should start with sopping up the new puddles . . ." Carrying the wet towels, he trotted out of the room as he talked and returned with his arms full of fresh, dry towels.

Sure, yes, of course, they should clean the sitting room—the rugs were soggy with seawater—but . . . "*Or* we can try to open more broken doors. See if Auntie Zee is behind any of them." She thought of his father and wondered which door he was behind—but Auntie Zee herself hadn't been able to reopen that portal. First find Auntie Zee. That felt achievable. And necessary.

"Oh, whoa, yes! Auntie Zee!"

She almost smiled. He'd been as flustered as she was.

"Think of how happy she's going to be when she learns that you inherited her ability," Jack said. "She might even forgive us for blatantly violating every single rule she's hammered into me since my dad and I came here." Using a towel, he began excitedly and haphazardly dabbing at the seawater. "But if she's behind a closed portal, she could be anywhere. Where do we even start?"

Calisa saw a flicker out of the corner of her eye, and she glanced out the window. The stone statue had drawn closer to the porch. She must have been eavesdropping—the window was open, and Jack and Calisa hadn't kept their voices down. She could have heard every word. Could she be trying to enter? Did she want to help?

Trusting her instincts, Calisa crossed to the front door and opened it. "Do you know where Auntie Zee is?" She deliberately turned away, watching through the sitting room entryway as Jack spread towels over the damp rug to soak up the excess water. On the lobby wall, the smoky mirror was dark.

When she turned around, the statue's head was dipped down. *Yes.*

Oh wow. Why didn't I think of this sooner? She knew why she hadn't: living statues weren't supposed to exist. Asking one for help just wasn't something she'd normally think to do. "Jack?" Calisa called.

Dropping a towel onto a chair, Jack trotted over to her.

"She knows where Auntie Zee is." To the statue, she said, "Where? Can you point?" To Jack, she said, "Turn around. She'll answer if we aren't looking."

He turned around with Calisa.

A second later, Calisa peeked back at the statue. "She's pointing!" Straight behind them, toward the kitchen. "One of the cabinets? The pantry? The supply closets? Washer-dryer closet? Do you want to come inside and show us?"

"She can't do the stairs," Jack said. "It's the pedestal."

Her ankles flowed into the slab of granite at her base. Of course she couldn't do stairs. She'd need to be carried. "Would it be okay if we helped you inside?" Calisa asked.

Both of them turned away, then looked back.

The statue had inclined her head *yes*.

Together, huffing, Calisa and Jack hoisted the statue inside the foyer and set her down. She was far heavier than she looked, and Calisa wondered where she'd come from—had she been made this way? Who'd made her? How and why had she come here? All more questions than they had time for now.

She turned away, and when she looked back, the statue was pointing again, more clearly, toward the kitchen. They hauled her into the kitchen and positioned her facing the stove. From there, she pointed into the corridor of supply closets. Again, they dragged her forward.

Finally, she pointed at a single door: the third closet on the left.

Calisa grinned. This was it! They were going to find Auntie Zee!

She swung in front of Jack and kissed him again. He kissed her back, sweetly and deeply, his arms cradling around her.

In a murmur, he asked, "Do you think we need to kiss every time you open a portal?"

"Is that a problem?" she asked, between kisses.

"Definitely no, but"—he kissed her again—"you already unlocked your power. Your mom implied that was a"—another kiss—"onetime thing." Now he kissed her neck, light kisses like a hummingbird drinking nectar. She felt her heart flutter like it had wings. "You should be able to open portals"—more kisses—"on your own now."

"Are you interrupting this with logic?"

"Um, no?" He kissed her lips again.

This time, when they broke apart, Calisa stepped back with her hand on his chest. "Stand near me and think nice thoughts." Her head felt as if she were swimming, and she swayed a little.

He was right: Mom-Kate had said that it took an epiphany to unlock the power, but there was nothing about needing an epiphany each time she tried, so these kisses were, theoretically, wholly unnecessary.

I regret nothing.

She approached the closet door and opened it onto shelves of folded sheets and quilts. Clearing her mind as best she could, she ran her fingers over the doorframe, touching every inch as her mom had instructed her.

She then closed the closet door.

Out of the corner of her eye, she noticed that Steve had waddled into the hallway. He must have come in through the front door—they'd left it open when they hauled the statue inside. He plopped down next to her and nibbled nonchalantly on his hind talons.

"If it doesn't work . . ." Jack began.

"It will work," Calisa said. "It will *open*." As she said the word, she pulled open the linen closet door, and a silvery shimmer swirled within the doorframe.

"Oh wow," Jack said behind her.

"There's no guarantee Auntie Zee is on the other side," Calisa cautioned him. "The statue could be wrong." She glanced back at the statue, who had put her hands over her eyes while they'd been kissing.

She's not wrong. There were windows everywhere, and the statue was always watching. She could have seen Auntie Zee walk through this door. Feeling hope bubble up, Calisa grinned.

She held out her hand, Jack took it, and together they stepped into the portal. Colors blurred around them, and all sensation vanished except the feel of his hand in hers—and then they were through. She inhaled salt air before her eyes adjusted to the swath of blue.

On the other side, they stood on a cliff covered in seagrass. It overlooked the ocean, broad and blue and beautiful. Wind blew her hair into her face and against her cheeks. She thought it looked a bit like Ireland, or it would have if it weren't for the very obvious sea serpent out in the waves.

"Is that . . ." Jack began.

"I think so. Do you think it prefers to be called a sea serpent or a sea dragon?" Calisa asked, eyes wide. She watched its silvery form as it dove between the waves. She couldn't hazard a guess as to how large it was—at least the size of a cruise liner.

She saw a flicker out of the corner of her eye. She glanced to her left as Steve settled on a rock. He lifted a wing as if in a wave. "You weren't supposed to come with us," Calisa said.

He let out a little burst of flame.

"Yes, very nice, but you should go back," she said. "We don't know if this is safe."

Steve ignored her.

Out in the ocean, the sea dragon breached and then dove into a wave. Its tail flicked toward the sky. "All right," Calisa told Steve, "but stay close, okay?"

Opposite the portal was a winding dirt path that led down toward the shore. Nestled between the rocks below was a village, just a few homes clustered around a dock. "It looks like our world," Jack said. "But if this is our world, then why—"

"Not our world," Calisa corrected. "Sea dragon."

"Oh, right. Do you think Auntie Zee is down there?"

"Only one way to find out. Come on, Steve." She patted her shoulder, and the winged lizard flew up and settled on it. He wrapped his tail around her neck like a scaly necklace.

They began walking down the path. The wind blew sea mist off the ocean, and Calisa felt coated in a thin layer of salt, not unlike the upholstery in Auntie Zee's sitting room.

Halfway down, she felt a sudden wave of dizziness. She reached out to steady herself, and Jack caught her arm. "You okay?" he asked.

"Just . . . one sec . . ."

It faded. She took a deep breath of salty sea air.

On her shoulder, Steve chirped worriedly.

"I'm fine," she said. "Let's keep going." She didn't know what that was about. Maybe they were at a different altitude here? Or maybe there was something in the air that was messing with her balance. Jack seemed fine, though. She shook her head to clear it and marched onward. In a few minutes, they reached the edge of the village.

At the edge of town was an empty house: broken windows, a brick chimney covered in lichen, and a front door that swung wide in the wind. Inside she could see an overturned table and a thick layer of dust, as well as an old-fashioned TV with a shattered screen.

The second house looked lived-in. It had an herb border in front that looked well cared for (after all their yard work, she could tell immediately that someone had weeded these plants), as well as a pair of boots next to the door, but the windows were dark and there was no sign of movement.

The third building was larger and had dirty white walls, heavy shutters that framed the windows, and a trellis with roses so deeply red they looked black. It was three stories tall and boasted an array of antennae on its roof between its brick chimneys. An inn, maybe? Or a restaurant? It had a stone sign planted in front of it with no words but an image of a turtle. Warm amber light glowed in the windows, and Calisa heard the buzz of voices within.

Calling something unintelligible to someone inside, a woman came out backward. She was carrying a basket on her hip, and she turned as soon as she was through the door—and froze. She stared at them, and they stared at her. Her eyes were black, her hair was white, and instead of skin she was covered in silvery scales, not unlike the sea dragon. Without a word, she darted back inside the building.

“Okay, so they’re not overly friendly here,” Calisa said.

Close to her ear, she heard a rumbling from Steve’s stomach vibrating against her neck and wondered if that was his version of a growl.

“Should we leave?” Jack asked.

“Auntie Zee could be in there.” Or she could have passed through. Someone in this village might have seen her and know where she is. “We have to try to talk to them.”

“She literally saw us and fled.”

“We could try a different house?”

Before they could decide what to do, the woman rushed out again, this time pulling a man with her. He also had silvery scales, as well as a white beard that was so fine and wispy that it looked to be made of silk strands. They halted and stared at Jack and Calisa. Pointing at them, the woman flapped her hands and began whispering urgently to the man.

Calisa stepped forward and cleared her throat. “We’re looking for an older woman, my great-aunt. Everyone calls her Auntie Zee. We think she might—”

Staring at Jack, the man interrupted. “You’re right. He looks just like Thomas.”

Thomas? Who—

Beside her, Jack went as still as the statue. “You know my father?”

Exhaling so loudly that she sounded like a gust of wind, the silvery-scaled woman pointed toward the water. She had light webbing between her fingers. “He’s on the sea.”

Calisa turned to look out at the white-crested waves. The

clouds had gathered above them, and it looked as if it was about to burst into rain. The horizon was streaked with gray and purple. For all she knew, that was how it always looked here.

Jack's father?

Was this why the statue had pointed to this door? Not because of Auntie Zee, but because of Jack's father, Thomas? Could this have been the door he'd gone through, the one that Auntie Zee hadn't been able to open? Her heart pounded so fast that it felt ready to fly out of her rib cage. She couldn't imagine how Jack must be feeling—the hope leaping inside him so hard it had to hurt.

"He's been missing. . . ." Jack's voice cracked. He swallowed hard, as if the words were lodging in his throat. "He was supposed to be gone three days. It's been three years. We opened the portal. . . . She opened it. . . . This is Calisa. I'm Jack, Thomas's son. What do you mean he's on the sea? Doing what? When will he be back?"

"He'll be back with the tide," the man said. "He's taken to fishing. Has quite a knack for it. Rigged up a better kind of net with a pulley. He's been talking about designing a new kind of lobster trap. You're his son?"

Jack nodded, as if unable to speak.

"Extraordinary."

"He'll be so pleased," the woman said, pressing her hands to her heart. "Overjoyed. You cannot imagine what he's gone through, thinking he'd never see you again."

"I'm sorry," Calisa said, "but who are you?"

"I'm Vela, and this is my brother Enkle," the woman said. "We run the Seaturtle Lodging House." She waved at the building behind them. "You can stay here, have a bite to eat, while you wait for him to return."

"How long will it be?" Jack asked. "Is there a way to tell him I'm here?"

Enkle squinted at the cloudy sky. "It's not advised."

Vela said kindly, "Your father, when he arrived . . . You should know he tried desperately to return to you. He journeyed . . ."

"So far. So very far," Enkle said.

"Beyond what is known." Vela gestured broadly at the cliffs and beyond. "He was gone for months at a time, searching, always searching . . . always returning when his search failed."

Calisa watched Jack. He was drinking in every word, blinking hard to fight back tears. His hands kept curling and uncurling into fists, and she wanted to wrap her arms around him, but she didn't. She was ready, though, if he needed her. This had to feel overwhelming—to find out now that what Jack had feared, that his father hadn't been able to find another portal, was true. . . .

"After failing again and again, he returned to us and resolved to wait here," Vela said. "He believed the portal would reopen. He never quit believing."

"I confess we did not," Enkle said. "We thought he'd baked in the sun too long. . . ."

"Or drank too much of the sea," Vela said.

"Or stared into the eyes of a sea snake," Enkle said.

Jack looked dazed.

"Sea snake," Calisa repeated lightly, eyes still on Jack, ready to be there if he needed her. She couldn't tell if he was about to fall apart from fear or explode from hope. "I admit I was rooting for 'sea dragon.' It's a cooler name."

"Our dragons fly, not swim," Enkle said. "It wouldn't make sense to give them both the same name. You should know that, given the little dragon you carry." He held a finger out toward Steve.

Catlike, or more accurately, dragon-like, Steve sniffed it and then let out a puff of smoke.

Calisa stared at Steve. "Little dragon." In retrospect, it was obvious. She'd just been too busy and too distracted to properly think it through. "Okay, that tracks." To Jack, she said, "Told you Draco fit him."

Jack shrugged. "I still think he's a Steve."

To Enkle, Calisa asked, "Is Steve from here?" She twisted to look again at the little dragon on her shoulder. He'd quit rumbling once Vela and Enkle had started speaking to them. "Is this your home?"

He didn't reply, of course.

"Doesn't look like one of ours," Enkle said. "Ours aren't that small."

Calisa wanted to ask a thousand more questions about dragons and sea serpents and their world and why they didn't have other portals and what their lives were like. *Another time.* "Jack's dad—do you have a way to contact him and tell him to come back to shore?"

"We don't know how long the portal will stay open," Jack explained.

He's right. It had closed on Jack's father, and Auntie Zee had been unable to reopen it. What if it closed again, trapping them inside? She hadn't considered that possibility when they'd walked through, but then she hadn't known this was *that* portal. A shiver ran through her. She thought of her moms and how worried they'd be. "We can't stay."

"Please," Jack said.

Both Vela and Enkle looked alarmed. "Of course," Vela said. "We should have thought of that. You can't linger." She nodded at Enkle. "We'll sound the horn. Your father will come."

CHAPTER TWENTY-THREE

As they followed the two silvery villagers to the end of the dock, Calisa shot another glance at Jack. She couldn't imagine everything he must be feeling right now—so close to a reunion with his father. She wondered if she should step back, let him have the moment to himself.

"Are you okay?" Calisa asked. "Do you want to be alone? I could return to the portal. I'll wait for you there, if you want this moment with your dad."

He was staring straight out at the water.

He took her hand.

On her shoulder, Steve let out a tiny chirp, as if he wanted to say he was here too.

Vela and Enkle halted at the end of the dock beside a curled horn. It was taller than Enkle, and it curved out over the water. The mouthpiece was framed in gold, and the horn itself looked like mother-of-pearl. Calisa wondered what sort of creature it had come from. She didn't ask, just filed it away to ask later.

It occurred to her that she was collecting far more than a summer's worth of questions. Every person she met, every realm she visited, led to a dozen more.

"This horn summons all the fishers to the dock. It's used for storm warnings, as well as the start of festivals," Vela explained. "If we blow it, your father and the others will know to return to dock."

"Then blow it," Calisa said. "Please. Jack and his father have waited long enough."

Jack seemed unable to speak. He was clutching her hand hard.

Vela and Enkle exchanged glances, and she wondered why they were hesitating. She had no way of knowing how long the portal would stay open. Didn't they understand that?

"He won't be the only one to return to dock," Enkle explained.

"We'll apologize to the other fishers," Calisa said. She'd blow the horn herself if she had to. Jack deserved to see his father, and his father needed to know they were here—and then they all needed to get back before the portal closed again. Surely that was worth missing some fishing time. She could pay them all back for the lost fish in chocolate cake. Or whatever.

Vela shook her head. "You don't understand. It won't be just the fishers who come." She exchanged another glance with Enkle. "Thomas wasn't afraid at the first horn blow. Perhaps these two won't be afraid either. Look what she carries on her shoulder as if it were a tame pet."

"His name is Steve," Calisa told them again.

“See, she’s even named it,” Vela said. “She’s brave enough, and he only wishes to be reunited with his father. All will be well.”

Enkle said to Calisa and Jack, “If you are calm, it can be beautiful.”

Okay, this was sounding ominous. Maybe they weren’t worried about lost fishing time. Calisa began to feel a tickle of nervousness. She noticed her hand was sweaty, squeezed by Jack. “What can? What’s going to happen? Who’s coming?”

But Vela had already placed her lips on the mouthpiece. She blew, and a low note unrolled across the waves. The water rippled as the sound spread.

The note seemed to grow louder, echoing like thunder in the belly of a storm—it echoed off the cliff faces, and it was reflected back by the sea.

Vela stepped away from the horn.

“Now what?” Calisa asked.

Steve let out a nervous chirp.

“Now? We wait,” Enkle said. He crossed his hands in front of him. Vela stood beside him, her hands also crossed. They both looked out at the waves.

Calisa scanned the ocean, looking for ships. She wondered how far out the fishers sailed, as well as what kind of fish they caught. What was in these waters? They’d mentioned a lobster trap, which indicated they at least had crustaceans in common. Unless their word for lobster actually meant an entirely different creature, and the portal magic was just doing its best to translate. She didn’t know if . . .

The sea began to churn.

A tentacle flailed out of the waves, followed by a second tentacle. "Whoa," she breathed.

"Uh, Calisa . . ." Jack said, strained. "Is that a . . ."

She was fairly certain the word was *kraken,* no translation needed.

Beyond the kraken, she saw a silvery sea snake, perhaps the same one they'd seen from the cliffs, swim closer to shore, winding through the waves. It was at least twice the length of a bus. A second sea snake, golden in color, followed. It was even larger, and when it raised its head out of the water, Calisa saw rows of swordlike teeth. Soon, the sea around the dock was filled with massive creatures.

Vela and Enkle continued to stand side by side, motionless, with their hands crossed, looking out across the water. Steve buried his face into Calisa's hair.

Calisa tried to convince her heart to stop galloping as the sea around the dock continued to fill with sea monsters. The waves battered at the pilings, and water sloshed onto the boards. What if one of the tentacles smacked down on the dock? It would break it. A single sea snake could swallow it, if it wanted to.

But it didn't seem to want to.

The monsters swarmed, but they didn't attack.

It occurred to her after a few more moments of not being eaten that the sea monsters looked as if they were dancing. Not to music, but within the waves. They wove between each other, the snakes winding into elaborate braids that then unraveled.

The tentacles undulated, causing the waves to pulse against the current.

"They come," Enkle said.

"Steady. You may find this startling," Vela warned them.

More startling than dancing sea monsters?

The fishers looked, at first, like figures standing on an island—an island that was moving toward the dock at high speed. But what was propelling them? They were scurrying over a rounded surface that looked like an inverted boat. As it drew closer, Calisa saw the "boat" lift its head out of the water.

"That," Jack said in a strangled voice, "is a very large turtle."

It was. A turtle. And extremely large. It carried at least a dozen figures on its back as it swam toward the dock. When it was closer, Calisa saw its face, as gray as granite and as wrinkled as Auntie Zee's. Its eyes were a swirl of black and gray, reminding Calisa of the portals.

The sea snakes and krakens parted to allow the vast turtle to approach the dock. Calisa noticed that near the tail a contraption was lashed to the enormous shell—it had pulleys and netting like on a fishing boat back home. Beside it was a man without scales.

Jack lurched forward. "Dad!"

Vela and Enkle caught him on the edge of the dock as one of the kraken snapped a tentacle up. "Calm," Vela cautioned in a soft, steady voice. "You don't want to flail like a fish. Accidents have happened."

Jack froze and just stared.

Behind them, Calisa watched as the island-like turtle swam close to the dock, and the fisherfolk clambered off the shell. "What's the emergency?" one of them asked.

"Who's this? Another scaleless one? Hey, Thomas, this one of yours?" a woman called.

The man by the netting held his hand over his eyes to shield them from the sun. "What did you say? Is it an emergency or a festival?"

Jack seemed frozen. So Calisa waved. "Hello!" she called. "Hi, Jack's dad!"

"He's lost his glasses," Jack said in a strained voice.

But it didn't matter. Thomas was climbing over the shell, and the other fishers—who *had* seen Jack, recognized the resemblance, and put two and two together—were all helping him along, offering him a hand, half shoving him over the shell, until Jack's father reached the dock and slid the final bit of distance to dismount from the shell.

Now he could see his son.

The two of them stared at each other.

And then they were crying and hugging and talking so fast that the words spilled over each other, churning like the waves in the monster-filled sea.

Soon, the shoreline was filled with celebrants. Someone called for a feast, and within half an hour, tables were set up and piled high with breads, jams, fruits, and other treats that Calisa didn't recognize. Musicians hauled instruments out of their houses, while others knocked on doors, calling everyone outside for a celebration: a father and son reunited!

"Shouldn't we be getting back to the portal?" Calisa whispered to Jack.

"If my dad's not worried . . ."

His dad had been the one trapped here for three years. She supposed he knew far more about how the portals worked than she did. She told herself to relax and celebrate. This was an unexpected victory.

Off the shore, the sea monsters careened through the waves, while the villagers tossed them fish heads and fish tails and other bits of leftover food, as if they were feeding sea gulls at the beach.

In front of the lodging house, one villager played a three-pronged flute, while another beat the rhythm on a drum set made of barrels and shells. A third played an instrument that resembled a cello but only had three strings. Others took turns singing—some well and some not so well. Sitting on a bench with Jack and Calisa, Jack's dad joined in on one of the songs, and the tune was so catchy that Calisa hummed along until she'd heard enough that she was able to jump in on the chorus.

When the song ended, Thomas leaned toward them. "I'm sorry. I know you're Jack's friend, but who are you? And is that a dragon on your shoulder? I've never seen one that small."

Calisa noted he had the same eyes as his son, though his were red-rimmed and had wrinkles that curled around them. "I'm Auntie Zee's grandniece, Calisa. And this is Steve. He's . . .

a guest at the inn, sort of. Or he came with a guest. He seems to like me."

He squinted at her. "I remember you. You were"—he gestured to about half her height—"smaller the last time I saw you. Little Cali. Jack, you remember, don't you?"

"Hmm?" Jack was distracted by a plate of shrimp speckled with spices.

"The two of you got into mischief." Thomas laughed at the memory. "Little Cali wanted to climb her first tree, and you decided to help her. But there were no trees that were good for climbing near the house—pines and birches are lousy climbing trees, but there was a maple tree in the back garden with potential, except its lowest branches were still too high. Calisa here had the bright idea to reach it from the roof of the greenhouse. . . ."

Jack looked at her, a smile on his lips. "That was *you*?"

"What happened?" Calisa asked. "I don't remember."

"Jack found you a ladder, and instead of leaning it against the tree . . ."

"The idea was to climb onto the roof of the greenhouse and then jump onto the tree," Jack said. "It seemed sensible at the time."

Calisa winced. "Which of us fell?"

"Neither, actually," Thomas said. "But you did get stuck."

"And we were too embarrassed to call for help, or too certain we'd get in trouble," Jack said. "So we stayed up in the tree until after the sun set, long after, when our parents noticed we hadn't come in for dinner and went out to look for us."

Huh. She had a vague memory of that—being in a tree with a friend while the stars came out overhead. She'd assumed it was a tree. There weren't trees like that in Brooklyn. Or so many stars. "I'd decided you were an imaginary friend," Calisa said to Jack.

"Very real," he said.

"I'm glad." She smiled at him.

"How long did Auntie Zee say she could keep the portal open?" Thomas said as he took three honey-coated pastries from a tray. He passed two to Jack and Calisa. "We don't want to risk cutting it close if she isn't back to full strength."

"She didn't open it," Jack said. "Calisa did."

Pastry frozen halfway to his mouth, he looked alarmed. "You? You can open portals?"

"I've done it twice now." Calisa felt all the worry she'd shoved away crash into her like a wave on the shore. She glanced up at the cliffs, but she couldn't see the portal from here.

Thomas surged to his feet. "Then you don't know how long you can hold it open."

She jumped up too, and Steve chirped querulously from beside a tray of shellfish.

"This realm is far from ours," Thomas said. "It takes extraordinary strength to hold a gateway across this distance. If you don't know yet how strong you are—we need to leave. Right now." He hastily whispered to his friends and then hugged several of the villagers.

Her heart thumping harder, she wanted to drag him and Jack away as quickly as possible, but she tried to be patient. He'd lived among them for three years. He deserved a moment.

But if he thought the portal could close . . . *I don't want to live here for three years. Or at all.*

While Thomas finished his goodbyes, Calisa scooped up Steve and deposited him onto her shoulder. He had a crawfish half shoved into his jaws. He swallowed it quickly and strained his neck toward the tray of food. "No, we're going home," she told him.

As another round of food was brought out on oar-like platters, they finally slipped away from the festivities. Carrying Steve, Calisa hurried after Jack and Thomas as they wound up the dirt trail toward the portal. She had to jog to keep up. She put one hand on Steve to be sure he stayed attached. She was not going to leave him behind.

Puffing as he climbed with long strides, Thomas was saying to Jack, "I tried to return, but there's no nexus here, or if there is, it's too well hidden. I couldn't even find a hint of one. I bribed travelers to keep an ear out. Chased after rumors. In the end, though, there wasn't anything to find. So I returned here. Tried to start over, build a life." He glanced back down at the village, and Calisa saw a flash of emotions: sorrow, fear, hope, regret, guilt. "It's a good place filled with good people."

"You'll be able to come back and visit here," Calisa said, "now that the portal's open."

"Auntie Zee must have been so pleased to finally have a successor." Thomas was trying to sound cheerful, conversational, but Calisa could hear the worry threaded through his voice, and it made her heart pound faster as if it were shouting, *Hurry, hurry, hurry!*

"Actually, she doesn't know yet," Jack said. "She's . . . been gone."

Thomas's smile dropped. "What do you mean 'gone'?"

"She was supposed to be back days ago," Calisa said, keeping a hand on Steve. "But no one's seen her in any of her usual supply places. . . ."

"Then we have to hurry." Thomas picked up the pace to a near run.

In minutes, they were back at the portal. It still shimmered, and Calisa felt a bolt of relief shoot through her like lightning. It looked exactly the same as when they'd left it. She wondered if it would show any sign it was about to collapse, fading or wavering, or just vanish like a popped bubble.

Glancing one more time at his home away from home, Thomas hesitated. The music from the fishing village rose toward them, filled with the sound of his friends talking and laughing. A flute soared in a melody high above the singers, while the drumbeat matched the rhythm of the waves crashing on the shore.

He then looked at his son.

And he walked through. Jack followed immediately after.

With one more glance at the sea writhing with dancing serpents, Calisa stepped through into the inn. Steve clung to her shoulder as the iridescence folded around them.

In less than a breath, they were back in the Faraway Inn.

"All this time away," Jack said to his father, "did you find what you were looking for?"

Thomas looked around him like he'd woken from a dream

and wasn't sure if this was real life yet. His eyes swept over the closets, the laundry machines, the window with the view of pine trees. "Yes," he said at last.

"What were you looking for?" Calisa asked.

"A remedy. To save the inn. To save Auntie Zee."

CHAPTER TWENTY-FOUR

"Save her?" Calisa asked. "From what?"

Thomas scowled at the portal that had consumed three years of his life and didn't answer.

Calisa wasn't certain whether to repeat the question or let him have a moment to cope with his obvious trauma. But she had to know: Save Auntie Zee from what? She knew the inn had to be rescued—from neglect, from entropy, from bankruptcy and closure and failure, but what was wrong with Auntie Zee?

Eyes still glued to the swirl, he demanded, "How long has Auntie Zee been missing?"

Jack answered, "She's been disappearing for longer and longer since you've been gone, but this is the longest stretch by far. Nearly a week."

Calisa shook her head. It didn't make sense. Why would Auntie Zee take off just when the inn needed her most?

Especially when Jack needed her? Had she been trying to find Jack's father? Or just escaping her responsibilities because they'd become too overwhelming? *What if Jack was right and she doesn't want to be found? Ever?*

"Has she explained why?" Thomas asked.

Jack shook his head. "You know her."

Thomas snorted. "True."

But I don't, Calisa wanted to say. She looked from Jack to his father and back again. Jack was staring at his father as if he was afraid he'd vanish if he quit looking at him for even a second. She wasn't sure he'd even blinked since they'd been reunited.

On her shoulder, the little dragon shifted his wings, and his talons dug into her shirt. She was certain she'd have holes in the fabric, but she didn't care. She reached up to scratch Steve's neck. "Save Auntie Zee from what?" she repeated louder.

"From time," Thomas said.

That wasn't an answer.

He clarified. Sort of. "From the decay of her portal magic due to the passage of time."

Calisa closed the door with the swirling iridescent portal that led to the sea serpent world. On an impulse, she cracked it open again—still active. She closed it. She didn't know what he meant by the decay of her magic, but that was secondary to the need to find her. "Okay, what portal would she most likely have gone through?"

"None of them," Thomas answered immediately.

He was wrong about that. They'd searched every inch of

the inn. She wasn't anywhere nearby, unless she'd run off into the forest like Melidor, but Calisa couldn't picture that.

"How do you know that?" Jack asked.

"I know her," Thomas said. "If I had to guess, I'd say she's been trying and failing to rescue me. She's exhausted herself. She's here in the inn, trying to recover, trying to find her way back to herself, embarrassed by her failure, unwilling to admit her weakness, even though I've told her time and again there's no shame in not being superhuman." He pivoted and stalked toward the kitchen. "She's never liked to admit she can't do something, never wanted to ask for help, never considered that she's—"

Jack scurried after him and nearly crashed into his father when he suddenly halted. Behind Jack, Calisa peeked into the kitchen to see what had startled Thomas.

The statue stood in front of the sink, her hands clasped over her heart as if she was hoping hard and her eyes squeezed shut as if she was afraid to see.

Calisa wondered if Thomas knew she was alive and aware and—

"Evela." His voice was an exhale.

"She was the one who helped us find you," Jack said. "We wouldn't have even known which portal to try. In fact, we thought she meant—"

"Close your eyes," Thomas ordered Jack and Calisa.

Calisa obeyed. She waited for him to tell them to open their eyes, but he said nothing. She heard the soft murmuring of Thomas's voice, too quiet for her to make out the words. He fell silent, and she peeked one eye open.

The statue, motionless, had her arms around Thomas, and his were wrapped around her in a tight embrace. Her head was inclined against his shoulder.

"Your eyes are open," Thomas accused.

It wasn't a question. "Sorry. I didn't—"

The floor suddenly tilted oddly, and her knees felt flimsy, as if her joints were watery. She put her hand out against the kitchen wall.

"Calisa?" She heard concern in Jack's voice. She tried to turn her head to look at him, and her knees buckled. Steve squawked in alarm. She felt the brush of his wings on her cheek.

And then she saw Jack moving toward her, but he was tilted.

A pool of darkness was rising up from the bottom of her vision. "Jack—"

She felt the dragon's talons pierce her shoulders as he squawked wildly. The floor loomed sideways, filling her vision, and the wooden birds on the kitchen clock all turned their heads to look at her . . . and then everything was soft darkness.

Calisa woke in Jack's arms, which was lovely, but why? She stared up at the kitchen rafters, admired the lack of cobwebs, and thought that this was a strange place for a nap.

"It worked," Jack said. "She's awake."

She blinked as Thomas's face came into view behind Jack's. He peered down at her. "Luckily, she only needed a drop. You wore yourself out, couldn't you tell?"

"I . . . what? Did I faint?"

"Worse," Thomas said grimly. "You drained your power. Only one way to restore it, and you apparently haven't been taught how. Well, only one way *aside* from the extremely rare flower that I went in search of. . . . You're lucky that I found it, and you, in turn, found me." He shook his head before she could speak. "Auntie Zee will explain everything. For now, *don't* open any more portals until you know how to heal yourself magically."

"Heal myself?" None of this made sense. Her head was throbbing, and she had a faint taste of cinnamon in her mouth. She licked her lips. It wasn't quite cinnamon. It was sharper. "What did you give me?" Her throat felt scratched, and her voice sounded as if the syllables had been rubbed over a cheese grater. She swallowed and then winced. Whatever it was had *not* gone down smoothly.

"Felitris juice," Thomas said. "It's what I went into that realm for. Very rare. Extracted from a flower that only grows under ridiculously specific conditions that no one's been able to replicate. It's the only known substance that can restore an equally rare power like yours."

"But what happened to Calisa?" Jack said. "Why did she collapse like that?" His arms were still around her, solid and comforting and warm and nice.

Exactly what I want to ask. Her tongue felt thick, though, and she felt as if her thoughts were swimming in goo. Her left shoulder ached, and she wondered where Steve had gone. He'd been on her when she'd collapsed. She hoped she hadn't fallen on him. Tilting her head back, Calisa scanned the kitchen—ah, there. Steve was perched on one of the rafters above the sink, looking down at her with worried eyes. His wings were spread wide, and smoke seeped out of his mouth. She smiled so he'd know she was okay.

The smoke dissipated.

She wondered how hot his flame was and if he could control it yet. *If he could, I could toast s'mores.* A little giggle escaped her lips, and then she wondered if she'd hit her head. It was so difficult to focus. *Ooh, or make a real crème brûlée with the crispy caramel top. Yum.*

Thomas was talking. "It's draining to open portals. Literally, it drains you. The farther the realm from ours, the more tiring it is to maintain a doorway. I wasn't running errands for the inn all those times I left. I was looking for felitris juice, to help Auntie Zee replenish her power faster. She's weaker than she used to be. It's age. Comes for us all, and Auntie Zee has handled it better than most, but even she with her boundless energy isn't immune to it."

Her eyes blurred, and his words faded into a fuzzy murmur.

His voice became crisp again: ". . . She told me that she could only hold it open for two days while I searched. It should have been plenty of time—I knew precisely where to find the flower, and she'd deliberately opened the portal close to its location—but it was raining when I emerged, and the path down to the shore was slick with mud. I slipped. Over the cliff. I broke my leg and knocked myself out. By the time the villagers had nursed me back to health, the portal had closed. She must have been too weak to reopen it. It's a very distant realm."

"I opened it," Calisa said, her words slow as she tried to form them with her gummy-feeling mouth. She touched her left shoulder. There were holes in the fabric, and she felt wetness. She pulled her fingers back and saw blood. Startled, Steve had dug his talons into her when she'd fainted. She remembered that. "Ow."

Kneeling next to her, Jack pressed a wet paper towel to her cuts. She winced.

"You're young, full of untapped strength, but you still have limits," Thomas said. "Looks like you hit yours. That realm is very far, so it's not a surprise. You said that Auntie Zee has been missing more and more? I believe she must have been trying to reopen that very portal, exactly as I feared, but lacked the strength to succeed. Each time, she exhausted herself more, until at last she didn't have the strength to turn back."

She tried to focus, but it was so hard to string his words together. She felt as if they were swimming in her head. Whatever medicine he'd given her hadn't cured her perfectly. She did remember that the last time they saw Auntie Zee, Jack had been upset about his father.

He stood up. "She usually likes the sitting room."

"The sitting room has been damp lately," Jack said. "And we haven't seen Auntie Zee in days. I told you, we've looked everywhere. Even through the portals." To Calisa, he said, "I don't know that you should stand up yet."

Using Jack like a ladder, Calisa was struggling to rise. He helped her balance. Once she was back on two feet, she felt steadier. "I'm fine."

Above her Steve warbled.

She looked up at him again and repeated, "I'm fine."

Thomas was already marching out of the kitchen.

Jack kept his arm around Calisa as they hobbled after him. She wondered if the statue, Evela, was trailing behind them, and she intentionally didn't turn around, so that Evela could follow. She also had about a thousand questions about the statue and her relationship with Jack's dad, as well as a thousand questions about Auntie Zee, the portals, the magic, and the whatever juice. *And me. I never faint.* She had never felt this weak before. It was like someone had sucked all the energy out of every one of her muscles and left them floppy.

Ahead of them, Thomas checked the dining room, then the sitting room, and last the library. Calisa paused to sag against the wall in the lobby. Jack stayed with her. Beside them, the shadowy mirror swirled.

"Hey," Calisa said to the mirror, "do you know where Auntie Zee is?"

Always.

Wait. *What?* Really? "And you didn't think to tell us while we were running around looking for her? For days?" Calisa demanded. She tried to peel herself off the wall to glare at the mirror, but she felt too wobbly. She clutched both Jack and the wall, bracing herself. "Why didn't you say anything?"

Not my problem.

She glared at the shifting shadows within the mirror. She was tempted to lift it off the wall and shake it. It had known all along? While they were panicking and worrying? And Kendra was nearly flooding the inn? "It will be your problem too if the inn closes, you—"

From the library, Thomas said, "Ah, there you are, Zee. Jack and Cali had me worried."

Auntie Zee! But . . . they'd passed the library on their way to the portal. She would have noticed if Auntie Zee were just chilling on the window seat with a book. Also, why hadn't Auntie Zee spoken up when they were hauling the statue through the inn? Or when Kendra was soaking everything? She had to have noticed that they'd been in the middle of an emergency.

Calisa, with Jack's help, hobbled forward. Leaning against the doorframe, she peered into the library. "Huh," Jack said. "Um, Dad?"

There was no Auntie Zee.

Only the elderly white cat, Portia, curled on the window seat.

Calisa looked at the cat.

The cat looked back at her.

She couldn't be . . . "You're not implying that Auntie Zee is . . . a *cat* . . . Are you?" It felt like a ridiculous question, but given all that she'd seen . . .

"No, of course not," Jack said immediately.

Thomas shrugged. "She is what she is."

“What?” Jack said. “Portia? She . . . what?”

Calisa looked over her shoulder. The mirror was only smoke, wordless and unhelpful, but the statue, Evela, had followed them as far as the lobby.

Her head was inclined: *Yes.*

CHAPTER TWENTY-FIVE

Okay.

Auntie Zee was the cat.

Was that really any more odd than any of the other magic she'd seen?

Yes. It is. A lot odder. "Auntie Zee?" Calisa said, squatting in front of the cat. "Is it really you? Um, meow once for yes, twice for no?"

The cat began to lick her paw.

"That's her," Thomas said. "She takes that form to recover her strength—it's what enables her to heal and recharge—but she must have been too worn out to change back. She warned me once that could happen, if she overextended herself. One of the reasons I needed to find the remedy." He knelt beside her and lifted the medicine to her face. "I found it, Zee. I'm sorry I couldn't bring it to you earlier. But I found it."

She lowered her paw and licked the medicine from the dropper.

Calisa leaned against Jack and whispered, "Did you know?"

"Not a clue," Jack said, also in a whisper. His eyes were round, and his jaw dropped as they both gawked at his dad and the cat. "Though, in retrospect, I can't remember ever seeing Portia and Auntie Zee in the same room together, but I thought that was just the cat being a cat."

She could understand that.

"In my defense," Jack said, "it is a far better disguise than Clark Kent as Superman."

Also, agreed.

She stared at the cat, wondering if Portia was about to shapeshift into Auntie Zee like some bad CGI effect. She felt another laugh tickle at her lips. It was too absurd, too unbelievable. Just too much. Other realms, a pet dragon, a moving statue, a sea witch, and now this? "Where do her clothes go when she transforms?"

Jack's eyes widened, and then he spun around quickly to stare at the bookshelves. The library ladder scooted closer, as if hoping he'd climb it. He pretended to study the book spines.

Calisa was about to ask another question when the cat's fur rippled. It looked as if water were moving beneath her skin. The air around her shimmered, and suddenly it didn't seem so funny anymore. This was happening. It wasn't a joke or a trick; it was magic. And it was right here in front of her. She felt her heart thump faster, and she gulped oxygen as if there weren't enough left. She clung to Jack's arm as her knees wobbled again.

Rising, Thomas moved to beside the statue and took Evela's motionless stone hand. He watched silently.

And the cat *unfolded*.

It reminded Calisa of origami in reverse—white fur unfurled, flat as a cloak, and the cat's face lengthened and paled and then stretched again. The cat's body blurred, a column of fuzzy white, and then the white faded away.

A moment later, Auntie Zee was slumped across the window seat, crumpled within a paisley housedress with white buttons. Her white hair was awry, like untamed fur, and her eyes were closed, near buried within the folds of her wrinkles.

Kneeling, Thomas touched her hand. "Zee."

She was breathing, shallowly, but Calisa could see her chest rise and fall. Unable to stop staring, Calisa elbowed Jack. "You can turn around."

Jack turned. "Auntie Zee!"

Her eyelids flashed open. "Much too loud."

"Sorry," Jack whispered.

"How do you feel?" Thomas asked gently.

"Thomas. You're home." She reached up toward his face and then stopped an inch from his cheek. "Unless this is a dream." She pinched the wiggly skin on her upper arm. "Not a dream." She tried to push herself up to a more seated position, and her arms wobbled, her elbows caved, and she flopped backward.

Gently, Thomas helped her sit. He plumped pillows behind her.

The library ladder shifted back and forth as if it wanted to help. "Calm yourself," she told it. It subsided, slightly vibrating. "Explain," Auntie Zee ordered Thomas when she was comfortable, with several pillows propping her up. "I lost you. Yet you're here."

"It wasn't your fault," Thomas said. "It was an accident. Shortly after I arrived in the other realm, I suffered a fall—there are cliffs, and it was raining. I was knocked unconscious, in the cold rain. It took days for the villagers to nurse me back to health. By then, the portal had closed—"

"Yes, yes, but you found the remedy, and you made it back," Auntie Zee interrupted. "How?"

He glanced at Calisa.

Auntie Zee leveled a gnarled finger at her. "Explain, girl."

And so Calisa did, starting at the moment she realized this was not an ordinary inn. Halfway through the retelling, she felt Jack take her hand. She left nothing out, except for the details of the kiss. She glossed over that with just a mention—enough of a hint that Auntie Zee rolled her eyes. When she got to the part about how they searched the realms for Auntie Zee, the eye roll became a full-out scowl.

"You shouldn't have risked yourselves like that," Auntie Zee said.

"We needed you back," Calisa said. "The inn needed you back."

"Bah, the inn is doomed anyway."

"It doesn't have to be." Calisa didn't know why she was feeling so angry, but she was. Furiously, incandescently angry all of a sudden. It felt as if the frustration and disappointment and *feelings* that she'd been shoving down since the start of the summer were bubbling up into her throat and popping in her brain.

"You know nothing about it, child."

"You could have explained that sometimes you get stuck as a cat," Calisa said. "You could have told me how it worked. And what to do." She'd been lied to again and again, her questions unanswered, so little explained, when she could have been trusted to make her own decisions about her summer, her life, her future. She could have been told she had this portal magic, trained to use it, warned that it could cause her to faint . . . or become a *cat*?

The glare hardened. "It's not your problem or your responsibility. I would have recovered enough to transform back eventually."

Calisa crossed her arms and glared back just as hard. "And what would have happened to the B&B in the meantime? What about the guests that are still here? They'd just have to fend for themselves? Do you think they'd ever want to stay here again after that?" If she'd just trusted Calisa . . . or Jack! He hadn't known that Auntie Zee was here all along, or that she was trapped in feline form, or that his father had gone to search for a cure for the overuse of portal magic. All of that would have been useful information for him to have.

"It's *my* bed-and-breakfast."

"You still need help," Calisa said. "If not from me, then from someone. Thomas. Or Jack. Or whoever. But you don't need to do it by yourself." She *couldn't* do it by herself.

"I always have."

"So? Things change." It was a cliché, but the truth of those two words hit her like a fist to the stomach. She thought of Ethan. She'd wanted that to be forever, but now that it was gone . . . He was the past, and that was okay. *That* had been her epiphany in the closet doorway while she'd kissed Jack. *Everything changes, and it's okay.* And a huge reason why it was okay: she hadn't had to go through it alone. She'd had Jack. And Steve. And her moms and Crystal and Maddy back home. Even Melidor and Mulligan and Kendra had helped in their own ways. "There's nothing wrong with asking for help. Or not even asking—you don't have to ask. There's nothing wrong with *accepting* help."

"You don't know what it's like—"

Calisa cut her off. "To feel helpless? Powerless? Sure, I do. Anyone who's been disappointed by someone knows that. You don't have to be a thousand years old to discover that people can suck."

"I am *not* a thousand, and it is my own self that's disappointing me. My own body."

"How's that different?" Calisa countered.

"Because it means that I'm dying."

Thomas and Jack both gasped.

Narrowing her eyes, Calisa crossed her arms. She wasn't buying it. Yes, she could believe Auntie Zee occasionally turned into a cat, but dying? She was too stubborn for that.

Auntie Zee waved her hand at Jack and his dad. "Not right this second. But I'm far closer to death than any of you. My strength—it's not what it used to be. I recover slower than I used to, if I do at all, and I have to accept that. I am old, Calisa. Old. I won't be around forever."

Calisa wondered if Auntie Zee had always been this

dramatic. Sure, she was older, but she wasn't dead yet. How could she abandon all of this, everything she'd worked for and built? Just because she didn't want to accept help? "You're here now, and you can't give up."

"It's not giving up to accept the inevitable. It's practical. I am slowing. Someday I will be gone. Someday this inn will close. Perhaps it's reached that point. I remind you that it's my inn, my decision."

It was her decision, but it was so hard to watch her make what was so obviously the wrong one. All she had to do was accept help! How was that so terrible? Three people were right here, ready to help. Plus the statue. And the ladder. Even Steve, in his own way. Probably not the mirror, but everyone else.

On the other hand, she did have the right to retire. People did that. Calisa felt a tickle of doubt. What if Auntie Zee had reached that point? She knew her own limitations. Every business owner probably did reach the point where they were ready to quit. *But she shouldn't leave carnage in her wake.* If she were to retire, she should do it in a way that didn't destroy the inn. Sell it to someone who could keep it magical. Ensure that Jack and his dad weren't instantly homeless. Create something that lasted. Retire happily, not in defeat.

"Do you *want* it to close?" Jack asked.

"Of course not, silly boy," Auntie Zee said. "This is my life's work. I wanted it to outlast me, but I know my limitations and it's foolish to continue on—"

Calisa cut in. "Did you ever think that the B&B isn't just yours?"

Her great-aunt frowned. "Of course it is."

"It's also Jack's home. And Thomas's," Calisa said. "It's a sanctuary for your guests. Look at Melidor—she needed the space from her family before she could decide what she wanted for herself. And Kendra is under so much pressure from her responsibilities. She needed a break from them, or she risked burning out. Mulligan—he needed somewhere to figure out the solution to his problem with Zef, and time and space to forgive himself. Those are just the guests that I know." She didn't mention herself, but she'd needed the inn just as badly as any of the others did. "This place has so much to give so many different people. Everyone needs a place where they can escape and just breathe."

"Don't you think I know that?" Auntie Zee wagged a finger at Calisa. "I've been here far longer than you. You have no business swooping in here and thinking you know better than your elders. I have been running this inn on my own—"

Thomas interrupted. "You haven't been on your own."

Him, she listened to.

Auntie Zee opened her mouth and shut it. "You're right, and I'm sorry." She reached her hand out to him, and he clasped it. "Thomas, I am sorry I wasn't able to bring you home sooner."

"You tried," he said gruffly.

"It did not open. Until her." Auntie Zee studied Calisa.

Calisa bit her lip to keep from saying anything. She'd said enough already. Probably too much. She felt the weight of questions pressing against the back of her lips. She'd been barreling forward, guessing about how everything worked and what it all meant. She'd been lucky. It could have been so much worse. She could have visited unfriendly worlds. She could have been trapped behind a closed portal, unaware how to access her magic or that she even had any.

She felt a weight on her shoulder as Steve landed and settled in. There was a stab of pain as he kneaded his talons in the spot where he'd pierced her before, but she managed not to flinch. She liked the comforting weight of him on her shoulder.

He was a reminder that she'd done something right in all her flailing around. He'd been lonely, attached to someone who didn't want him and didn't appreciate him, and now he had her.

She waited for Auntie Zee to say something, to yell at her, to send her home.

"I had thought I was the only one left, at least in our family," Auntie Zee said at last.

"Only one what?" Calisa asked.

Auntie Zee smiled, a little sadly. "It appears it skipped a generation. I hadn't known that was possible. I was so afraid of disappointment that I didn't even let myself hope—that's why I wanted you to leave when you first arrived. I didn't dare hope."

That was so close to an apology. Calisa opened her mouth, but Auntie Zee wasn't done.

"I should have realized when the teapot responded to you that you weren't like your mother." And then she said it: "I'm sorry. Can you forgive me? I should have explained, should have tested you immediately."

Calisa felt the last of her anger drain out of her. She hadn't expected a full-out apology, especially not after she'd just finished admitting to all the times she'd broken Auntie Zee's two simple-to-follow, straightforward rules.

"Your mother should have told you about all of this before

you even came," Auntie Zee said, her voice still full of regret. "I wonder who she was more afraid of disappointing: you or me."

"Auntie Zee." Calisa tried to make her voice quieter, calmer. "What . . . how . . . ?" She didn't even know how to frame the question she most wanted to ask.

Gently, Auntie Zee said, "I am a traveler cat."

"A what?" Jack asked. Calisa was grateful to him for voicing the question. She had so many battering through her skull that it felt like she couldn't speak.

"It is a type of witch. Very rare. I was born with the ability to open and close portals."

A witch. "And the cat part of it?"

Now she smiled more broadly. "It's how a portal witch recovers her powers. I have to transform into a smaller body, specifically a cat. It allows the magic to replenish—there's less energy required to keep a smaller body alive. As for *why* a cat . . . I suppose the universe has a sense of humor. Cats are known for always being on the wrong side of every door."

Jack's father snorted—an almost laugh.

"Dad? You knew about all of this?" Jack asked. "About traveler cats and Auntie Zee and how the portals work? Why didn't you ever tell me?"

"I'm sorry. . . ."

"I told him not to," Auntie Zee said. "You didn't need to know, and I . . . I suppose I've become used to keeping this inn's secrets. I figured, what good would it do for Jack to know?"

It would have helped when they were on their own and Kendra was panicked about the portals and they'd known nothing about how the portals worked. It would have helped if Calisa had known there was a chance she had this power too. It would have helped if they'd known to talk to the cat!

"The fewer people who know, the better," Auntie Zee said. "People aren't always kind when they discover you have a power they don't. It . . . changes things."

Calisa thought of Mom-Kate. Was that what had happened between them? Maybe Mom-Kate had left because she couldn't handle not being a traveler cat. Or maybe Auntie Zee had pushed her away because she was afraid she wouldn't be able to handle the disappointment.

"You truly went from realm to realm to search for me? Without any knowledge of what you'd find?" Auntie Zee asked Calisa and Jack.

Calisa couldn't read her emotion this time. She didn't seem to be angry anymore. Surprisingly, Calisa realized she didn't feel angry anymore either. "Um, yes?"

"The unearned confidence of youthful ignorance is remarkable." She shook her head.

"It's because of Calisa's bravery that you're back," Jack said. "It's because of her that my dad is home. And I believe that if you give her a chance, she can save this inn. *We* can save it."

Auntie Zee raised both her eyebrows. "You do, do you?"

"Her idea about a grand reopening," Jack said. "It's a good idea."

"A lot of people out there know you," Calisa said. "They know this inn. If we invited them . . . said we were taking new reservations for a grand reopening. Made it an event."

"We've already done a lot of work fixing up the inn," Jack said. "Calisa has cleaned all the front rooms, she's restarted afternoon tea with cake, and we've restored a lot of the outside."

"It looks a lot less like it's being eaten by the forest," Calisa said. "The guests like it. If we tell other people that the inn has been restored and is ready and waiting for them, just as much a peaceful refuge as it used to be . . ."

She couldn't read Auntie Zee's expression. The innkeeper could squash the idea right here. She had the right to close the inn and retire if she chose, but Calisa didn't think that Auntie Zee wanted to let it just crumble away, her life's work.

"Thomas, what do you think?" Auntie Zee said. "Is it a fool's plan?"

Both Calisa and Jack looked at him. On Calisa's shoulder, the little dragon made a whirring chirp that sounded like a question, and she saw the ladder give an extra shake. The statue, of course, was motionless and silent, and she didn't bother looking back at the mirror. Everyone had an opinion, but it was Auntie Zee's choice, and she was looking to her old friend.

"I think you have been given a second chance, one you thought was lost," Thomas said. "What you choose to do with it is up to you."

Auntie Zee snorted.

"Yes, you should do it, you stubborn old woman," Thomas said, but there was a softness and affection in his voice. The ladder wriggled back and forth.

"Ask the mirror," Auntie Zee said to Calisa. "If that old pessimist thinks I should . . ."

Calisa stepped into the lobby. "Mirror, mirror . . ."

It already had its answer displayed within the smoke:

Save the inn.

Obviously.

CHAPTER TWENTY-SIX

Over the course of the next week, Calisa and Jack returned to the various realms they'd visited to spread the word and take reservations: a room to a fishmonger couple from the mermaid-friendly village, one to the bone-like creature who covered its body in the pelt of a bear, another to the family made of bark and leaves, and another to the jewel-drenched fae queens from the Night Market.

Every time they returned to the inn between trips, Auntie Zee put them to work on preparing. Sitting on a cushioned chair behind the lobby desk, she issued orders while sipping tea from the enchanted teapot:

Excess seawater needed to be mopped up.

Towels stacked and folded in the bathrooms.

Pillows fluffed and bedsheets smoothed.

Bathrooms sprayed with room freshener made by mermaids.

Otherworldly flowers that smelled like sunshine on a perfect

July day should be tucked into glass bottles and placed in every guest room on the mantel and windowsills. A sprig of lavender on each bed. Check for cobwebs. Lay a piece of fresh firewood in each hearth for the firebird—that was, Auntie Zee said, part of their arrangement. In exchange for fresh logs, it would flit around the bed-and-breakfast from fireplace to fireplace and send up sparks when Auntie Zee was needed. The number of sparks would indicate which room number required the innkeeper's attention.

As Calisa passed through the lobby with an armload of towels for Jack—he was finishing soaking up what remained of Kendra's disaster—she asked, "What about the mirror? How does it help with running the inn?"

"It doesn't," Auntie Zee said. "It's just an asshole."

I heard that, the mirror wrote.

Auntie Zee laughed. "The mirror is my security system. It watches the lobby and lets me know if it spots any threats to my guests. In exchange, I offer it a respite from people who want to ask it stupid questions because they read a ridiculous fairy tale and think it has opinions on human beauty."

Calisa laughed and then saw she was serious. "Not sure it's totally doing its job. It didn't alert you when I stole . . . *borrowed* . . . the inn's logbook. It had to have seen me pluck it out of the portal."

Auntie Zee shrugged. "As I said, it's an asshole."

In my defense, I thought it would be funny.

"How is that a defense?" Calisa asked.

In small letters: **It was objectively hilarious.**

Hobbling out of the lobby, Auntie Zee grunted at the mirror.

After tossing the towels to Jack, Calisa followed her aunt into the kitchen. "The first thing to know about running a bed-and-breakfast," Auntie Zee said, "is that you must be both visible and invisible. The guests should feel catered to but never smothered. . . ."

Calisa wondered if she should be taking notes.

She continued on with the advice—answering questions that Calisa hadn't even thought to ask about maintaining an inn with otherworldly guests—before concluding with: "We will, of course, need to fill the pantry before the influx of guests begins."

From under the sink where he was working on the plumbing, Thomas called, "Make me a list. I'll visit Rin's stall in the Night Market after I'm done with this."

Carrying an armload of damp, salty towels, Jack popped into the kitchen before heading for the washing machine. "You are *not* going through a portal again." He and Calisa had done all the inviting and making reservations. This was the first time the possibility of his dad venturing through had come up.

"That's not how you talk to your father," Auntie Zee admonished as he sailed by. "You have been spending too much time with my grandniece."

Thomas slid out from beneath the sink. "It's not your decision to make. I have been visiting the Night Market for longer than you've been alive."

Calisa located a pad of paper and a pencil. "Jack's right. You aren't going through a portal anytime soon. We'll get whatever is needed. You have to stay put." She leveled a look at Thomas. "For Jack."

Huffing, Thomas began, "Everything I do is for Jack, for this place, for Zee, for our futures. If you think I'll let my son take risks—"

Jack called over his shoulder, "You were gone for *three years*."

His father fell silent.

Calisa held the pencil poised over the paper and asked with a steel edge to her voice, "Auntie Zee, what do we need?"

She thought she heard Auntie Zee give a quiet grunt of approval.

With the full supply list in hand, Calisa and Jack (and Steve, riding on Calisa's shoulder, as usual) returned to the Night Market. Working at his stall beneath an array of lanterns, Rin was delighted to see them and even more delighted when they showed him the list from Auntie Zee and explained about the grand reopening. "She is truly a marvel. I had worried . . . Well, never mind an old centaur's worries. Passion cannot be stopped. It shines through, despite adversity. You know that's how you achieve happiness, having a purpose in life, and she found hers with that inn. The last time I saw her, though, she was certain that the inn wouldn't last much longer. May I ask what caused this change?"

"She got help," Calisa said simply.

"Ahh, I see. Beautiful." He read through the list, nodding at each item. "The breads, the pastries, yes—I will bring them myself."

"How much?" Calisa asked.

Rin waved his hand airily. "For the witch of the inn, it's a gift."

Jack frowned. "She won't want—"

"Please, let me do this for her," Rin said. "For years, decades, lifetimes, Auntie Zee has been sending customers my way. She is responsible for a significant portion of my family's wealth. It was that wealth that helped save my daughter's life—when they said a miracle couldn't happen, it paid the best doctors. Truly, I owe her my happiness: my purpose, my family. Did she tell you it was she who introduced me to my wife? My Veracitu. It was Auntie Zee who brought her to the market, to me. We've been married twenty-eight years now, and we'd never have had all those years together without Auntie Zee. In fact . . . so many people have stories about her. She doesn't know the good she's done, the lives she's touched. Let me share this list. I know others feel the same as I do. She has done more than she knows, and she's never allowed us to show our thanks."

Calisa was silent. She was both surprised and unsurprised—she'd known the Faraway Inn was special and that others cared about it too. Here was proof. "Are you sure? It's a long list. Auntie Zee gave us lercats. . . ."

"It would be my greatest pleasure."

"And the other vendors?" Calisa pressed. "They won't want anything in return?"

"What we want," Rin said, "is for the inn to continue."

All right, then. She glanced at Jack.

"Auntie Zee . . . isn't exactly good at accepting help," Jack said. "She only barely agreed to let us move forward with the reopening, so I don't know how we'll get her to agree to accept all of this."

That was a problem, but they were talking about a gift. You didn't need permission to give a gift. "What if we just sneak everything in? Let it be a surprise."

"She won't be happy," Jack warned her.

"Outwardly, she'll grunt, but inwardly, she'll be happy," Calisa said. "Or she will be if she lets herself." And the inn needed this—the kindness of others. It could give them the boost to change the reopening from a risk to a sure success. "It's not a comment on her independence. It's a thank-you."

He thought about that for a moment and then nodded. "You're right."

She reveled in that. Not everyone would be able to say that so simply—to think about what she had said, take it seriously, and then change their mind. It made her want to kiss him right here and right now. Instead she said to Rin, "Can you be ready and by the portal at . . . What time is it here at our sunrise?"

"Your sunrise is our moonrise."

"I'll open the door on the other side at your moonrise," Calisa said.

"Wait, what if Auntie Zee stops you?" Jack asked. "If she figures out—"

"That's why I said 'sneak.' She can't stop me if she doesn't know."

Smiling broadly, Rin wagged his finger at her. "I like you. You have style. You will make an excellent heir to Auntie Zee."

Calisa laughed. *Heir to Auntie Zee.* She'd barely convinced her great-aunt to allow her to stay for the summer. It didn't seem likely that Auntie Zee would want her to come back after all of this was over, despite her earlier apology.

Except that I did inherit her magic.

She sobered.

She hadn't had time yet to think through what that could mean for her and for her future. *I'm part witch.* She'd proven it by opening portals, and Auntie Zee had said in no uncertain terms that she'd inherited her special ability. *I'm a traveler cat?* She didn't feel particularly feline. Or witchy. But then again, she had worked magic. That much was indisputable. She'd have to think about what it all meant when she had a moment to breathe, after the grand reopening.

She left the list with Rin and tugged Jack with her, back toward the portal. Now that this was all set, there was plenty more work for them to do at the inn. "He loves Auntie Zee," she told Jack. "I think she should be allowed to see that for herself." Auntie Zee claimed she knew that guests needed her inn, but Calisa doubted that she really *knew* how much her B&B mattered to people—how much *she* mattered to people.

And how much the inn had come to matter to Calisa herself.

Hesitating, she leaned against Jack and said, "I don't want to go back."

"I know, but Auntie Zee needs us. And my dad—"

She cut him off. "I mean *home*. My home. Brooklyn. After the summer ends . . . I don't want this to end."

"It's not ending yet," Jack said. "We've got the grand reopening to get through. Can we focus on that and not think about what comes after?"

And then he said the words she didn't know she wanted him to say:

"I don't want you to leave either."

Hand in hand, they walked back to the portal. Steve rode on Calisa's shoulder, and she thought he seemed noticeably heavier. She wondered how much he was going to grow, and then she wondered if she was going to be around to see it. And then she wondered if Steve was going to expect to go with her to Brooklyn, because that wasn't going to work at all.

Future Calisa problem, she told herself.

"Maybe sometime after the reopening, we can come back to the Night Market?" Jack suggested. "Not for any purpose. But just, you know, as a date? A second date. I mean, if this counts as a first date."

She smiled. "I'd like that."

Together they walked through the portal back to the inn.

CHAPTER TWENTY-SEVEN

At dawn, Calisa opened the closet door and walked through to the Night Market. Stars twinkled overhead and the endless music of the market drifted up to her. True to his word, Rin was waiting with baskets strapped like saddlebags to his horse half. Behind him were a half-dozen others carrying crates, baskets, and bags.

"You did it," Calisa said.

"Did you doubt?" Rin asked.

She smiled. "No."

Chattering, they all followed her back through the portal. "Thank you for coming," she repeated to each of them as they arrived, laden with far more supplies than they'd requested.

"Pleasure to be here." "'Course. It's Auntie Zee." "What a charming place." "My pleasure." "Happy to." "Glad to do it." "Hope it helps." "The figs are fresh. Wait a few days on the peaches." "Anyone bring the starseed?" "Hey, watch your pack." "Where should I put these?" "Glad to help." "It's an honor." The smells of baked bread and spices and flowery fruits that she couldn't name saturated the air, and the chatter of the voices blended into a pleasant hum. She'd never imagined so many vendors would come. Auntie Zee was going to be . . . *Probably pissed, but she'll live.*

Once they were all through the portal and crammed shoulder to shoulder in the guest room, Calisa lifted her voice. "If you'll follow me . . ." She led the way out into the hall, down the stairs, and into the kitchen. She felt a bit like she was leading a parade, especially with the clatter of Rin's horse hooves on the stairs. All they needed was their own marching band.

"What is all this?" Auntie Zee cried. She was at the stove, an apron wrapped around her waist, stirring a pot of golden syrup that smelled like honey and lavender.

Smiling broadly, Rin trotted across the kitchen and kissed her on the cheek. "Happy reopening day, Auntie Zee," he wished her. He then deposited his baskets of sugar-covered pastries on the butcher block island.

The other vendors repeated the greeting, each kissing her on the cheek and delivering baskets of ruby and golden fruit, fat berries, fresh-baked breads, honeyed pastries, packets of spiced meat, and jars of pearly beverages. Soon the parcels, jars, baskets, and crates were piled as high as the rafters, and the sweet and savory smells were thick in the air. Inhaling, Calisa thought it was like being inside the most delicious café in the world. *In many worlds,* she corrected herself.

Auntie Zee was glaring at Rin. "I can't afford all of this! Calisa, what did you do?"

"All I did was say yes." Calisa stepped sideways so that a

tower of baskets blocked Auntie Zee's view of her. She truthfully had not expected the vendors to all be so generous. She marveled at the bounty. This was phenomenal. Their guests would feast!

"We will take no payment," Rin said.

Auntie Zee let out a strangled noise halfway between a yelp and a snort, and Calisa peeked out around a bread sculpture of a swan to see what she'd do next.

"We will also take no objections and no refusals," Rin said, grinning at her. "Our gift to you for years of patronage."

She put her hands on her hips. "I am not a charity."

Clasping his hands to his heart, Rin trotted forward. His hooves clicked on the kitchen floor. "Let us do this, dearest Auntie Zee. It is truly our pleasure. You have touched each of our lives, and it's finally our chance to thank you."

Others echoed him, each of them repeating that it was their pleasure and honor.

Before Auntie Zee could marshal up an argument or refuse the gifts entirely, Rin gave her a jaunty wave and trotted out of the kitchen. The stream of vendors filed out after him.

Hurrying ahead of them, Calisa scurried up the stairs to the guest room. Thanking them each profusely, she held the closet door open as they went through the portal, Rin last.

At the closet, he winked at her. "Don't let her discourage you," he said. "She needs you. And she'll appreciate you eventually."

"Thanks," Calisa said. "For . . . all of this."

"You'll make a great witch of the inn, when it's your time."

Before she could do anything but gape at that, Rin trotted through. His tail flicked before it was swallowed by the iridescent swirl. She stared at the portal for a moment more, and then she decided to leave it open in case any other vendors wanted to come through to deliver gifts, before she headed back downstairs to the kitchen.

Auntie Zee was waiting for her. "Calisa. What did you do?"

Calisa halted in the doorway. "Rin offered, and I said yes." She'd already decided that if Auntie Zee was mad, she was going to pretend it was just her and Rin who had done this. She'd deny that Jack was even there. He didn't deserve any anger directed at him.

Seething so hard that she was practically hissing, Auntie Zee said, "I didn't want it spread around that I am in need of help. I have always stood on my own two feet and I always will."

"No spreading occurred," Calisa insisted. "They wanted to do this. They *like* you. Can't you accept at least *that*?" To be fair, Jack had warned her that Auntie Zee wouldn't be happy about this, but couldn't she at least see it was wonderful that so many *wanted* to help? She had people who cared and wanted her to be happy. Surely once she had a chance to think about it—

Auntie Zee snorted. "I'm not likable."

"That was a half-dozen people who think you are."

Despite herself, Auntie Zee smiled. It was, however, a somewhat vicious and not very mirth-filled smile. "You owe Rin now. I suppose that's your problem. He'll expect to be our primary supplier. You're going to have to keep visiting the Night Market."

That sounded great to Calisa.

Auntie Zee opened up the nearest basket, and the kitchen filled with the aroma of pastries—herbs, berries, and the thick smell of cinnamon. "Plate a reasonable amount and bring it to the dining room for the arriving guests. The rest of this we'll store for later."

Relieved that her great-aunt was done objecting, Calisa set to work, piling pastries on serving plates, arranging fruit, pouring the pearlescent juice into pitchers, and then arranging it all in the not-yet-used dining room. Joining them, Jack carried a stack of plates, while Calisa folded the napkins. She located a vase and filled it with flowers from the B&B's gardens, and then she ran the vacuum over the carpet an extra time. If all the guests who'd made reservations came, the bed-and-breakfast would be full. She didn't want a single one to be disappointed.

Once they'd finished setting out the welcome spread, they located tinfoil, plastic wrap, ziplock bags, and various containers and began bagging and boxing and sealing the gifted food to serve later. Soon, they fell into a rhythm: Calisa sealing the food into airtight containers and Jack finding room for them in the refrigerator or on the pantry shelves. It was almost a dance as they zigzagged through the kitchen and circled the butcher block island. Some food went into the refrigerator, some into the freezer—each item squeezed in like a complex puzzle—and the rest went into the pantry, labeled and on shelves: pastas and grains and rice, as well as potatoes and onions. She shelved several jars of sauces, as well as jams and preserved fruit. She began to feel like a squirrel stocking up for winter. The vendors had been *very* generous. There were even a few cakes to add to the chocolate one that Calisa had already baked.

Sitting on a stool watching, Auntie Zee muttered to herself throughout, but Calisa thought that her tone softened as she saw the wealth of delicacies that her old friends had sent. Every so often, she'd get up and begin to help. Just as often, Thomas would pass through the kitchen carrying his tools and bark at her that she needed to rest.

Finally, she sighed. "Oh."

Calisa wasn't sure what to make of that "oh." She thought maybe, just maybe, she was pleased? Or at least exasperated with a tinge of amused rather than furious?

"You are . . ." Auntie Zee began.

Calisa expected to hear any one of a variety of adjectives, but Auntie Zee simply sighed and walked away, leaving them to their unpacking.

Midafternoon, the guests began to arrive from various realms. Calisa scurried from closet to closet, welcoming them and guiding them to the lobby.

Seated at the desk in the lobby, Auntie Zee checked everyone in, writing their names into her registrar and handing them room keys. She offered to close and reopen their portals as needed, typically the closets of their assigned rooms. As soon as the administrative details were completed, Thomas and Jack carried the luggage to the various rooms, while Calisa invited the new guests to tea. The enchanted teapot hummed happily in the corner.

First to check in were a silent couple, whose shadows spoke for them. The wife sank into a chair in the sitting area with a cup of tea, while the husband browsed the library, to the delight of the ladder. His shadow commented on each book the husband touched.

Second was the young couple of fishmongers, who, from the number of times they paused to gaze into one another's eyes, looked to be freshly married. Auntie Zee didn't ask, and Calisa merely offered them each a slice of strawberry cake. Carrying their slices to the conch chair, they squished into it together, bumping each other with their elbows as they ate. When they opened their mouths, Calisa saw sharklike teeth.

Third was the bone person covered in the pelt of a bear from the realm with the labyrinth. Calisa couldn't tell if the pelt was fused to their bones or if they wore it like a cloak over their skeleton body. She supposed she didn't need to know.

"Should I offer them cake?" she whispered to the mirror, as the bone person thanked Auntie Zee for their key. They had no throat or internal organs that she could see. She wasn't sure if it would be rude to offer or not to offer.

Do it.

"You just think it would be funny."

Absolutely.

She rolled her eyes at the mirror.

Peeking into the sitting room, Calisa checked on the firebird again. Occasionally it would flit up the chimney and then return. Only once did it shoot sparks upward: five, which meant room five. Calisa alerted Jack, who went to check. "They want more pillows," he reported back before heading for the supply closets.

Next was the family made of bark and leaves. Their two twiglike children scampered out the kitchen door into the garden, where they were greeted by Melidor, who had booked a room for the weekend. She introduced them to her seedlings while their parents checked into their rooms.

Nearly two hours later, after the other new guests had settled into their rooms and were either relaxing in the sitting room or outside admiring the view of the mountains, the two fae queens arrived, sweeping through their laundry room–closet portal. Jack scurried to settle their belongings in the largest guest room, on the third floor, with a view of the mountains and a canopy bed.

Their faces were painted as before: blue for one and bronze for the other. Gold was laced through their hair, and their dresses were draped in intricate folds. Welcoming them, Calisa led them to the desk in the lobby.

"So this is the famous Faraway Inn," the bronze-painted queen said, no emotion in her voice. She ran a finger over the wall and sniffed it. "It is older than I expected." She studied the mirror, which today was a placid gray. "Shabbier."

The blue queen hissed, "Do not be impolite."

Cheerfully, Auntie Zee said, "I am older than I expected too. But time comes for us all."

The bronze queen let out a judgmental "Hmm."

The mirror displayed: **You don't have to stay.**

The words twisted into a language that Calisa didn't recognize, and the bronze queen startled. "Shabby *and* unfriendly. This is not what I expected."

Calisa glanced at Auntie Zee. What was she going to say? She couldn't offer to upgrade their room—they already had the nicest one, and they hadn't even seen it yet. Was she going to apologize for the mirror? Or for the state of the inn? Calisa and Jack had cleaned and repaired as much as they could, but the wallpaper was faded, the rug was frayed, and the wood on the stairs was chipped. There was no denying that the inn showed its age.

Calisa suddenly felt as if she'd failed. She hadn't done enough. It wasn't fit for royalty. So far, the other guests had seemed happy, but what if they overheard the queens and decided they agreed?

"Here is your next lesson in innkeeping," Auntie Zee said conversationally to Calisa. Raising her voice, she asked the queens, "Is all not to your liking?"

Behind the queens, she saw the new words display on the mirror: **I wish I could eat popcorn.** Wondering why it would say that, Calisa looked from Auntie Zee to the queens then back again.

The blue-painted queen glanced wistfully at the mostly eaten cake displayed in the sitting room, sliced for anyone who was still hungry. Strawberry jam had oozed out onto the platter, tempting someone to stick their finger into it and scoop up the strawberry-ness with a dollop of the creamy frosting. "Perhaps we could—"

The bronze queen held up a hand to silence her. "It is *not* to our liking. Do you know who we are?" She'd drawn herself up even taller, the top of her coiffed hair brushing the light fixture that hung from the center of the lobby.

"Yes," Auntie Zee said evenly. "You are unwelcome."

Her eyes widened. "What did you just say?"

"This inn is a sanctuary to those who need it and those who want it," Auntie Zee said, her voice clipped but polite. "It has stood as such for decades. If it is not what you need or want, then I am encouraging you to leave. There will be no charge, and you may, of course, help yourself to tea and cake before you depart."

She was *kicking them out*? Calisa felt her mouth drop open. She wouldn't have guessed that was her next innkeeper lesson.

"You dare—" the bronze queen began.

"You are in *my* realm," Auntie Zee said. "As host, I set the rules."

Stiffly the bronze queen said, "I acknowledge your dominion."

No wonder the mirror wanted popcorn. She looked at the queens, then at Auntie Zee, then back at the queens, ping-ponging between them as she waited to see who would speak next and what they would say.

The blue queen laid a hand on her coruler's arm. "My dear, I wish to stay."

"It is not suitable—" the bronze queen began.

"You can return home, if you desire," the blue queen said softly. "I am in need of a respite, and, yes, the accommodations may be different from what we're accustomed to, but I *want* different."

Auntie Zee held her pen over the logbook, neither writing

a name nor crossing one out. "A place like this inn," Auntie Zee said to Calisa, clearly not caring that the queens could hear her, "is what you allow it to be. It's a deep breath, but you are still the one who must breathe deeply."

A smile touched the blue queen's lips.

The bronze queen rolled her eyes hard. "You know I cannot say no to you, but I ask you to reconsider—"

"Hush. Come have some cake with me." Gently, the blue queen led her into the sitting room, joining the other guests. Calisa drifted into the entryway to watch.

By the fireplace, Mulligan was posed with one foot up on a stool as he recited what sounded like a Shakespeare sonnet to Zef. Kendra had claimed her usual conch seat, displacing the lovey-dovey couple with shark teeth onto a sofa, and was delicately eating a slice of cake while she dripped on the carpet. Her rest was officially over—her ocean needed her for the approaching hurricane season—but she'd returned for the celebration. She'd also already booked a stay for next summer, her usual room three.

As the two fae queens glided into the sitting room, the teapot poured them tea, and Jack scooted over to the cake to cut them slices. No one bowed or curtsied to them, but they were greeted warmly.

Aw, there was no screaming, the mirror pouted.

"Not everyone wants what we have to offer," Auntie Zee said to Calisa.

"I thought you'd . . . I don't know . . . offer them more? Talk up the inn? Give them a discount?" Calisa said. "Isn't the customer always right?"

Auntie Zee snorted. "That's bullshit. And the full quote is: 'The customer is always right in matters of taste.' You build what you want to build, offer it as widely as you can to whoever you think will appreciate it, and if other people like it or don't like it . . . that's on them. Not you."

She thought of Ethan. That sentence shouldn't have applied to him, but . . . it kind of did. He hadn't wanted what she built. And that was on him.

Jack laughed at something one of the guests said, and Calisa peeked again into the sitting room. He was chatting with the guests as he served cake to Zef. *He likes me as I am.* He saw her as she was. He listened to her. He never tried to change her. *He's what I need and want.*

As if he sensed her watching, he looked over. Calisa met his eyes and smiled, and he smiled back, instantly and fully, like he'd been ready and waiting for her to notice him.

"I think I understand," Calisa said to Auntie Zee.

CHAPTER TWENTY-EIGHT

A week after the grand reopening, Calisa made crème brûlée for the first time. Mom-Elise had looked up the recipe online and read it to her over the phone. She whisked, heated, baked, then cooled. Now she had a half-dozen ramekins ready for their tops to be crisped into caramel.

"Ready for your big moment?" Calisa asked Steve.

He waddled over to the six shallow dishes of custard and dipped his head.

"No eating," she said. "Fire."

Tilting his head, he looked at her quizzically.

"You can do it. Steady flame." She sprinkled spoonfuls of white and brown sugar over the top of each custard. "Come on, Steve. Fire."

He looked at the crème brûlée again, and she tickled under his chin. He chirped and wriggled his body, then he opened his mouth and a spurt of fire came out. She lifted each dish to the flame until the sugar top crystalized to a perfect golden brown.

“You’re magnificent,” she told the little dragon.

He preened.

Jack came in through the back door. “You let him inside again.”

“Yep,” Calisa said. She patted Steve on the head and then went to the fridge to fetch him a slice of meat that they’d purchased from the Night Market on their last visit. He took it daintily out of her fingers using his teeth, and she washed her hands before putting the perfect crème brûlées back into the refrigerator to chill until it was time for them to be tonight’s dessert. “How’s Melidor?”

“Nearly ready to return home, she says.”

“And the seedlings?”

“Loud.”

She’d heard them chirping and squealing when she woke up this morning. They sounded like baby birds crossed with the pop of bubble wrap. She wouldn’t have guessed they’d squeak like that, but she supposed it wasn’t anything she’d ever given any thought to before this summer.

“Steve, do you want to go play with the baby dryads?” Calisa asked.

He obediently flew out the back door as Jack held it open.

Jack crossed to her as she was putting the last of the crème brûlée into the fridge. “These look incredible,” he said, peeking over her shoulder. “Let me know if you need a taste tester.”

She turned to make a joke and the words fled from her mind. His eyes were warm and laughing, as they always were, and before she’d even decided to, she was kissing him in the chill of the open refrigerator door. His lips were warm and soft, and his arms wrapped around her and made her feel as if she were enclosed in the world's nicest blanket.

"Close the fridge door," Auntie Zee said testily behind them.

Calisa and Jack jumped apart.

"Sorry," Jack said and closed the refrigerator door.

"You should know better than to open and close doors carelessly," Auntie Zee scolded.

"It's a refrigerator," Calisa said. "Wait, can you turn a fridge into a portal? What about a car door? Does the car have to be parked, or can a portal be in motion? Can you have one on a plane?" As she rattled off questions, she scooted closer to Jack. She wasn't going to be embarrassed about kissing him. In fact, she was tempted to kiss him again right now, and Auntie Zee could do whatever she wanted. She had every intention of spending as much time as possible with Jack before the summer ended, and yes, that included kissing him at every opportunity.

Because time did move on, as Auntie Zee kept saying, and Calisa didn't want this summer to end.

She was trying so hard not to think about *that* Future Calisa problem. She didn't want to leave the inn. Didn't want to leave Jack. Or Steve. Or the firebird in the hearth. Or Auntie Zee. Or the statue. Or even the unfriendly mirror. She wanted her enchanted tea every afternoon. She wanted to bake cakes. She wanted to walk through portals into other realms. She even wanted to weed and clean the bathrooms, if it meant she didn't have to say goodbye.

"Your mothers have been pestering me about you," Auntie Zee said.

Calisa winced. She hadn't called home as often as she should have. She'd let them know that Auntie Zee was back, the grand reopening had been a success, and they didn't need to abandon work and rush up to Vermont, but after that . . . the inn had been full, and she'd had a lot of work to do. "I'll call them," she promised.

"You'll do better than that," Auntie Zee said. "Come with me."

Calisa glanced at Jack.

Rolling her eyes, Auntie Zee said, "Yes, he can come too, if he wants, at least for the first part. After that, he'll have to stay here." She hobbled out of the kitchen, through the lobby, and down the hall toward Calisa's room.

Calisa and Jack followed.

Over her shoulder, Auntie Zee said, "I have never made a portal in either a fridge or a car, but I suppose it's theoretically possible. Awkward, though, to climb in over the crisper into another realm. Closet doors are ideal choices."

The first thing Calisa noticed was that the red X on her door had been cleaned away, and now a bouquet made of acorns and pine cones hung in its place. Auntie Zee didn't wait for Calisa to unlock the door but instead strode inside as if she owned the place—which she did, of course. In the hearth was the firebird.

"Do you know what she's up to?" Calisa asked the firebird.

It danced over the logs, which wasn't an answer.

As if sensing her nervousness, Jack took Calisa's hand as Auntie Zee crossed to the closet door. It wasn't that she didn't trust Auntie Zee. She just didn't know what the innkeeper had in mind. First she'd been complaining that Calisa didn't call home enough, and now she was sending her off into an unknown realm?

"It's easy to open or close a portal that already has a designated terminus, given enough power and sheer dumb luck," Auntie Zee said, "but much harder to establish one to a new destination. Probably take you years to learn how. Luckily you're young and spry."

Years? Did that mean that Auntie Zee planned to train her? Long-term? They hadn't talked about it yet, not in any concrete way. She felt her heart beat faster. There was nothing she wanted more, but how would it work? Could she come back every summer? Would that be enough? She'd have to talk with her moms, but she thought they'd say yes. She wished she could be here fall, winter, and spring too, though. What if she visited every school vacation also? Would her parents allow that? Would Auntie Zee?

Auntie Zee touched each inch of the doorway, groaning when she had to bend to touch the floor and the lower parts of the sides. She hauled over a chair to stand on to reach the top. Huffing, she stepped up onto it and then wobbled.

Jack hurried over to steady her and the chair.

Auntie Zee grunted at him but didn't protest at the help. When she finished, she stepped down and puffed. "Silence. I have to concentrate."

Neither Calisa nor Jack had said a word. The firebird stilled, and the crackle of its flames quieted. Out of the corner of her eye, Calisa noticed that Steve had flown to her windowsill and was perched outside, watching. He didn't like when she ventured into other realms without him, especially if the other realms had treats.

Touching the doorframe lightly, Auntie Zee whispered to the doorway in a coaxing tone. She swayed slightly, and Jack glanced at Calisa. She shrugged. She didn't know if they should be letting her great-aunt do this or not. Last time she'd opened a brand-new portal, Jack's father had been lost for three years.

Auntie Zee leaned against the mantel with a gasp.

Flapping its flame wings, the firebird flew up the chimney in a whoosh of heat as Calisa started toward her. "Auntie Zee?"

Auntie Zee held up a hand to stop her.

"I'm getting my father," Jack said.

Before he could leave the room, though, the firebird flew back to the fireplace with a fiery *whoomp,* and Thomas arrived at a jog. "What are you doing?" he demanded. "You know you don't have the strength. . . ."

Huffing at him, Auntie Zee shrugged him off. "I can do this. Child's play." She pointed at Calisa and said, "You'll want to go through this one alone, girl. Trust me on this. Fewer explanations needed if you're solo." Without waiting for any questions or for Calisa to do more than glance at Jack and Steve, Auntie Zee drew herself up straighter than Calisa had ever seen her and commanded, "Open!"

She then sagged into a chair.

And she promptly shrank. Her clothes sprouted white fur, and her face reshaped itself into an elegant elderly cat. With dignity, the cat licked her paw.

All of them stared at her.

"Uh," Calisa said. She still couldn't get used to the idea that—*poof*—her great-aunt could become a cat. "Now what? Do we use the remedy?"

The cat lowered her paw and shook her head very clearly.

Thomas knelt beside her. "Give her a chance to rest. If it truly was 'child's play,' as she said, her magic should restore itself naturally."

The cat, Auntie Zee, licked her paw again.

"You should open the door," Jack said to Calisa. "See what she wanted you to see."

Right. Good idea. Certainly it was preferable to standing here imagining if she was going to transform into a cat next. She wasn't sure she wanted to sprout fur. Calisa opened the door to a pleasant pink whorl. It looked like raspberry jam being stirred into pink milk. She glanced back at Jack, Thomas, her cat-aunt, and the little dragon peering through the window. Trying not to dwell on what happened the last time Auntie Zee opened a new portal, she gave them all a wave, and then she stepped through the swirl.

And she walked into a very familiar place: the kitchen of her and her moms' Brooklyn apartment. Mom-Kate and Mom-Elise were seated at the table—Mom-Kate with her usual latte, and Mom-Elise with her phone. Both of them jumped up when Calisa stepped out of the bathroom doorway.

"Calisa!" Mom-Kate cried.

"What happened to our bathroom?" Mom-Elise asked.

Calisa laughed and then suddenly, inexplicably, found herself crying. Both of them rushed to her and threw their arms around her, drawing her close. "I'm okay," Calisa said, muffled, crying, into their hair and shoulders.

"Of course you are," Mom-Kate said. "You're home."

After she'd spent over an hour with them, telling them everything about her summer and the inn and Auntie Zee and Jack and Steve and her cakes and the Night Market and the baby dryads and all of it, Calisa invited them back to the bed-and-breakfast.

"Does Auntie Zee want us there?" Mom-Kate asked.

"Of course!" Calisa had no idea if she did or didn't, but why open the portal if she wasn't going to talk to Calisa's moms? Clearly it was time for a family reunion. Mom-Kate had reached out to Auntie Zee by sending Calisa, and Auntie Zee was reaching back by making this portal. Both of them wanted to heal whatever had broken between them. She was sure of it. Mostly sure of it.

She held both her moms' hands as they squeezed together through the doorway and popped back into Calisa's guest room, where Auntie Zee was napping in the chair, in her human form and beneath a quilt. Jack and Thomas had left, but the firebird danced over the logs, keeping watch as it always did.

Mom-Elise saw the firebird immediately. "Wow. I know you said . . . Mom-Kate has told me stories too . . . but to see with my own eyes . . ." She knelt beside the fireplace. "Absolutely beautiful."

Stretching its wings, the firebird pranced over the logs as if showing off.

Auntie Zee opened her eyes. "Ah, good, you're all here. We have a lot to discuss." She threw off the quilt and pushed herself shakily onto her feet. Without another word, she began shuffling toward the hallway.

Calisa saw her moms glance at each other, and she wished Auntie Zee had started off a bit more friendly, perhaps with a hello, so great to see you, sorry for holding a grudge for a decade. Still, it was an okay start to the reunion. She didn't seem angry that Calisa had invited her moms. So long as they all—

Mom-Kate crossed her arms and said in her mama bear voice, "Yes, we do have a lot to discuss. I heard you were ready to send Calisa back home as soon as she arrived."

Calisa cried, "Mom-Kate! That's not the most important thing that I told you. And besides, she didn't. I'm still here." In fact, if she thought back over it, Auntie Zee hadn't mentioned sending her home since the moment she'd relocated Steve to the greenhouse. That had been the turning point, though she hadn't known it at the time.

"Come to the sitting room," Auntie Zee ordered. "This won't be a short conversation." She waddled out of the room without even glancing back to see if they followed.

"Mom-Kate, Mom-Elise, please . . . just come talk to her, okay? For me?" She led them down the hall, through the lobby, and into the sitting room, which was thankfully devoid of guests. "Not a word," she said to the mirror as she passed it.

Who? Me? the mirror wrote. **I'm kindness personified.**

"You're not a person."

Rude. Also, accurate.

She shooed her moms past it. She didn't trust the mirror not to write something to upset her moms just for the amusement value. "Would you like some crème brûlée?" Calisa offered. "And tea?"

The firebird had already raced through the chimneys and was dancing on the log in the fireplace of the sitting room. Mom-Elisa halted to stare at the fiery bird again.

"Excellent idea, Calisa," Auntie Zee said, which was more praise than she'd ever heaped on Calisa and made her, if possible, even more nervous. What exactly did Auntie Zee plan to say to her moms? And what would her moms say back?

She hurried into the kitchen to fetch the dishes of crème brûlée that she'd made. She heard a tapping on the window over the sink and spotted Steve poking at the glass with his wing. "Yes, come in," she told him. "I need reinforcements."

Opening the window, she welcomed him in and patted her shoulder. He flew up and perched beside her neck. His scaled side felt like rough leather, and he smelled of dirt and pine.

Leaning out, she called, "Jack?"

He popped his head up from within the garden, where he was working with his dad. "You're back! Where were you? How was it?"

"Want to meet my moms?"

"Uh . . ."

"They're going to love you." Surely they wouldn't argue in front of Jack and Steve and the firebird, would they? She really wanted this to go well. It felt like the grand reopening all over again, except this time she had less control over it.

Jack handed his gardening gloves to his father and trotted inside. After he washed his hands in the kitchen sink, he helped her carry a tray of crème brûlée into the sitting room. As she passed the mirror, she whispered, "What did I miss?"

No drama yet. Just a lot of boring awkward staring.

"Good."

Are they going to fight? I want to watch a fight.

"Calisa?" Jack asked, nervous.

"It'll be fine," Calisa told him. "Just show them your smile."

I'm betting on Auntie Zee. She'd fight dirty.

Ignoring it, she walked into the sitting room. "Mom-Elise, Mom-Kate, this is Jack."

Setting down the tray of crème brûlée, Jack smiled at them and offered his hand to shake. "Nice to meet you, ma'am. Ma'am."

"We've met before," Mom-Kate said, shaking his hand and smiling at him. "You and Calisa once climbed a tree—"

"Is that—" Mom-Elise pointed to the little dragon on Calisa's shoulder.

"This is Steve," Calisa said. "He's my dragon." She'd told her parents about him, but apparently seeing him in the flesh—and in the scales—was a different experience. She wondered how much of her story they'd believed or even absorbed. It had been a lot. She considered whether she could have waited a few days before bringing them to the B&B. Perhaps they'd need more time to process everything.

Her moms exchanged glances, which made Calisa even more nervous. "Um, sweetie," Mom-Kate began, "we know that we said someday you could have a pet . . ."

". . . when we live in an apartment that allows them," Mom-Elise finished. "But I'm not sure any apartment lease allows for . . ." She waved her hand toward Steve.

"Well, they don't *not* allow it," Mom-Kate said to her.

"But a . . . I can't even say the word," Mom-Elise said.

"He's what's known as a draco minor, or micro dragon," Auntie Zee said briskly. "He won't grow much larger. But regardless, it's best if he lives at the B&B, where he can fly free outside whenever he wants, without the risk of being spotted by anyone."

Calisa put her hand up to scratch Steve's neck. She didn't like the idea of leaving him here without her. She'd gotten used to him always being nearby, and she knew he was attached to her.

"As you can see, the draco minor has formed an attachment to your daughter," Auntie Zee said. "They bond with one person at a time, and it would be cruel for Calisa to abandon him at this point. She should be the one responsible for training him, now that he's able to produce flame."

Wait, where was Auntie Zee going with this? Calisa looked from her great-aunt to her moms and then back again. Obviously she didn't want to abandon Steve. . . .

Mom-Kate rose to her feet and paced through the living room.

"Tea?" Auntie Zee offered.

The enchanted teapot rose into the air and poured.

"You're trying to overwhelm us with magic," Mom-Kate said, "with what you can offer Calisa that we can't." She glared at the teapot as if it had personally offended her.

"I think it's pretty impressive," Mom-Elise said mildly.

"But Calisa can't stay here permanently, no matter how much magic you throw in our faces," Mom-Kate said. "This was for the summer because you needed assistance. A temporary arrangement."

"I want to stay!" Calisa burst out.

"Out of the question," Mom-Kate said. She held up her hand before Calisa could argue. "You can stay the rest of the summer, and you can come back next summer—that's the inn's busy season—but that will have to be enough. She's about to start her senior year of high school."

"Auntie Zee needs to train me," Calisa said. *And Steve needs me. And Jack. And I promised Rin I'd spread his name . . . and . . . and . . . and . . .*

"You aren't dropping out of school," Mom-Kate said firmly. "You're finishing high school and then going to college. As *you* planned. You aren't sacrificing your future for someone who had no interest in you until you proved useful to her."

Ouch. Also, of course she wasn't going to drop out! But could she transfer to a local Vermont school? Or online school? Or . . . she didn't know. She thought of Crystal and Maddy, and the idea of switching schools, not spending their senior year together, made her heart ache. As badly as she wanted to stay here, she didn't want to leave home. Not yet. She was supposed to have one more year. She felt as if she were being ripped in two, bones split from flesh.

Auntie Zee agreed, "She has to finish school." She waved the words away as if it was a nonissue, already resolved. "And I did not have 'no interest' in her or you. You left."

"Because I couldn't stand the disappointment in your eyes," Mom-Kate said.

"You *left*."

"You didn't want me back," Mom-Kate said. "If you did, you would have reached out. Invited us back. Apologized—"

"Apologized?! It wasn't my fault you wanted what I couldn't give you."

Calisa felt any chance at a lovely family reunion with tea and cake shatter into pieces. The firebird seemed agitated, racing back and forth on its log, and Steve was digging his talons into her shoulder. She felt the same, like she wanted to dig her fingernails into the upholstery. She imagined the mirror in the lobby was enjoying this. *Probably making bets with itself.* "Mom-Kate. Auntie Zee. Please, could you . . . take a deep breath? For me? And for Future Calisa? I know that you've hurt each other. Disappointed each other. And that you have a lot to work through. But can we maybe not use me as a pawn to do that? I want to stay here, learn about"—she waved her hand to encompass the entire bed-and-breakfast—"all of this and all of what I am, but I also want to be home."

Auntie Zee folded her wrinkled hands on her lap.

"Uh, Calisa?" Jack said.

She glanced at him. "What?"

He looked very uncomfortable to be speaking up during all of this family mess. She was amazed he hadn't bolted already. "There's a solution. Um, I think."

"A very obvious solution," Auntie Zee said tartly.

Calisa opened her mouth to ask what and then she shut it. "Oh."

The portal. In her guest room. Which led to their kitchen in Brooklyn.

"Yes, *oh,*" Auntie Zee said. "Calisa will return home at the end of the summer, resume school, and then every afternoon—"

"After she's finished her homework," Mom-Elise put in.

"After she's finished her homework but before teatime," Auntie Zee said, "she comes through the portal to the bed-and-breakfast to train and to take care of her responsibilities here. She has a lot to learn if she's going to eventually become innkeeper."

Me, innkeeper! She remembered Rin calling her the next witch of the inn. That . . . would be amazing. This place could be her future. *The perfect Future Calisa problem!* If it was possible. If Mom-Kate and Mom-Elise agreed.

"She's still going to college," Mom-Kate said.

"And she should," Auntie Zee said. "There are programs in hotel management, if she's so inclined. I recommend she at least take business courses. We can establish a portal to her dorm room, though you may have to arrange for her to not have a roommate, but these are details that can be worked out, if you're willing to allow it."

Her moms were looking at one another.

Calisa felt as if her brain was whirling as much as it was when she'd first discovered this was a magical inn. She couldn't pluck one coherent thought out of the tornado.

Jack spoke up. "No one has asked the most important question."

All of them looked at him.

"Does Calisa want this?" He flushed red. "I mean, she's got Auntie Zee's traveler-cat-whatever powers, but a month ago she didn't know anything about this inn or the realms or any of this. Just because she can do it doesn't mean she wants to."

"No one else can," Auntie Zee said.

Mom-Kate held up her hand. "Jack's right. It's her choice. Her future."

Leaning forward, Mom-Elise said to Calisa, "You can take time to think about it. You don't have to make a decision quickly. You have the whole rest of the summer. In fact, you have as long as you'd like. Unless Auntie Zee needs you to decide immediately?"

"I won't be retiring just yet," Auntie Zee said. "Now that Thomas is back, and I have both him and Jack to assist me, I'll be fine for a while."

"You could hire someone else too," Calisa suggested. "Now that the inn is flourishing again. Rin could help you find someone trustworthy if you ask him. . . ."

Auntie Zee glared at her. "I'll think about it."

That was better than a no.

"Regardless, your moms are correct," Auntie Zee said. "You should think about what you want before you decide. It is not a small responsibility. It's a brand-new purpose." All of them looked at Calisa with various expressions of concern, interest, and, in the case of Auntie Zee, complete confidence that she knew what Calisa would say.

Calisa rolled her eyes. "Obviously," she replied.

CHAPTER TWENTY-NINE

September came quickly.

Calisa wrote her college application essays about her summer working at her great-aunt's inn, leaving out everything magical. She applied to every school that had hotel management courses, as well as a few with business majors and minors. It didn't matter where she went—Auntie Zee could make her a portal. By the time she graduated, she expected to know how to establish her own portals, in addition to opening and closing existing ones.

For now, though, she had senior year of high school ahead of her. Her friends Crystal and Maddy were thrilled she'd met a new guy and instantly began to plot how to coax him to Brooklyn for senior prom at the end of the year. Whenever she mentioned Steve, they assumed he was another guy in Vermont, and Crystal kept pestering Calisa for an introduction.

Calisa, though, kept the inn's secrets from everyone. It had to be that way—the Faraway Inn needed to be kept safe, for everyone who needed it.

And there were a lot of people (and beings) who needed it. Thanks to word spreading about the success of the reopening, it was booked for most of the summer and half the fall, especially during peak fall foliage weekends in October—many were repeat guests from prior years, but several were new, drawn by Auntie Zee's reputation and word of mouth spread by the vendors in the Night Market.

She only saw Ethan at a distance until the second week of school, when he was waiting for her outside the bodega downstairs from her family's apartment. As soon as he saw her heading for the stairwell, he jogged to catch up to her.

"Hi, Ethan." She didn't feel the urge to say much else. He had apologized, after all, earlier in the summer. She didn't need anything more from him. She checked her heart to see if it still felt sore, and she felt a familiar what-could-have-been ache. It was surrounded, though, by thoughts of what she needed to do this afternoon at the inn for the guests, what cake she'd bake next, whether anyone had fed Steve yet, and when her and Jack's next trip to the Night Market should be.

"Calisa!" Ethan said. "You've been avoiding me."

She hadn't. She just hadn't tried to see him. "Not really."

"I think we need to talk."

Calisa considered that—did she want to hash through everything that had gone wrong? It wasn't all that complicated, actually. "I don't know what there is to say," she told him honestly.

"I'm hoping we can still be friends," Ethan said.

"I . . ." She stopped, thought about it, and then smiled sadly at Ethan. Not unkindly. "We aren't enemies. I don't hate you."

"That's a start," he said.

"And an end," Calisa said. "Ethan, you should find a way to move on. We're the past. I have a different future now."

"Yeah, I heard you met some guy—"

She stopped him. "Ethan."

He waited for her to say whatever she was going to say. She thought of how much it had hurt when he'd betrayed her, how it had felt like her future had popped like a bubble, how she'd had to redefine who she was and what she wanted. She'd fled Brooklyn because of him. Changed her whole summer because of him—her whole life. She should have feelings about all of that. And she did.

"Thank you," she told him.

"For what?"

She didn't elaborate. He'd shaped her life. Broken her heart. And when it had healed, it had become like those Japanese vases glued together with gold, more beautiful because of their breaks. Not that she wanted to go through that again. But she wasn't going to regret it either. She liked who Future Calisa was. "Goodbye, Ethan."

She walked toward her apartment lobby.

He followed her.

Glancing back, she saw the moment he was distracted by a siren on the street. She concentrated as Auntie Zee had taught her, tapping into what was inside her. . . .

When Ethan turned back, all he saw was a gray cat strolling away.

Calisa whispered "Open" to the apartment bathroom door, and then she stepped through to Vermont. Outside her window, the mountains were already painted with golds and reds and oranges, in between the deep green of the pine trees. Yellow birch leaves stood out like candle flames between them. The apple tree in the yard sagged with fruit, nearly ripe.

She closed the door and the portal, restoring both the closet on her side and the bathroom on her parents' side before she ventured out to the lobby. "Hey, mirror."

Ugh, you're back.

"Love you too." She passed by the mirror and headed for the kitchen. "What kind of cake should I make today?" she asked Jack. She had a stack of recipes that she wanted to try out. "Apple cake? Are the apples ripe?"

He grinned at her. "Guess who booked a room for the weekend?"

She had no idea. "A unicorn?"

"No."

Pity. She would've liked to meet a unicorn, if they existed. Her eight-year-old self with a collection of unicorn stickers would have been thrilled. "Are they real? If they are, we should definitely visit a realm with unicorns and invite them to the B&B." So far, she had notes on twenty-five realms, but as she understood it, there were an infinite number.

Not all of them reachable with her level of magic, but still, it wasn't impossible. Ooh, she'd have so many questions for them!

"We'd have to build a stable," Jack said, "or at least a unicorn-accessible room."

That could be done, probably. She'd watched a centaur clomp down the stairs, so a unicorn wouldn't be that much of a reach to make it equine-ready. "Who? Give me a hint."

"Melidor," Jack said.

That wasn't a hint. It was an answer. But it didn't matter, since she was happy to hear it. She hadn't seen her dryad nieces and nephews in weeks, and she couldn't wait to see how much they'd grown. Could they talk yet? Did they have leaves? Flowers? "With her babies?"

"She said they want to see their favorite aunt," Jack said.

"All right, then, apple cake it is!" She grinned back at him but didn't move toward the bowls or the ingredients. Instead she crossed to him and wrapped her arms around his waist. "First, though . . ." She kissed him.

He kissed her back with just as much enthusiasm. She felt as if she were bathed in sunlight, the warmth of summer spreading into autumn. Her hands ran up his back and into his hair. He cradled her close, and she thought of nothing and everything all at once.

When the kiss ended, he answered her earlier question, "The apples aren't ripe yet."

"Then we'll have to go somewhere they are," Calisa said with a smile.

Jack smiled back, and she felt her insides melt like chocolate in the oven. "Night Market?"

"Night Market," she agreed.

"While we're there, we can bring back some more of Rin's pastries—those were a hit with the new guests in room nine. Plus Steve will want more sliced meat. . . . Wait, I'll make a list." He fetched a piece of paper. "Okay, what else do we need?"

She rattled off the ingredients for apple cake, as well as for tomorrow's breakfast. "Do you think there will be dancing at the Night Market today?"

His eyes lit up. "I think we should see."

"I think so too." Calisa took his hand as he tucked the list into his pocket. Steve swooped down from the rafters and settled on her shoulder.

Hand in hand, Calisa and Jack strolled out of the kitchen. She waved to the mirror as they went by. Upstairs, they entered the empty guest room, and Steve chirped at the firebird waiting for them in the hearth.

Calisa opened the closet door. A familiar portal swirled in front of them.

"Ready?" Calisa asked.

"Always," Jack said.

Together they walked through the iridescence. Overhead the full moon shone on the Night Market, and the familiar chatter of vendors and their customers drifted up to them.

Steve launched himself into the air and chirped happily.

Beside the portal, Jack spun Calisa in a twirl, catching her in his arms. She laughed as they half danced and half slid their way down the grassy slope. When they reached the tents, she wrapped her arms around him. He smiled at her, and she drew him close.

While the little dragon flew in circles overhead, Calisa kissed Jack. He tasted like an epiphany. Like chocolate cake with raspberry jam. And like a future she wanted.

ACKNOWLEDGMENTS

Everyone should have a great-aunt with a magical inn. Also, a pet dragon. And enchanted tea.

That's why I wrote this book: I believe that everyone deserves a magical escape.

The word "escape" (or "escapism" or "escapist fiction") often gets said with a dismissive air, as if it's a negative—a sign of weakness or an unnecessary luxury. But I think that's a mistake. Escape is a beautiful and essential tool that enables us to cope with the world more effectively. It's a deep breath before the plunge. It isn't a display of weakness; it's a gathering of strength. It's taking a moment to remind yourself that there's good in the world—that there's wonder and magic and friendship and love and kindness and cake.

While I was writing my first cozy fantasy, *The Spellshop,* I thought a lot about giving readers an escape, and I started thinking that there is one group of people in particular who needs a sanctuary and doesn't often get one—a group who often isn't allowed control over their own lives, much less the state of the world: teens. I decided that I wanted to write a YA cozy fantasy as a gift to teens who need a moment to breathe.

So if that's who you are, please know that I wrote this book for you. Please know that there is good out there—and also cake. Please know that there is light after the darkness, and there will always be another door to open.

And if you're not a teen and you're reading this . . . well, it's for you too, because everyone deserves cake. Especially chocolate cake with raspberry filling.

I'd like to thank my amazing agent, Andrea Somberg, and my phenomenal editor, Lydia Gregovic, as well as all the other incredible people at Delacorte and Penguin Random House. Thank you for believing in me and in this book! Thank you for bringing my quirky little bed-and-breakfast to life!

And thank you to my husband, my children, and all my family and friends. I am so lucky to have you in my life! You are my sanctuary, my deep breath, and my cup of (enchanted) tea!

ABOUT THE AUTHOR

SARAH BETH DURST is the *New York Times* and *USA Today* bestselling author of more than thirty books for adults, teens, and kids, including cozy fantasy *The Spellshop*. She's been awarded the American Library Association's Alex Award, the Libby Book Award for Best Fantasy, and the Mythopoeic Fantasy Award. Several of her books have been optioned for film and television, including *Drink Slay Love*, which was made into a TV movie and was an answer on *Jeopardy!* She lives in Stony Brook, New York, with her husband, her children, and her ill-mannered cat.